FOREVER ENCHANTED

MAGGIE SHAYNE

AVON BOOKS NEW YORK

This is a work of fiction. Names, characters, places, and incidents either are the product of the author's imagination or are used fictitiously. Any resemblance to actual events, locales, organizations, or persons, living or dead, is entirely coincidental and beyond the intent of either the author or the publisher.

AVON BOOKS
A division of
The Hearst Corporation
1350 Avenue of the Americas
New York, New York 10019

Copyright © 1997 by Margaret Benson
Inside cover author photo by Karen Bergamo
Published by arrangement with the author
Visit our website at **http://AvonBooks.com**
Library of Congress Catalog Card Number: 96-97087
ISBN: 0-380-78746-6

First Avon Books Printing: April 1997

AVON TRADEMARK REG. U.S. PAT. OFF. AND IN OTHER COUNTRIES, MARCA REGISTRADA, HECHO EN U.S.A.

Printed in the U.S.A.

RA 10 9 8 7 6 5 4 3 2 1

"I TRIED TO LEAVE YOU, PRINCESS, BUT YOU WOULDN'T ALLOW IT."

"Nonsense!"

"You clung to my neck and muttered my name. You asked me to hold you, begged me not to go. I think you must have been dreaming."

"I think, Tristan, the only one dreaming in this room is you. Why would I ask you to hold me when I can't bear the sight of you?"

"I can't imagine, Bridín. But I know what I heard. It seems fairly obvious you're not being quite honest."

"You're the liar here, Tristan, not me."

"I'm not lying about this, at least. I want you, Bridín. You are a fire in my blood and you always have been. Just as I am burning in yours. Admit it."

"I'd sooner be tortured by hot coals," she whispered, but her eyes were focused on his lips, and she was yearning for their touch against hers. Starving for it.

"Liar." He gave her what she couldn't ask for, then.

And how she burned for him.

Other Avon Contemporary Romances by
Maggie Shayne

FAIRYTALE

Chapter One

TRISTAN OF SHARA, master of all he surveyed, drew his mount to a halt and watched the one woman who could take it all away from him, fighting for her life.

The three men who'd cornered her in the forest were common garbage. Criminals who didn't give a damn who ruled the realm, so long as they could roam free. He knew their type. This trio happened to be Albinon, but their kind existed in every race. They were the selfish ones who lived without a conscience or a single moral fiber. They took what they wanted without remorse. And he had a fair idea what they wanted from Bridín, could guess it by the gleam in their pink eyes.

He watched as Bridín was backed up against a rough granite wall while the three closed in around her. She held her chin high, meeting their eyes with a defiant stare and a toss of her honey blond tresses. The pendant she wore caught the moonlight and glinted. The pendant that would protect her from Tristan. It would do her little

1

good against those three. Its fairy spell was meant for him, and his kin, and any he sent to do his bidding. And only for them.

She was Tristan's sworn enemy. She was the one obstacle to his dream of a peaceful reign, a kingdom no longer divided, a faithful following. The one thing he'd wanted all his life. The thing he now held in his hands, though his grasp, he knew, was tentative. Because of her.

He should turn the black stallion around right now, and let them have her. They'd kill her when they'd finished with her. There was no doubt of that.

His horse, Moonshadow, stomped a forefoot and tossed his head, shaking his wild mane in excitement.

Tristan dug his heels into the animal's sides and drew his sword. It hissed against its sheath as he pulled it free, and the men froze where they stood. Bridín's gaze lifted, met his, held it. The moonlight bathed her face and shone its reflection in her eyes, transforming them into blue flames.

He couldn't look away. This was the first time he'd seen her since she'd escaped him a month ago. And for the briefest of moments he had the most ridiculous feeling that he'd missed her. His heart leapt in his chest at the sight of her, as if he were glad to see her again. Foolish, of course. He shook the odd notion away and broke eye contact with an effort. Looking into the eyes of a fairy princess was too dangerous, and he wasn't foolish enough to linger in the fiery wells of her eyes. It was not the first time she'd tried to enchant him that way. Pity she still hadn't realized his will was far too strong.

Instead of proving it by holding her fairy eyes with his, he leveled his gaze as well as his sword on the nearest ruffian, easing Moonshadow forward until the tip of the blade touched the man's chest.

"We seen 'er first," the Albinon blustered, backing up a step and scanning Tristan head to toe as if taking his measure.

"Do you know," Tristan asked slowly, "to whom you speak?"

The man's pink eyes narrowed in his pale-skinned, utterly hairless face. "Don't know, don't care," he said, and then he spat on the ground. "Only know there's three of us, against one of you. You'd best be on your way."

Moonshadow was well trained, and took another step forward at the merest nudge of Tristan's knees; just enough to keep Tristan's blade in contact with the man's chest.

"You ought to kneel," Tristan said, twisting the blade against the man's ragged shirt, "when approached by your prince."

The man blinked and stared up at Tristan, eyes widening. Tristan slanted a glance at Bridín, but she only glared at him, her eyes sparkling with defiance.

From the corner of his eyes, Tristan saw the man's two companions fall to their knees at once, groveling in the rich black soil. Very slowly, this one, their apparent leader, genuflected as well.

But Tristan's gaze never left Bridín's. "Well?" he asked her.

She stepped forward, her jaw tight. No flowing

gowns for the former heir to the throne of Rush, he noted. No, she wore garments more suited to life in the forest where she hid out with her band of rebels. Tight-fitting leggings and a tunic of leafy green, with a belt at her small waist and a scabbard at her side. An empty scabbard. Her knee-high boots were of soft brown suede. She moved forward to stand at his horse's side. A warm breeze lifted her golden hair and sent a strand blowing across her face. Fists anchored on her hips, feet set apart, she gazed up at him like a warrior goddess.

"I'll never kneel to you," she seethed, eyes flashing. Then she turned to the closest of the bowing criminals, planted a booted foot against his backside, and gave him a shove. He landed on his face in the dirt. "Nor should you! Fools! Don't you know me? I'm Bridín of the Fay, daughter of Queen Máire, and your rightful ruler!"

"Gods of Rush have mercy," the toppled man muttered as he slowly righted himself, back-handing dirt from his mouth. He got to his feet, looking from Bridín to Tristan and back again as he retreated. "We're no part of this fight," he said, his voice dropping to a fear-filled whisper. "Have at it, kill each other if you will, but leave us out of it!" Whirling, he raced away into the sheltering trees.

As Tristan sat silently upon Moonshadow, his gaze riveted to Bridín's, the other two did as their companion and scattered away. He didn't try to stop them. He didn't care where they went or what they did. They represented no challenge. Killing them would have been like picking off songbirds with a slingshot. Too easy to be sporting.

Bridín, on the other hand, was a worthy opponent. So much so, it was going to be almost sad to see her conquered in the end.

"So," he said softly, caught in the trap of her blue eyes like a fly in a spider's web, and hating his own inability to look away. "You did make your way back here."

"No thanks to you."

He didn't dismount. It would have done little good anyway. As long as she wore the pendant, he couldn't touch her. Couldn't harm her. And she knew it.

All the same, she edged sideways and bent to retrieve her gleaming sword from the ground where it lay. She didn't sheathe it, he noticed. And then he frowned, because as she bent, her pewter fairy pendants swung free, and he saw that she wore two of them now. But the other had belonged to her twin.

"Your sister?" he asked automatically.

"Very good, Tristan." Straightening, she wiped the gleaming blade free of dirt with the edge of her tunic. "That note of concern in your voice sounds almost genuine." She smoothed her long hair away from her face, holding the sword in one hand, studying its sheen. "Brigit is fine. Living a mortal life with her mortal husband and their baby son on the other side."

"Loyalty, it seems, is not one of her strengths." He'd fully expected both twins here plotting against him. But there was only one. Only Bridín.

Her eyes snapped up to meet his once more.

"This is not her battle, Tristan. It's yours. And mine."

"As it's always been." Tristan dismounted slowly and saw the wariness in her eyes. When his feet touched down she backed up a step, lifting her sword.

"No closer," she said.

A warrior goddess, yes. A fierce fighting woman, the sort of which legends were made. Standing there with that sword at the ready, her slender hands curved around its hilt, long fingers almost caressing the gilding there. That rough stone wall behind her, glittering with the crystals embedded in its granite face. Like her. Rugged beauty. Unattainable treasure. Gemstones embedded in rock. If he were a painter, he'd capture her just this way. Standing there armed and defiant. Beautiful and deadly. She took another step backwards as he advanced.

Tristan frowned and shook his head. "Don't tell me you're afraid of me now. You never were before, Bridín. Nor did I ever once give you reason to be."

Her sparkling blue eyes narrowed on him. "You brainwashed my uncle," she said in a voice low and trembling with anger. "You convinced him I was insane and in need of constant care. Made me a prisoner in my own home from the time I was seven years old, Tristan, and set your own people to guarding me there in the mortal world. All to prevent me from returning to Rush and taking my kingdom away from you." She tossed her head in the same agitated manner his stallion did when he smelled battle. The wind took a few more strands of spun gold and whipped them into motion. "And you say I've nothing to fear."

He shrugged and stepped closer. She held her ground this time, bending a little more at the knees, and lifting her sword a bit higher. "It was a cruel step to take," he said. "I admit that. But my choices were limited, Bridín. I was barely grown, a boy of seventeen with the responsibilities of an entire kingdom. My brother advised me to have you murdered and be done with it. Surely, given the choice, you'd have preferred your childhood prison to death?"

"Given the choice," she whispered, "I'd prefer to see you beheaded."

He lifted his brows. "You know that's a lie."

She averted her gaze abruptly. And Tristan was glad. There was nothing more disturbing to him than staring into those mesmerizing eyes of hers. Many a man, mortal and otherwise, had lost his soul in such a way. And while Tristan had long since become convinced he was not susceptible to her fairy allure, looking into her eyes still had an unsettling effect on him. Like staring too long at the sun.

"I took care of you, Bridín. Saw to it you had every comfort. Surrounded you with mortals who adored you. The nurse, Kate. And the old man. Razor-Face, wasn't it? Whatever became of him?"

He saw the defensiveness that clouded her eyes and the sudden tensing of her fine jaw. She'd loved the old man dearly, and now had the look of a she-wolf protecting her cub. "Raze is nothing to you. Your battle is with me, Tristan, and me alone." She met his eyes again. "I will have my throne back," she said. "And I'll see you and your followers driven from Rush once and for all. My kingdom—"

"*My* kingdom," he said, "is no longer called Rush, but Shara. As it was a thousand years ago when your family drove mine out and took it from us by force. For ten centuries, Bridín, my people had been condemned to live in the darkest part of the forest, where even the sunlight fears to venture. A prison too cruel for the most vile criminal. One that doesn't even compare with your own limited freedom as a child under my care."

"Your *care*?" She tossed her head. "I didn't have limited freedom, Tristan, I had no freedom. And your *care* was nonexistent. You were my captor."

It was a lie. He had cared for her. Always. But he would not stoop so low as to admit that.

"The blood of my ancestors cries out to me for justice, woman, and I will not ignore their pleas. I cannot. Ruling the kingdom is my sole reason for existence. It's the only reason I was born, and my father reminded me of that sad fact often enough so that I will not forget. The kingdom is Shara, its rulers are Sharans, and will be forevermore. And if you try to take it from me . . ."

He let his voice trail off, unable to complete the sentence. She knew it; he could see that in the glint of victory in her eyes.

Boldly Bridín stepped forward. She slid her sword smoothly, slowly, into its sheath, and stood so close to him, her chest nearly touched his. And she tilted her head back and looked into his eyes. "If I try to take it?" she asked him. "Go on, Tristan of Shara. Tell me what will happen if I try. You'll kill me? Is that what you were about to say?"

He parted his lips, but no words escaped. Her eyes . . . Gods, the power in her eyes! He wanted to grip her slender shoulders and shake her until she understood that fighting him would be useless. He wanted to toss her over Moonshadow's saddle and carry her back to his castle to fling her into the dungeons where she could no longer torment him this way. But he could not. So long as she wore the pendants, he could not lift a hand to her.

But she could touch him if it pleased her. And she did. She lifted her hands to either side of his face and slipped her fingers into his hair. "You can't hurt me, Tristan. Because for all those years you kept me prisoner, you were feeling the allure of the fay, though you'll deny it with your dying breath. You felt it. You know you did. You tried to get inside my mind, the way you did the mortals. So you could alter my thoughts as you did theirs. But instead, it was I who touched your mind, Dark Prince. And you can't get me out of it now."

"You're wrong," he said, but his words were harsh and coarse.

"When I pretended to be sick, you took me to a hospital," she went on. "Even knowing it was likely a trick on my part, you took me. You couldn't do otherwise. You couldn't stand to see me suffer and think I might die. And even now, Dark Prince, even should I take these pendants from around my neck at this very moment, you couldn't harm me. I told you I'd own your soul, Tristan. And I do."

"You own nothing!" he said, but he felt her words sinking into his flesh like blades, before melting into pools of molten steel that burned him inside. And her scent, the scent of the forest where she lived, and something else, drifted up into his nostrils and made him dizzy. Dammit, she was using the most powerful weapon of the fay against him, and he was succumbing when he'd deemed himself immune to it!

"No?" she asked. And she lifted her head, pulling his down to her, and touched her lips to his. He stood rigid, fighting her magic with everything in him. But she moved her lips, opening and closing them over his mouth, sucking at it as if it were a moist plum.

He couldn't touch her. He couldn't . . . he mustn't . . .

His back bowed over her, and he dropped his sword to the ground. His arms slid around her waist, and he pulled her body tight to his. His lips parted and he kissed her. For the first time in all the years he'd known her, he kissed her the way he'd always fantasized. Plunging his tongue deep inside and tasting the honeyed recesses of her mouth. Feeling her heart pound against his chest and her hips arching against him, and her hands clawing at the richly woven fabric of his tunic where it lay upon his shoulders. As if she'd like to rip it from him. She shuddered in his arms, her taut body going soft, molding against his. She opened her mouth to him, and her fingers tangled and tugged his hair. And he wanted her then. Be it by fairy magic or . . . or something else. He wanted her more than he wanted to breathe again.

Then suddenly she pulled her mouth from his, turned her head away, and whispered, "Enough."

And as soon as she said it, some invisible force pushed him backward. His arms fell to his sides, and his heart thundered like the hooves of a thousand stampeding horses. "Gods," he muttered, still struggling to catch his breath. In all his imaginings . . . it had never been . . . like that. And then he frowned, because he'd bypassed the enchantment of those pendants, somehow. "I touched you," he said, lifting his brows in question.

"Only because I allowed it." She was breathing hard and fast, and her face was flushed. She didn't meet his eyes.

It dawned on him slowly, gradually, but when it finally did, he knew he was right. As maddening as the kiss had been for him, it had been equally so for her. *At least* equally. Gods, she looked as if she were having trouble standing, as if her knees would buckle at any moment.

"You wanted it, too," he whispered in disbelief, stating his thoughts aloud to see her reaction. A pretty reaction, it was. Pretty and pink and suffusing her face with denial and fury. He smiled very softly, stepping around her, better to see the effect of his words on her averted face.

"And now perhaps you know what I've always known, Bridín." It was only a small lie; he *hadn't* always known. But he should have. "That in attempting to invade my soul, in attempting to charm me with those magical fairy's eyes, you inadvertently gave me access to yours. This power you have over me . . . it's two-pronged. It runs both ways, my fay princess. And you could no more allow harm to come to me than I could to you. You let me into your soul, Bridín. And I'm not leaving."

She shook her head, her gaze averted. A trembling hand rose, and her fingers pressed to her lips . . . as if in wonder. "No."

"Yes."

"You're wrong. I care nothing for you! I'll fight you, Tristan, and I'll win. Rush will never be yours."

"It's mine now."

"That's a lie! There are constant uprisings, constant skirmishes in the outlying villages. My people will never bow to your rule."

Tristan lowered his head. It was true. There hadn't been true peace in Rush—in Shara—since his father's armies had retaken it more than twenty years ago. But Tristan knew his duty, he knew why his father had begot him. Tristan of Shara had been bred and born to be king, and to hold the land his father had taken. If he couldn't manage it, then he might as well not be alive. His father had made sure he understood that. So he would do it. Fulfill his destiny, live up to the part he'd been born to play. Serve his people by seeing to it they never had to return to that land of darkness to which they'd been banished so long ago.

His mission in life was all there was. All there would ever be for Tristan. He'd had this lesson drummed into his head from the time he was old enough to talk and listen. He'd been denied everything else. Love. Affection. Recreation. Friends. None of that mattered. His indoctrination and training were all he'd needed, according to his father, and they had served him well.

Until now.

Well, he had a plan. He'd always had a plan. And that was why he'd taken Bridín prisoner and kept her all those years. Not to prevent her return. But to put it off ... until he could convince her to return with him, at his side. At the point of his sword, if need be, but at his side nonetheless.

"There *will* be peace and harmony in Shara again," he told her. "Your people *will* bow to my rule and cease their senseless rebellions ... just as soon as they see their beloved princess kneeling before me. Calling me king."

She jerked her head around to face him. "I'll die first."

"I'll see to it you're given that option. When the time comes." He retrieved his sword from the ground, lifted it, aimed its tip at her throat.

She jumped out of reach before he could slice those pretty chains and leave her unprotected and utterly at his mercy. He sighed in disappointment. If he hadn't been such a fool, he'd have ripped the pendants free when she'd kissed him, instead of dropping his weapon and groping her like a buck in rut. Physical desire meant nothing, dammit. Securing his hold on the throne was all that mattered, and all that should be on his mind.

He wasn't even certain he *could* break the chains and free her of those pendants, given the power of enchantment in them. But it might have worked.

As long as she wore them, though, she was safe. Tristan turned away from her and easily swung into the saddle. He was disgusted with himself for forgetting his mission, even for a moment, and disgusted with her for being the cause of his error.

"When you attempt this foolish coup you're planning, and fail, Bridín—when you're utterly defeated—come to me, and I'll dictate the terms of your public surrender."

He kicked the stallion's flanks and pulled on the reins. Moonshadow whirled and galloped away, leaving the beautiful fay princess shouting obscenities after them.

Bridín stomped into one of the many caves that lined the forested hillsides of Rush. She swore as she entered, drawing the gazes of everyone present. But she only looked back at them, and in a very loud, very firm voice announced, "We attack the city at dawn."

She saw Raze's reaction. He lowered his head and shook it slowly back and forth, rubbing the graying stubble on his chin with one hand. The others only remained still and silent, watching her, awaiting an explanation.

It was her cousin Pog who slowly rose from the stone slab where he'd been resting. He paced toward the small fire that danced and snapped in the center of the floor, providing the hideaway with warmth and light, and he studied its flames, and then her face, for a long time. She knew all too well what he was doing, and avoided his eyes. Not that it helped.

"You . . . you've seen him. The Dark Prince."

The fay male's powers of discernment were incredible. Pog was gifted, far more than most. And as a third cousin or some such, he'd been leading the forest dwellers in her absence. It had been he who'd brought them to these natural catacombs, and then converted the place into a virtual fortress city. It had been he who'd kept them busy, inciting villagers to revolt against Tristan's rule in order to keep the interlopers off balance and preoccupied. And it was he who'd kept her followers loyal to her. All had been ready for her return. Many had been waiting for a very long time.

She owed Pog a great deal. But right now she felt nothing but irritation with him. "What difference does it make whether or not I've seen Tristan of Shara," she snapped.

There was a gasp, and all eyes turned on her.

"My lady," Pog said softly. "You break the laws of your ancestors by speaking the Dark One's name. It's been outlawed for centuries. Since the banishment of his people to the Dark Side. You know that."

"And a stupid law, it is," she replied, tossing her head, and refusing to apologize. "What harm can speaking the man's name possibly do?"

No one spoke. They only stared. Drawing a deep breath, Pog turned to the few others who had gathered here. "Go. The princess Bridín and I would speak alone."

One by one they shuffled out. All manner of beings, from the hairless, pink-eyed Albinons, to the pint-sized Wood Nymphs, to the fay folk. Until only Raze and Pog remained in the room with her.

"All right, Bridey-girl," Raze said. "Tell us what happened." He sat in a stoop-shouldered pose on a stone, and didn't bother getting up.

She pursed her lips, staring into the flames. "Nothing. I met him in the forest and we quarreled. Nothing more than that."

"You seem awfully angry over a mere quarrel," Pog observed, tilting his head as he paced a circle around the fire. He was lean and graceful, long-limbed and light. He could move through the forest without making a sound, nor was he likely to be seen with his leaf-colored garments and bark-colored curls.

His fragile appearance might be misleading to some. But not to Bridín. She'd come to know him well since her return, and she knew he was powerful, both in physical and magical strength. Slow to anger, but impossible to fight once his mind was made up.

So she'd best make her arguments and make them well. "I'm not angry at all," she said softly. "I simply believe the time is right. Our archers have been honing their skills. We've made enough arrows to fill every quiver, Pog. We have weapons enough to fight six wars. We've gone over our plans again and again. I see no need to put this off any longer. We attack at dawn, while those Sharans sleep off their ale."

Pog frowned and tilted his head. "What makes you think they'll imbibe on this eve more than any other?"

"Today is Tristan's birthday, Pog." She

averted her eyes. "I was reminded only when I met him in the forest."

"His birthday?" Pog seemed amazed. "How in the world did you know—"

"I was his prisoner for seventeen years," she explained, still not meeting Pog's gaze. "One comes to know a person fairly well in that amount of time. I know Tristan as well as he knows himself. He is three and thirty today."

Pog looked at her, a cloud of concern darkening his brown eyes. "Too old to remain a prince. He ought to be king at his age."

Raze frowned hard. "But he can't be king until he marries. That's the way the law here works, isn't it?"

"Yes," Pog told him. "That's been the custom for as long as anyone can remember. The question is, why hasn't he married? What is he waiting for?" He looked at Bridín. "You say you know him better than anyone, my lady. What say you?"

She shook her head. Bridín had her suspicions, topmost being that the man had a heart of stone and no woman in her right mind would wish to be his wife. His only care was for the kingdom.

They had much in common in that regard. For taking the kingdom back from him was the only thing in the world she ever cared about.

"I don't know why Tristan hasn't married, nor do I care. The point I'm trying to make is that the prince's birthday celebrations will last long into the night, and at dawn his men will likely be inebriated and unconscious. Even those who might wake will be too ill to fight. You know soldiers and their love of any excuse to indulge in drunken revelry."

"Yes." Pog nodded hard. "Yes, I do believe you're right," he said at last. "I'll call a council meeting. Inform our forces to make ready."

"Good," she said. She turned to go, wishing only to curl up in a warm blanket and try to sleep, but then she paused, looking back at Pog once more. "Just one thing," she said.

He lifted soft brown eyebrows and waited.

"Tristan is not to be harmed."

"My lady?" Pog's eyes were round with confusion.

She hated the way he was looking at her. As if she were insane. And she searched her mind for all the logical explanations she had thought of for this command. But they seemed weak now. "Sparing his life will ease the minds of those who've been loyal to him. They'll be grateful to us, and more willing to bow to my rule. And . . . besides, if we keep him in our dungeons, then others of his family—that blackhearted younger brother of his, for example—will not dare attempt to retake our city, for fear we'd harm him at the first sign of trouble."

Pog tilted his head, and she knew by the narrowness of his brown eyes that he was trying to read her thoughts.

"If those reasons are not good enough, Pog, then this one should be. I am your princess and it is my command."

He bent his head. "Yes, my lady. It shall be done."

"Make sure of it," she said, and then she turned to go. She left the main room by one of the many tunnels that opened off it, and headed through the smoky torchlight into her chamber. She paused once on the way, when she heard echoing footfalls scooting off down another passage. Small footfalls. Light ones, like those of a child. Snatching a torch from the wall, she followed the sound, but saw no one.

She sighed hard and shook her head, telling herself she was only nervous. And then she went on to bed. But she didn't sleep.

Each time she closed her eyes, Tristan's voice came back to haunt her. Or his touch. The feel of his mouth on hers and the shock of the intense reaction she'd had to it. Gods, his kiss had left her weak and longing . . .

She swallowed hard. He'd been right. She couldn't see him harmed any more than he could lift a hand to her. And it made no sense. She hated him. *Hated* him. He'd kept her prisoner in the mortal world until she'd become old enough and smart enough to escape him. He was ruling the city that rightfully belonged to her. His father's troops had murdered her mother in the battle to retake that city.

And yet . . . and yet she couldn't see him harmed. The very thought made her heart feel heavy and tight.

Damn him. Damn him.

Chapter Two

TRISTAN TWISTED BENEATH the covers, but the brush of cool satin against his naked flesh only made matters worse. He couldn't stop thinking about her. Bridín. Her tiny waist entrapped in his arms and her breasts pushing against him. Her mouth. The taste of it. The way she'd shuddered, and sighed, and blushed in his arms.

Gods! She was his sworn enemy. Always he'd been aware of his weakness where she was concerned. He'd never been able to bring himself to simply have her killed and be done with the only true threat to his rule. And he'd known, for weeks now, the location of her forest hideaway. Yet he didn't tell anyone he knew. Even his second-in-command, his own brother, Vincent. Only Tate knew, and that was because he'd been the one to discover the honeycomb of caves in the hillsides. Tristan didn't inform his knights, didn't launch a raid. All because Bridín would likely be killed in such a mission, and he couldn't stomach the thought of that happening. Nor could he tell his men that he wanted her life spared. If they realized his weakness for their enemy, they'd turn on him, and his reign would end in mutiny.

No. He'd risked all he cherished to spare her life, in the hopes she would give up her foolish notions of retaking the kingdom. He prayed that would be the case.

But deep down, he knew better, didn't he? Because no one, not even Bridín herself, knew her heart the way he did. And he knew she'd never give up without a fight. Never.

He closed his eyes. He ought to be up, dressing in his royal finery for the revelry of tonight's celebration. The celebration and feasting and merriment were things he'd just as soon do without, but his men needed the break from the tension. Constantly putting down rebellion had taken its toll on them. And his birthday was as good an excuse as anything else to let them cut loose and have some fun. He'd thought a short nap might better prepare him for the night ahead, but of course, he couldn't sleep. And he knew too well that none of the perfumed whores paraded before him tonight were going to remedy what ailed him.

Not now that he'd tasted her. He didn't think he'd ever know a good night's rest again. And yet his own reaction baffled him. He knew he was stronger than her fairy allure. Was certain of it. Why, then, did he feel this need to have her in his arms again? Why couldn't he stop thinking about that kiss?

A tap at his chamber door stirred him, and he sat up in the bed, pulling on a purple satin robe and belting it tight as he slid to his feet.

As a precaution, he drew the small dagger from beneath his pillow, and stood to one side of the door. As ruler of Rush, he must be careful, for there were others besides Bridín who would take his throne if they could. Why, some even suspected his own brother of plotting his fall. He smiled wryly at that ludicrous notion, and shook his head.

"Who's there?"

"'Tis Tate, Your Majesty. I bring news."

Tate. Tristan smiled. Dear, overcautious Tate. He was the one concocting far-fetched theories about Tristan's brother, Vincent, among other things. Of course, being overly paranoid was a common trait among the Wood Nymphs.

Tristan opened the door, and Tate paused to peer into the room, as if checking for unseen enemies before stepping in and closing it behind him. He went directly to the bedside stand, picked up the single candle that burned there, and then touched its wick to every unlit taper in the room until the place glowed. The nymph hated the dark. Most did. And though he had to stand on chairs to reach some of the candles, Tate didn't stop until every last one was alight.

"There," he said, replacing the first and hopping into a chair that dwarfed him. "Much better. Are we alone?"

Tristan remained standing where he'd been as he watched Tate's antics. "Do you see anyone else here?"

"That doesn't mean we're alone," Tate observed, tilting his cherubic face to one side. He looked like an angelic little boy, with charcoal curls and bushy dark brows and thick-lashed black eyes. His chubby cheeks and a bow-shaped mouth made him appear to be a beautiful six-year-old.

He was, in fact, one hundred thirty-six.

And Tristan's most trusted friend. "You said you'd brought news," he said, lowering himself to the edge of his bed. "We're alone, Tate. What is this news?"

"The princess Bridín plans to attack at dawn."

Tate could have struck him and shocked him less. Tristan only gaped, shaking his head, searching for words.

"I know. It's the very worst of news. But it matters not, Tristan. You gave me your word twenty years ago when your father's troops first took this castle. You promised you'd never harm the princess. Doesn't matter if she leads the attack herself, you have to see she's safe."

"You know I won't hurt her."

"But will you protect her?"

Tristan lowered his head. "Tate, my friend, I don't believe I have much choice in the matter."

Tate frowned and searched Tristan's face, then shrugged. "It won't be easy. If your brother has the chance, he'll kill her out of hand—"

"Don't be ridiculous. My brother will follow my orders."

Tate met Tristan's eyes, his small black ones filled with foreboding. "You know better. He wants your crown, Tristan."

"He wants no such thing. You're always seeing conspiracy where none exists."

"Of course I do. And his constant complaining about your weakness in dealing with these little rebellions is not meant to weaken your authority with your own men, is it? No, of course not. The man is only voicing an opinion. Behind your back. Planting seeds of doubt in the men's minds with no intent of harvesting what grows there. He's—"

"He's my brother."

Tate shrugged and stopped arguing, and Tristan was glad. He didn't like arguing with the little man. Tate had a way of making Tristan feel like a naive little child with those knowing eyes of his. Worst of all, Tate was rarely wrong. But on this occasion, he must be. Vincent wouldn't turn on him. They'd suffered through their childhood on the Dark Side together, through their constant indoctrination together, lost their mother together, and then their father. And while neither of them tended to show emotion, having been taught that *feeling* was a weakness, Tristan couldn't help but believe his brother harbored some mild affection for him. He must. For if he didn't, then no one did. Vincent was all Tristan had, the only person in the world he'd allowed himself to feel anything for. He wouldn't betray him.

"Tristan?" Tate asked, interrupting his thoughts. "What shall we do about Bridín?"

Tristan sighed, lowering his head. "I suppose I should call off tonight's celebration, and meet with my lieutenants instead."

"If the princess is killed, there will never be peace in this land," Tate warned, hopping out of the chair and heading for the far wall as if to gaze out the window. "Those loyal to you wish her dead. And those loyal to her wish you dead. But beware, Tristan, my prince, for there are those loyal to another. And they would like to see you both dead."

"Another conspiracy, Tate?"

Tate gave Tristan a knowing look. "You'll see." And then he put one small hand against a block in the castle wall, and vanished. It startled Tristan, though he should be used to Tate's dramatic exits by now. The little runt had been a servant in this castle for nearly a century now. He knew every secret passage in the place, but refused to divulge the information, even to Tristan. And Tristan suspected he knew many other secrets as well.

Tate's loyalty was unquestionable. His allegiance, he claimed, was to Rush, and he'd serve whoever ruled, so long as they were good to the kingdom. His ancestors had served in this very castle when the last Sharan had held the throne. They'd witnessed the siege of the fay, and remained here when Bridín's forebears had banished them to the Dark Side of the forest. He suspected some of Tate's clan would be in this castle long after his reign was over, and even after that.

Pursing his lips, Tristan went to the spot where Tate had vanished and felt the stone blocks, touching, pushing, pulling. Nothing gave or wiggled. No hidden doorways opened. He smiled, shook his head, and began to dress.

Tristan stood at the head of the long stone table in the lesser hall, and kept his composure despite the looks of disgust on the men who sat before him. Some shook their heads and muttered while others only gaped. It was Vincent, his brother, who met his eyes, his black gaze penetrating. He held up one hand, silencing the mutterers. "Perhaps," he said softly, "my brother has a sound reason for this seemingly absurd request."

All eyes returned to Tristan. "I do," he said, and was grateful for his brother's faith in his judgment. "But first let me clarify. This is no request, but a command. One I expect to be obeyed."

"But, Sire," Murdock all but whispered. "Bridín of the Fay is your enemy. About to lead an attack against your kingdom, my lord. 'Tis treason, and punishable only by death."

Tristan nodded. Murdock was one of those closest to him, a man he trusted almost as much as Tate. The others at the table, well, they adored his brother, and because of that, they'd obey Tristan without question. Vincent had taken on the difficult task of choosing Tristan's closest advisers himself, long ago. And while Tristan had at first questioned some of the choices his brother had made, he'd been glad of the help. At the time, he'd been overwhelmed with his new responsibilities. As it turned out, the men had served him well.

"Your points are well taken, Murdock," Tristan said slowly. "But already there is rebellion in the kingdom. Many here will never stop seeing Bridín as their liege. If she dies in this battle, she'll become even more beloved to them. A martyr. A legend." He paced away from the table, his boots tapping over the stone floor. "We'll never know peace in Shara if she dies. But . . ." He turned to face them all again. "If she lives, if we spare her life, those same followers of hers will see us as fair and merciful and kind. And when their princess bows to my rule, they will do likewise. These constant uprisings will end, my friends. There will be peace in Shara at last."

Vincent rose slowly from his seat, his expression still mild, though Tristan detected the tightness of his brother's jaw. "By sparing her, my brother, there is some risk. I hope I won't be out of line by pointing this out to you."

Tristan nodded at his brother to go on, and Vincent did. "We might be seen, not as kind and merciful, but as weak, ineffective leaders unwilling to carry out our own laws. Our father taught us that one can only attain peace by conquest. Perhaps we should show these rebels what becomes of those who dare to challenge our rule, and make them cower in fear. I advise you to make an example of this Bridín of the Fay, and deliver a powerful lesson to the rest."

It troubled Tristan greatly to see most of them nodding in agreement.

"No." He said it loudly, firmly, as he took his seat at the head of the table. "I am the prince of Shara. When I take a bride one day soon, I'll be crowned your king. And I will not have the woman harmed. Many of you may disagree, and I have the deepest respect for your views." He met Vincent's eyes. "Especially yours, my brother. But nonetheless, this is my decision. When she attacks in the morn, Bridín is to be taken prisoner. And any man who harms her will wish to the gods he had not."

For the briefest of moments, he saw pure fury flare in his brother's eyes. But then Vincent dipped his head. "As you command, my prince."

Tristan tried to restrain the urge to sigh in relief. Thank goodness his brother hadn't chosen to argue with him, as he truly would have done had Tate's suspicions about him been true. The very mutiny Tate feared could have taken place right here and now. But it hadn't. His brother wasn't his enemy.

Bridín was.

Tristan looked at the others. "And the rest of you?"

"Your word is law, Prince Tristan," Murdock intoned. "Truly, I believe you are wise in this. I'll inform my troops."

"Thank you, Murdock. The rest of you, do the same. Be sure every fighting man knows my wishes in this matter. And then rest. At two hours before dawn, you're to have your troops in place to defend Shara. When Bridín's army attacks, they'll find themselves surrounded so quickly and effectively, there may not be need to shed so much as a drop of blood. And if that's so, then it's all the better for the kingdom."

The men exchanged glances, troubled glances, but no one spoke against him.

He drew his sword and held it up, high above the table. "For Shara!"

And each man at the table rose and did likewise. "For Shara!"

Vincent watched his brother leave the lesser hall, followed by Murdock, and then Tate, who was never far from Tristan's side. He went to the door, as if he'd leave as well, but only remained until his brother rounded a corner and vanished from view. And then he turned back to the two men who remained. Tristan's lieutenants, yes, but placed in that position of trust and power because of Vincent's pull with his brother. They were his men, not Tristan's, though his trusting brother was too naive to realize that.

"If this spectacle was not enough to convince me of it, nothing ever will be," he said softly, turning to step back inside. "My brother is not fit to rule Shara."

"Too soft," said Llewellyn. "He'll make our kingdom a laughingstock, and ripe for attack from other enemies even more powerful than the fay."

Kenniwick nodded. "I agree. But what's to be done, my liege?"

"He seeks to spare Bridín because of the people's love for her. But the fair Bridín will not be loved by her people much longer," Vincent said, pacing slowly and rubbing his chin as he formulated a plan. "Take some men out tonight, Llewellyn. Only those whose loyalty you can be sure of. Dress them not in the blue and gold of Shara, but in poorly spun clothing of green, such as that forest dwelling band of fay folk might wear. Ride your mounts without saddles. And see if you can round up a golden-haired harlot whose assistance can be bought. She's to ride with you, at the front of your troops, with her tresses fully visible, as you burn at least three of the outlying villages. Preferably those most dense with Bridín's loyal ones."

Llewellyn met Kenniwick's eyes across the table, then slid his gaze to Vincent's once more. "Sir?"

"When she attacks Shara proper at dawn, it should be fairly obvious that she led those raids on her way here. Those who live will blame her. There will be none left to defend her when she's captured at dawn. I want her brought to me in chains. Not to my brother, but to me. When I'm forced to kill her in defense of my own life, I will be cheered by the people of Shara. And when Tristan condemns me for my act, as he will, fool that he is, he'll be guilty of treachery against his own kingdom, and his own brother. Particularly when it's made public that he's known of her whereabouts for weeks now, and could have prevented the havoc she's wrought."

Kenniwick shook his head, looking down at the floor. Llewellyn's face split into a broad grin. " 'Tis genius, my lord. The crown will be yours."

"As it should have been from the start. The fates were mistaken in allowing my brother to be born first. But we can alter the fates, my friends. And we will." He turned to Kenniwick. "In the morn, as soon as Bridín's army is sighted entering the city, you are to distract my brother. Tell him a second group is approaching from the rear and lead him there. In his absence, Llewellyn, you are to order the men to attack Bridín's forces. There will be no mercy, no chance for surrender. I want them dead. All of them."

Bridín felt a chill of foreboding slide up into her nape as she led her ragtag army right up to the gates of Rush—now known as Shara—and found those gates open and unguarded.

And she should have turned back, right then. But she didn't. Swords drawn, archers poised and ready, they walked their horses quietly beneath the portcullis and into the city proper. And when the last horse was clear, the portcullis slammed downward and mayhem erupted. Soldiers in full armor seemed to emerge from every door and window. Arrows rained death from the slits in the tower walls, and shouts and cries filled the night air, followed shortly by the stench of warm blood. Horses bolted and reared, screaming in fury. Bridín's mount threw her to the stony ground, and she rolled to her feet in time to duck a powerful blow.

Her men fought... Gods, how they fought. And then Pog, her cousin, had her in his deceptively slender arms, dragging her out of the fray and through the open door of the castle, into its great hall.

"Damn you, Pog, release me!" She twisted free, but Pog only closed and bolted the huge wooden door, then blocked her escape with his own body.

She lifted her sword. "By the gods, step aside, Pog, or I'll do you harm!"

"No, my lady! 'Tis a trap, can't you see that? You'll be killed, and what good will you be to your people then?"

A cry cut the night, and Bridín's head came up sharply. "They're dying out there! Pog, let me go!"

"Too late, lady. There's nothing you can do for them. They'd want you safe, and for Rush, I'll see you are. I swear it! Come, we must find a way out of here." He took her arm, his strength overpowering her as he pulled her through the great hall and into a vaulted corridor opening out to its rear. He was heading for the kitchens, at the far end, she realized, and the door that opened into the rear of the castle. But she couldn't go. She couldn't simply leave her men to die alone. She couldn't—

She turned, managing to tug free of his grip once more, and tried to run, but a terrible thud and a dull groan brought her up short. "Pog?" she whispered, and turned slowly to see her best friend lying still on the stone floor. Above him, a man whose face was little but purest evil stood holding a torch in one hand, and a bloody mace in the other.

"You're to come with me, Bridín of the Fay."

"No!" And she turned to flee.

"Wait," he shouted, and raced past her, to the door Pog had bolted, flinging the bar away and shoving it wide. And Bridín stared out into the dawn, at the mayhem of the battle.

"Those men in the courtyard will be killed," the man rasped. "Already many lie dead. They are surrounded, you know. Outnumbered and outarmed. Come with me, and I'll call my troops off. Run, and I'll leave them to die."

Bridín wanted to run out there and help her people, but his body blocked her escape, and common sense intervened. She couldn't save her men by going out there. He motioned her inside, closing and bolting the door again. She could no longer see the carnage, but she could still hear it. The clanging of swords and the hiss of arrows. The cries of the dying, some of those voices all too familiar. "All right," she cried, lowering her head. "Call them off, please!"

And the man was turning around, leading her

back down the corridor. "A wise decision, my lady."

A stone in the wall moved, and for an instant Bridín swore she saw a child peering out at her. But then the apparition vanished, leaving her alone with this villain.

"Call them off," she said, looking at the man again. "Please, do it now. And take me to your prince! I must speak with Tristan."

"You'll find, my lady, that Tristan will not be of much help to you after today. Better you speak with me."

Bridín frowned in confusion. The man guided her through a doorway into a small chamber of stone, and then yanked the door closed so that it hit her body with an impact so forceful, her head cracked against the wall. He jammed the torch into a wall bracket, cast his mace to the floor, and drew a sword of black steel.

She tried to back away from him, but was already pressed to the wall. "You . . . said you'd call them off."

"I lied," he said, and he smiled.

"I don't understand. Who are you? Where is Tristan?"

"I am Vincent, my lady. Tristan's brother, and soon to be ruler of Shara. But first . . ." He lashed out with his sword, slicing through the chains of her pendants. Bridín cried out and tried to catch them, but they fell to the floor and lay there, sparkling in the torchlight. "But first, I have a problem to solve." She swallowed hard as she saw both his cruel hands tightening around the hilt, saw him lifting the sword high. And then it

was descending on her and she knew the blow
would sever her head.

"In here, my lord! He took her in here!"

She heard the voice coming from the corridor,
and then the door crashed open. Tristan's eyes
flashed to hers, and to the blade. All in the space
of a heartbeat. Vincent paused with the blade in
the air.

"What the hell are you doing?" Tristan
shouted.

"What you should have done long ago," Vincent spat, and then he swung hard, and the
sword descended on her.

"No!" The word seemed torn from Tristan's
throat as he leapt between Bridín and her mur-
derer, and the blow caught him high on the
shoulder. She heard the crunch of bone, and saw
the blood. Tristan's blood. He sank to his knees
in front of Bridín, reached back with the one arm
he could still use, and pushed her toward the
window. But she was paralyzed with shock and
horror.

"Damn you, Tristan!" Vincent shouted. "Get
out of my way!" Vincent lunged forward, one
fist shoving Tristan as if to move him aside. But
Tristan caught his brother's arm and held him
with so much force, his entire body trembled.

"Run," he whispered, glancing up at her only
briefly. Their eyes met, and held. "Run, Bridín,
now!"

Then Vincent glared down at his brother,
yanked his arm free, and lifted his sword once
more, over Tristan's weakened body this time.

Pog staggered into the room and grabbed Bridín around the waist, shoving her hard toward the room's single window.

"No!" she cried, staring back at Tristan, who knelt defenseless at his brother's feet. But Pog was stronger than she, and he shoved her through the small window at the far side and then leapt out after her. The last thing Bridín saw as she was forced to make her escape was Tristan's blood-soaked hand, closing around her two pendants.

"Guards!" Vincent bellowed from the doorway. He made not one move to help Tristan to his feet, or to stanch the flow of blood from his body. There was a stampede of feet, and then men, his men . . . his brother's men . . . crowding into the room.

"Your prince has betrayed you!" Vincent roared. "That fay woman was here, right in our hands, and he helped her to escape!"

"Vincent," Tristan attempted, but it was a weak effort.

" 'Tis true," a voice said, and Tristan looked up to see Kenniwick, one of his most highly placed lieutenants, standing over him. "I saw the whole thing. Tristan attacked his own brother in defense of that treacherous beauty. He's obviously fallen victim to her fay charms and spells."

"I can't believe it," another muttered. "After what she did! The villages she burned last night? The men she murdered? Even her own, some of them!"

" 'Tis treachery," said another. "Treachery."

"Take him to the dungeons," Vincent declared.

Several men gripped Tristan and hauled him from the floor. He couldn't stand upright. His weak legs wouldn't hold him and his feet slipped in the pool of his own blood. He clasped the pendants tighter in his fist to hide them, and again met Vincent's eyes. "You . . ." he said. "My own brother . . ."

"I'm no brother to a traitor," Vincent said. "Take him away."

And they did it! They obeyed his brother. Tristan was dragged, bleeding, down into the pitch black dungeons, and tossed into a cell. The barred door was slammed and locked, and he was left there. And he knew full well he'd been left to die.

Tate had been right all along. His brother had craved the throne, and now he would have it. He lay on the floor, eyes closed in pain, the blood loss weakening him more and more by the second. And in the darkness, he thought of Bridín. The way she'd looked—every bit as defiant and strong as ever—even as his brother's blade swung toward her.

He'd never known a woman like her. He was convinced now that there simply *was* no other woman like her. And he hoped to the heavens that her man had got her to safety and out of Vincent's reach. He hoped she was all right.

He supposed it was foolish to be worried for her safety when his own was in such great question right now. Then again, worrying for himself would be a fairly useless exercise. He wasn't going to survive the night.

"Gods," he muttered. "Gods, I should have listened to Tate. Why didn't I listen?"

"Because you're a bloody fool, is why." The scrape of stone from above was followed by a small, lithe body sliding down a length of hemp and dropping to the floor. "But perhaps now you'll listen to old Tate."

Tristan straightened, staring in shock, first at the little man, and then at the passage opening into the ceiling above him. "How . . . ?"

"Never mind how." Tate pulled a small pouch from his tunic, and from it removed a large, rusty-looking needle and a handful of what looked suspiciously like horsehair. "Best find something to bite down on, my friend. This isn't gonna tickle." He crouched beside Tristan and tore the sleeve of his bloodied tunic away.

"And don't go faintin' like a woman on me, Tristan. We'll be needin' to make our way out of Shara tonight."

"I can't. I'm too weak, Tate. I'm not sure I'll even survive."

"You won't if you stay here, that's sure. That brother of yours wants you dead."

"He'll find me if I leave."

"Not where you're goin', he won't. And he's not likely to make a big show of searching for you, either. Wouldn't do for him to admit he'd let two prisoners escape in the space of one night."

"You know him so well, do you?"

"Better than you do, Tristan."

That, Tristan thought, was painfully obvious.

"One hundred men." Bridín sat with her back braced against the cool stone wall of the cave, staring into the firelight without really seeing it.

"One hundred men, Pog. Gods forgive me, what have I done?"

"Ninety-eight, my lady," Pog said, and he poured her some of the soothing herbal brews that the Wood Nymph Marinda was so talented at concocting. He hung the pot over the fire again and brought the mug to Bridín, pushing it into her cold, bloodstained hands.

All through the long day she'd been working in the makeshift hospital, which was really no more than a large, hidden cave with supplies of bandages and healing herbs and spring water. And volunteers. Plenty of those. Some had managed to escape the slaughter that had taken place in the courtyard this dawn. But most of those who had were injured. Senselessly.

"And what you have done is precisely what your followers have been clamoring for you to do. You led them into battle in an effort to reclaim the kingdom. 'Tis what they wished."

"But I failed." Her head fell forward, shoulders sagging under the incredible weight she felt pressing them down. "All those lives were lost because I failed."

Pog paced back and forth slowly, the small fire between them. " 'Tis quite obvious to me, Your Highness, that the Sharans knew we were coming. We walked right into a trap," he said. "And that means that we were betrayed. Someone told of our plans. Our attack was doomed from the start. It was not you who failed, Bridín, but the one who betrayed us to them."

She closed her eyes tightly, recalling the pain she'd seen and heard and smelled in that courtyard, and shuddering. "I'd never have believed him to be so utterly ruthless," she whispered. "To take us all prisoner, yes, but not to butcher so many men that way. By the gods, once his troops had mine surrounded, there was no reason. He could have ordered us to lay down our weapons, and we'd have had no choice. But this . . ."

To her surprise, a tear rolled down her cheek. Her heart felt heavy with a disappointment she could not explain. Not so much at losing the battle, though that ate at her too, but at what felt oddly like betrayal. Betrayed by her archenemy. And how much sense did that make?

"I suppose I shouldn't be surprised, though," she whispered, thinking out loud. "It was he who arranged for the car accident that took my adopted mortal parents when I was little more than a child. Why should I be shocked by the depths he'd sink to now?"

"It makes little difference, Bridín, at this point. Doesn't matter anymore just what Tristan of Shara is capable of."

"Of course it matters!" Her head came up fast, eyes focusing for the first time on Pog, but her mind was far away. In that little room. Tristan, no matter how ruthless she knew him to be, had stepped between his brother's blade and her own neck. He'd saved her life.

She recalled very briefly the hatred she'd seen flashing in Vincent's eyes when he hit Tristan. But shook her head against the memory. Surely that blow cutting Tristan to the bone had been an accident. He'd lunged in front of her too quickly, and his brother hadn't had time to pull back. There was no more to it than that.

"When I see him again," Bridín said, putting his heroism out of her mind because of the odd feelings it invoked, and thinking instead on his savage butchery of her loyal ones, "I'll ask him why he found it necessary to be so merciless. I'll make him tell me how he rationalizes such brutality, how he manages to sleep at night with so much blood on his hands, how he—"

"No, my lady. I'm afraid you won't."

She blinked at Pog over the yellow-orange dancing flames, sending him a silent question with her eyes.

"We had word an hour ago, Bridín." He came around the fire and dropped to his knees in front of her. With his slender, graceful hands he took the untouched broth from her, set it aside, and then held both of her hands in his. She frowned, trepidation sending chills up her spine. "This will not be easy for you to hear, I know. But . . . Vincent made a public address tonight. He said . . . he said that Tristan is dead."

Her heart seemed to halt abruptly as her mind absorbed those words. The entire world ground to a stop, and she felt dizzy, as shocked as if he'd struck her. "Dead?" she said, when she could finally speak again. "No. No, he isn't dead, Pog. I'd know if he were." Pog looked at her, cocking one brow. She went on. "I mean . . . I saw him, Pog. You were there. It was only a blow to the shoulder."

"Which cut clean to the bone, lady. He'd nearly bled out before we even made our escape."

"He is not dead!" She got to her feet, began pacing, and automatically reached up for her pendants. When nervous, she was forever sliding them back and forth on their chains. But this time she found nothing there, and blinked down in shock. And then the memory came. Tristan lying on the floor. Tristan closing his hands around her pendants in that pool of his blood. Meeting her eyes, his own dulling already, and whispering at her to run.

Slowly she lowered her hand from her throat. "He can't be dead," she whispered. "He has the pendants. You know full well the strength of their healing power."

"Only for one who knows how to use them, my princess," Pog said softly, rising and standing before her, facing her with solemn eyes. "Tristan wouldn't give up the kingdom, Bridín. You know that. Not for anything."

"Of course I know that. That's what drove me to this foolish attack."

"Well, he's given it up now. His brother claimed the throne of Rush . . . the Rush they call Shara . . . today. He's ruling now. And Tristan . . . Tristan is gone."

She met Pog's eyes, and felt her own begin to burn and sting. Nothing else would have convinced her . . . but this . . . What more evidence was needed? Tristan wouldn't give his throne to his brother, not voluntarily. It must be true. He must be . . .

"Gods, Pog, do you realize the implications? That blow Vincent struck his brother . . . It might not have been accidental at all!"

Pog lowered his head. "There have been rumors, my lady. Rumors of Vincent hungering for the throne, and plotting against his brother. Tristan refused to believe them, I'm told."

Bridín tried to remain rigid. Stoic. But failed, and finally sank to her knees, buried her face in her hands, and sobbed with such intensity, it felt as if her body were being torn apart.

Pog let her cry for a short time. Then he knelt in front of her, slid his arms around her, held her tight. "There, now. I know, darling. I know you loved him."

She snapped her head up hard and fast. "Loved him! I hated him, hated him with everything in me, Pog, and for most of my life. And I always would have."

Pog lowered his eyes, not commenting.

"It's unfair, that's why I weep! Unfair that the man I so enjoyed hating has been taken from me. Unfair that I've been denied the chance to beat him fairly in this battle for Rush. And utterly unfair for anyone, even the devil himself, to be so thoroughly betrayed by his own brother. That's why I cry, Pog. And for no other reason!"

Pog nodded.

"But now . . . now, this Vincent. He must be exposed for the traitor that he is, Pog. Tristan's death must be avenged, and by the gods, I'll be the one to do it!"

"No."

She blinked twice, and stared at him. "What do you mean, no?"

"I mean no. Bridín, you are our princess, our leader, and we love you."

"Why are you speaking in the plural, Pog?" She looked around him, seeing no one.

"Because this is not my decision, my lady, but one reached by all of us. Vincent is vicious. Tristan never would have harmed you. Never. We all knew that. But Vincent . . . Gods, lady, he murdered his own brother for the crown. And now he'll hunt you down like a rabbit."

Bridín narrowed her eyes. "Let him try," she whispered.

"No, Bridín. We're not going to let him try." She shook her head.

"There's no time to argue. Tristan knew where these catacombs of ours were. He'd known for weeks."

"He . . . ?"

"He wouldn't mount a raid, nor would he allow anyone else to do so, because he knew the danger to you in such an effort."

She rolled her eyes. "You give him more honor than he ever possessed, Pog."

"Nonetheless, we have no way of telling who else he shared this information with. If Vincent knows, we can expect a raid at any moment. And that's not a risk we're willing to take."

"So we'll move. Deep into the forest. We'll regroup, heal our wounded, build more weapons—"

"Before your dear mother died, Bridín, she knew you'd need help one day. And she made me give my vow to protect you when you returned here. Even if it meant disobeying your direct orders. I swore I would do so, and that's what I'm doing now."

Bridín took a single step backwards. "What are you saying, Pog?"

He drew a deep breath, squared his shoulders. "Come in here, please, Marinda," he said loudly.

Stiffening in shock, Bridín whirled to see what

appeared at first to be a little girl, slowly entering the cave. But she wasn't a little girl at all. With long, dark curls and huge brown eyes, smooth skin, and slight stature, she was a Wood Nymph. The one so skilled at making healing potions and brews. One of the ever-young creatures of the forest, the most highly psychic beings in the universe.

She wore a leaf green tunic and hose, like everyone else, for camouflage. In her small hands she carried a smooth, round ball of quartz crystal. The fire leapt and danced its reflection in the clear stone, and sparkled on the fissures and facets inside it.

Marinda bowed deeply. "Your Highness," she said. "I have a message for you. It comes from your sweet mother, Máire, whose beautiful face I have seen here in this scrying crystal. And you must heed her words, my princess. She's very emphatic about that."

Bridín's hands touched her cheeks. "My mother? You've spoken to my mother?"

"It's she who has spoken to me, my lady Bridín. Or rather, her magic. She infused this stone with her magic when she was still with us. And it's that magic that speaks to you now. In her stead, because she can't be here to advise you herself."

Bridín rushed forward, dropping to her knees in front of the childlike woman, taking the crystal ball from her hands and searching its depths. "Mother! Are you there? Can you hear me? Mother, please, tell me the truth. Tell me . . . is Tristan truly dead? Can it be true? Is he really gone?'' She shook the thing and stared some more.

''My lady, please. You must understand, your mother isn't living inside this crystal. But the ball is simply a conduit through which I can communicate with her essence . . . that part of her she left behind when she empowered this stone.'' The Wood Nymph held out her hands, smiling gently. Closing her eyes to hide her tears, Bridín returned the ball to her.

Walking in tiny steps, Marinda moved past her to set the ball on a flat stone, near the fire. Then she sat down on the other side of it, and Bridín went closer to look over her shoulder. The way the firelight illuminated the crystal was a form of magic in itself.

Marinda stared for a long time, and then nodded. ''Your mother's magic says it is true, my lady. She says, 'The Tristan you knew is gone.' ''

No doubt. Not anymore. Bridín's knees buckled and she sank to the floor. She couldn't stop the tears this time, so she didn't even bother to try.

Bridín. Do not weep, my beloved daughter.

Her head came up sharply. That was the voice of her mother. She knew it was, somewhere deep inside her. And as she looked, she saw a face, hazy, but there, wild red hair and blue, blue eyes, and a gentle smile, deep inside the ball.

''Mamma?''

She looked at Pog, but he seemed to have frozen in time, sitting utterly still on the far side of the fire. And Marinda, too, had become a tiny statue.

Bridín's gaze returned to the crystal, to her

mother. "Mamma, what should I do? I feel . . . Gods, Mamma, it's so confusing."

I know, darling. That is why I've come to you now. Heed my words, Bridín. Do as I say and do not let your pride prevent your obedience. For I am your mother, as well as your queen.

"I'll listen, Mamma. I promise."

You must go now. Return to the other side, the world without magic, the mortal realm, my Bridín. And there you must remain.

"But I can't! I only just came back, Mamma, and the people . . . they need me."

They need you alive, my child. And the evil Vincent will see to it you are not, if you remain. You cannot retake the kingdom alone. There is someone awaiting you.

"Who? I don't understand."

A man, Bridín. A man who will return with you, and who will fight for Rush alongside you, and who will rule by your side. You must return to the mortal realm and wait for him. When you find him, you will know. Marry him, Bridín. Be his queen. Make him your king. And return triumphant to the thrones of Rush.

Bridín lowered her head, shook it. "I need no man's help, Mamma. I can retake the kingdom on my own, and I will."

No, my darling. That I cannot allow. Pog is under my command. The magic I left behind, that which speaks to you now, guides his actions, though he knows it not. And he will force you bodily through the doorway and into the world beyond, if I will it.

"But, Mamma, I must stay."

No, Bridín. You must go.

"How will I get back?" she cried. "Mamma, I

cannot come back without my pendants! And I don't have them anymore! Mamma! Wait!''

But the image of her mother faded from the crystal ball, and Bridín was left more confused than ever before. Pog seemed to rouse from his frozen state, and so did Marinda. She rose, and turned, her ball once again in her hands. "For you, my lady," she said, bowing her head and extending her hands toward Bridín. "Take it with you, and my blessing with it."

Bridín took the ball, handling it with great care and reverence. "Thank you, Marinda. But I'm not going anywhere."

"Yes, you are, my lady," Pog said, and Bridín felt a warning chill race into her nape as Marinda quickly scurried away.

"No, Pog," she said.

But Pog shouted all the same. "Men!"

And there was the thunder of booted feet, and within seconds Bridín was surrounded . . . by her own people. "You can't do this!" she shouted. "This is treason!"

"Forgive me, Bridín," Pog said, and his soft voice was actually wavering. "But somehow I am certain this is the only way. I love you, dear cousin. And I am also certain that one day you'll thank me for this rash action I now take." Then he nodded to the men who surrounded her. "For the princess's own protection, we must act. Take her, now, by force if necessary, to the portal deep in the forest . . ." He drew a deep breath and sighed. "And force her through to the other side."

Chapter Three

SHE TRIED TO return through the portal, but it was no use. She was met with a solid wall of resistance, invisible but powerful, and put there by her mother for her own protection. She knew that, but felt far from grateful as she sank to the ground and closed her eyes in abject defeat. For all her life, she'd existed for the moment she would return to Rush. She'd plotted and planned for that day. And now she'd lost it. It was yanked from her grasp and smashed to bits. Her dearest enemy murdered by his own blood. And she was left with nothing. *Nothing.*

"My lady Bridín! Wait!"

Bridín's head came up sharply, just as the tiny Wood Nymph, Marinda, stumbled from beyond the invisible curtain, clutching the crystal ball in her arms as if she were carrying a baby. To most eyes it would seem she'd simply appeared there. And that shimmery veil in the air would seem no more than mist or heat waves or some mortal thing.

Marinda caught her balance and, wide-eyed,

looked around her. They were in a tiny clearing, no more than a patch of forest grass big enough for a humble picnic. The cave stood at Bridín's back. She knew it well.

"My goodness," Marinda said softly. "The other side doesn't seem much different at all!"

"We're not on the other side, Marinda. Nor are we in Rush any longer. This is . . . It's nowhere, really. It's an in-between place."

Marinda's eyes narrowed as she scanned the ground. "It is a circle," she said softly, and clutching the crystal still, she walked the border of this nowhere place, her tiny feet moving through the deep blue-green grass. She moved along the inner edge of the shimmering, transparent veil. Only now did Bridín realize the portal was curved. A half circle made entirely of her mother's magic. It ended where the cave began, but the cave's entrance bowed inward, making the other half of Marinda's circle.

"There's no wind here, my lady Bridín. Have you noticed? Nor warmth, nor cold."

Bridín tilted her head to one side, studying the childlike creature curiously. She didn't see what difference it made whether this spot in between the worlds was circular. Yet she wasn't willing to discount Marinda's observations. The woman was too highly skilled in the mystical arts to be taken lightly. So she remained seated, and she remained silent, and she waited.

Marinda returned to the center of the clearing and lowered her crystal ball to the flat stone there, which looked to be some sort of marble, nearly overgrown now with grass and soil. Bridín hadn't even noticed it before. But Marinda had seemed to know it would be there without even looking for it. She just brushed the dirt and growth aside, and placed the crystal there as if it belonged. Then she rose again and pointed. "The stone face of that cave marks the northernmost point of the circle," she said very softly. And then she looked to her left, eyes narrowing as she bent forward to look closer. And then she nodded. "See there? That tiny spring of water bubbling from the earth at the west?" She pursed her lips and walked to the right, and then dropped to her knees, her hands feeling the ground. "If I'm right, then . . . Ah, yes!" She held up a feather she'd located, smiling brightly. It was bright yellow and seemed as light and fluffy as down. "A feather in the east. My lady, this is indeed a place of great power."

Bridín looked around. "I hadn't realized that, Marinda. But what are you—"

"The south, though," Marinda mused, pacing back to the exact point where she'd entered. "There ought to be fire in the south. Or . . . or something."

"It's fascinating, Marinda. But what are you doing here? Why did you come through after me? The other side is no place for a wood nymph."

Dropping to her knees, Marinda clawed her fingers into the soft earth, scooping up handfuls of sod and filtering it through her fingers. "Of course," she said brightly, brushing at something. She turned and held the huge, sparkling gem in her palm. "A diamond."

"Of course," Bridín sighed.

Marinda turned again and reburied the blindingly brilliant stone where she'd found it. Then she rose, slapping her hands one against the other to clean the rich black earth away.

"Marinda," Bridín began.

"Yes, I know, my lady. You want to know why I followed you."

"Yes."

"Well, you left your scrying sphere behind. Your crystal ball," she said, when Bridín lifted a brow. "And you'll need it."

"What for?" Bridín asked.

"I don't know just yet. But I know you will." She smoothed her knee-length tunic over her green hose. "So let's be on our way, then."

"Marinda . . ." But the little nymph was already light-stepping past Bridín. She paused at the mouth of the cave and peered inside.

"Is this the way to the other side?"

"Not for you," Bridín said, getting to her feet and joining Marinda there. "You must go back. The mortal realm is no place for you."

Marinda looked up at Bridín, her huge brown eyes so lovely, and so filled with the wisdom of the ages. She only looked like a little girl if one didn't look too closely. Staring into her eyes was like looking into the eyes of time itself. She tossed her raven curls and lifted her chin. "I'm coming with you, my lady. You are my princess, and where you go, I go."

"It isn't safe."

"You will need me."

"Marinda—"

"I can travel freely back and forth through the portal, my lady. I can keep you abreast of what's happening in Rush, and deliver messages from you to your people." She tilted her head and looked into the cave once more. "Pog thinks it a fine idea. Your mortal friend, Raze, wanted to come with you. But as you know, a mortal can only pass through the veil once. Raze would have had to stay on the other side forever if he'd returned with you now. And since he knows you'll be back, he chose to await you there." She shook her head. "That old mortal adores you, my lady."

"I know." Bridín had hugged him desperately before they'd forced her through the veil. But even Raze had agreed that it was for the best. She'd been stunned.

"Besides," Marinda said, "I've always wished to see the other side."

"Pog is lucky I didn't do him harm," Bridín said sharply, drawing the nymph's gaze back to her. "I'd like to throttle him for this."

"He was only obeying your mother's wishes," Marinda said. "The wishes of his queen, my lady. He loves you deeply, you know."

Bridín softened, unwillingly. "I suppose that's true enough." She studied the small woman, drew a deep breath. "I suppose you'll pass as a child, so long as no one looks too closely. But you'll have to play the part, Marinda. And promise to return should I decide it's too dangerous for you to stay. Agreed?"

Marinda nodded. "Of course, my lady."

Bridín nodded. "All right then. You may come with me." Bridín picked up the crystal ball and tucked it into the cloth sack that had been pressed into her hands as she was delivered through the portal. Then she turned and took

Marinda's hand. "Come. This is the way."

Marinda's excitement was impossible to conceal as she walked at Bridín's side into the dark cave, all the way to the wider space at its rear. They circled the room once, clockwise, and then returned to the entrance. Bridín had to crouch to fit through, but Marinda was small enough to walk upright. They emerged again, into a rain-wet, dripping forest that looked like the one they'd been in before only on its surface. Any person of magic would know right away that it was not the same.

"So this is it," Marinda said, sounding unimpressed as she glanced up at the gray storm clouds above. "Where do we go from here?"

Bridín smiled very slightly, for the first time in many hours. "To my sister," she said softly. "It's been months since I've seen her. And I have not yet seen my newly born nephew." For a moment, the memories of the battle . . . of the blood . . . of Tristan's eyes meeting hers as he lay dying, clouded her eyes and made her stomach convulse. But she shook the sadness away and started forward, through the forest, over the path her sister's husband had shown her long ago.

Brigit sat by the fire, singing softly and rocking her tiny baby in her arms. But her song stopped abruptly as a shiver of apprehension danced up her spine. It was the second time she'd felt this way in the space of the past twenty-four hours. Something was wrong. She felt it in her soul.

Adam rose and came to gently take the sleeping child from her lap. He bent to kiss the baby's forehead before taking him to his cradle. He tucked a blanket over the baby and then returned to his wife, kneeling in front of her.

"What is it, Brigit?"

She met his eyes and smiled. "You know me too well," she said softly.

"Well enough to know when something's bothering you. Come on, tell me. What's going on?"

Brigit closed her eyes. "I wish I knew." She took his hands and let him pull her to her feet. Then she drew him to the big window that looked out over Cayuga Lake, and leaned into his strong embrace as she stared out at the pouring rain pummeling the dark water. "Something's happening. I don't know what, but—"

Her words were cut off by a soft rapping at the front door. And she whirled, her eyes widening, and whispered, "Bridín!" She pulled free of Adam's arms and ran from the study, through the double doors into the living room, and then flung the front door open.

Her sister stood on the step, rain-drenched and so, so sad. Her long golden hair hung down her back, clinging to the Robin Hood–like clothes she wore. My God, she had a sword belted around her waist!

Brigit shook herself, and wrapped her arms around her sister's cold, wet shoulders, pulling her close, hugging her hard. "Bridín. Thank God you're here. Come on, come inside, get warm."

Bridín did so, and then Brigit realized her sister wasn't alone. There was a breathtakingly beautiful little Wood Nymph at her side. "Come, both of you," Brigit said quickly, and she tightened her arm on her sister's shoulders as she pulled her inside.

Adam closed the door behind them, gripped Bridín's hand, and squeezed it hard. "God, it's good to see you," he said. "Come in by the fire. You're soaked to the skin. Are you all right?" He glanced down at the Wood Nymph and smiled. "You poor little thing, you must be half-frozen." Adam snatched a blanket from the sofa and gently draped it over the little woman's shoulders, then he ushered them both into the study, he and Brigit both talking at once.

Bridín pulled free of him and remained where she was, standing near the door, looking into her sister's eyes.

Brigit glanced at her husband, and he nodded, understanding her unspoken message. "Come along," he said to the Wood Nymph, who nodded and went with him, leaving Brigit alone with her sister.

"What's happened?" she asked softly.

Bridín stared into her eyes for a long moment. And then she fell into Brigit's arms, her shoulders shaking with sobs, her tears warm. "He's dead, Brigit. That bastard Tristan of Shara is dead. And I ought to be happy. I really ought to be . . ."

Brigit closed her eyes and held her sister tighter.

Tristan sat close to the small fire's glow. It wasn't cold in the forest. He shouldn't be shivering. But he was, and even the snapping flames couldn't chase the chill away.

He'd nearly died. Probably would have if not

for Tate's perseverance. The childlike man had made poultices of herbs and roots and soil, and had packed them over the hastily stitched wound in Tristan's shoulder. He'd changed them every hour, even through the nights. He'd brewed a foul-tasting tea and forced Tristan to drink a cupful at regular intervals, but refused to say what went into it. As bad as the stuff tasted, Tristan wasn't sure he wanted to know. Tate had also taken great pains to repair the broken chains of Bridín's two pendants. And then he'd fastened them about Tristan's neck, and warned him sternly never to remove the charms.

It was the most bitter irony, Tristan thought now as he stared into the dancing flames. For years he'd plotted and schemed to find a way to get hold of the pendants, to remove them from Bridín's throat. Now he had the things. But he'd lost his kingdom.

"To my own brother, no less," he muttered. "Tate was right all along."

"Of course Tate was right." Tate's voice came from the forest beyond the firelight, and startled Tristan. Tate stepped into the circle of yellow glow. "Tate is always right," he said. "You'd best remember it from now on."

"I think," Tristan replied, "that this is one lesson too hard learned to be easily forgotten."

Tate smiled and moved closer, leaning over the rickety tripod fashioned of tree limbs, and removing the small tin pot.

"Have you had your tea yet tonight, my lord?"

"Of course," Tristan lied, slanting his gaze at Tate's face to judge whether or not he'd be believed.

"Of course," Tate repeated, and he filled a tin cup, replaced the pot on its hook above the flames, and turned to press the obnoxious concoction into Tristan's cold hands. "Drink."

"First tell me what you learned on your reconnaissance mission, little friend. What is the situation?"

Tate sighed heavily and sat down beside Tristan. "She's fine," he said with a knowing glance at Tristan. "Escaped your brother unscathed, thanks to your foolish heroics."

Tristan closed his eyes and felt every tense muscle in his body relax. She was alive. Thank the gods.

"Knew you'd be glad to hear it, seeing as how you nearly got your head lopped off to save her."

Tristan didn't like the speculation he saw in his friend's big, dark eyes. "You're the one who made me promise to protect her," he said, smiling. But then all thoughts of mirth fled him. "I couldn't just let him kill her, Tate."

"Nor am I saying you should have. But it would seem to me there might have been a less life-threatening way to intervene."

Tristan lowered his head. "It didn't seem so dangerous at the time. I never believed my own brother would strike me down."

"But you believe it now."

"I have no choice but to believe it." He lifted his head again, searching Tate's eyes. "Where is she? Is she safe from Vincent?"

Tate shrugged. "Depends on how determined he is to have her, my lord. She's left. Gone back to the other side."

Tristan frowned. "She couldn't have. She wouldn't have left Rush. Not for anything." He couldn't believe it was true. That Bridín could walk away, knowing he was languishing in his own dungeons while his brother accused him of treachery. Unless . . . unless he'd misjudged her all along. Perhaps she really did hate him as much as she claimed.

"No, Tristan," Tate said softly, putting a hand on Tristan's uninjured shoulder. "It isn't that at all."

Tristan rolled his eyes. "Stop reading my thoughts, nymph."

"But they make for such interesting reading." Tate grinned at him, but then his face turned serious again. "Your brother has announced to the kingdom that you're dead, my lord. Bridín . . . Well, they say she took the news very badly."

"Did she?" And just why should that bit of news make him feel so good?

"Yes indeed. I'm told she collapsed in grief, and cried enough to flood the rivers. Her followers forced her through the doorway, Tristan. And you know she cannot return without the pendants."

Tristan nodded. "Good, then. At least I don't have her to worry about. Only my traitorous brother." But he wasn't thinking about his brother. He was thinking about Bridín. Had she truly grieved for him? Cried for him?

"Drink your tea."

Grimacing, Tristan sipped at the stuff. The taste sent a shudder through him, but he took another drink. Whatever it was, it seemed to be helping. Or . . . something was.

"We need to make a plan, Tate. I've been thinking on this, and I know there have to be knights in the kingdom who will believe my version of events over my brother's. We have to find them, contact them somehow, and let them know I'm not dead. And we need to begin gathering evidence against Vincent . . . evidence that will prove—"

"No, my prince. That is not the way we'll retake the kingdom. For one thing, public sentiment has turned against you, and against Bridín as well." Tristan frowned, but nodded at Tate to go on. "The night before she attacked the kingdom, several outlying villages were raided and burned. The attackers wore the garb of the forest dwellers, and were led by a golden-haired female."

Tristan shook his head slowly. "Not Bridín," he said without hesitation. "No, she wouldn't turn against her own people. Not if her life depended on it."

"You're certain?" Tate asked.

"Of course I'm certain."

"You know her very well, don't you, my lord?"

Tristan closed his eyes, and instantly saw her as she'd been years ago. A golden child, held in captivity. By him, a prince only ten years her senior. Even then it had torn at him to have to keep her that way. But he'd had no choice. Her eyes . . . Gods, he could feel them staring into his, and into his soul, even now.

"I know her," he whispered, "better than anyone else ever has, or ever will."

"Good. That will make our plan a great deal easier."

Tristan's head came up. "Bridín has left the realm of magic, Tate. You said so yourself. She's no longer a part of this. It's between me and my brother now."

Tate got to his feet and paced in a circle around the fire, stopping again only when he arrived at Tristan's other side. "I'm afraid, my prince, that she is very much a part of it. A vital part." He held up a small hand when Tristan would have objected. "Hear me out, my friend. You know my advice is sound. You trust me, don't you?"

Tristan looked away with a sigh, then looked back at Tate once more. "You know I trust you with my very life. Go on. Tell me what you think."

"I think," Tate said, "that your brother's rule is solid. He's had months to plan for this, Tristan. Years even. From the very beginning he encouraged you to place his own closest confidants in positions of power and trust. Most of your own knights are truly loyal to Vincent. And now, with him blaming those raids on Bridín, and blaming her escape on you . . ." Tate sighed and shook his head. "No, Tristan. I fear you'll never be able to regain the throne. Not alone, at least."

Tristan got to his feet, careful not to use his left arm, or even move it. "If not alone," he said, looking down at Tate, "then how?"

"As king," Tate said, tipping his head back so he could meet Tristan's eyes. "And for that, my lord, you will need a queen."

And his meaning was very clear in that moment. Too clear. "No," he said. "Bridín would never agree to—"

"Bridín won't know, my lord. Not until it's too late."

Sighing in frustration, Tristan began pacing. "You speak nonsense, Tate."

"No, Tristan, I speak with the wisdom of a hundred thirty years, plus six. I, too, have been devising a plan. And mine is far superior than anything else we might attempt. The lady Bridín has had a message from beyond, from her very own mother, through the magic of a scrying crystal. She's been told she must remain on the other side until she finds a man who will return as her partner, her husband, and her king. She knows not who this man will be, only that she will find him in the mortal realm."

Tristan's head came up, but he did not turn around. "She's gone there to . . . to seek a husband?"

"She was given little choice, my lord. Don't you see the opportunity this presents to you? Especially since the Tristan she claims to hate is a man she believes to be dead."

Tristan turned slowly, staring at Tate in disbelief. "You're suggesting I go there, find Bridín, and somehow trick her into believing I'm someone else? Trick her into marrying me, Tate?" He shook his head. "It's impossible."

"Now, Tristan, would I suggest it if it were impossible?"

Tristan blew air through his teeth and lowered his chin.

"My lord, I have magic in me. This you know, as you've always known it. I can alter your appearance. Not to any great extent, but slightly. Enough to fool her."

Tristan's head came up slowly. "And can this magic of yours also make the woman love me, Tate? Enough to marry me? Enough to place in my hands the crown she considers hers alone?"

Tate shrugged. "I'm a Wood Nymph, not a god. That part will be up to you. Although . . ." He bit off the rest of whatever he'd been about to say, and gnawed his lower lip. "Think of it, Tristan. The two of you together . . . Nothing could stop you then. Not even the machinations of your brother. If the people saw you, hand in hand, they'd believe you. Don't you see?"

The plan, Tristan had to admit, held certain appeal. Ah, but it would never work. Bridín would know him. She'd *know* him.

"Eventually, perhaps," Tate said, reading his thoughts yet again. "That only means, my lord, that you will have to work fast. Before she realizes the truth."

Tristan stared into the fire, but he was seeing Bridín's eyes. "And what then, my friend? What happens when she does realize the truth?"

"That will be a problem we'll have to deal with when it happens. One step at a time, my lord."

Grating his teeth, Tristan paced. "I don't know," he said.

"It's the only way," Tate said, and the tone of his voice left no room for doubt.

Closing his eyes, and praying he wouldn't live to regret it, Tristan said softly, "The only way.

Well, then I suppose we don't have much of a choice, do we, Tate?''

"No, sir, I don't suppose we do.''

Tristan nodded once, firmly. "Then so be it.''

Chapter Four

BRIDÍN WAS GLAD of her sister's help before long. Brigit had held her through that first long night as she'd poured out the tale of all that had happened. The comforting Brigit gave was like none she'd known before. Not since their precious mother had been taken, murdered, her body disposed of by those cruel invaders so that they couldn't even wish her a proper farewell. Having Brigit's arms around her that night was very much like having her mother back again. And she'd needed it. Desperately.

Of course, she'd had to pull herself together eventually. Brigit told her she would heal, but Bridín doubted it. Even the hours she'd spent snuggling tiny nephew Jonathon failed to take away the pain. And it shouldn't hurt this much. She hadn't lost the kingdom forever. She'd get it back.

Slowly she put her lingering, illogical pain aside. She had to begin to make some sort of life for herself here in this realm devoid of magic, while she sought this man she was supposed to wed. And Brigit had helped her with that as well. She'd given her clothing and helped her to find an apartment of her own. Of course, she'd have rather had Bridín live with her and her precious little Jonathon, and Adam. But Bridín had insisted on finding her own place. There was always a slim chance Vincent would attempt to hunt her down, and she wouldn't dream of putting her sister and family at risk by living with them.

So with Brigit's help, she'd achieved independence. Even found employment in a shop a few doors away from her sister's.

She'd never realized how very little she knew about existing alone in the mortal realm. Though she'd lived here from infancy, she'd been Tristan's prisoner for most of that time. He'd seen to it she had everything she needed . . . right down to the movie projector and reels upon reels of Disney films he'd procured for her when she was very young. And beautiful clothes to wear. And servants to see to her every need. A tutor to educate her. A cook who could make her mouth water just from the aromas of the meals as they were prepared. And his own constant guardianship, as he'd always called it. The older she became, the more often he'd neglect his duties of running her kingdom, to come and watch over her. To sit and share a meal with her, or slip into her bedroom and look on her as she slept. When she'd changed from adolescent to young woman, something else had changed as well. The energy between them had altered. And she'd known his desire for her, recognized it. She'd never admitted that she felt similarly drawn to him. But she had. And those feelings haunted her now.

Familiar tears burned in the backs of her eyes, and she chided herself inwardly. Tristan was gone. Just one of the obstacles standing between her and her throne removed, and certainly nothing to mourn over.

He was gone.

She closed her eyes and sighed, popping them open again when a warm hand closed on her shoulder from behind. "Bridín, you've been polishing that same cluster for ten minutes. You keep it up, you'll rub it down to a handful of amethyst dust."

She blinked and looked down at the large, glittering rectangle of amethyst in her palm. "I'm sorry, John," she said. "I drifted off, I guess."

Her employer smiled at her and took the stone from her palm, turning to place it just so inside a glass case lined with other glittery crystals and countless pewter figurines. Wizards. Dragons. Fairies with painted butterfly's wings as big as their entire bodies.

Bridín glanced at the latter and tried to stifle an ironic smile. Everyone in Rush knew that only fay folk of royal blood and purest magic were born with wings. And her dear mother had been the last of those. The bloodline was mingled with mortal blood in Bridín and her sister, whose father had been mortal. No wings. And if there had been, they'd have been thin and filmy and light.

A gorgeous young female customer breezed in, smiled brightly at John, and then headed to the room in the back to check out the candle collection.

"So how's the new apartment?" John asked,

with the briefest nod at the pretty woman in the back.

Bridín shrugged. "Small for the two of us, but I suppose it's better than a cave."

John's dark brows drew close and he tilted his head to one side. "You know why I'm glad I hired you, kid? 'Cause you're an oddball. I like that in a girl." He winked and headed behind the counter when the telephone there started ringing.

Bridín studied John for a long moment. When her sister had brought her here in response to John's HELP WANTED sign, she'd taken one look at him and thought he might just be the one. He was handsome, and could, Bridín suspected, charm the venom from a cobra. In fact, she'd even secretly hoped he'd turn out to be the one. He was pleasant and kind and intelligent, and the two of them got along from the start, with an easy, almost immediate friendship.

But as it turned out, he was married. Moreover, he had children. And if that hadn't been enough . . . well, she'd had Marinda consult the crystal on the matter. And the ball, Marinda said, had turned a cloudy shade of deep gray, which was a definite "no."

John caught her gaze and gave her his sexy smile. Bridín sighed. Six months in this realm, and still no sign of this mate she was supposed to be awaiting. She was eager and more than a bit nervous about meeting this man who would help her to reclaim her kingdom. Eager because the sooner she found him, the sooner she could return home. Nervous because it would be difficult to follow through with the plan. Marrying a man she did not love had never been part of Bridín's vision for her future. And there was no doubt in her mind that she would not love him.

Clamping down on a twinge of envy for John's wife, she turned to see if she could help the pretty woman in the back. The girl looked to be of college age. Probably a student from the nearby university. She seemed friendly and sweet and greeted Bridín with a bright smile.

"Is there anything I can help you with?" Bridín asked.

"Just looking," she replied, stroking the bumpy back of a gleaming, brightly colored wax dragon. "I just love this shop. It must be sheer heaven to work here."

Bridín smiled back at her. Young people reacted pretty much the same way to this place. They liked the New Age music John always had playing. They liked the smell of the incense he kept burning. They liked the jewelry and tiny collection of crystal skulls and the 3-D posters. But basically Bridín suspected they liked John. Brigit had been brilliant when she'd suggested this place to Bridín. There was magic here. One could almost taste it.

"Ooooh, look at the stones!" the girl said, and went hurrying back into the main room, making a beeline for the amethyst cluster Bridín had been polishing when she'd first come in. "Can I see that one, please?"

"Of course." Bridín took a key from her pocket, opened the case, and removed the deep purple stone, placing it in the girl's hand with care. The girl sighed as she held it and looked at its facets flashing up at her.

"One of the most powerful stones in the place," John called, hanging up the phone and coming around the counter. "Look at that tallest point in the center. See the shadow inside it? That's special."

The girl blinked, narrowing her eyes and staring.

"Actually," John went on, "I was thinking about keeping that one. It's very potent. I can tell. That stone could really open up some psychic channels . . . probably do some healing work, too. No doubt in my mind. And—"

"How much?" the girl said, drawing her now awestruck gaze away from the stone.

"For you," John said with a wink, "fifteen bucks."

"I'll take it." She hurried over to the counter and set the stone down. John slanted a triumphant glance at Bridín. She only smiled back at him and shook her head.

The man knew as much as any mortal could know about spells and magic and crystals and herbs. She still hadn't decided whether he believed any of it, though.

As John rang up the sale, and then carefully wrapped the stone and boxed it, the girl turned to Bridín and held out a hand. "I'm Tiffany," she said.

Bridín took the proffered hand and gave it a friendly squeeze. "Bridín," she replied. "Pleased to meet you." It was only as the girl took her package and turned to go that Bridín caught the faintest vibration of deceit emanating from her. But it was so brief, she couldn't be sure.

* * *

Tristan waited in a booth at a place called Hal's Deli; he sipped coffee that should have been licensed as an addictive substance, it was so good. Tate sat across from him, and Tristan suspected every mortal in the place thought he was a little boy. Tristan's little boy. The idea was so funny, he would have laughed aloud . . . if he hadn't been so damned nervous.

He'd known well enough where to look for Bridín when his shoulder had finally healed and his body had fought off the infection that had set in shortly thereafter. Near her sister. And sure enough, he thought he'd finally tracked her down right here on Ithaca's Commons. A woman fitting Bridín's description was, he was told, working at a New Age shop known as 3-D Lite. Being that it was only a few doors down from Brigit Malone Reid's flower shop, Akasha, he was nearly certain the information was correct. And in a moment he'd know for sure.

"Don't be so nervous," Tate whispered across the table. "And for the fourth time, get me a cup of that coffee. It smells incredible."

"Children don't drink coffee, Tate. Be quiet and drink your milk."

Tate scowled. Then the pretty young thing they'd been waiting for sauntered in and headed for their table. She slid in beside Tristan and smiled at him. A smile she intended to be beguiling, Tristan knew. It had no effect on him. None whatsoever. And for a moment, he wondered why.

"Well?" he asked her.

"She's tall, very slender, has golden blond hair that reaches past her waist, and eyes that are so blue, they make the lapis lazuli in the case look dull." The girl opened the bag she was carrying and removed a small box. Then she lifted the lid and fingered a pretty purple stone. "She was very nice," she added absently.

"And?" Tristan prodded.

Her head came up. "Look, I like her. You're not . . . like, a stalker or anything, are you? Because I won't be—"

"I'm not a stalker," he promised. "I'm an old friend, just as I told you. But I don't want to make a fool out of myself by blundering in there until I'm sure she is who I think she is."

"The girl you knew when you were kids," she finished, repeating his own cover story back to him.

"Exactly."

It was an awkward way to be sure, but he had to know before he saw her. He had to be prepared. And he couldn't send Tate in, because if she looked closely at him, she'd recognize him for what he was.

"Okay," the girl said. "She told me her name is Bridín."

It seemed to Tristan that his heart stopped beating just then. He'd found her. Gods have mercy, now he'd have no choice but to set this ludicrous plan into motion.

"Well?" the girl said.

Tristan fumbled in his pocket, pulled out a twenty, and laid it on the table. The girl snatched it up, quickly replacing her rock in the bag. She looked at him expectantly.

"That's all," he said. "You can go."

She shrugged, got up, and left them alone.

"So," Tate said. "We've found her."

Tristan closed his eyes. He'd led armies into battle with less churning in his stomach. "Tomorrow," he said. "I'll see her . . . tomorrow."

Vincent of Shara was a man content with the way things had turned out. So much so that he nearly purred with it. He'd convinced the entire realm that his brother was a traitor, and that he'd died by the hand of fate itself. He'd convinced them that Bridín, the beloved of nearly all of the fools, had betrayed them, turned against her own people in a fit of rage and frustration. And that now she had fled them all, abandoning them to save herself.

And they believed him. Left with no one else, they'd turned to him for advice and solace and guidance. Leadership. "They love me now," he muttered, as he sat in the royal bedchamber that had, until recently, belonged to his brother.

"They fear you," said his first knight, Kenniwick.

Vincent smiled and sat up a bit straighter on the satin-covered settee that rested near the hearth. "What difference does it make? They obey me. That's all that matters."

"For now it is, my lord. But it could come to matter—and most easily."

Kenniwick seemed agitated, his stance constantly shifting, and his hand opening and closing over the hilt of his sheathed sword. Vincent detested bad news. Therefore his men detested the job of delivering it. He tilted his head, narrowed his eyes. "If you have a message for me,

Kenniwick, then deliver it and be gone. I've appointments to keep, you know."

Kenniwick swallowed hard, no doubt knowing exactly what sort of appointments Vincent referred to, and no doubt disapproving. Too bad. He was the ruler now. Prince, for the moment. King, when he found a woman worthy of him. And even then he'd continue the practice Kenniwick found so distasteful. The law that allowed for it was still on the books, one of the few "barbaric" codes his softhearted brother hadn't eradicated—but only because it had somehow slipped past his notice.

"You Majesty," Kenniwick said, bowing low. "Reports on your brother's whereabouts have come in. It's been confirmed, Sire. He's returned to the other side."

"Good riddance, then. Let him remain there."

"But, my lord, should he return—"

"Should he return," Vincent said, getting slowly to his feet and leveling his harshest glare on his knight, "he will be killed."

Kenniwick swallowed hard, nodded fast. "Of course, Your Majesty. That would be your intent. But you promoted me to this position because you sought my counsel, and I feel that in this matter I ought to speak it. You may take my advice or leave it by the wayside, but I'd be slack in my duties did I not—"

"Stop the jabbering, Kenniwick, and say whatever it is you have to say. Dire predictions of doom, no doubt." Vincent absently released the large gold pins holding his cloak to either shoulder, and let it fall to the floor. The servants would care for it later. He paced to his nightstand and dropped the baubles into the hand-tooled box there.

"The other side, my lord, is also the place to which the lady Bridín has fled."

"So?" he asked, fingering trinkets, and wondering which of the royal jewels he would wear on the morrow.

"My lord, should the lady Bridín and Lord Tristan join forces to overthrow your reign..." He paused there, and when Vincent turned it was to see Kenniwick shaking his head. He looked up, met his sovereign's eyes. "Do you see the danger, Sire?"

Vincent rubbed his chin. "I suppose there might be *some* risk," he said thoughtfully. "Do you suppose the people would heed their words, did they speak against me as one?"

"I fear so, my lord. If Tristan and Bridín both spoke publicly about what truly happened here, they would likely be believed."

There was a sound from beyond the closed door, and Vincent smiled softly. When he pulled it open, two armed guards stood there, clasping two women, one who struggled and one who wept. Vincent tilted his head, and the guards shoved the women inside, pulling the door closed.

"My lord," Kenniwick whispered. Vincent didn't turn from his perusal of the tender female flesh, however. He held one slender arm in each hand, gripping hard enough to bruise, and he let his eyes roam his night's entertainment, head to toe.

"Speak your mind, Kenniwick, and then be on your way."

"My lord," he repeated, full voice this time. "It might be wise to refrain from practices which . . . vilify you in the eyes of the people. Perhaps did you show mercy, or kindness to them, they would return to you loyalty should ever you need it."

"The law clearly states," he said slowly, "that the king has the right to take the virgins before they are given over to their husbands."

" 'Tis an antiquated law, my lord. Not practiced in centuries."

"But still written," Vincent said. "What I do is perfectly legal and right." He looked at the women, the sniveling one with raven hair, and the other, who held her chin high and stared at him with fire in her eyes that matched her fiery red mane. "Remove your clothing."

The dark-haired one returned to sobbing. But the one with the strength in her eyes glared at him. "Your reign will be a short one, Vincent of Shara," she hissed from between clenched teeth. And as she spoke, she tore the dress from her own body and flung it at his feet. "Do your worst, but know that I will have vengeance."

She was perhaps the most strikingly beautiful creature he had ever seen in his life. Fire and brimstone in her, and courage he found nothing less than amazing given the circumstances. She stood there, naked before him, as well as the two guards and Kenniwick. And yet she remained rigid, proud. There was no hint of shame in her. Nor should there be. Hers was a body that made him ache with yearning.

"What is your name, defiant one?"

" 'Tis not who I am, Sharan, but what I am that ought worry you."

"You're fay, aren't you?" He studied her, the rounded curves of her. "And no trembling virgin, either. You fay women conceal the truth of your age from maiden to crone. A man never knows what he's getting."

She narrowed her eyes. "Tell me, great king. Do you prefer that I fight you wildly, or comply to your every request willingly tonight?"

Vincent's brows rose. One corner of his mouth pulled into a smile. "You interest me, Fay woman. You're saying you'll comply with my every request?"

"Let this other one go free," she said softly, "and I'll give you the pleasures you've known only in your dreams, if then, Sharan. You'll never know a night as erotic as this one I will give to you." She glanced toward the other woman, cowering in fear. "Or keep her, and I will become as limp and unresponsive as a wet leaf, and you will never know what you denied yourself. 'Tis up to you."

Vincent swallowed hard, unwilling to let her have any say at all, but so aroused by her challenge that he didn't care. Without looking away from her, he whispered, "Kenniwick, take the weak one away. Do what you will with her. And see that I'm not disturbed until further notice."

"Sir," Kenniwick said, hastening forward to gently take the arm of the weeping woman, and guide her toward the door. "But about the other matter, Sire. We must take action to assure that your . . . enemies do not join forces in conspiring against you."

"Yes, fine," Vincent muttered, and licked his lips. "Send assassins to . . . to the place where they are. Kill them. Kill them both."

"Yes, Your Majesty."

Kenniwick backed out of the room, bowing, guiding the woman, and pulling the door closed all in one graceful round of motion.

Vincent smiled. "Fight me," he said softly. "And make it good, or I'll have her brought back."

"So long as you have me here, you loathsome cur, you'll have no desire for any other."

So she was doing this to protect the young women of the villages from his attentions, was she? He almost believed she could live up to her wild claims.

"If you're as talented as you would have me believe," he said, "you might well hold my interest for a good many days."

"Do you expect me to be pleased by the honor?"

He reached for her. She struck him hard across the face, with the clawed end of her fingers. He felt the cuts, felt the blood beading and rolling down his cheek, and his smile widened.

Chapter Five

THE BELLS JANGLED , announcing that a customer had entered. Bridín glanced up from the shelf she'd been arranging to see John busy unpacking and shelving a new box of books on spirit guides and channeling. Busier than she was. Sighing, she set a pewter castle in the center of the shelf, and turned to glance toward the newcomer.

He looked up at the same moment, and their eyes met with an impact so powerful, she felt she'd taken a blow. The shock! She jerked backward in sheer reaction, and a silent cry was wrung from her soul. Her hand hit the little pewter fantasy scene she'd been painstakingly setting up, and figurines flew everywhere. The man froze where he was, his eyes wide and unblinkingly fixed on hers.

John stood up fast, looking from one of them to the other, his frown finally settling on Bridín's face. "Honey, what's wrong? You okay? Jesus, you look like you've seen a ghost."

Bridín blinked her vision clear and narrowed her eyes on the man whose entrance had so shocked her. "For just a moment," she whispered, "I thought I had." She tilted her head and stepped closer to the man. Tall. Broad in the shoulders and narrow in the waist. He wore modern clothing, worn indigo jeans and an army green T-shirt. High-topped black boots with long laces. A brown leather belt.

Still closer she stepped, her gaze raking his features. So like Tristan's . . . but different. His hair was the same wavy mass of black satin, but cut short, and so much tamer. And he wore a very close-cropped coat of dark whiskers on his face. Like a shadow of darkness—the visual evidence of the darkness she'd always sensed shadowing Tristan's soul.

Only . . . this wasn't Tristan. Tristan was dead. The scrying crystal, and her own mother's magic, had told her so. Tristan was dead.

She moved until she stood very close to him. And she saw the minute differences. The shape of his jaw, not as sharply delineated as Tristan's. And his cheekbones were softer, too. His lips seemed less full to some degree, and his brows curved differently.

In fact, the more she told herself this man wasn't her Tristan, the less he resembled her nemesis. Until she was left wondering how she could have looked at this stranger and seen Tristan's face. Then she met his eyes again, and she knew why. It was those eyes, coal black and full of mystery, heavily fringed, and hard and icy cold. A layer of frost sealing in the emotions that stormed and burned underneath. The pain. The hurt. And the passion.

That was where the resemblance was strongest. In the eyes. And if she blocked out the rest of him and only focused on his eyes, it was almost as if she were looking at Tristan again.

And that disturbed her.

He smiled, and the resemblance vanished. He seemed kind, and gentle just then. Nothing like the man she'd known. "I frightened you," he said in a voice that came out as soft as goose down. Deliberately so, she thought. "I'm sorry."

She shook her head, feeling foolish. "You remind me of someone . . . someone I knew once."

"Really?" he asked, lifting his brows. "Who? Someone you were fond of, I hope."

She lowered her head. "Someone I hated with a passion," she told him. "I only just realized how very much I miss the bastard."

He tipped his head to one side. "You miss a man you hated?"

"Hated with a passion," she said. "It's the passion I miss." She looked up at him again and felt her lips pulling into a slight smile. "Gods, how I loved fighting with him."

"Did you win these fights?"

He seemed genuinely curious. "That's just it," she said. "He didn't live long enough for either of us to be declared the victor." She sighed. "Life seems rather boring without him." When she met his eyes again, they were bright, sparkling. "I'm sounding quite insane, aren't I?" she asked. "Never mind. You're here to buy something and I'm here to sell it to you."

"Actually," he said, his voice dropping low, "I'm not sure why I'm here."

"No?"

He shook his head. "I was passing by and I

was overwhelmed with the urge to come in here. Odd, isn't it?"

Gods! Could he be the one?

She blinked and took a step backward. Not him. It mustn't be him. She couldn't bear to be with a man so much like Tristan.

"Anyway, now that I'm here, I could probably be persuaded to make a purchase. Why don't you show me around?"

Her heart was hammering against her rib cage. She tore her gaze away from his dark one, and sent a pleading glance to John.

John gave her an imperceptible nod and set the box he'd been unpacking aside. "I'll show you around, Mr. . . ."

The man's eyes darted around the shop, lighting on the case of crystals. "Stone," he said. "Christian Stone."

"Call me John." Her savior stepped between the two of them, to shake this Christian Stone's strong hand. "My assistant here was just heading out on her lunch break, and I don't want to lose her, so I don't dare keep her any longer. Go on now, Bridín, honey. Get something to eat. See you later." He winked.

Bridín sighed in abject relief, and slid past the disturbing stranger toward the door.

"But I can't let her just leave," Stone said softly.

She froze with her hand on the door, goose bumps racing up and down her spine. Gods, he even *sounded* like Tristan. Softer-spoken, yes, but . . .

"At least, not until I help fix the mess I created."

She turned, then watched as the man crouched down to begin retrieving the toppled figurines from the floor, gathering them into his hands one by one, rising again and spilling them onto the glass shelf. His hands mesmerized her. Long fingers, elegant, like the hands of a wizard, as he set up the pieces again. The castle in the center. The wizard with his comically pointed hat, and the tiny bit of a crystal ball balanced in his palm, beside it. Tiny cottages with trolls and goblins surrounded the castle. And then the fairies, one by one, set up around the outskirts of the tiny village.

Frowning, she stepped forward. "That's not quite right," she whispered.

He turned to face her. So close she could feel his breath fanning her face. "No?"

"No." Tearing her gaze from his, she reached for the fairy with the butterfly's wings, and placed her beside the castle. She took the wizard and placed him outside the village where the fairy had been. Then she took the dragon he still held in his hand and placed it next to the wizard.

"Now, that hardly seems fair," he said.

"Why not? Any wizard worth his salt could slay a dragon."

"And if he's not so great a wizard?"

"Then the dragon will eat him."

He studied the scene, tilting his head, rubbing his chin. "How about a compromise?" He picked up the wizard and set him again beside the little castle, close to the fairy's side.

Bridín's stomach twisted into a hard little knot, and she blinked at an inexplicable burning in her eyes. "Why . . . why did you do that?"

He shrugged. "Seems to me that they'd stand a better chance of slaying that dragon if they worked together."

She searched his face, and her hands grew damp.

"Now that that's finished," he said, surveying his work, "how about that lunch?"

"L-lunch?"

"I was on my way to grab a sandwich myself before I wandered in here. Why don't you join me?"

John cleared his throat, breaking the spell this stranger's familiar eyes had on her. And Bridín looked his way. "Bridín's not in the habit of going out with strange men, Mr. Stone. Wouldn't be wise, in this day and age. I'm sure you understand."

Stone smiled when she looked back at him. "I wasn't suggesting she get into my car and let me drive her away to the middle of nowhere. Just a sandwich. At Hal's. We can walk. Look outside, Bridín. The Commons is crowded with people. You'll be as safe as a princess in the hands of her prince."

She felt her eyes widen, knew she'd drawn in a sudden breath.

"Bridín?" John asked.

"I . . . I can't. I have . . . to see someone. Maybe another time." Bridín was not the kind of woman who ever allowed as senseless an emotion as fear to invade her mind. But it was there now. Senseless, yes, but huge and vivid and real.

Disappointment clouded his eyes. "Well, I'm not one to beg," he said. And she could have sworn a hint of anger tinged his voice. Very unlike the sad expression on his face. He closed his hand around hers, sending warmth and a tingling sensation right up her arm. "I'll see you again, though," he promised.

Her hand trembled in his, and she drew it away quickly, hoping he hadn't noticed. "I have to go," she said, and hurried to the door.

"She knows!" Tristan slammed the door of the suite and turned to glare at Tate's surprised expression.

"Impossible," Tate said, crossing his arms over his chest and scowling.

Tristan sighed, lowering his chin and shaking his head. "Maybe not on the surface, Tate, but somewhere inside her, she knows me. She recognized me the second she looked my way." He crossed the hotel-issue carpet to the wet bar at the far end, took a dewy pitcher of iced tea from the minuscule refrigerator, and filled a glass. "Gods, I've never seen Bridín so shaken."

Tate shrugged and planted himself in the modular sofa's corner seat. It dwarfed him, soft brown plush hugging in on him from all sides. "She doesn't know, Tristan. She can't know. She might have thought she recognized you at first, but her common sense would have ruled it out right away. I told you, she believes you to be dead."

Tristan sighed. "Maybe so. But believing me dead, Tate, is a far cry from believing this *new* me to be the man she's come to find." He took a long, deep drink from the glass. Icy, sweet tea bathed his throat.

Rubbing his chin, Tate nodded. "She refused to go out with you, then?"

"Of course she refused. She's afraid of me." He gazed down into the amber liquid. "Hell, she was never afraid of me before. Even when she was my captive."

"And curious?" Tate said. "You did as I suggested, didn't you, Tristan?"

Sighing hard, Tristan nodded. "I sprinkled my sentences with veiled references to Rush, yes. Which only seemed to shake her further." He recalled the way she'd removed the pewter wizard from the vicinity of the tiny castle, and placed the poor bastard beside the dragon instead. It had angered him. Bridín *always* angered him.

"So she's curious. No doubt she'll consult that crystal ball she has with her tonight. Ask it whether you're the one she's been instructed to seek."

Tristan set the glass on the bar with a bang that sent droplets up to sprinkle his wrist. "And no doubt the ball will tell her that I am not."

"Did you follow her when she left? Find out where she's staying?"

Glowering, Tristan met Tate's eyes and nodded once.

"Good. Give me the address."

Tristan came forward. "Why do you want it, Tate? It's over. She's probably already looked into her magical little orb and learned—"

"It amazes me, Tristan, how very little you know of the ways of my people."

Tristan tilted his head.

"She has a Wood Nymph with her. A powerful one, yes, but, my dear misinformed prince,

Wood Nymphs only scry by night. By moonlight, if possible. Marinda—powerful though she is— will wait until nightfall to consult the crystal. And by then . . . it will be gone."

Tristan blinked in surprise. "You're going to steal it."

Tate smiled. "So the ball won't be ruining your chances to make our plan work. Bridín will have only her own instincts on which to rely. But this is as much as I can do for you, Tristan. You're the one who has to convince her. Charm her."

"Charm a woman I detest," he muttered, shaking his head and pacing the room's center. "I can think of more pleasant chores."

"Make her fall in love with you, Tristan. At least convince her to care for you in some way. Make her believe you're the one she's been waiting for. Your kingdom depends upon it."

Tristan closed his eyes.

"And remember my warnings. The nymph Marinda, she must never set eyes on you. She'll know you at once if she does. We're not as easily fooled as you gullible wizards and fay folk."

"You set such easy tasks for me, Tate. Make a woman who hates even my memory fall in love with me. Make her believe I'm someone else. And never set foot in view of the woman she lives with."

"There is some encouraging news, my lord."

His polite form of address, Tristan knew, was as close to an apology as he was likely to give. "Please, enlighten me. Good news, I need."

"I've found us a house."

Tristan's head came up, and for the first time,

a genuine smile pulled at his lips. "Tell me about it."

"It sits high above Cayuga, on an island. Isolated, as you suggested. In fact, I'm certain it's invisible to mortal eyes. Shrouded in mists, you know."

"Tate, this is the mortal realm. There are no enchanted castles here."

Tate only shrugged. "Enchanted or not, it's quite fit for a prince of Shara, if I'm any judge of houses."

Tristan frowned and tilted his head. "Sounds a lot like the home of Bridín's sister, Brigit."

"Oh, no, Tristan. Not at all. That place is so . . ." He made a face. "*Contemporary. So mortal.* No, it's far from there. Just off the opposite shore, on a sliver of an island far out into the waters. As close to a castle as anything to be found on this mortal continent."

Tristan nodded. "I'd like to see it."

"All in good time, my lord. For now, we have work to do. The both of us. Now, stop pacing and sit still so we can discuss tonight's strategy."

"Marinda!"

The tiny woman went rigid at Bridín's shrill cry. She was turned away, facing a bright, sunny window and holding a watering pot over a gargantuan fuchsia that had been but a slip last week.

Bridín crossed the room, her steps rapid, and took the pot from Marinda's little hand.

Marinda looked up, all brown-eyed innocence. "I know you said no magic here, my lady, but the plant only needed a bit, and—"

"Oh, gods of Rush, Marinda, I don't care about the *plant*."

Tipping her head to one side, Marinda searched Bridín's face. "What is it then?" She frowned. "By wands and cups, lady, you're white as a snowdrop! What's happened?"

"A man. He came into the shop today and . . . Gods, Marinda, he can't be the one. He mustn't be the one. Get the crystal. Hurry!"

Marinda shook her head from side to side, clucking like a wet hen. "Now, Bridín, dear, you know the magic is strongest by night. Under the moon, the crystal will—"

"Get the crystal, Marinda. *Now*."

Marinda swallowed hard, bobbed her head, and rushed off. She wore no shoes, so her steps were quick and soundless. Forest green tights in a little girl's size, a pleated plaid skirt, vanished into the master bedroom. Moments later she returned with the beautiful quartz sphere cradled in her hands. "It might not work. Daylight and all. It simply isn't done, you know."

Bridín wiped her sweaty palms on the legs of her stirrup pants and went to the window to draw the drapes. Then she locked the apartment's door and extinguished the lights.

"Better?" she asked, sorry she'd snapped at her friend, but desperate for an answer all the same.

"Perhaps," Marinda said. She opened a drawer and took out a blue candle, struck a match and lighted it. Then she placed the ball carefully in the center of the floor, with the candle at its back, and folded her legs beneath her to sit before it.

"Well?" Bridín moved behind her, dropping to her knees to peer over Marinda's shoulder.

"Sit," Marinda said softly. "Relax yourself, my lady. Tension is no more conducive to scrying than daylight is. Breathe deeply, slowly. And tell me about this man."

Bridín sat. She drew a deep, cleansing breath, released it.

"Close your eyes, my lady."

Bridín frowned at her. "I didn't have to close my eyes before."

"It wasn't the middle of a sunny afternoon in a world without magic, before. Now, do you wish to know the answers or don't you?"

Sighing, Bridín closed her eyes. She tried to envision the man called Stone so she could describe him to Marinda. But all she could see were his eyes. Tristan's eyes.

"He . . . he reminds me of Tristan," she said in a whisper.

She heard a soft gasp, and *sensed*, in the way of the fairy, that Marinda was staring at her, and paying no attention at all to the crystal.

"Does he?"

Her voice sounded wary, as well. Bridín opened her eyes to peek, and Marinda jerked her gaze back to the ball, where it belonged. Her small hands hovered over the ball, as if in an attempt to draw the magic out of it. But Bridín had the distinct feeling she wasn't really trying.

"Well, then, it's no wonder you hope he isn't the one."

"I couldn't be with him, Marinda. I couldn't marry this man."

"Not even for your people, Princess Bridín of the Fay? Not even . . . *for Rush*?"

As a not-too-gentle reminder of her duties, it did the job. Bridín braced her spine and stared at the crystal. "I would do anything for Rush," she whispered.

"Perhaps, my lady, your vow is about to be put to the test."

Bridín blinked and turned to stare at Marinda. But Marinda's wide, unblinking eyes were fixed on the crystal though it wasn't glowing as it had before. "Marinda?"

"Close your eyes, child!"

Bridín did, and Marinda began to speak slowly. "The man you met today is not what he seems," she said, her voice taking on the soft monotone Bridín knew well. "He is a man of shadows. With great pain in his heart. But he is also a man of destiny. And his destiny, Bridín, is twined with your own."

"No," Bridín whispered.

"Make him fall in love with you, Princess. Make him your husband. And make him your king."

Bridín's heart knotted in her chest. "Not him," she moaned. "Gods, why must it be him?"

"It must."

Bridín opened her eyes in time to see the candle flicker and die, though there wasn't even a breeze in the room. She blinked at Marinda, then at the ball. "I don't believe it," she said. "I . . . I want to see for myself!"

Marinda clutched the crystal to her breast, her eyes round and hurt-looking. "You distrust me, my lady?"

"I . . ." Bridín shook her head hard and averted her eyes. "No, of course not, I just . . ."

Marinda brushed a hand across her forehead and her eyes fell closed.

"Marinda? Gods, what is it? Are you all right?"

The small woman nodded. "The magic . . . it's exhausted me, my lady. If you insist on seeing the crystal's message with your own eyes, I fear it will have to wait until later, when I feel stronger. This mortal world . . . My, but it's draining to my soul."

She took the crystal with her and wandered from the room. And Bridín tried to tell herself that it wasn't a trace of guilt she'd seen in Marinda's eyes just before she'd turned away.

Chapter Six

THE FIRE ALARM went off just before dusk. Marinda had been in the small kitchenette peeling vegetables for dinner and insisting she'd be ready to give the scrying crystal another try as soon as it was fully dark. Bridín had been pacing restlessly, trying to consign herself to the fact that she might actually have to marry this man. Charm him. Make him care for her. A man who reminded her of Tristan so much that it was painful.

Painful? What a foolish notion.

"What is it!" Marinda shrieked when the piercing alarm rent the silence of their apartment. She came rushing from the kitchen with her hands pressed to her ears and her eyes as round as silver dollars. "Make it stop, my lady!"

The shrill bell continued ringing, though, and Bridín put her arms around the small woman's shoulders, bending down to do so. "Hush, Marinda. It's only the fire alarm."

"Fire?" Marinda cried, dropping her hands and staring up at her. "*Only* fire?" She pulled free, swinging her head this way and that. "Where? Where is the fire?"

Gripping her hand, Bridín tried to calm her. "It's probably nothing, darling. Come, we're supposed to go outside when the alarm sounds. Just in case."

"Oh, my," Marinda said. "Oh, goodness. Oh, my. Hurry then. Hurry."

Together they walked into the dim hallway, closing the apartment door behind them. They took the stairs down to the first floor and moved quickly past the line of mailboxes on the wall. Bridín sniffed the air, but smelled no hint of smoke. Still, best to err on the side of caution. She clung to Marinda's small, chilled hand as they stepped out the double front doors and onto the front stoop. Their apartment was actually the second floor of a three-story house. She imagined, in better days, it had been one large home.

On the sidewalk they were joined by the elderly Mrs. Fletcher from the floor below, and the two young men who occupied the floor above. Mark and Reggie held hands and stared up at the building they called home. Bridín resisted the urge to smile at her own tunnel vision. She'd considered them both as possibilites for the man she would marry for the good of her kingdom. Perhaps it was best that she'd finally found the One. *If*, indeed, she had. At least she would no longer have need to consult the crystal about every male she met here.

Screaming sirens brought her gaze around, and she saw large red vehicles crowding to a stop out front. A dozen men in yellow coats and odd-looking helms poured from the noisy machines and made their way into the building. A car pulled in behind them, and another man, dressed unlike the rest, emerged. He started for the building, then paused near her side. "Is there anyone still inside?" he asked.

She recognized his voice, blinked in surprise, and turned to stand face-to-face with him. "Stone? What are you doing here?"

"Bridín! This is your building?"

She nodded.

"Are you all right?" His hands clasped her shoulders, squeezing gently to emphasize the concern in his voice.

"Of course." She narrowed her eyes at him, wary of his presence. "But what are you doing here?" she repeated, glancing down at his attire: jeans and a sweatshirt. "You're not a firefighter."

"No. But I know how to care for wounded. I saw women and children standing out here, saw the firefighters, and thought I might be of some help."

She tilted her head to one side, still suspicious of him. "That's a very noble thing to do."

He smiled a little, and her stomach tightened. "If it made you think I'm noble, dear lady, then it was well worth the effort."

Was he—what did they call it—*flirting* with her?

"You're shaking. This frightened you more than I did this morning, didn't it?"

She lifted her chin. "Nothing frightens me."

"No?" He lifted one brow in a way that reminded her so much of Tristan that she sucked in a sharp breath. "Then why wouldn't you have lunch with me?"

She held his gaze. "I told you, I had to see someone."

"And tonight? Do you have plans to spend time with someone tonight?"

"Yes," she said. Grating her teeth and stiffening her spine. "As a matter of fact, I do."

He sighed and lowered his chin.

She hoped she hadn't just dashed her chances, in case he truly was the one. "Perhaps . . . some other time?"

He met her eyes, looking triumphant. A look that frightened her. "I hope," he said, "you won't make me wait too long." Then he looked past her as she struggled to understand what he'd meant by that remark. The firefighters were coming out of the building, shaking their heads and muttering. Stone left her to speak briefly to one of them, then returned to her side. "False alarm," he said. "You don't have to be afraid anymore."

Oh, if he only knew. She was more afraid now than ever. But she'd die before she'd let him see it.

Marinda managed to extricate herself from Mrs. Fletcher's grasp, and was coming toward them.

"I have to go, Bridín," Stone said. "But . . . I'll see you again. And . . ." He reached into a pocket, extracting a card with a telephone number scrawled in black ink. "Keep this. In case you change your mind."

She looked at the card and wondered if he always carried his number scribbled on a scrap in his pocket, or whether he'd had this on hand just for her.

He turned and hurried back to his car just as Marinda reached Bridín's side again. She was jarred away from watching his taillights fading in the distance by a tug on her oversized shirt.

"That was him, wasn't it?" Marinda asked.

Bridín nodded. "Yes. That was him." The others were already filing back inside. The firefighters climbing back into their trucks, rumbling away. Bridín sank onto the top step, lowering her head to her hands. "Oh, Marinda! What am I going to do? I know nothing about feminine charms or womanly wiles. Even if he *is* the one, how will I manage it? How will I go about making this man fall in love with me?"

The sound of Marinda's laughter was like a silver bell in the night. "Bridín. My dear, sweet princess. You're a *fairy*! Enchanting men is what fairies do best."

Bridín swallowed hard. Yes, she knew about the allure of the fay. She'd even employed it . . . long ago. When she'd foolishly tried to soften her captor's heart toward her. Her captor. Her beautiful, dastardly captor. "Tristan," she whispered. Something wet rolled down her cheek. She swiped it away angrily, refusing to admit, even to herself, that it was a tear.

"You are a fairy princess, sweet Bridín. You'll get through this, because you know you must."

Sniffing, Bridín nodded and got to her feet. "Come, then. Let's consult the crystal once more. I don't wish to put myself through this unless I know I have to."

"Still doubting me, my lady?"

Bridín looked down at her. "The crystal told you his destiny and mine were tangled, Marinda.

But it didn't say straight out that he was the one I am to marry. You said that on your own."

Marinda lowered her eyes guiltily. " 'Twas what I felt."

"Don't forget, Marinda, I have magic in me, too. You shouldn't try to deceive me."

"It wasn't that—"

"So we consult the ball again." Bridín turned and led the way back up the stairs and into their apartment. Marinda followed her into the bedroom where the crystal was kept, resting beneath a black velvet cloth on the dressing table.

But when they entered the room, the crystal was gone.

Bridín heard Marinda's sharp gasp. But she didn't believe what she was seeing. Not until she'd turned the apartment upside down searching for it, without success.

"It's no use, my lady. The crystal has been stolen. I can't believe—"

"This is terrible," Bridín whispered. "Gods of Rush, how will I ever know now?"

She paced the floors in anguish as Marinda tried uselessly to comfort her. And finally she sank onto the sofa, feeling utterly defeated. "There's only one thing left for me to do," she said softly.

"And what's that, my lady?"

"I have to see him. The ball . . . it seemed to indicate . . . that he might be . . ." She sighed, lowering her head. "I have to rely on my own judgment now. Or at least until we get the crystal back again, Marinda. I'll see this man. I'll . . . I'll test him. Try to learn whether he is, indeed, a suitable king for Rush. Whether he's even capable of ruling. And perhaps my fay sense will tell me all I need to know.''

''Perhaps,'' Marinda said. ''It is a good plan, Bridín.''

Bridín looked at her questioningly, but Marinda only nodded hard. ''Yes indeed. A good plan.''

Closing her eyes and biting down on her lip to battle her fear, Bridín took the card he'd given her from her pocket, and reached for the telephone.

Tristan tucked the pendants he wore inside the collar of his white cotton shirt, shrugged into the lightweight, camel-colored jacket, and then struggled for twenty minutes with the ridiculous necktie, before tossing it to the floor and cursing it.

''Don't give up so easily, Tristan.'' Tate opened the menswear catalog and thumped his forefinger against the model on the slick, glossy page. ''You have to look like this.''

''To hell with looking like that. I'll go without the noose.''

Tate opened his mouth to object, but Tristan silenced him with a glance. Tate shrugged, and smiled. ''All right, fine. Now, remember all we've discussed. The flowers. The wine.''

''Alcohol goes straight to the heads of fay folk, Tate. You know that.''

''My point exactly.'' Tate winked and strode over to the table where Bridín's recently liberated crystal ball rested. He stroked it lovingly. ''I was good, wasn't I? No one even saw me.''

''You were good,'' Tristan conceded. ''But I

truly doubt Bridín needs that ball to see me for who I am."

"So move quickly, Tristan. Before she sees anything. Sweep her off her feet, as they say here."

Tristan grumbled, checking the collar once more to be sure the pendants were out of sight. "I should take these things off," he said. "It's foolishness to wear them."

"And take the chance she might find them and take them back?"

"How could she possibly—"

Tate crooked his eyebrows. "Same way I found her crystal. She's not a fool, Tristan. No, you keep those pendants on at all times. It's far safer that way."

Tristan shook his head. As he left he could still hear Tate's voice calling after him not to forget the flowers and the wine. Not to forget to show his best side. To impress her. To convince his worst enemy that he was fit to rule his own kingdom.

She was nervous. He could see it at a glance. Of course, she would be nervous. He was nervous, and he was Tristan of Shara! He'd never, in all the years he'd known her, expected to be dealing with her like this. Romancing her, charming her, seeking to please her. The woman who'd cost him his throne. What he'd rather be doing was throttling her.

And even as he thought these things, he knew they were not true. He wanted her, just as he'd always wanted her. Hating her, just as he'd always hated her, did nothing to tame that desire.

Bridín stepped out into the apartment's corridor, pulling the door closed behind her, when he rang her bell. She didn't invite him inside. Which was just as well, if he was to keep that little Wood Nymph Marinda from setting eyes on him. Bridín's eyes, those sparkling sapphires, were dilated. Wide and expectant. And . . . and what was this? They were dusted with a trace of iridescent powder of the same golden hue as her glorious hair.

She'd painted her eyelids? And her lips as well, he noticed. For him?

The realization startled him, and made him take a better look. Then he wished he hadn't. The dress she wore was of a deep blue silk, and it hugged tight to her body, stopping at midthigh. Her long, elegant legs were encased in silk stockings that glimmered and shone, and made his fingers itch to run over them. And the top of the dress . . . well it seemed to be missing. No sleeves, nor straps of any kind. It barely covered her breasts, squeezing them so tightly that the creamy mounds spilled above it. He couldn't take his eyes from the swell of them, not for a very long time. Not until she gently cleared her throat.

He looked up quickly, meeting her eyes, seeing a hint of smugness in her gaze. So she'd meant to distract him with the beauty of her shape. He should have expected as much from a conniving, scheming fairy.

"You look lovely," he forced himself to tell her. And it was utterly true. He simply hated this act of fawning over her.

"Thank you." Her gaze shifted downward, toward his hand at his side, and he belatedly remembered the flower. He held it up, and she took it from him, burying her nose in the red rose's soft petals and inhaling its scent. "It's perfect," she whispered.

"Like you," he said. And he managed not to grimace as he blurted the compliment. Her face colored nicely, though, so it must have sounded sincere. It was, in fact. She was quite perfect. She'd always been.

"I'll wear it tonight." She met his eyes and smiled slightly, oozing fay charm and trying to make him feel her allure. It wouldn't work, he vowed. It had never worked in the past. He was not susceptible to her magical enticements. His desire for her was a purely physical one. She'd never mesmerize his heart. He wouldn't forget his goal here. Trick her into marriage and then force her to return to Rush . . . to *Shara* to help him regain his kingdom. Nothing more.

There was nothing more. His throne, his kingdom, was all that mattered. His father's lessons echoed in his ears, even now. And he'd learned them too well to forget. Shara was his destiny. He was born to keep that kingdom for his people, and that purpose was his only one. He had no time for distractions of the heart.

She snapped off the rose's long stem, and placed the blossom in his hand. He looked down at it, then up at her again. "Will you pin it on for me?"

All innocence. The vixen. "What shall I use for a pin?"

She lifted her hands to the back of her head, and a second later her golden locks fell free, spilling over her shoulders. Gods, but she did have beautiful hair. She held up a single hairpin. And he took it from her, commanding his fingers not to tremble.

Slipping the rosebud's now stubby stalk into the hairpin's tight grasp, he reached out and attached it to the very center of the dress. The backs of his fingers brushed over warm, silken breasts as he did so, and he closed his eyes for just one brief moment, savoring the firm roundness he touched. Then he bit his lip and drew his hands away. She would not enchant him.

"Where are we going tonight?" she asked, her voice coming out slightly hoarse. She cleared her throat.

"That's a surprise," he told her, taking her hand, ignoring the perfect fit of her hand in his. He led her down the stairs and out the front door. And then he heard her gasp very softly, and looked at her to see those eyes widen as they took in the limousine that waited at the curb. "Surprised?"

She nodded. "You shouldn't have . . ."

"Oh, but you don't know my plan, beautiful Bridín."

She looked at him, tilting her head to one side so that her golden hair slid down along her bare arm. "Your . . . plan?"

"To sweep you off your feet." He released her hand and moved to the car, opening its rear door and holding it for her. "Your carriage awaits," he said. Just as he had rehearsed with Tate, though he knew too well that Bridín of the Fay was far too sensible and practical a woman to fall victim to such flimflam efforts at seduction.

She smiled, a trembly little smile, and got into the car. Graceful as a dancer, she sat, then drew her long, silk-encased legs in after her. Scowling at his physical reaction to the way the woman moved, Tristan ordered himself to stop looking at her legs, and got in beside her.

There was a tap on the apartment door, and Marinda scowled at it, not answering. The tap was repeated, though, more demanding this time. It was then followed by a voice. A voice she knew well. "It's me, Marinda. Open up, will you?"

With a gasp of alarm, Marinda leaped off the sofa and hurried to release the locks. She stared, wide-eyed, as the man pushed past her to come inside.

"Well, close the door, for the love of Rush! We can't be seen together."

Marinda pushed the door closed, but kept one hand on its knob. "You shouldn't come here! My lady Bridín might return at any moment!"

"Nonsense." His tone was harsh, but his eyes soft as they searched her face. And then he smiled. "I've missed you."

Marinda's anger vanished when he opened his arms. She curled into them and kissed his cheek. "Oh, gods, but I've missed you, too, you scheming devil."

Tate held her tightly for a long moment. When he released her, she looked up into his eyes. "Tell me," she asked him. "How go things on your side, love?"

"Ah, the fool still thinks he hates her. But I've convinced him she's his key to the kingdom." He stroked her hair. "I've also convinced him that you will recognize him should you see him, so he's making efforts to steer clear of you."

"Ah, that's a relief. Wouldn't he be surprised if he were the one who recognized me, instead? He's seen us together more than once, on the other side."

"Yes, and he's too smart a man not to figure out our plan if given the slightest clue." He hugged her tighter. "And what about Bridín?"

"Resistant," she said. "Refusing to believe he's the one. Praying he isn't. I still think it would have worked better to do this without the disguise, Tate. Her heart belongs to Tristan, though she'd deny it with her dying breath. She'll not give it to another."

"But he's not another. That's the beauty of my plan."

Marinda shook her head and paced away from him. "She mourns him so. In secret always, but oh, how she mourns him! It's cruel to let her go on believing him dead."

Tate sighed. "It will only be for a short while, sweetheart. Just until they're safely wed." He came up behind her, closing a hand on her shoulder. "It will have to be a short time, love. I'll not put up with this separation for much longer."

She turned and fell into his embrace, returning his hungry kiss with all of her heart. When he lifted his head away, she whispered, "Are you certain they'll be away for a while?"

"Certain," he replied. "Tristan has a full evening planned for his bride-to-be. Though I imagine he'll be grating his teeth all through it." He grinned at her. The dimpled, devilish grin that had won her heart ages ago.

She took his hand in hers, and drew him across the floor. "Come along, then," she whispered, "and remind me why I took you as husband."

He was a charming man. A handsome man. An interested man. She ought to be feeling more enthusiastic about all of this. After all, if she had to marry, then wasn't it good that at least her husband would be a pleasant companion?

The answer should have been yes, but for some reason, it wasn't. She felt it would have been far easier if she'd hated the man on sight. She didn't like . . . liking him.

He took her to a fine restaurant, escorted her to a private table near a bank of windows that overlooked the lake. He sat across from her and ordered expensive wine. Ah, at last, something she didn't like about him.

She frowned as the waiter scurried away to do his bidding, and he met her gaze. "Something wrong?"

"I do not drink wine," she told him.

"Oh." He did not apologize.

"You might have asked first," she said. And she saw a flare of anger appear in his eyes, and mentally added a short temper to his list of faults. And then she caught her breath, because those faults of his were so similar to Tristan's. Only . . . Tristan's list was much longer than this man's could possibly be.

But the anger she'd managed to rouse in him was carefully banked. In less than a second, he was smiling again. "I'll send the wine back. Order whatever you want to drink."

She nodded regally, and flipped open the menu the waiter had left her. But she wasn't really scanning the items listed. She was, instead, wondering if perhaps this man had other faults, things that would make him unsuitable to rule Rush at her side. She felt a little brighter, deciding tonight would be the perfect time to begin her task of trying to find out. He might have family he wouldn't be able to leave behind. Or other responsibilities. A job he couldn't give up. He might be stupid, or careless. He might lack the authoritative demeanor that was required in a king. He might be . . . she shuddered at the thought . . . a *pacifist.*

The waiter returned with wine in a bucket of ice. And Bridín's date held up a hand before he could even place it on the table. "We've changed our minds," he said. "Take the wine back."

"But, sir, I've already opened the bottle—"

"*Take* the wine *back.*" The look in his eyes seemed to be all the encouragement the waiter needed.

"Of course, sir. What would you like instead?"

There went her theory that he was lacking an authoritative demeanor. Bridín sighed heavily, then realized both men were looking at her. "Oh. Yes. I'll have a tall glass of cranberry juice with a splash of . . . that stuff you people are always . . . ginger ale. That's it. A splash of ginger ale."

The waiter looked at her as if she had a third eye growing in the center of her forehead. Bridín lifted her chin and fixed him with an imperious glare, invoking her own authoritative demeanor. "Is there some problem with that?"

"No. No, of course not." He gave his head a shake and turned to the mysterious Mr. Stone. "And for you, sir?"

Keeping his eyes fixed to hers, Stone said, "Whiskey."

"I don't blame you," the waiter muttered as he nodded and hurried away.

Bridín had the feeling she'd just been insulted. But since the fellow returned in record time with their drinks, she decided to let it slide. She turned on her brightest smile, and devoted her attention to the man across from her. After all, it was her responsibility to see to it that the man who would be king of Rush was fit for the job, was't it? She owed it to her people.

"Tell me about yourself, Stone," she said. "Do you have any . . . family here?"

"Here in Ithaca?" he asked, then looked slightly amused as she searched her mind for the proper answer. He saved her from it, though, a moment later. "Actually, the only family I have is a brother. We . . . er . . . don't get along."

So no family bonds tied him to the mortal realm. That was good. Wasn't it?

"What do you do for a living?" she asked.

He frowned a bit. "I'm independently wealthy," he returned. "Is this a date, dear Bridín, or a job interview?"

She lifted her brows in surprise. Really, he wasn't being very cooperative. Then again, she supposed most women he dated were more interested in seducing him than in his personal background. She shrugged. "I'm only curious."

He took a large gulp of his whiskey, and set the glass down. "Should I be flattered?"

She lowered her eyes. "Of course."

That seemed to please him. Or maybe it didn't. There appeared to be a mingling of emotions in his eyes when she looked up again.

"Any other questions, my lady fair?"

She blinked, taken aback by the form of address. But it must be coincidence. Of course it was. What else could it be? "Actually, yes," she said, and she traced the moisture on the rim of her glass with the tip of one finger. "I was wondering about your arm."

"My *arm*?"

"You tend to favor it, as if it's injured or weak," she pointed out. "Do you have some sort of physical infirmity?"

"*Infirmity?*"

She only nodded and waited for him to explain, lifting her glass to her lips and taking a long sip. He downed the remainder of his drink and signaled the waiter by holding up the empty glass. A full one was quickly brought to replace it. Then he stared at her, stared *through* her. "I think I know what you're trying to ask me," he said finally, and that glint of anger had returned to his eyes. "Don't worry yourself, Bridín. The injury that makes me favor my left arm didn't affect anything *vital.* I'm still perfectly capable of satisfying the needs of a woman."

The glass she clutched in her hand gave under the pressure of her grip and shattered. Bits of glass and cranberry juice rained down on the table. Instinctively she turned her hand, palm up, and stared down at the pool of red liquid cupped in her palm.

Stone came around the table and knelt beside her, snatching her hand with one of his, and yanking a white linen handkerchief from his pocket at the same time. He blotted the red from her palm. She yanked her hand away, clutching the hankie, and glared at him.

"You are a pig," she whispered.

He shrugged. "It was a logical conclusion. Look at it from my point of view, Bridín. First you wear a dress that barely conceals your . . . charms . . . and then you ask about my physical prowess—what was I supposed to think?"

"You dare . . ."

"Yes, I do. I dare just about anything."

She narrowed her eyes on this man. Then slowly they widened. Hadn't she once heard Tristan use that same particular phrase? No. It had to be her imagination making him seem so . . . so achingly familiar.

He took her hand again, cradling it in his with her palm turned up, and gently pried her fingers open so he could examine the wound. She let him this time. He peeled the hankie away. "There . . . there's no cut," he said, frowning.

Bridín took the red-stained handkerchief from him with her free hand, held it over her palm, and squeezed until some of the liquid spilled back into her palm.

"You rushed to my aid prematurely, Stone. It was only cranberry juice. You see?" She now cupped a few droplets of the juice in her palm, to show him his mistake.

"I see," he said, and his eyes darkened so suddenly that she couldn't take hers away. "But perhaps I'd best make sure." And then he bent lower, and pressed his lips to the very center of her palm. With his lips and his tongue, he drank the droplets from her palm. White heat raced up her arm, eliciting a shudder of desire that nearly shocked her speechless. Gods, she hadn't expected *that*!

The waiter hovered behind him, eagerly asking if she was all right, if he could do anything to help, if they'd like him to call for their car so they could leave early.

"No," she said softly, her eyes still fixed to the man kneeling before her. "No, I'm fine. Simply clean up this mess, and bring us our meal."

The waiter looked intensely disappointed. But he did as she requested.

When the glass was gone, and the table restored to order, their food was delivered. Far faster than she would have expected it. Stone didn't eat, though. He sat there drinking his whiskey and staring at her.

"We got off the subject of our discussion," he said finally. "Tell me, Bridín, why is it you were asking about my arm?"

"I told you," she whispered. "I was only curious."

She was still shaken by her own unexpected reaction to the touch of his mouth on her skin. She only shrugged. She'd run out of questions, for the moment. She no longer cared whether the man would make a suitable king. She felt troubled, almost guilty, but she couldn't identify the reason for it.

She picked at her food, having lost her normally ravenous appetite, and finally pushed her plate away.

"Dessert?" he asked.

"No, thank you."

"Coffee, then?"

She shook her head.

"We didn't get off to a very good start tonight, did we, Bridín?" She licked her lips, not answering. "There is a spot above the lake where I'm told the young people go for midnight trysts," he said softly. "I'd like to take you."

She looked up quickly, eyes wide. "Wh-what?"

His smile was slow and dangerous. "Take you to see it. I've heard it's the most beautiful place for miles around." He reached across the table and closed his hand around hers. "I want to get to know you, Bridín. Really know you. I want to spend time alone with you, just the two of us."

She knew the spot he referred to. She'd seen it once, when she and Brigit had taken little Jonathon there for a picnic. That had been by daylight, of course. She could picture it by night. Secluded. Bathed in moonlight. Waves crashing against the shore far below. She could picture the two of them there, together . . . alone. A tiny ball of need formed in the pit of her stomach, and she snatched her hand away.

"I think . . . another time, perhaps. I . . . I'd like to go home now, if you don't mind."

She peeked up at his face to gauge his reaction, saw disappointment in his eyes, yet again. But also a hint of relief. "I do mind," he said. "But if it's what you want . . ." He nodded to the waiter for the check, then looked at her again.

"You are going to see me again, aren't you, Bridín?"

She swallowed hard, and nodded. "Yes."

He looked as if he'd been half hoping she'd say no.

Chapter Seven

THE NERVE OF her. The very nerve! Questioning him as if he were some knave petitioning her for knighthood. It infuriated him to have to be interviewed for a position that was rightfully his. It enraged him that the decision as to whether or not he was fit to rule would be made by her. And it baffled him that he'd had such a strong reaction to seeing her palm filled with what he'd mistakenly thought to be blood. Why was he forever feeling the urge to protect her, anyway?

Damn her with her haughty, arrogant ways, and her icy stare. Damn her. He was liking this plan of Tate's less and less with every moment he was forced to grovel for the affections of his enemy. Force would be far preferable to this nonsense. Hadn't he learned anything from his father? You didn't ask for what you wanted, you simply took it. By fair means or foul. And while he'd never agreed with his father's views in that regard, they were beginning to make more and more sense to him now.

Damn, if only Tate weren't always right. If

only he didn't trust the man so implicitly . . . but he did. And so he'd give the plan a little more time. Not much. But a little.

He held the car door as Bridín emerged, and then walked beside her into the building and up the two short flights to the second floor. And then he stood there, outside her door, feeling ridiculous and ill tempered, and knowing he had to grovel just a little bit more.

"I want to see you again, Bridín," he forced himself to say, and he hoped he sounded appropriately humble to suit her.

"I know you do," she replied.

Tristan grated his teeth. "Tomorrow is Saturday. If you're not working at the shop, perhaps we could—"

"No. Not tomorrow."

She was pushing him to his very limit. He *would not* beg. He held her gaze. "Why not?"

She frowned. "I didn't realize I was required to provide a reason."

"Humor me," he ground out.

She smiled . . . at his frustration? Probably. But maybe not. Her smile grew a bit wistful, and her gaze turned inward. "Tomorrow is going to be my first carnival," she said, and her voice softened to match her expression. "I've always wanted to ride a roller coaster. And since my nephew's first birthday is tomorrow, I have the perfect excuse." She closed her eyes. "I won't have a lot of time to spend with him before I have to go back . . ." Her eyes popped open, and she cut herself off before she finished. But he knew fully well where it was she planned to be going back to. "Anyway, while his aunt is here, little Jonathon is going to do every single thing I dreamed about doing when I was a little girl ... everything I wasn't allowed to do."

He felt as if she'd kicked him. A blow seemed to land at his solar plexus and radiate out in waves of stunned awareness. "You ... you dreamed of going to a carnival?"

She nodded. "Doesn't every child?" Then she shrugged and shook her head. "I led a rather ... sheltered life then. My ... *guardian* didn't let me out much."

He searched her face for signs of deceit, or some kind of trickery. But he saw only longing in her eyes. The childish longing for a ride on a roller coaster. Gods. She turned and reached for the doorknob. But he caught her arm, stopping her. She looked up, wide-eyed.

"What else did you dream of doing, Bridín?" Frowning, she tilted her head. "Tell me," he said. "I really would like to know."

Shrugging, sighing, she nodded. "The zoo," she said very softly. "I never set foot in a zoo, though that idea has lost some of its appeal now that I'm grown. I'm afraid now I'd be compelled to turn all the animals loose." She glanced at him, but he nodded for her to go on. "The circus," she said. "One of those fast-food restaurants where they put little toy treasures into the children's meals. A movie theater. A public school." Her voice wasn't hushed anymore. It was becoming just a little bit strained now, and she let her body go soft, and leaned back against the wall. "A junior prom. A slumber party. A ..." She blinked rapidly, straightened, and averted her eyes.

But not before he'd seen the sheen of unshed tears there. He'd done this to her. *He'd* denied her all of those things. He'd taken . . . Gods, he'd robbed her of her childhood. In very much the same manner he'd been robbed of his own. That he'd never thought of this before—it ate into his soul like acid now. He'd soothed his conscience by giving her everything a child could want or need. Or . . . he'd told himself that's what he'd given her. Dammit, he was only just seeing that he hadn't even come close.

She'd grown into a woman who hated him. A woman who was his most deadly enemy. A woman who had cost him his throne. But perhaps he'd had more than a small part in creating the woman she'd become.

It was a concept that shook him to the roots of his soul. It altered the way he saw *everything*. He wasn't even certain how it changed things, or to what extent, but he knew it did. He felt like a warrior too long at battle. Shocked and disoriented. Unsure.

He *hated* feeling unsure.

He moved closer to her and, catching her shoulders, turned her slowly to face him again.

She'd dried her eyes, of course, but the signs of the momentary weakness were still there. She lifted her chin, caught his gaze. "Don't pity me, Stone. And don't think I'm one of those weak and weepy females who are comforted by a simple hug from a man."

"I wasn't going to hug you."

"No?" She glanced down at his hands on her shoulders, then looked at him again, brows lifting.

"No. I don't know where you come from, Bridín, but I'm told that around here, it's customary to reward a man who takes you to an expensive dinner in a limousine, with some small token of gratitude."

Her eyes narrowed. "A bit of a ludicrous custom, don't you think?"

"Maybe, but it's the custom, all the same."

"And just what sort of *token* were you expecting?"

His gaze slid down to her lips. Full, and moist. And he remembered the last time he'd kissed her in the forest. Her reaction. If nothing else worked to entice her, the physical desire that flared between them when they kissed should do the trick. "Nothing so great. Only a good-night kiss."

She tilted her head, thinking about it. He saw her eyes rest on his lips, saw her soft pink tongue dart out to moisten her own. Finally she shrugged. "All right, then. You may kiss me."

She said it as if she expected him to fall on his knees in gratitude. Deprived childhood or no, the woman was a witch.

He silently vowed that next time, *she'd* do the asking. And then he slipped his arms around her, very slowly, letting his hands slide down to her waist, and run around it, to settle at the small of her back. He pulled her closer, gently closer, until her body touched his, and then he lowered his head, holding her gaze until her eyes fell closed. He met her lips, tasted them, and shivered. Gods, what touching her did to him! He nuzzled her mouth until it parted, giving him more access to the sweetness he craved. And then he took that sweetness.

He caught her tiny moan, inhaled it, and felt the response beginning to shiver through her body. She pressed closer, so slightly it was barely palpable, and she moved her mouth against his. He tasted her with his tongue, and she melted, letting him press her hips tight to his, letting him lick inside her mouth deeply, tilting her head back to invite more. Her hands clung to his shoulders, and her fingers splayed in his hair.

And then she jerked herself out of his arms with such a sudden burst of strength that he almost lost his balance.

Her eyes glistened. Her cheeks glowed. Her breaths came quick and short and shallow. Eyes darting over his face, wide with some kind of horror, she shook her head side to side slowly. Then she brought her hands up to press her fingertips to her lips, and she whispered, "How could I?"

"Bridín . . . Bridín, wait!"

But she'd already whirled around, yanked the door open, and vanished inside. And he was left with a curious and ever-growing feeling of . . . betrayal. How could she? she'd asked herself. He was asking the same thing. How could she kiss another man the way she'd kissed *him*? How could she lose herself in the arms of some stranger named Stone, every bit as madly as she'd lost herself to the embrace of Tristan of Shara?

And how could he feel suddenly flung into competition . . . *with himself?*

*   *   *

Bridín leaned back against the door she'd slammed and felt the locks she'd turned digging into her shoulder blades. How could she?

Gods, when she'd been in his arms, crushed to his body and melded to his mouth . . .

She closed her eyes and shook her head. She couldn't have!

Oh, but she had. She'd thought of Tristan. Fantasized him. Drawn him up out of her memory and slipped him into the place of the man she'd been kissing. In her mind, in her heart, it hadn't been Stone holding her at all. It had been Tristan . . . just the way he had done in the forest. Just the way . . .

Just the way Stone had done, seconds ago.

Frowning, Bridín pushed herself upright, away from the door, and paced across the carpeted floor. Was it her imagination . . . her errant memory? Or had Stone's kiss truly been as much like Tristan's as it seemed? Gods, unless she'd lost her mind entirely, the two even *tasted* the same.

She stopped short as her stomach knotted. Closed her eyes. Licked her lips. Tasted him . . . tasted them . . . again. Sweet. Minty. Erotic as musk. The knot moved lower, pooling in her loins, and she had to bite her lip to keep from moaning.

She might well have hated Tristan. Detested him right up to his dying day. But she'd also wanted him. And he'd known it. He'd felt it, too.

And despite the fact that they were sworn enemies, he'd been the only man who had ever made her feel that way. So now . . . now that this newcomer, this Stone, was stirring similar responses from her . . . she felt . . . almost . . .

Guilty.

She closed her eyes and bit her lip as the word whispered through her brain. But that was it. That was it exactly. She felt guilty. As if she were cheating on a lover. Ridiculous!

She shook her head at the absurdity of it all, and headed through the apartment to peer in at Marinda as she slept. Sensing her there, Marinda parted her eyes a minuscule amount and muttered, "So? Is he or isn't he?"

"He might be." Bridín leaned her forehead on the cool doorjamb. "I'm still not certain."

"More tests are in order, then?"

She nodded. Tristan was gone. She had to accept that, and deal with this Stone, this man who was very nearly as infuriating as Tristan had been.

Gods, but she missed fighting with him.

"Yes, Marinda," she whispered, and the thought brightened her a bit. "Yes. More tests." She smiled very slightly. Watching him deal with the *tests* she had in mind would be the most pleasant part of this entire ordeal.

In the dream, she was in a dark room. A dark, chilled room, with a hard floor littered in dried rushes . . . She could feel them beneath her small bare feet.

My goodness, why were her feet so small?

Of course. She was a little girl. And she was here in Rush, in one of the rooms of her family's very own castle. Only . . . only . . .

A terrible panic swept her heart like a killing frost, and she felt the tiny organ's beat become a staccato tattoo. She couldn't breathe. Her stomach cramped. Something horrible was happening. Something . . .

She looked up, and saw the blade of a mighty broadsword flashing down at her. And for just an instant, she envisioned her own head rolling crookedly across the floor and spinning as it came to a stop.

But the blow never came. And when she had the courage to peek and see why not, it was Tristan's face before her, not a deadly blade. His eyes met hers, probing them. He held to his shoulder with one hand, and blood pulsed through his clothing and flooded over it. In his other hand, the wounded one, he clutched her fairy pendants.

She held his gaze, searched his eyes. "You died for me," she whispered to him.

"Because I loved you," he replied. And then his beautiful, soulful eyes fell closed for the very last time.

"No," Bridín whispered. "No . . . no . . . *No!*"

She sat up in bed, drenched in sweat and shaking like the tiniest twig of a giant maple when the winds are harsh and biting. She trembled right to her soul. And Marinda was there, beside her, pushing her hair away from her face, dabbing at her tears with a paper tissue from the box beside the bed.

"There now, my lady. There. It was only a dream, my friend, nothing more. Just a dream. There now."

Bridín sniffed and drew her knees up to her chest, hugging them. She couldn't believe the tears she shed. Her face was soaked and felt swollen. Her nose ran. She rocked back and forth, hating that she was crying like a silly little girl, and she stammered, "It isn't true, Marinda!"

"Of course it isn't," Marinda soothed, having no clue, Bridín knew, of what she spoke.

"Tristan of Shara *never* loved me!" she shouted. "It's a lie!"

Marinda straightened away, searching her face with a scowl, and then reaching out to snap on the light. "Now, Bridín, suppose you tell me who it is who's doing the lying? Who says the Dark Prince ever loved you?"

"*He did!*" Bridín blinked, sniffed, rocked some more. "In the dream, he did. He said he loved me . . . as he lay there dying by his brother's own sword. He said he saved my life because he loved me. But it's not true, not one word of it, I tell you!"

Marinda smiled and shook her head. She stroked Bridín's hair until Bridín finally stopped rocking. Then Marinda eased her back down to her pillows, and tucked her covers over her. She left for a moment, and returned with a hot cloth, which she used gently on Bridín's stinging face. "It was but a dream," she said softly. "But a dream. Your own mind . . . or your conscience, lady, rising up to torment you. He never told you that he loved you, did he? He didn't say a word as he lay there . . . except to tell you to run. And he didn't die until later in the day."

Bridín nodded and let her eyes fall closed as the hot cloth settled across her forehead, and Marinda began rubbing tiny circles over Bridín's temples with her fingertips.

"Why do you suppose he did it, Marinda?

What would make him leap in front of his brother's sword the way he did?"

"Who's to say what makes any male do anything?" she asked, rubbing, still rubbing. It felt good. The tension seemed to ease away from Bridín's brain, melting into Marinda's fingers.

"He thought Vincent would pull back. He didn't think he'd be killed."

"That might very well be it, child," Marinda said.

"Or maybe he . . ."

"Maybe he what, dear?"

Bridín opened her eyes, but all she saw was the look in Tristan's that last time he'd looked into hers. As he lay there, dying, telling her to run. He hadn't spoken the words of her dream . . . but a fairy could see a man's heart by gazing into his eyes. And she'd seen his that bloody dawn. It had simply taken her this long to realize exactly *what* she'd seen there.

She swallowed hard, but it didn't help. The tears flowed anyway. She felt as if her heart were being slowly crushed in a gauntlet-clad hand. He'd loved her. The foolish arrogant bastard had *loved her*.

And she'd never known. Not until he was gone far, far from her reach. No wonder he'd never been able to bring himself to do her harm. No wonder. Why hadn't he told her? Why hadn't he simply . . . Ah, but what difference would it have made if he had? It wasn't as if she returned his tender feelings.

She hadn't.

She *didn't*!

* * *

"Physical lust, that's all it is." Tristan returned to the hotel suite, poured himself some coffee from the fresh pot Tate had left warming for him, and paced the tiny kitchenette. "Powerful, yes. But that's to be expected when dealing with her kind."

"Talking to oneself is considered a sign of mental illness in these parts, my lord."

Tristan whirled around quickly, slopping hot coffee onto his hand, and then hissing a few choice curses. He banged the cup down and thrust his hand under the faucet, cranking the cold-water tap with the other hand.

Tate only chuckled and fixed himself a cup of the tasty brew. "So I take it the evening out wasn't exactly a rousing success?"

The burning eased. Tristan shut the water off, walked to the breakfast bar, and sank tiredly onto a stool.

"Land sakes, Tristan, she didn't beat you with a mace, did she?"

He grimaced at his friend. Then shook his head. "Tate, have you ever had a child?"

Tate's eyes rounded, and Tristan thought it was his turn to slop the coffee. He set it down instead and clambered his way onto the stool beside Tristan's. Then he punched Tristan's arm. "Guess the date went far better than I could have hoped, eh? You're a sly one, I'll say that for you."

Tristan rolled his eyes. "This has nothing to do with the *date*, my friend. I'm thinking about Bridín. I had control of her from the time she was just a bit of a thing. Hell, I was little more than a brat prince myself. Only ten years her elder."

Tate nodded. "I know the tale, Tristan. You got

into her uncle's head. Convinced him she was a little off, and that she had to be kept under careful guard for her own protection."

Tristan nodded. Then he grimaced. "I'm only just now beginning to realize how . . . how cruel that was."

"Cruel?" Tate's head came up, eyes as curious as a little bird's. "As I understand it, the child was lavished with attention."

"The attention of strangers. Her uncle was rarely there. Her only family were her nurse and the old man. Raze."

"No fault of yours," Tate said. Then he sipped. "Her uncle could have stayed around. You didn't make him go away and leave her, did you?"

"No, but I've no doubt she suspects I did." He lifted his head suddenly. "She believes I had her adoptive parents killed, you know. She's always believed it."

Tate twisted his lips to one side, a sign of deep thought. "You . . . um . . . ever tell her otherwise?"

"Defend myself?" He sniffed. "Never."

Tate rolled his eyes, sipped his coffee. "So what is your point? You feelin' guilty about her upbringing now?"

Tristan shook his head. "Not guilty," he said, and knew it was a lie. "Well, not exactly. But I'm beginning to think I may have had a hand in creating my own devil."

"Not much you can do about it now, though."

"But there is." Tristan smiled slightly, and then more fully as his plan became clear in his mind. "Yes. There is, Tate, don't you see? I'm supposed to be wooing her anyway. I can try to make up for some of what she missed."

Tate bobbed his head forward, lifting one hand cuplike to his ear. "Eh?"

"Don't you see? All those things she said she'd dreamed of . . . the things she was denied. A circus. A zoo. A hamburger and French potatoes with a free trinket in the box."

"Tristan, are you all right? She didn't put some kind of drug into your wine, did she?"

Tristan only smiled, feeling as if a huge burden had been lifted from his shoulders. "It's her secret childhood dreams I'll be fulfilling, Tate," he said, and he slugged down the rest of the coffee and turned toward his bedroom, feeling for the first time as if he might be able to sleep tonight. "It's the best possible way to win her heart."

"Is it now?"

"Of course," Tristan said, stepping through the bedroom door. "Why else would I bother?" He nodded good night and closed the door. And then he drew a deep breath, held it . . . and sighed from the core of his heart. Who was he kidding? He wasn't going to do this because it would win her. He was going to do it . . . to make it up to her. To make it up . . . not to the imperious princess who wanted his throne . . . but to the beautiful golden child who used to look at him with so much awe in her eyes.

"I will make it up to you, Bridín," he whispered to that little girl's image in his mind. "I promise."

Chapter Eight

"I'M SO SORRY , Bridín," Brigit's tinny voice said over the telephone. "I know how much you were looking forward to this."

Bridín shook her head, plastering her brightest smile in place before remembering that it would do little good. Her sister couldn't *see* her. "Stop apologizing. Jonathon is what's important here. Are you certain he's all right?"

"I told you, it's just a slight cold. He'll be fine."

Biting her lip, Bridín clutched the receiver more tightly. "But he's three-quarters mortal, Brigit! And you know how fragile mortal children are. Much more than any fairy's child." She paced until the tug of the telephone cord made her turn and start back. "If only I had our pendants. We could do a healing on him and—"

Soft laughter came from the phone, halting Bridín's nervous pacing. "I fail to see anything funny about this, Brigit!"

"Sorry," her sister replied, getting her humor under control, though it sounded as if it cost her a great effort. "I'm still not used to the way you think."

"And what way is that?"

"In terms of magic and the great mysteries," Brigit said.

"And you, my dear sister, think like any common mortal." Bridín was more than a little bit offended. "Have you lost all your fay sense?"

"Not all," she said, and Bridín could hear the smile in her voice. "But we don't need the pendants to take care of Johnny. He has something better. It's called a pediatrician."

"You're laughing at me, aren't you?" Bridín asked. "As if I don't know about such things. I lived here most of my life, Brigit. And I know about mortal medicine. I also know it's a Saturday."

"Well, this pediatrician takes calls on Saturdays. Especially when they come from worried mothers. And he says Jonathon is just fine. He just needs to stay out of the autumn wind, is all." She drew a deep breath. "And I wasn't laughing at you, Bridín. You know I'd never do that."

Bridín sighed. "Yes, I know. I'm sorry if I'm a bit testy."

"How's the husband hunt coming? Beginning to get to you, is it?"

Bridín opened her mouth to reply, then changed her mind. There was no use in worrying her sister over her own emotional state. Particularly when it was such a foolish one. Tristan was dead and gone. What he'd felt or hadn't felt for her was completely irrelevant. All she did now, she did for the good of Rush. Nothing else mattered.

"Bridey, hon? You okay?"

"Fine," she said. "Have you ever known me not to be?"

"Are you sure? You sound a little . . . odd. Is it . . . Have you found him?"

"I . . . I have to go, dear. Marinda's calling. She's probably blown something up with that microwave oven again." She replaced the receiver in its cradle, then stood staring at it for a long moment. Had she found him? It was a good question. And a disturbing one. Far more disturbing than it ought to be.

The sound of a knock at the apartment door stopped her from dwelling on it. Marinda was still in bed, sleeping as soundly as if she'd had as eventful a night as Bridín. Sighing heavily at the suddenly dreary outlook for the day ahead, Bridín walked to the door and pulled it open.

The creature standing there looked, at first glance, like an explosion of velvety red roses with legs. But then the flowers were lowered a little, and she saw those familiar ebony eyes and felt a stab of pain. "Stone," she said. "You must be an incredibly early riser."

He looked worried. "I didn't wake you, did I?"

"And what could you possibly do to rectify it if you had?"

He held up the flowers again. "Offer a bribe in exchange for forgiveness, of course."

Twisting her lips into a grimace, she took the flowers from him, then stepped aside to allow him to come in. He seemed to hesitate, glancing into the room as if to inspect it first. "Are . . . you alone?"

"My bevy of lovers left at dawn," she told him. Then she remembered Marinda, and added, "And my . . . roommate is still sleeping."

"I promise to be quiet." He came in, closing the door behind him, and followed her into the kitchen.

Bridín became suddenly, acutely conscious of her state of dress. She wore a lilac-colored satin robe, with nothing beneath it, and only a single sash to hold it closed. And she knew he had to be aware of it.

Nothing to be done about it now, short of making a cowardly dash to the bedroom. And Bridín never ran from anything. So she forced an outward appearance of calm and located a large clear glass vase in a cupboard, filled it with water, and stood at the sink arranging the roses. One of them drooped, its blossom too heavy for its skinny stem. Automatically Bridín ran her fingers over the weak stalk. "Little flower, hear my song. A fairy's touch will make you strong," she said, and then plopped the suddenly perfectly straight and tall rose in with the others.

Then she closed her eyes and slowly released her breath. What was she thinking? This mortal was standing right behind her, lounging in the doorway, watching and listening. What would he think?

Bridín cleared her throat, lifted her chin, and turned around with a bright smile. "Just a little nursery rhyme," she muttered. "I don't know what made me think of it."

He smiled back at her. A knowing smile. It sent a shiver down her spine. "Is that coffee fresh?" he asked then, nodding at the full pot on the counter.

"Of course." She turned again, to take cups from a cupboard, filled them, and then carried them to the breakfast bar. The room was too small for a table. She sat on one stool, and the dark man sat on the one right beside it.

"I'll drink it fast," he promised, reaching for his mug, drawing her gaze to his strong, graceful fingers. The gesture made her remember how he had kneaded her waist when he'd kissed her. It made her remember Tristan.

Tristan had loved coffee. Good coffee. Black, no sugar, and hot enough to scald his tongue.

Then Stone took a huge gulp of the steaming brew, ignoring the sugar bowl and creamer on the table.

She swallowed hard and sweetened her own coffee, then poured the heavy cream until it was caramel-colored. Then stirred, waiting for it to cool. "No need to hurry," she said absently, looking again at his eyes.

"No?" He set his cup down. "I thought you'd be getting ready for your outing with the nephew. Jonathon, wasn't it?"

His mention of her ruined plans brought her thoughts back to the present. "Oh. No, we had to call off our carnival adventure. Jonathon has the sniffles and his mother thinks he should stay out of the wind."

Stone frowned at her, his brows bunching. "But you were so excited about it."

She shook her head quickly. "That was just foolishness. I can't imagine why I went on and on about it the way I did last night. I really don't care one way or the other."

"And you really are a terrible liar."

She looked up quickly, and those probing black eyes grabbed hers and wouldn't let go.

"Let me take you, Bridín."

She blinked in surprise, taken totally off guard. "You . . . you want to—"

"I want to take you to the carnival. I've never been to one either, you know."

"No. I didn't know."

"Of course you didn't," he said. "So I've made up my mind. I'm going to one, and I'm going today." He tipped his cup to his lips and drained it. Bridín took a sip of hers, and burned her tongue. "So?" he said. "Are you coming with me or not?"

She wanted to go. It was silly for an adult woman—a princess, no less—to be feeling excited over such a childish outing. But she was. She told herself it would be practical to go with him. She needed to spend time with him. She'd be able to observe him a bit more, see whether he'd make a suitable king. She would be able to test him, perhaps. To learn the depth of his courage, his strength, his wisdom. She would be able to . . . she smiled, dipping her head . . . she would be able to ride a roller coaster.

"Bridín?"

She cleared her throat, wiped the giddy grin from her face, and lifted her head again. "All right," she said. "It will take me a few minutes to get ready. Will you wait?"

"If I can have another cup of that coffee," he told her.

*   *   *

Bridín of the Fay, coldhearted, haughty, troublemaking, vengeance-seeking, deposed ruler of Rush . . . screamed loudly enough to damage his hearing. Her long, sunset-colored tresses snapped like whipcords, and she clung to his hand, then his arm, then snagged his waist and buried her face against his shoulder as the tiny car in which they sat plunged and dipped and lurched around curves.

Tristan was very glad he'd skipped breakfast this morning. Yet he managed not to flinch or make any startled sounds like the ones that kept emerging from her pretty lips. He knew that even in this exhilarated state, she'd be watching, observing, judging whether his courage was up to the level needed to rule Rush beside her. And though his head was spinning and his stomach seemed to be following the path of the twisting tracks, albeit at a slower speed, he refused to give any clue to the woman beside him. Instead, he sat very still, noticing how tightly she'd wrapped her arms around his waist. Feeling the silken tendrils of her hair that fluttered against his face. Smelling her. Hearing the soft little cries she made each time the car jerked in a new direction, and thinking how similar they probably were to the cries she would have made had he been making love to her.

Her face remained pressed to his shoulder. He could feel her mouth, parted and moist, just beyond the thin barrier of the T-shirt he wore. And while telling himself that these sensations, and the stirring in his loins, were no more than evidence of her fairy magic, enchanting him—despite his vow that it wouldn't—he encircled her shoulders with one arm, and squeezed her a little bit closer. He lowered his head, until his nose and his lips touched the top of her head, and remained there, eyes closing, stomach clenching.

So swamped with physical sensations was he that he didn't even notice when the ride slowed and stopped. Not until she lifted her head slowly to blink up into his eyes as if just rousing from a long slumber. And he realized that she'd stopped stiffening and tensing and crying out at some point. That she'd just relaxed there in his embrace, and that maybe . . . maybe . . . she'd been as lost in sensations as he'd been. He searched the sparkling sapphire gemstones the gods had given her for eyes, then lifted his gaze higher at the sound of a throat clearing.

A young man stood there holding the safety bar open, waiting for them to exit the car so the next eager couple could climb aboard.

Tristan lowered his eyes to Bridín's again and, hating to break the moment—the first moment in which she'd seemed at all susceptible to his efforts at seduction—was forced to do just that. The carny was waiting. Not so patiently by the look of him. He hooked a finger under Bridín's chin, lowered his head to whisper to her. And she closed her eyes, obviously expecting the touch of his lips on hers rather than the soft voice in her ear. Good, he thought. Good.

He bent so close, his lips brushed her tender earlobe, and whispered, "Time to get off now, my lady fair. But we'll ride this one again, if you like."

She started in surprise, and jerked her head

around, seeing the young man who stood in front of the car for the first time. Her cheeks flushed with color, and she got up hastily, hurrying down the steps, clearly a bit embarrassed.

Tristan trotted down the grated metal steps as well, and fell into step beside her. Her suede walking boots were turning a pale shade of gray from the midway's dust. And her tight-fitting jeans, too, seemed to have absorbed a good deal of the stuff. None of which did a thing to detract from her allure. Every man she passed turned to look at her. And it occurred to Tristan that she wasn't even aware of what she was doing. The enchantment seemed to exude from her pores like some sort of musk, drawing men the way the scent of a flower draws the honeybee. Most fairies were fairly harmless unless they consciously chose to turn on the allure. But with Bridín it was just there. She wore it like a nimbus that was with her wherever she went. And she wasn't even aware of it.

She looked up at him, smiling. And he could do nothing less than smile back. Her eyes sparkled, her cheeks glowed, and her hair sailed in the hot-dog-and-popcorn-scented air. The tin-can music blasted from a dozen attractions, all of it blending into a cacophony of noise that didn't even seem unpleasant. It belonged here. The dust did, too. And the crowds, and the spilled drinks and tired mothers and noisy children. All of it combined to form the very soul of this place.

A carnival. He was suddenly very glad he'd experienced this.

"What next?" he asked her. "We've ridden on every ride at least once and played every trickster's games. What else would you like to do, Bridín?''

Smiling still, she searched the crowd, then pointed. Tristan looked and saw a small child in a stroller, clinging to a fluffy pink bunch of something, and burying his face in it. The child was clearly in ecstasy.

''What in the world—''

''Cotton candy,'' Bridín said. ''I'd like to taste it.''

He lowered his head in a miniature bow, then straightened and began looking for a cotton candy stand.

And that was when he heard the screams.

He whirled quickly and saw the woman, saw her eyes, which was all he needed to see. ''Timmy! *My God, Timmy!*'' she shouted again.

Tristan followed those stricken eyes, and saw the young boy, far too young to be on that Ferris wheel alone, but there alone all the same. The machine had stopped with the boy at the very top, and the child was now dangling from the car.

Tristan took another step forward.

''What the hell—'' someone shouted.

''He dropped his bear,'' the mother said. ''He leaned over to try to catch it. God, somebody get him down!''

''Who the hell let him on there alone?'' a man said, clearly accusing the younger one who was running the ride.

''Hey, he was tall enough,'' the kid said, gesturing toward the wooden sign that read, IF YOU'RE NOT AS TALL AS ME, YOU CAN'T GET ON THIS RIDE.

"I only turned my back for a second," the woman went on.

And still the child dangled.

Bridín clutched Tristan's arm, squeezing it. He could hear the child crying, see him twisting and shaking as he dangled by his hands. His own magic didn't include any spells for making children float. But he could see that it wouldn't be impossible to climb up to where the child was. He turned to meet Bridín's eyes, and she seemed to read his mind. She nodded once. Tristan moved forward.

The carny reached for the control lever. "I'll just bring him down, nice and slow."

"No!" Bridín stepped in front of him. "If you move it, he'll fall." Tristan heard this, then felt her eyes on his back as he gripped the cross pieces of the machine, pulled himself up, and began his climb.

"Just let him hold on," he muttered.

Then Bridín's whisper, which he shouldn't have been able to hear, reached him anyway, filling his mind and echoing through it.

> "You are but a little child,
> always meek and always mild,
> tossed by fate whose will is wild.
> But magic makes your body strong,
> your arms will hold you all day long,
> if you would heed the fairy's song."

Yes, Tristan thought fiercely. *That's it, Bridín. Help him, help him hold on until I can get to him.*

He climbed faster, driven onward by the pathetic cries of the frightened little boy, which grew louder the closer he got. "I'm coming for you," he called. "Hold on. I'm almost there."

He swung for the bar closest to the child, gripped it, and pulled himself up beside the little boy. Hanging by one hand, he wrapped the other around the child and, grating his teeth, boosted the boy back into his seat.

A swell of cheers rose from the midway as Tristan pulled himself into the car as well, and when he looked down, he saw that a huge crowd had gathered. The mother was sobbing in relief now, her face nearly covered by her two hands. Bridín stood below, too, looking up at him with a pleased smile on her face as she dusted off the little boy's teddy bear, which she'd apparently just picked up from the ground.

Tristan turned to the dirty, tearstained child. "You're going to be all right," he told the boy. "See? Your mother is right down there waiting. You'll be with her in—"

But his words were cut off when the little one suddenly hurled himself into Tristan's lap. Two small arms snapped around his neck, and a sobbing little face soaked his shirt. There was nothing he could do but hold the little fellow as the Ferris wheel moved slowly around, lowering them again. He looked for Bridín, thinking that if this little episode didn't make him seem like a suitable husband for her, then nothing would . . . but when he finally found her again, his attention was grabbed by something else.

Everyone else in the crowd that surrounded her was looking upward, focused on the child. Smiling and clapping or looking relieved. But one form stood apart from the rest. He was dressed all in black, and he wasn't smiling. He wasn't looking up, either. He was staring at someone else in the crowd. And that someone ... was Bridín.

Damn. He might be overreacting. Or that might be one of his brother's scouts, sent to find her. His fingers itched to hurl a bolt of blue fire at the man and kill him where he stood. But of course, he couldn't be sure the fellow was any threat. He might not be here to kill her. Perhaps only to see that she had no plans to return. Or perhaps he wasn't from the other side at all, but simply a man caught in the web of Bridín's charms. He couldn't just go around blasting the innocent.

The ride reached bottom and stopped. Tristan got to his feet, still cradling the child in his arms, and carried the tot to his waiting mother. She took the boy, hugged him, cried, blubbered her thanks over and over. Tristan was oblivious to most of it. His gaze remained focused on Bridín's admirer, but he lost sight of the man even as Bridín herself made her way to his side, elbowing through the crowd to do so.

It seemed at first, as she rushed toward him, that she would throw her arms around him and kiss him breathless. It was as if she caught herself at the last possible moment, and came to a grinding halt only inches from him. But her eyes still shone with pleasure, and her lips were parted in a breathless smile. "You saved that little boy's life."

"And you helped," he said.

Frowning, she tilted her head. "What in the

world do you mean by that?" A tiny widening of her eyes signaled her alarm.

Tristan shrugged. "Well, you stopped that fellow from turning the motor back on. Besides, I only did it to impress you. If you hadn't been here—"

"You'd have done the same," she said.

He put a casual arm around her shoulders, turned her toward the exit, and walked at a brisk pace, keeping his eyes on the people around them, watching for the man he'd seen.

"This upset you," she said, and when he looked down it was to see her studying his face.

"What makes you think I'm upset?"

"The way your dark eyes are darting all around. The way you're dragging me along the midway at the pace of a racing horse. The way you're holding me so tight to your side that you're leaving finger marks on my arm."

He slowed his pace, eased his grip. "Sorry."

She lifted her brows, looking regal again. "*And* the way you've forgotten all about my cotton candy," she added. But then she dropped the royal despot imitation, and smiled. "But that's all right. That little scare made me lose my appetite. I can see you're shaken. Perhaps we should leave."

"I'm not shaken," he told her. "I don't *get* shaken." He stopped, seeing a cotton candy booth off to the right, and turned her in that direction. "And your appetite is not an issue here. I don't think one eats something like that stuff out of hunger." He stopped by the booth, ordered a large cotton candy, then leaned against the counter, watching Bridín as she watched the person inside. The girl whisked a cone-shaped bit of cardboard around inside a spinning pan, and the pink fluff seemed to take shape by magic.

When it was finished, she handed the thing to Bridín. Bridín studied it for a long moment. She opened her mouth and approached the fluff, then back off and tilted her head in another direction, approaching again, until she finally picked a bit of the stuff off with her fingers and popped it into her mouth.

"Oh!"

Tristan lifted his brows, waiting for the verdict.

"It *melts*," she told him, popping in some more. Then she pulled off another piece and held it out to him in offering. Leaning forward, Tristan took the fluff from her fingers with his mouth. And it did indeed melt. And it was indeed sweet. But not as sweet as her. So when she would have drawn her hand away, he caught it in his, and brought it back. And he took her forefinger into his mouth, gently sucking the stickiness from it. And when he finished, he did the same with her thumb. Her cheeks got pinker than the candy, and her eyes, those glittering sapphires, darkened to midnight blue, and her lips parted on a soft, surprised sound that was half gasp and half groan.

When he finished, she lowered her hand to her side, and with it, she lowered her eyes.

"I think you're right," he told her. "I think we should leave now. There are . . . other things I want to do with you today."

She blinked and looked up fast. "O-other things?"

Tristan smiled, knowing fully well she'd drawn the conclusion he'd wanted her to draw. "Yes," he said. "The place with the golden arches for lunch, and then the zoo."

She looked as if he'd sprouted a second head. "I . . . I don't . . . understand."

"What's not to understand? I'm sweeping you off your feet, Bridín. You might as well just relax and enjoy it. Because it isn't going to end until . . ."

"Until . . . what?"

He shrugged, lowering his head. "Until you tell me to go away," he said, finally. "Until you tell me that you aren't feeling . . . any of the things I'm feeling."

Holding his gaze, lifting her chin, she whispered, "And what if I never tell you . . . to go away?"

He smiled at her. "Then . . . then I guess you're going to wake up one day to find yourself sharing cotton candy with a very old man."

Her brows drew close, and he saw moisture spring into her eyes. She lowered her head, but he caught her chin, lifting it again. "I'm moving too fast," he said. "Frightening you, aren't I? We barely know each other, and I'm talking about forever already. I'm sorry."

She lifted one hand to his cheek, caressed him there. "I feel as if . . . as if I've known you all my life," she said softly. "But that wasn't you. That was someone else."

Tristan felt a hard knot form in his stomach.

Someone else? Did she mean *him,* Tristan? Or . . . or could there be another?

Someone jostled against his side, alarming him and reminding him sharply of the man he'd seen watching her so intently. There was a small chance she could be in danger here.

"I don't mind that I remind you of someone else," he said. "As long as there's only the two of us now." But he did mind. He minded a great deal. He minded that she was responding so easily and so powerfully to him, when she thought him to be a stranger. He minded that she'd never looked at him as Tristan the way she was looking at him now.

"To the golden arches, then," she told him.

He nodded, taking her hand and leading her away as she munched on her cotton candy.

Chapter Nine

"WELL? HAVE YOU decided yet, Bridín? Has he passed your tests and proven himself worthy of the throne of Rush?"

Marinda had met Bridín at the door when Stone had dropped her off. Now she was following her through the apartment like a lonely puppy eager for a pat on the head. Bridín sailed into the bathroom, started the water running in the tub, and added lavender-scented oil.

"Well, where shall I begin? We got to the carnival and there was a game to test a man's strength. It involved hitting a small peg of some sort with a giant of a maul, and seeing the power of one's swing measured on a meter." She stirred the tub's rising water with one hand to mix in the oil.

"And?"

"Well, naturally, I suggested Stone try it." Bridín straightened away from the tub, and turned to walk out of the room. Down the hall to the bedroom, with Marinda on her heels. "He made the meter's arrow go all the way to the top, where it rang a bell. I do believe it would have gone higher, if there'd been more room."

"So he's plenty strong enough, despite that weak arm of his," Marinda almost sang.

Bridín pulled her satin robe from the closet where she'd hung it this morning. "But there's more to ruling a kingdom than physical strength, Marinda. So very much more. A king must be skilled in many other ways."

"As well I know, my lady."

"There was also an archery game. Simple thing, really. Any child could have hit the targets with the blunt-tipped arrows. They were little more than ten feet away. But still, I thought I might study his form as he took aim, so again I suggested we play the game." She tilted her head. "And you know, I got the feeling he sensed I was testing him. Yet he agreed readily enough."

Slinging the robe over her shoulder, she bent down to pull the matching slippers from beneath her bed.

"The arrogant show-off insisted on standing fifty feet from the targets, though. Made the carnival workers clear a lane for him, so he wouldn't hit anyone accidentally. And then he shot three times, hitting the bull's-eye with each shot. The third arrow hit directly between the first two."

"Very impressive," Marinda said. "Skilled in battle."

"At archery, at least," Bridín put in. She carried her slippers and robe up the hall, crossed the living room, and went back into the bathroom.

"Well, yes," Marinda said. "I don't suppose you had opportunity to test him any further today. The rest can wait, I suppose. But these are good signs, aren't they? They all point to him as the one."

Bridín hung the robe on the bathroom door. Then she set the slippers down and headed out again, aiming for the kitchen this time. Marinda was right behind her, but getting a bit breathless. "I thought I was through testing him for the day," she said. "But then he went and rescued a small child who'd fallen from one of the rides. Risked his life to do it, too. I suppose he thought I'd be impressed." She ran water into the teakettle, set it on the stove, and turned on a burner. "No, that's not true. I believe he'd have done the same whether or not I'd been there to witness it and be impressed by it."

"And were you, my lady?"

Bridín sighed deeply. "Yes, Marinda. I was. I truly was."

"Ahhh," Marinda whispered. "He's the one. I'm sure of it. There's no doubt in my mind."

Closing her eyes, Bridín muttered, "I wish to the gods of Rush that he weren't."

"But why?" Marinda's voice rose an octave, and Bridín's eyes shot open again of their own will.

She took a teacup and saucer from one cupboard, and a chamomile tea bag from the canister on the counter below. "Because . . . I like the man, Marinda. He . . . he stirs something in me that I haven't felt before . . . except . . ." She bit her lip and carefully unwrapped the tea bag from its protective white paper, then concentrated fiercely on unwinding the string and leaving it to dangle over the edge of the cup.

"Except for when you were with Tristan," Marinda said softly. "You don't have to try to hide it from me, child. These eyes only look young. They're old, my lady, and they know what they see."

Bridín turned to face her, finally ready to admit the suspicion that had begun to keep her awake nights. "I think that I might have been in love with Tristan, Marinda." She lowered her head, shaking it slowly. "But he's gone, and now I'm feeling something very similar happening to me again. And it doesn't seem right, somehow, that I should feel . . . that way, for another."

Marinda shook her head slowly. She reached out to take Bridín's hand in her tiny one, and gave a gentle squeeze. "Don't feel guilty, my lady. You've done nothing that should make you feel that way. Nothing at all. Only sought to fulfill the edicts of that crystal."

The teapot didn't whistle, just hummed a bit. But Bridín didn't like it too hot, so she moved to take the kettle from the stove, and filled her teacup with steaming water. Sighing, she leaned an elbow on the counter, resting her cheek in one hand and slowly dipping the tea bag with the other. "I'm not even certain it's Stone I'm having feelings for, you know. It might be just that he reminds me so much of Tristan."

"So perhaps it's those parts of him you're falling in love with, lady. And there's nothing wrong with that."

She finally stopped dipping. She took the tea bag out, squeezed it between two fingers, and then carried her cup with her, walking slowly back into the bathroom. "I don't want to fall in love with *any* parts of him," she said, shaking her head in frustration. She set the cup on the tub's edge and reached in to turn off the water. Then she turned and sat down beside her teacup. "That wasn't part of the plan, you know. I wanted a man I could respect. A man I could trust. But I didn't want to love him. This was to be a marriage of convenience, not one of . . ." She bit her lip.

"Not one of passion?"

"Damn you for your mind-reading, Marinda."

Marinda shrugged. "Force of habit, my lady."

But her eyes were kind as they met hers. And Bridín found herself blinking away tears. "I'm frightened, Marinda. I've never been so frightened before."

"It's natural to be afraid, dear."

"I hate being afraid." She clenched her jaw, then lifted her chin. "But I'm a fay princess, and I'll do my duty, despite my fears. If he's the one, then I'll marry him."

"And what more must he do to prove he is the one, if I might be so bold as to ask?"

Bridín rose, and turned, unbuttoning her shirt as she did. "Well, I only know he's brave and strong, and a very good shot," she said. "I need to know that he's wise, as well. And fair-minded. And honest. Above all else, he has to be honest."

"Oh, my," Marinda muttered.

Bridín glanced over her shoulder at her. "What's wrong with wanting an honest king?"

"Nothing, my lady. Seems reasonable. I was

only wondering why you place it above all else, in your list of requirements."

"Because," Bridín said, continuing to release buttons, "if Tristan had been honest about his feelings for me, then just think how different things might have turned out. But no, he had to insist he was my enemy and claim he hated me. And what happened? He died." She felt her shoulders begin to tremble, felt the tears sting her eyes. And the next thing she knew, she was on her knees beside the tub, with her face in her hands sobbing her heart out and muttering, "He died. Oh, Marinda, why did he have to go and do that?"

"My lord, can't you take a single day off from this pursuit of the lady Bridín? I've made all the arrangements and the house is ready for us. You know how cramped I feel in this apartment. I detest it. I'm used to vaulted ceilings and gilded halls."

"And secret passages and hideaways. I know, I know, Tate. But this is important. It finally seems that I'm making some headway with her."

Tristan rested on the sofa with his arms folded behind his head and his feet crossed at the ankles. Tate had commented that he had the look of a man well pleased with himself, and if he did, then well he should. He *felt* pleased with himself. "I do believe this plan of yours might just work after all, my friend," he said to Tate. "She's responding to me."

"You think she's beginning to believe you're the one?" Tate asked.

"More than that. I think she's beginning to . . . develop feelings for me."

"Well! That *is* something to be pleased about." Tate came around the sofa and planted himself on the overstuffed chair opposite it. Then he tilted his head to one side. "So if we're so pleased about it, why are you frowning?"

He shrugged. He did not wish to discuss his feelings of uneasiness and betrayal with Tate. Not with Tate. Not even with himself. Hell, it made no sense to be jealous of his own alias, but he was. It was the only thing that detracted from the pleasure of seeing Bridín succumbing to his charms. This creeping, utterly foolish feeling that she was being unfaithful to his memory by falling so easily.

Ah, but at least it was *he*, and not some stranger. Not that she had any way of knowing it.

There it was again. He didn't think he'd ever fully trust the woman after this.

"So how long will it be, do you think, before she'll agree to be your bride?"

Tristan sighed hard, shaking his head. "I'd thought to give it more time," he said. "But now . . . now I think we may need to move a bit faster, Tate."

"Why?" Tate tilted his head, looking concerned.

"I think . . . I saw someone. A man, watching her today. Following us together."

"A mortal?"

Tristan shook his head. "I wasn't close enough to tell, Tate, but . . ."

"But?"

"I'm not sure. But I had an uneasy feeling when I saw him. Do you think he could be a scout of some sort, sent by my brother to track her down?"

Tate narrowed his eyes. "What did this man look like, Tristan?"

"I wasn't close enough to see his face."

"But his clothing . . ."

Tristan eyed Tate's worried face. "He was dressed all in black." Tate paled, and Tristan felt a tremor run through him. "What is it, Tate, what does this mean?"

Tate blinked, shaking his head. "It might not mean anything, Tristan. But . . . but black was the traditional color of a member of the brotherhood you banned when you inherited the crown."

"Brotherhood . . ."

"The Sharan Assassins," Tate said. "You never saw them in action, Tristan, so you wouldn't know what to look for. You only learned of their existence and ordered them to disband. They were a crew of highly skilled killers, created by your father long ago. Tristan, do you think your brother has sent them after you?"

"It isn't me I'm concerned about," he said, getting to his feet. "It's Bridín."

Tate leapt to his feet, hurried to the bedroom, and flung a case out from beneath the bed. "We'd best hurry, then," he said. "The mansion is far more defensible than this worthless hovel. We must move at once, Tristan. And we must get Bridín and Marinda there with us. Immediately!"

As Tristan watched, Tate began packing. "Marinda?" Tristan said. "Is that the name of the

Wood Nymph she has with her? I wasn't aware you knew the woman."

Tate froze in his work, his back to Tristan. "She's one of my own," he said, speaking very slowly, so slowly, Tristan began to wonder just how well he truly knew the female. "We're a close race. We all know one another. And though she's on the wrong side in this, my lord, I'd hate to see harm come to her . . . or any of my own kind."

Tristan put a hand on Tate's shoulder, stopping his work. "I'll take care of moving our belongings to the mansion, my friend. There's something else I need for you to do."

Tate turned slowly, staring up into Tristan's face. "What is it?"

"Go back through the veil, Tate. Return to Shara and try to find out if there's any reason for my concern."

Tate closed his eyes, released his breath slowly. "You want me to spy on your brother, find out whether he's activated the legendary Sharan Assassins and sent them here for her."

Tristan nodded gravely. "It's true that I banned the brotherhood when I took my father's crown," he said. "But perhaps they only went underground. I need to know."

Lifting his chin, Tate shook his head. "I'm sorry, my lord. But I cannot obey your command."

Tristan's eyes widened in shock. Tate had never . . . He wouldn't. "Explain yourself."

Tate lowered his eyes. "If you're moving our things, and I'm on the other side carrying out this mission . . . then who is to protect Bridín and

Marinda? Suppose that was a Sharan Assassin you glimpsed in the crowd at the fair? No, Tristan, the women shouldn't be alone. Not even for a short while."

Tristan shook his head. "You misunderstood me, Tate. Bridín is a warrior at heart, my friend. But even so, I've no intention of leaving her unguarded for another moment."

"Well, Marinda is not a warrior," Tate countered. "She's but a Wood Nymph, skilled at magic, not at battle. And I'll not leave her unprotected, nor even trust her life to you, though you know I'd place my own in your hands in an instant."

Tristan tilted his head, studying his friend's determined eyes. "I'm going to them right now, Tate. I'll bring them here with me to get our things."

"Unless it's already too late."

The thought of it shook him. As he hurried from the room, he went on, but knew he was trying now to convince himself more than Tate. "I'm telling you, Bridín is more than capable of protecting herself, as well as her lady. They're safe. They have to be."

"I don't know," Tate said, hurrying after Tristan. "I only know I won't be all right until I see for myself that Marinda is, and that she remains so."

"I never should have left her," Tristan said. "She shouldn't be alone. Neither of them should. My God, Tate, they've been unguarded for several hours already." He dove into his car, Tate climbing in the other side, and they sped into the night, Tristan battling nightmarish images all the way there of what he might find in Bridín's apartment.

Bridín came awake at a subtle sound. A scraping, as if . . . as if a window were slowly sliding open. Frowning hard, she slipped out of bed, reached for the light, but then stopped herself. An extra sense of some sort, like the danger sense of a spider, told her not to turn the light on. Not to make a sound, in fact. And she got very quietly to her feet and walked with the typical light step of a fairy, not making a single noise as she crept to the doorway of her bedroom and gripped the cold metallic knob in her warm palm.

She twisted, and pulled, very gently. The door opened but a crack, and Bridín peered out through it, but saw only the darkened hallway standing empty and alone. Still, an icy finger traced a shivery path up her spine. Something was wrong.

Pulling the door open further, looking up and down the hallway first, she stepped out of the room. And her first thought was of Marinda, sleeping alone in her own bed next door. So she stepped silently to that door, and opened it to look in on her friend. Marinda seemed fine, sound asleep on the small bed, bundled up in covers and hugging her inanimate pillow. The window beyond the bed was closed, and the moonlight from without spilled through, making grate-shaped shadows on the bed and on Marinda's sleeping form. She loved the moonlight, Marinda did. She'd like that it bathed her as she slept.

Bridín backed into the hall, locking Marinda's door from the inside before pulling it closed once more. Then she began her silent trek again, heading for the living room this time. From the hall where she stood, swathed in shadows, the living room stretched out before her, with the bath to her left and the kitchenette to her right. Nothing. She saw nothing. The apartment door was still locked up for the night. All windows in here closed tight, by the looks of it. Only the bathroom remained to be checked.

Drawing a breath and telling herself that her fay sense was way out of kilter tonight, Bridín headed for the bathroom, and belatedly wished she'd remembered her big robe. It was chilly tonight, and she wore only a shiftlike nightgown of green silk, with spaghetti-thin straps that left her shoulders and arms bare. Her back and chest were barely covered, and her legs shivered from midthigh down to her undressed feet.

She checked the bathroom. Nothing. Good.

Releasing the pent-up breath she'd been holding, she turned and happily went back to her room, envisioning herself bundled beneath the warm blankets. She stepped into her bedroom and came to a stop as the pretty white curtains billowed in the gentle breeze that wafted in through the open window.

It was just as Tristan had reached the second-floor landing and started down its hall to her door—having very little idea what to do once he got there—that he heard her scream.

His heart leapt into his throat. The sound made his blood curdle, and he knew Tate had been right. And for a moment, for just one chilling moment, he traveled backward in time. He was standing in that chilled corridor outside the chamber in Castle Shara, hearing her cry out. He'd smashed through the door then, only to see a blade swinging in a deadly arc toward her throat. It had nearly killed him to see that . . . Death, licking its lips at the thought of a taste of one so sweet.

With a fierce growl he slammed his shoulder against her apartment door, half expecting to see a similar sight.

But as he stumbled inside, he saw nothing. No one. He could hear the frantic pounding coming from one of the bedrooms, and heard the Wood Nymph's cries. "My lady, my lady! What is it! Let me out! Help!"

And then a crash . . . the sound came from Bridín's bedroom. Tristan's heart leapt into his chest and he lunged forward, kicked the door in, and saw her.

She stood with her back against the wall, and the man before her, his face invisible beyond the black mask he wore to cover it, lifted his sword. "I execute you in the name of Vincent, prince of Shara!"

"No," Tristan shouted, and he hurled himself forward.

She saw him from the corner of her eye, and it was as if she were reliving her worst nightmare. "Gods, no," she screamed as he lunged between her and the blade. "Not again!" And she launched herself at the attacker, her head and shoulders taking his midsection much as the football players did on television sometimes. She heard his blow land, heard the sickening wet sound it made, and Stone's grunt of pain. But the attacker went down onto his back on the floor. And Bridín landed atop him. She thrust her hand downward, found the dagger in his boot, yanked it out, and buried it to the hilt with a neat upward thrust just below the rib cage.

The man groaned once, and then lay still.

Bridín pushed herself up, and turned to see Stone lying on her bedroom floor, clutching his arm where it pulsed blood, and staring up at her with eyes so familiar . . . so very familiar . . . and so pain-filled.

A great wrenching sob was torn from her chest and she flung herself down to the floor with him, pulling him into her arms as the tears flowed and the sobs grew more and more forceful. She held him, kissed him. "Please don't die," she cried. "Please . . . please don't die. This can't happen. Not again. I can't bear for it to happen again."

And gradually she felt one of his hands stroking her hair, and heard him whisper into her ear, "Bridín, it's all right. Shh. It's only a small cut. All blood and no substance, I swear it. I'm fine."

She lifted her head, searching his face in disbelief. "You . . . you're all right?"

He nodded. "Look." And he lifted his arm for her inspection. Bridín turned her attention to it, tearing the fabric of his shirt away, then ripping a bit of the silk from her own nightgown to press to his wound.

"It's true," she whispered. " 'Tis not a mortal wound."

"No."

"You're not going to leave me just when I've begun to know you, are you, Stone? You're not going to go away just when I've begun to . . . to love you?"

He blinked at her. "Love me? You . . ."

"Please!" She caught his good hand in hers, and clutched at it with both of hers, drawing it to her lips to press desperate kisses to his knuckles. "Don't tear my heart away, like he did. Don't make me care only to go and get yourself killed. I thought it would kill me before. It surely would this time."

He pulled his hand gently from her grasp and cupped the back of her neck. "Bridín," he whispered, and he drew her face close to his, and kissed her. Kissed her deeply, and gently, and with ever-increasing passion. Kissed her the way Tristan had done. The way she'd dreamed of him doing again. And she still felt guilt for caring so deeply for another. But she couldn't let another man slip away from her before she'd had the chance to tell him the truth of her feelings. Before she'd made him admit to her the truth of his own. She wouldn't miss another chance to feel . . . to feel *this*.

When he finally drew his mouth very slightly away from hers, she whispered, "Say it, just once. Tell me you love me, Tristan." And then she bit her lip, and her eyes flew wide.

But he didn't look angry. He didn't look furious or hurt or even confused. He looked . . . he looked amazed. Hadn't he heard her? She'd called him by another man's name! She'd called him Tristan. Why wasn't he shoving her away or berating her?

"I'll do better," he whispered, and it was as if he hadn't even heard what she'd said. Or hadn't understood. Perhaps his wound was more serious than she'd realized. Perhaps the blood loss or the pain had made him . . .

"Marry me, Bridín."

Her thoughts came to a sudden halt at his words. She blinked down at him. "M-marry you?"

"Be my bride."

She blinked rapidly, and felt a shudder work through her body. This had happened far more quickly than it was supposed to. She hadn't even had time to prepare him, to explain about Rush and its need for a king. She hadn't . . .

"Say yes, my love, before I bleed to death."

She stared down at him, in awe. And then, smiling tremulously, she nodded. "Yes. Yes, but only if you still want me after I've . . . after I've told you . . . some things."

"I've always wanted you," he whispered, then grated his teeth and clasped at his arm. "Nothing you could ever tell me would change it now."

She glanced down at the blood soaking his arm, saw it pooling in a small puddle on the floor. "I'll get bandages," she whispered, still not believing the extent of her feelings for this stranger.

"Not yet," he said, struggling to his feet, reaching down for her and pulling her to hers. "I need to hold you, Bridín. I need to feel you touching me. Gods, I thought I'd lost you when I saw . . ." He stopped talking, pulling her tight to his chest and kissing her. His good arm held her hard, crossing at the small of her back, while his injured one held her more loosely, his hand massaging the swell of her buttocks and pulling her close to his groin. His tongue drove deep into her, and she felt as if he were . . . he were marking her as his own. Relishing his victory. Branding her. Possessing her. And a tiny feeling of unease sneaked into her psyche, robbing her of the tingling pleasure the kiss invoked, and replacing it with foreboding.

"No," he muttered, when she would have pulled away. "Don't stop, Bridín. I need you. Gods, you've no idea how much . . ."

The confession seemed wrung from the depths of him, rather than simply spoken. It was more than passion she saw in his dark eyes as they stared into hers. It was longing, and hunger, and a need that went to the core of him. He was breathless and clinging to her as if for salvation. And she couldn't turn away from him. She couldn't.

He kissed her again, and she felt something inside her slowly melting away. A fiery heat took shape in her belly and spread its flaming fingers outward, and she curled her hands at his nape, her fingers threading into his hair. His mouth slid over hers, tracing a hot path over her jaw, down to her neck. He nibbled her there. Her hands moved to his chest, as if to push him away. But she couldn't . . . she couldn't. And instead she found herself running her palms beneath the collar of his shirt, pushing it down and away from him and lowering her lips to the column of his throat. The salty taste of him drove her mad with desire. She kissed a trail down the front of his neck, nuzzling the shirt open still further . . .

She opened her eyes as an icy chill swept away the heat his touch had created. And she saw the twin pendants he wore. Her pendants. In her mind's eye she saw the scene playing out once again in her memory. Tristan lying there, his hand closing around those necklaces in a pool of his own blood.

She bolted upright, pulling away from him, eyes widening as she stared at him—at his face. At his eyes. At the necklaces.

He blinked, confused. And then it was as if sanity hit him, because he glanced downward at the pendants on his chest, and stiffened.

His face seemed to swim before her, just for a moment. And she felt dizzy as she blinked her eyes clear again. But she wasn't seeing whatever magic he'd used to conceal himself from her now. Not anymore. She was seeing him as he truly was.

She was seeing her nemesis. Tristan of Shara, the Dark Prince.

"Tristan," she whispered. And she blinked, but his image remained the same. Anger rose to engulf her. Her hand moved without her volition, and she struck a blow to his face that rocked him backward, as if she could somehow slap the truth away. But it remained. "How could you!"

Chapter Ten

STUNNED. TRISTAN STOOD still, unable to move or take his eyes from her face. His own cheek bore the imprint of her hand, he knew. He felt the stinging rush of blood coloring his skin. But it wasn't the blow that rendered him motionless. It was the pain he saw in her eyes. Devastation. Tears, shimmering and glinting on the sapphire surface of fathomless pools. Anger was there, too, of course. A rage so deep, she trembled with it. But the anger was the reaction he'd expected. The hurt . . . that came as a surprise.

Tate cleared his throat, and the tension stretched taut between them snapped. Tristan glanced toward the door, where the nymph stood beside the small female, Marinda. Tate met his eyes, nodded once, as if to say he was aware of Bridín's discovery, then looked beyond him, toward where the dead man lay on the floor.

"Where there is one Sharan Assassin, there will soon be more," Tate said, his voice low and grim. "We have to leave this place."

Tristan nodded, and reached out to clasp Bridín's arm, but she jerked free as if his touch offended her. "You can't think I'd go anywhere with *you*."

He met her furious glare. "You have no choice, Bridín. You heard what Tate said. There will be others. You're not safe here."

She took a long backward step, and stretched out one hand, palm up. "Give me my pendants."

"Why, Bridín? So that you can fasten them around your pretty neck and feel invincible? So that you can return to the other side and launch another foolish campaign against my brother, only to be killed this time?"

Her eyes narrowed. "He can't hurt me if I wear them."

"He sliced them from your throat once, Bridín. He'll do it again. You underestimate Vincent of Shara."

"And *you* underestimate me." She thrust her hand at him.

Tristan closed his eyes. "I can't give them to you, Bridín."

Her hand fell slowly to her side. "You mean you won't. And it isn't because they'd protect me from your brother, is it, Tristan? It's because they'd protect me from you. At least admit the truth. But I forget . . . honesty is not your strong suit, is it, Dark Prince?"

Lowering his head slowly, he released all his breath. Then raised it to face her angry countenance once more. "I have a place for you, where you'll be safe, Bridín. Come with me now."

"Never."

"Dammit, woman, put aside your bitterness

and use your common sense! Your stubborn pride will get you killed.''

Trembling like a small, frightened rabbit, Marinda stepped up to Bridín's side and touched her arm. ''He's right, my lady. It would be madness to remain and face those assassins alone.''

She slanted her gaze down toward the woman. ''Traitor,'' she whispered. Then she met his eyes again. ''I'm not going with you, Tristan. Get out. Get out now.''

He felt his shoulders slump. He hadn't wanted it to happen this way. He hadn't intended . . .

He lunged forward, gripped her shoulders, and turned her around fast and hard, pulling her back tight to the front of him and pinioning her arms to her sides with his embrace. ''I'm sorry, Bridín. But I can't leave you behind to die. Not now.''

She twisted and pulled against him, but of course, her struggles were useless. And a second later, Tate was beside him, handing him a roll of gray tape. Tristan gathered both her hands in one of his, and used his free one to bind them in front of her. He returned the tape to Tate. ''Her ankles,'' he ordered. And as Tate dropped to his knees to obey, he added, ''Not too tightly, Tate.''

Bridín's hair touched the side of Tristan's face as he held her from behind. And despite her wretched behavior, he was resisting the urge to rub his cheek over hers. To dip his head and taste the salty sweet skin of her neck. He hadn't meant to feel anything for her. That hadn't been a part of his plan. But he was beginning to wonder whether he had any choice in the matter. And whether—maybe—his father had been wrong when he'd told him so often that his only destiny was that of ruling Shara. That it was his only purpose in living. Maybe . . . there was more than that to his life.

"So it begins again, does it, Tristan? Once more you become my captor, and I your prisoner."

"I'm taking you only to keep you safe, Bridín. Tate tells me this place is like a fortress. You'll be protected from Vincent's men there."

"And who will protect me from you?" she whispered.

"You've never needed protecting from me," he said, bending close to speak softly into her ear. "Never, Bridín. You know that."

Tate finished with her ankles and rose, tossing the tape onto the bed. Tristan turned Bridín halfway around, then bent at the knees and scooped her up into his arms. He was doing it. He could barely believe he was actually doing it, taking her prisoner, taking her to this house Tate had found. But by the wings of the gods of Shara, he had no idea what he was going to do with her once he got her there.

He glanced back only once, from the bedroom doorway. The dead Sharan Assassin still lay on the floor, his spirit, no doubt, awaiting release. Tristan pointed his right index finger at the body. "Go now," he said firmly. "Body to the land of its birth, and soul to the place of atonement, reflection, and peace. I release you. Go." A shaft of pale blue light cut a path from the tip of Tristan's finger to the forehead of the man on the floor. And then the light spread, engulfing the man. It grew brighter, until it was blindingly white, and then it faded, and vanished. When it left, no trace of the dead man remained.

He looked down at her then, and caught Bridín staring at him, eyes wide with some sort of wonder. She blinked, and shook her head. "It really is you," she muttered. "You're alive. All this time I . . . and you were alive."

He said nothing. Just carried her out of the apartment and down the stairs, out to the car he'd left waiting. Tate opened the door, and Tristan eased Bridín into the front seat, sliding her all the way over to the passenger side, before settling himself behind the wheel. Tate and Marinda got into the back. Silent, but often exchanging glances that seemed to speak more loudly than words.

Wood Nymphs were highly psychic, and Tristan suspected they were having a thorough conversation back there. He wished to the gods he could hear it.

Bridín stiffened as the car came to an abrupt halt in the middle of what appeared to be no more than a dense forest. Tristan had driven them away from the city, then taken back roads, each one narrower and less traveled than the one before. Until he'd come, finally, to this mere dirt track in the middle of nowhere.

"You said it wasn't far," she accused. "You lie. We've been driving forever."

Tristan looked over at her . . . and she caught her breath again, as she had each time she'd glanced up to see him. *Him.* The Tristan she'd believed dead and gone. Alive, and every bit as arrogant and beautiful as he'd been before. Gods, how she hated him.

"I drove around for a long time, Bridín, just to be sure we were not followed. It isn't as far as it seems." He opened his door and came around to her side, scooping her up once again.

"This foolishness is unnecessary," she told him. "Put me down, Tristan, and remove this wretched tape. I can walk on my own."

He shook his head. "If I put you down, you'll either strike me or kick me, or both, and then you'll run off. Besides, I like holding you."

"Swine!"

"You like it, too, Bridín."

"Liar!"

He only smiled at her in the dimness of the moonlight, and carried her through a stand of fir trees along a nearly indiscernible path. She heard the sounds of lapping water, and scanned the area ahead. The lake. He was bringing her to the lake. Gods, if only she were home, in the enchanted forest of Rush, she'd summon a serpent or a lake sprite to come to her aid. As it was, there was nothing here to help her but a few fish and perhaps a frog or two. Then as he carried her closer to the water's edge, she stiffened, wondering if she was about to be tossed into the icy waves, bound and helpless. But of course, Tristan would never harm her. He couldn't, or she strongly suspected he'd have wrung her neck long ago.

A small, wooden boat bobbed in the water. And he walked into the water up to his knees, to lower her gently onto its foremost seat. Then he gave a mocking bow. "The lady Bridín, princess in exile, must sit in the front, as befits a fairy of her stature," he said. "Would that I had velvet pillows to cushion her tender rump."

"Bastard," she snapped.

He laughed, and turned to help Marinda into the boat, then Tate. He untied the ropes that held the vessel in place and climbed aboard himself, sitting in the center, his back to Bridín's. Hefting the oars, he slid them into the oarlocks, and began rowing them away from shore.

Bridín sat straight and tall in the bow, clinging to her dignity like a protective cloak. Mists rose from the moonlit water, making it impossible to see far ahead. Or even behind them to the shore. It was as if they'd been swallowed up in an invisible world of fog and madness. She lost her sense of direction, couldn't tell where they were going, and wondered how in the world Tristan could.

Tristan. Alive. The bastard. She'd kill him herself when she got free of this tape. She would. All this time she'd believed his lies. Thought him to be another man—the man destined to rule Rush at her side. The irony of it! If she'd only had her crystal, she could have ruled him out right away, but since it had been stolen . . .

Her eyes widened, and she turned to glare at his back. "It was *you*, wasn't it? You stole my scrying crystal!"

He glanced over his shoulder at her. "I made Tate do it, yes. But I guess it would be safe to return it to you now."

"Damn you, Tristan! That stone was the only way for me to find the man I am to marry."

He let go of the oars, letting the boat drift, as

he turned around to face her. He gripped her shoulders, and his black eyes blazed into hers. "Haven't you figured it out yet, Bridín? *I* am the man you're going to marry."

"Never."

"It's the only way to wrest Shara from my brother's rule," he said.

"Rush," she told him. "The name of my kingdom is *Rush*."

Their eyes clashed, and neither blinked. "It's the only way," he said softly. "I'll find a way to make you see it."

"You'll get me to the altar, Tristan, but only if you knock me unconscious and drag me there."

"Shrew." He turned away quickly and began rowing again.

Bridín turned as well, but she was shaken. Did he really think he could force her into marriage? Force her to make him king of Rush? Gods, the man must be insane.

The mists seemed to part then, and she saw the shape rising like a miniature castle from the midst of the water. It rested on a jutting island that rose from the lake's surface like a finger pointing to the heavens. It rose high and steep, almost volcanic in appearance, and she wondered why the place wasn't visible from the shore of Cayuga. But it couldn't be, or she'd have seen it before now.

Beaching the boat on a rocky, inclining shore, Tristan tied it, and then scooped her into his arms once more. The path, when she saw it, frightened her. For it curved in a spiral that completely encircled the jutting shape of the land, again and again. So steep was the rise that only this way could one make it to the top. The wind rose and whipped her hair, chilling her to the bone, and reminding her anew of the thinness of the silk shift which was all that covered her. She could hear it whistling and moaning as it buffeted the rocks, and the crashing of the water below.

She was shivering by the time they reached the flat summit, and surprised to see that they were above the mists now. Moonlight fell like the goddess's kiss to bathe the area, and she saw that it was smooth and level, and covered in a blanket of green grass and wildflowers. And right in the center was the building. No tall, pointed towers like Rush Castle, but a square building all of small gray stones. Like a monastery of old. A single watchtower seemed to jut from the center of the flat roof.

Tristan went still, staring at the place as if stricken.

"This place is surrounded by magic, lady," Marinda whispered from behind her, as Tristan set her on her feet. "I'd heard a few such places existed in the mortal realm, but I'd never truly believed . . ."

She looked at Tate, brows lifted.

So did Tristan. "I can see you know more of this place than you've told me, my friend. Come on, out with it."

Tate shrugged. "Does it seem familiar to you, Tristan?"

Tristan narrowed his eyes. "Sickeningly so."

Tate nodded. "I thought as much. It's said this place was built by a wizard, one of your own race, Tristan, exiled from the other side long ago.

The cloak of his magic remained long after his death. To mortal eyes, this place remains invisible."

Tristan sighed. "I don't like this, Tate. But I suppose we have little choice at this stage. And with any luck, the mists will help conceal this place from the Sharan Assassins when they come looking." He opened the huge front door and stepped inside, pulling Bridín in with him. Then he turned to the other two. "Tate, if you would, hide the boat so that our guest won't decide to borrow it. Marinda, you may see to your lady's comfort, if you wish."

"If that means I can remove the tape, my lord, then I'll do so at once."

He nodded, and Marinda was instantly at Bridín's side, peeling the tape from her wrists. It pulled at her skin, and she winced, but kept her lips sealed. She wouldn't let him know it hurt her. She wouldn't let him know *he'd* hurt her.

Marinda repeated the painful procedure, freeing Bridín's ankles, as Bridín rubbed at her wrists and watched Tristan's every move. He used the old, dry tinder wood to lay a fire in the stone hearth, then ignited it with no more than a flick of his fingers. Warmth surged through the large room, caressing her chilled flesh, and Bridín instinctively moved closer to the fire.

He stood where he was, watching her approach, waiting. She didn't stop, but moved as close as she wanted, and then stood staring into the flames and absorbing the heat.

"What now, Tristan?" she asked him softly, not looking at him.

"I honestly don't know," he replied, his voice

as soft as hers. He reached out, as if to stroke her hair, but she pulled away before he could touch her. His sigh was deep and long. "All right. I suppose we all might as well get some sleep, for now. It's been a long night, and dawn isn't far off."

Bridín glanced around the main room with disdain. Aside from a few meager furnishings, the place was barren. A large, circular concavity of a room. All of stone. And cold in its darkness as well as its chill. "And where am I to sleep? On the stone floor?"

Tristan's lips pulled tight. "Tate hadn't finished preparing the place for habitation yet, but he tells me there are blankets and a few oil lamps scattered about. And I know just the chamber for you . . . Your Highness." He held out a hand. "Come."

Her hand trembled at the mere suggestion she place it in his. But she didn't do it. She only nodded. "While I'm your prisoner, Tristan, I've little choice but to do as you wish. But you should know I'm only biding my time. And sooner or later, I'll escape you. Just as I did before."

He shrugged and reached for her, grasping her hand in his and pulling her from the room and up the curving stone staircase behind him. She wondered briefly how he knew this place so well if he'd never yet been here. Tristan had said it seemed familiar. She'd have liked to ask him about it. But it would wait. Conversing with him civilly wasn't something she felt up to doing, just now.

At the top he turned down a long hallway, passing several doors only to stop at the very last one. And then he flung that heavy wooden door open, to reveal to her a room nearly as barren as the one below. A fireplace gaped in the wall like the jaws of death itself, black and barren. A bed stood in the room's center, unmade, but heaped with folded blankets, sheets, and pillows. An oil lamp sat atop a large trunk, with a box of wooden matches beside it. Through the leaded glass of the small, square window, moonlight spilled in, bathing the room in silver. And she saw the broadsword standing up in a far corner, leaning against the stone wall, as if in repose. Or waiting for its owner's hand to curve around its hilt. She recognized that sword. Tristan's.

"This . . . was to be your room?"

"Leave it to Tate to choose the right one. His psychic powers never cease to amaze me."

"Then . . . it was your room?" His words only confused her all the more. He spoke as if he'd lived here before.

"Still is," he told her. "I can't risk letting you out of my sight, Bridín. I know how clever you are, how bold. And how determined."

He pointed a lazy finger at the stack of fragrant wood that lay ready in the grate, and it flickered to life as if on its own. "Besides," he said, "we need to talk."

She closed her eyes tightly, trying to gather her composure. He couldn't stay here with her. Not now. She couldn't think with him so near, couldn't begin to.

"Bridín?" He came nearer, his hand touching her face, as if in concern. And the heat of his fingertips warmed her cheek. She nearly pressed closer to that touch . . .

Her eyes flew open and met his. "If there is a shred of decency in your black soul, Tristan, then leave me. Bind me up in that wretched tape again. Chain me to the walls if you must, but leave me."

He searched her eyes, and she saw his resistance there.

"You've taken everything from me," she whispered. "My childhood, my kingdom . . . even my heart."

"Your heart?"

Her eyes burned, but she blinked against their stinging. "You made me fall in love with an illusion. A man who didn't exist. And now I'm left with nothing, Tristan. Nothing."

He flinched, she thought, though he did his best to hide it. "The man you fell in love with was no illusion, Bridín. It was me."

She shook her head. "No. *You*, I detest. I could never love a man who has robbed me so thoroughly. Even my freedom is yours to control . . . *again*. Leave me with something, Tristan. Take everything else away, but for the love of Rush, leave me with my dignity." Her voice broke, and she turned away abruptly. "I want to be alone when I fall apart. Give me that, if nothing else."

He stepped close behind her, his hands closing on her shoulders. "Bridín, I—"

"Please!"

His hands fell away. She heard him step quietly to the door, but she didn't turn to watch him go. Her spine remained rigid right up until she heard the hinges groan. The door closed softly, and the warmth seemed to flee the room. Her composure went with it. Every muscle, every bone, melted as Bridín sank slowly to the floor, her legs folding beneath her as if they'd turned to liquid. She curled her arms to pillow her head, and lay there, limp, lifeless. And the tears came.

Tristan paced the front hall, alternately cursing and pushing his hands through his hair.

"My lord?"

He stopped, brought up short by Tate's interruption.

"The boat is hidden, and Marinda settled in an upper chamber."

Tristan only nodded, closed his eyes, and resumed his pacing.

"I'm sorry, Tristan. It seems my plan has failed miserably."

"Failed? Gods, Tate, it more than failed. It's a complete disaster." He tipped his head back, gazing at the ceiling with teeth grated. "She hates me, Tate. She'd no more agree to marry me than she would leap from the damned watchtower."

"No, my lord, I believe you're mistaken there."

"I'm not mistaken. I know what I see in her eyes when she looks at me."

"You'll change her mind, then. Tristan, despite the current state of things, our goal remains the same. We must retake Shara—"

"The hell with Shara!"

Tristan stopped pacing. He stood very still as his own words echoed to the heavens in the large, empty hall. He could barely believe he'd uttered them. What in the name of hell was happening to him? His entire focus had shifted, altered somehow. Until the brokenhearted female upstairs had somehow replaced his own kingdom as his first priority. Gods, it was ridiculous.

But true, nonetheless.

"She'll come around," Tate said. "Give her time."

"We don't have time." Tristan shook away the image of the pain in her blue eyes, and tried hard to fix his attention on matters of more importance, though they seemed somehow trivial now. "We've no idea how things go in Shara. What my brother's rule has done. What we'll be facing when . . . *if* . . . we return."

"Easily remedied, Tristan. I'll go back," Tate said, as if it were all very simple. "And with your permission, Tristan, I'll take Marinda with me. It has become dangerous for her here. And there's no need in risking her life by keeping her. On the other side she can blend in with her people. Vincent will take no notice of her there. But should his assassins find her here . . ."

Tristan nodded. "Yes, you're right. She'd be executed out of hand. They won't risk leaving anyone alive who might carry the tale of my brother's duplicity back to the people of Shara. Yes, Tate, take her."

Tate nodded. "I'll return, my lord, as soon as I've learned all we need to know. Meanwhile, it would be best for you and the lady Bridín to remain here. Venturing out, even once, could very well reveal your whereabouts to the assassins."

Tristan nodded. Much as he detested the notion of hiding from anyone or anything, he needed to consider Bridín's safety as well as his own. If they killed her, his only chance of regaining the throne would die with her.

And so would my soul.

He blinked, and gave his head a shake. Foolish notion.

The tears gave way at last with the first light of dawn creeping over the leaded glass in the small, square window. She thought perhaps she'd cried until there were no tears left inside her. And finally she fell into an exhausted, troubled sleep, right there on the floor where she'd been. Too drained to move. Not caring that it was chilly or that her fire was dying to mere embers. Not bothering to reach for a blanket, though several were stacked only a few feet away on the great bed. She didn't have the energy to breathe, let alone move.

She could not make sense of her feelings. The anger was logical and right, as was her hatred for Tristan. But beyond all of it was another emotion, more powerful than any of those. And it was this one that confused and confounded her.

It was an overwhelming sense of relief . . . even joy . . . that Tristan was alive. She fell asleep still trying to understand that odd feeling.

Later, much later, as she shivered in her sleep, she felt warm, strong arms sliding beneath her body. Felt herself being lifted, then lowered into a nest of softness. Something soft covered her, and she burrowed into it, rolling onto her side and sinking her burning face into what felt like eiderdown.

And as she sank more deeply into the warm velvet embrace of slumber, she dreamed. She dreamed of Tristan. Tristan, stepping into the path of a blade that would have killed her. Tristan, clutching her pendants in a pool of blood, and whispering at her to run. Tristan's eyes, betraying his secret love for her. And then again, all over again. Stepping in front of the blade, taking the blow, to save her life.

Only this time, as he sank to the floor, wounded and bleeding, Bridín—her dream self—sank to her knees beside him, and cradled him in her arms. "You're alive," she whispered. "Thank the gods of Rush, my love, you're alive!"

"Not even death could take me from you," he whispered.

"Don't go, Tristan. Don't leave me. Don't ever leave me again."

"I'm here," he said softly. "I'm right here. I'm not leaving."

"Hold me." And tears filled her heart until they spilled over, leaking into her eyes, flooding them.

But his arms encircled her, held her tight to him. And his hands stroked her hair. And her sleep became peaceful again, and serene.

She woke some time later, to the brilliance of sunlight streaming over her face. And to the embrace of Tristan of Shara, her lifelong enemy.

He sat on the bed, his back against the headboard. And she lay curled atop him, her arms locked around his waist, and her face cradled by the firmness of his belly. His arms held her there, and one hand continued gently stroking her hair, over and over, as if he did it without thought.

Slowly she realized that parts of her dream hadn't been a dream at all. He'd moved her to this bed and then stayed with her, held her like a child in his arms while she slept.

Bridín felt warm and safe here, this way. But that feeling was wrong. She shouldn't allow herself to be deceived by sensations. What lay between her and Tristan was no more than a physical craving. She sat up, stiffening her resolve, but somehow unable to meet his eyes.

"What do you think you're doing?" She smoothed a hand over her hair.

His forefinger lifted her chin, forcing her to look at him. "I came to check on you, and found you on the floor, Bridín. Shivering and crying in your sleep. So I put you to bed."

"An act which would have been noble, coming from any other man," she said. Though her voice didn't carry the right amount of censure. It was too soft and too hungry. "But of course, you're no gentleman, are you, Tristan? Otherwise you'd have covered me up and left me here, rather than climbing in beside me."

Her accusation didn't seem to bother him. He never even blinked, just held her gaze steadily. "I tried to leave you here, Princess, but you wouldn't allow it."

"Nonsense!"

His brows rose. "You clung to my neck and muttered my name. You asked me to hold you, begged me not to go. I think you must have been dreaming."

"I think, Tristan, the only one dreaming in this room is you. Why would I ask you to hold me when I can't bear the sight of you?"

"I can't imagine, Bridín. But I know what I heard. It seems fairly obvious you're not being quite honest. Is it your conscious mind or your dreaming one that's lying, I wonder?"

"You're the liar here, Tristan, not me."

She moved to the side, ready to slide from the bed to the floor, but Tristan caught her shoulders and pulled her to him. His arms slid around her, until her chest was pressed tight to his and his mouth was only a breath away. "I'm not lying about this at least. I want you, Bridín. You are a fire in my blood, and you always have been. Just as I am burning in yours. Admit it."

"I'd sooner be tortured by hot coals," she whispered, but her eyes were focused on his lips, and she was yearning for their touch against hers. Starving for it.

"Liar." He gave her what she couldn't ask for then. His arms hooked under hers, and bent upward so that he cupped her head with his hands. She couldn't have turned away if she'd wanted to. But shameful as it was, she didn't want to. He brought her closer and claimed her mouth, kissing her hard. And yet not hard enough. She should be struggling, she thought. She should pull herself free and slap him. But instead she felt her lips tremble and then part. And she felt him breathe the word "yes" into her mouth, before forcing it open even further, taking her with his tongue. Stabbing fiercely in a slow, deep rhythm that was filled with innuendo and promise and threat.

And gods, how she burned for him. Ached for him.

She clung to him, not kissing him back because she couldn't move. Not the way he held her and ravished her lips. It was all Tristan. And it made it easier that she didn't have to comply and that she couldn't pull away even if she'd wanted to. This way she'd never have to admit, not even to herself, how much she wanted this. Craved this.

He lifted his head at long last, but only to dip it to her neck, and nuzzle her there. He pushed the strap of her shift aside with his mouth and nipped at her shoulder, and upper arm, and then, sliding lower in the bed, his hands at her back pulling her down atop him, he moved lower. His wet mouth moved hotly over her breast, through the silk. He scraped a path with his teeth, bumping to a stop at the tautness of her pebblelike nipple. And then he caught it with his tongue. Licked at it, wetting the silk. Pushed and pulled, and suckled her hard. And then he bit her there, and she gasped in pleasure and a tiny, shivery bit of pain. He heard her gasp, stiffening for an instant, holding her there throbbing between his teeth, then biting down harder.

She cried out, and it seemed to galvanize him. He gripped the fabric in his teeth, growling deep in his throat, and tore through it. She felt her breast fall free, naked and vulnerable, against his face, and she started to pull away, but he didn't let her. His hands held her tighter still, yanking her down to him, and his head rose from the bed, and he clamped his mouth over her breast and fed there like a man starved for her taste. With his hand he pulled her other breast free, and then moved to feed at that one. Pulling hard, nipping, working her until she was wet from his mouth and aching with need.

The shift tore open, down the center, as he slid one hand between them and yanked at it. And his mouth followed the path of the tear, tongue darting downward, wet and warm against her belly, moving lower, wetting her panties, biting at the elastic of them, pulling and letting it snap back. He mouthed her as if he were devouring her, and she told herself to stop this insanity before it was too late. But it was already too late. She could feel his mouth on her and it was already far, far too late.

He bit through the material, tearing her panties, shredding them with his teeth until she was naked. And he kissed her. Soft, teasing kisses. Then his fingers parted her folds, and he kissed her again. A hot little trail of quick, hard kisses. She groaned and pulled away. His hands gripped her buttocks and he jerked her down hard and fast, and locked his mouth to her quivering flesh. And he wouldn't release her. He refused. There was a feeling of invasion as he forced her open, and thrust his tongue upward, filling her with it, taking everything she had, devouring her very soul, it seemed. She felt her body begin to clamp in on itself, felt the tightening, and the trembling. Again she tried to pull free, but this time his teeth closed on the tiny nub that was the center of her need, and he nibbled at it until she stopped pulling. Until she settled herself down. Until she relaxed her clenching thigh muscles and let them fall open wider. His hands squeezed her buttocks in approval, and then his tongue stabbed her again. He bathed her with it, thoroughly, until she was completely unable to move or think or feel anything beyond this mouth on her. And then he seemed ready to give more. He moved again, harder this time, hurting her so deliciously that she cried out loud.

She screamed as her body yearned and reached and hungered for something she couldn't imagine. And then she found it. Her soul exploded as the orgasm seared through her. She heard her own anguished cries, but they seemed to come from somewhere far away. There was only one plane of reality. That place where he touched her. That place where he was. The universe was centered right there.

And then she collapsed atop him, shuddering and shivering and unable to move. He slid up her body, his lips blazing a trail with his kisses. His arms wrapped around her, he cradled her head to his chest, and he whispered something in her ear. Something . . .

"I love you, Bridín."

She stiffened, her glorious, glowing body cooling at a rapid pace. "Don't—"

"It's true. I want you to marry me. Now. Right away."

The chilling of her heated flesh was complete. Bridín slid away, and sat up in the bed, staring down at him. "Are there no depths too low for you to sink, Tristan? Is there anything you wouldn't do, any lie you wouldn't tell, to get my throne again?"

He sat up, too, his eyes narrowing, sparkling. "This has nothing to do with the throne," he said. "This is just you and me, Bridín, and it always has been. You know that. Dammit, in your heart, you know that."

"I only know you want the crown," she whispered, her throat tightening. "And by marrying me, you think you can get it."

He lowered his head, sighing hard. "And what could I do to convince you that you're wrong, Bridín?"

She dipped her head, her eyes focusing on the pendants that hung around his neck.

Tristan closed his eyes. "I can't."

She nodded. "I know you can't. Giving them back would end your power over me."

"And leave you free to run from me," he said. "Straight into the arms of death." He shook his head. "Ask something else of me, Bridín. Anything else."

"Let me go," she whispered.

He was silent as he met her eyes. "All right. Your point is taken. There's nothing I can do to prove myself to you. Not now. But I will, Bridín. I will convince you in the end. And you will marry me. We'll return to the kingdom together, you and I, and we'll stir the people to revolt. My brother will be proven the liar and traitor he truly is, and he'll be ousted. And then you and I will take our places on the castle throne. We'll rule as equals, as king and queen of Rush."

She blinked and turned away. He'd said *Rush*. Not Shara, but Rush.

"I know you don't believe me, Bridín. I only wish there were some way I could gain your trust."

She wanted to trust in him. Everything in her cried out to do just that. Even with all she knew. Her own weakness toward this man frightened her right to the core of her being. "And how am I to trust the man who took my kingdom? The man whose father murdered my mother? The man who held me captive from earliest childhood, after murdering my adoptive family, Tristan! The man who lied to me and deceived me and let me go slowly insane believing him dead!" Her hands curled into fists and she let them fall forcefully against his chest. "Do you have any idea what that did to me, Tristan? Do you know how I grieved for you? I thought you were dead, and you let me go on thinking it!"

He caught her fists in gentle hands. "I didn't understand. Darling, I didn't know it would cause you grief. I thought it more likely to cause you to celebrate."

She shook her head. "You lie. You knew."

He closed his eyes slowly, nodded once. "You're right. I knew. I'm sorry."

"It's too late to be sorry. I could never trust you now, Tristan. Never."

"But, Bridín, there's so much you don't know. The way your adoptive parents died—I had nothing to do with that. It was a car accident, just as you were told."

She closed her eyes, because her last remaining doubt was erased. He was lying now just as he'd been lying all along. And she'd so wanted to believe him. "You see?" she whispered. "Still you lie to me. The brake line on my family's car was cut, Tristan."

"No." He shook his head as if in disbelief.

"I was seventeen when I found out. I'd . . . I'd started to let myself doubt the things I knew to be true, you see. That you were evil, and cruel, and a killer. I'd started to . . . to fantasize about you. To think I'd been wrong about you all along and to believe that I was falling in love with you, Tristan. Raze was the only one I trusted enough to tell. And he couldn't stand by and see it happen. So he convinced a friend to help get the facts for me, and that's what they found out. The brake line was cut. My parents were murdered, and the case was never solved.''

He blinked twice, staring at her. "I swear to you, Bridín, by the wings of the gods, I swear, I did not kill your family. I couldn't have, even if I'd wanted to. I—"

"You did whatever you had to do to get what you wanted. And what you wanted was to prevent me from returning to Rush to reclaim my throne. And you did it. Just as you're doing it now. You lied and cheated and killed to do it, and you're doing it again. No, Tristan. Don't ask me to trust you. Not ever.''

Tristan lowered his head, and she could have sworn she saw moisture in his eyes when he lifted it again, then got up and left her there, alone.

More alone than she had ever been in her life.

Chapter Eleven

HE'D NEVER BEEN so aroused in his life. And he'd never been so angry. Gods, she was determined to disbelieve him! To distrust him! To credit him with the sins of the universe in addition to his own. It was as if she were seeking out reasons to hate him.

He pounded his fist down on the mantel of the front hall, grimaced, and lowered his head to that fist.

"Perhaps, my lord, she seeks reasons to hate you because it's the only way she *can* continue to hate you?"

Tristan turned, spied Tate standing near the door amid a pile of boxes, and frowned. "What are you doing here? I thought I sent you back."

"That you did, my lord, but before I left you, I thought you could use some supplies. Might make things a bit easier until my return."

Stepping closer, Tristan saw piles of his belongings packed in those boxes. And in others, he saw things that must be Bridín's. The crystal scrying sphere nestled at the top upon a cushion of silk that could only be her clothing. She loved silk. He looked at Tate again. This was his not-so-subtle way of suggesting it was time the crystal be returned to its owner. The thought sent a tremor through Tristan. If that ball told her the true identity of this man fate dictated she marry, he might lose her forever.

"You've been back at the apartment? Tate, you could have been seen. Followed—"

"I'm a Wood Nymph. No one follows me unless I allow it. I was careful, Tristan, you have my word. No one saw me."

Tristan lowered his head with a sigh. "Thank you, my friend."

"Marinda is waiting in the boat," he said.

Looking up, Tristan probed his friend's shuttered eyes. "You knew her before we came through the portal, didn't you?"

"Does a male ever truly know any female?" He turned and left through the front door, pausing just beyond it for only a moment. "We towed a second boat out here, though I'm sure you could probably have conjured one on your own. It's tied up in the cave, should you have need of it. Though I think it would be for the best if you two remained right here, out of sight, until I return with word."

Again Tristan nodded. "No action on my part would be wise without intelligence, Tate. That's why I'm sending you."

"I won't let you down."

With a nod, he hurried off, disappearing down the slope and its corkscrew path.

Alone. Alone in this miniature castle, with Bridín, a woman he . . . what? She'd been right before. When he'd told her he loved her, it had probably been a lie. Though he couldn't be certain of that. It seemed to Tristan that the way he felt for her was as close to love as anything he'd ever felt before, or was likely to feel again. Certainly he *liked* her. Despite her biting temper, he found he enjoyed spending time with the woman. Missed her when he was not with her. Wanted her with every cell in his body when he was with her. Couldn't bear the thought of lifting a hand to harm her, much less permitting anyone else to do so.

So if that wasn't love, he didn't think he'd ever feel the tender emotion. He needed her, as well. For Tate had been accurate in his predictions. He couldn't take the throne away from Vincent on his own. Couldn't stir loyalty among the people . . . not the way Bridín could. Hell, no one could stir devotion in men the way she could. She made a man feel damned . . . protective of her. At least . . . that was the way she made *him* feel.

Damn. He needed a plan of action, and he needed it now. But how could he win the trust of a woman who believed him guilty of so many wrongs—many of them justifiably?

Not the murder of her family, though. Not that. Perhaps if he could prove his innocence to her . . .

Ah, but how? They'd been dead for so long. Twenty years and more. Solving a crime so old would take a squadron of investigators. And that was something he didn't have. Hell, he couldn't even leave this place without risking her life.

What, then?

As he paced, Tristan absently fingered the pendants that dangled at his throat. Then he stopped, realizing what he was doing. No, he couldn't give them to her. She'd flee him, and he'd be unable to stop her, even to touch her. His stomach rumbled, and he let go of the necklaces, sighing hard. Food first. He might come up with some solution to this impossible task before him eventually, but meanwhile, he'd think better with some sustenance in his belly.

Though it wasn't food alone he hungered for.

He closed his eyes, recalling against his will the sounds of Bridín's sighs, the texture of her skin, the taste of her musk. The feel of her. Her scent. Gods, he'd wanted her. And could have had her, very easily, this dawn. Yet he'd known her resistance, her unwillingness, and something inside him had been unable to take full advantage of her body's betrayal. Something he didn't understand, for he knew full well that—physically, at least—she'd wanted him, too.

Bridín snatched the comforter from the bed and wrapped it tight around her when she heard him at the door. Then he entered, and fixed her with that somber gaze that sent shivers right down her spine.

He held a platter in one hand, and a swath of fabric over his arm. And he came in slowly, watching her almost warily.

"What do you want now?" she asked as he closed the door behind him. "Haven't you shamed me enough, Tristan?"

"There's no shame in you, Bridín. Nor should there be. I only showed you a small portion of the pleasures you could know each night of your life. If you wanted to." He set the plate on the trunk that rested beside the bed. "As to why I'm here again, I brought food. And clothes." He dropped the pile of garments on the bed, and then he sat on it, the wretch.

"Marinda would have brought me the food and the clothing as well. If you've come, you have other reasons." She stood near the fire she'd rekindled, her back warm from the flames, her belly warming from some other source.

He lowered his head. "You can't bring yourself to believe a single word I utter, can you, Princess?" Sighing, he faced her, his chin coming up, his eyes guarded. "Marinda is no longer here. I sent Tate back to the other side, and it was his desire to take the woman with him, to remove her from the danger we're facing here."

Bridín blinked in shock. "Marinda . . . left me?"

"I don't believe Tate gave her much choice in the matter."

"If he harms her—"

She stopped speaking when Tristan shook his head. "I believe the two . . . are well acquainted. Though for reasons only a Wood Nymph would be likely to understand, they chose to keep that fact from us. Regardless, I believe Tate's concern for Marinda's safety is genuine. He's an honorable man, Bridín. He'd no more harm Marinda than . . . than I would harm you."

"He's your man," she snapped. "And I'd no more trust him than I would you. I warn you, I hold you responsible for her safety."

He shrugged. "As the rightful leader of Shara, or Rush, or whatever you choose to call our kingdom, I'm already responsible for her safety. As well as the safety of all who live there."

"You are *not* the rightful leader!" She strode two steps nearer before freezing in her tracks, fear making her feet turn to stone. Being close to him was not in her best interests. "I am."

"We both are."

She closed her eyes, turning her back to him and holding her blanket tight to her shoulders, as if by doing so she could shut out the intensity shining from his black gaze. Though she couldn't, of course. She saw that gaze even when he wasn't in the room.

"The throne of Rush belonged to my mother," she told him, though she was well aware he already knew. "And her father before her, and his before him. It was handed down to me by birthright, as firstborn of the fay queen. And I will have it again."

He rose slowly and came close to her. She didn't turn. Refused to turn and face him. Nor would she cringe away from him like a coward. No, she stood her ground. Stiff and rigid. Fearing that he would touch her. Fearing that he wouldn't. He stood so close she could feel his heat, searing her even through the blanket she wore like armor. He did not touch her. And yet it was very much as if he did.

"The throne of Shara belonged to the grandfathers of my grandfathers, more than a thousand years ago," he said. "Long before any of the fay race had ever set foot on its enchanted ground. The homeland of your people, legend says, was a mystical island that moved with the tides, an island shrouded in mists to protect it from prying eyes. Much like this tiny island we're on right now, only larger. Some say it still exists, drifting along at sea. A few mortals even claim to have glimpsed it moving amidst the fog, only to find nothing there when they dare venture nearer."

Bridín wanted to cover her ears and refuse to listen to him. But she, too, had heard whispers of the fairy isle. Though she'd always believed them to be myths, and not the actual history of her people.

Tristan's deep voice came softly, his warm breath bathing her ear as he leaned in close to speak to her. "No one knows what caused your people to leave their magical island. Perhaps the land simply dried up. Or maybe there was a split among factions. Perhaps your family were never truly of royal blood at all, Bridín, but left that island because they wanted to be. They wanted a land where they could make themselves kings—"

Bridín whirled to face him, her cheeks burning with anger as she flung the blanket from her shoulders and stood before him in her torn silken shift. "Look at me, you treacherous liar!"

And his dark eyes heated, burned over her flesh. She'd made a mistake, she knew that now, but she wouldn't back down. The shift had been ripped down the center, and it hung open, clinging to her breasts but leaving the skin between them naked to his gaze.

"I *am* of royal blood," she told him. She drew her fingers over her skin, just above the blond curls, tracing the shape of the berry-colored birthmark she'd been branded with since birth.

"And this mark is the proof of that, as you know fully well. Only a fairy of royal blood bears the scarlet crescent."

He was silent. Just stood there, burning her with his eyes. Eyes that seemed pained for just a moment.

Sighing hard, Bridín strode past him, yanking at the clothing he'd piled on the bed. She found panties, and stepped into them, then let the shift fall from her shoulders and pulled the simple black dress over her head. Its long sleeves and full skirt did little, though, to erase the chill from her bones.

"For whatever reason," Tristan began again, though this time his voice was hoarse, and roughened, "your people left their isle when it came within reach of the shores of Shara. They came in boats. They came with armies, and with the power of their magic, and they took the kingdom by force. Those who fought them were killed, and those who resisted their brutally won rule were banished. My family—the royal family of Shara—was exiled, sent to live in the darkest part of the forest you call Rush. Even our name, the name of Shara, was outlawed, never to be spoken within the city walls again."

She said nothing. She had no defense against his charges. She knew it was true. All of it.

"Do you have any idea, Bridín, what it is like for a child to grow up in a world of darkness? A land without the sun's gentle kiss? To feed on the watery, white-livered vegetation that is all that can grow in that land?" He sighed deeply, heavily, and bent to toss another bit of wood onto the fire. Then he straightened again, staring pensively into the flames as she stood watching him, unable to look away.

"Our people were defeated because they did not know the ways of magic," he said, speaking slowly. "But they learned. During those ten centuries of exile, they drew down the power of the night, which has a magic all its own. They made of themselves a race of wizards, and built a temple where the most powerful were to reside. And when a child was discovered to have powers stronger than most, he was taken from his family and sent to live there, among the masters. Where his every day was spent in lessons and practice and indoctrination. Where he'd be grilled constantly in the single goal of our people. To one day retake Shara from the fay . . . at any cost."

Bridín felt a lump form in her throat. She tried to swallow, and couldn't. "You?" she whispered.

He turned to face her. "I was the eldest son of our king, Bridín. And gifted in the dark arts as well. I was considered the most important of all the novices at the temple, and I was treated to more intense . . . *teaching* . . . than any other. They told me I had but one reason for existing, Bridín. And that reason was to hold my kingdom for my people."

"You were taken from your family? From your mother?" She bit her lip. Why was she asking him about this? Why was she feeling any sympathy at all for his childhood when he'd robbed her of hers?

"Just as you were, Bridín. I know of that particular kind of grief. And because I know it so well, I could never bring myself to inflict it upon another. I had no hand in your mother's death that night my father's armies laid siege to Rush. And I had no hand in the killings of your adoptive family, either. I couldn't."

She closed her eyes, telling herself she'd be a fool to believe him, and bit her lip to keep from asking the questions that he'd started swirling in her brain. And yet the words spilled out all the same, in a voice soft with some emotion she didn't dare to name. "How old were you when they took you from your mother, Tristan?"

"Five . . . or perhaps six years of age. I don't really remember. And it doesn't matter now."

"You do remember. I can see it in your eyes."

He shrugged, and averted his gaze.

"Where is she now, your mother?"

"She . . ." He paused, cleared his throat. "She took ill and died while I was at the temple. My second year there, I believe." Then he gave his head a shake, and met her eyes once more, his own having gone as cold as ice. But it was thin ice. Just a single layer, placed there deliberately in an effort to conceal the pain underneath. But he couldn't hide it. Not from her. "The point of the tale, Bridín, is that Shara is as rightfully mine as yours. More so, in fact. You should be grateful of my offer to share its rule with you."

Bridín stiffened. So they were back to the same argument once again. "Your offer to share the ruling of Rush is based solely on your own desire to have the throne back, Tristan. Don't pretend it comes of your endless generosity. You know full well you have no chance of ousting your brother without my help."

"Nor do you without mine."

She crossed her arms over her chest, lowered

her gaze. "So this talk of love . . . It was but another ruse to convince me to agree to this proposal of marriage. Just another tool in your cache of weapons to be used in regaining the throne."

"It was . . . whatever you believe it to have been."

"I believe it to have been an outright lie."

He shrugged and walked past her, picked up the platter of food, turned and held it out to her. "It's cold by now. But you should eat, Bridín. You'll need all your strength when we return to claim our kingdom."

"I have not agreed to join forces with you, Tristan. You assume too much." She looked down at the plate, but he still held it there, so she took it and went to sit on the trunk that was the only piece of furniture in the room besides the bed. And she didn't want to be on that bed. Not with him so close.

The cold scrambled eggs and toast stuck in her throat, but she forced them down all the same. He was right, she would need her strength. She'd need it to carry out her escape.

"When I rule my kingdom once again, Tristan, I'll see to it your people are allowed to remain there, as my subjects. They'll never again be banished . . . so long as they pledge fealty to me."

"You are an arrogant little witch," he told her. "But you will agree to wed me, Bridín. You can hate me forever, if you like. But you will be my wife, and my queen. Think of it as a marriage of convenience. Think of yourself as a martyr, if you will. That would suit your haughty self-image, wouldn't it? Marrying me could be your great sacrifice for the good of the kingdom."

"I don't need your permission to hate you, Tristan. I've been doing so quite well without it. And will continue to." She finished the food and reached for the glass of milk that rested on the platter. She took a large drink, and then frowned. "It's sweet. What is this?"

"Milk and honey, my lady. The traditional offering to invoke the goodwill of fay folk."

She scowled at him, but sipped some more. It was good. Setting the glass down, she got to her feet, picking through more of the clothing on the bed. Nightgowns and robes, and a pair of those denims she'd grown so fond of during her time here. Some flat shoes, and blouses. "How did my things come to be here? We didn't bring any along."

"Tate fetched them for you. You can thank him when he returns with news of what we face in Shara."

So the Wood Nymph was on a spying mission. She'd guessed as much. "Did he bring . . . all of my belongings?"

Tristan cocked one brow. "Is there something in particular you're wanting?"

"My scrying crystal. I need it. You stole it from me, Tristan, and I want it back."

"So you can peer into its facets and try to discern the identity of this man you are fated to marry?"

"What good would it do me to know who he might be, while I remain here in captivity?" She lowered her eyes, sighing deeply. "No, Tristan, I want the crystal because in it I saw the face of my mother. She spoke to me through it, and I . . . long to see her again."

He stared at her for a long moment. "The crystal is in one of the boxes Tate brought along. If you want it, Bridín, it's yours."

She nodded, glad he wasn't going to argue over that. "There is one other thing I would ask of you," she said, wondering if it was wise to press her luck just now. But he looked at her, awaiting her request, so she pushed on. "My sister. She'll be concerned about me. I need to get word to her, let her know I'm all right."

"I'll have to think on it," he said. "There is no telephone here, and to leave the island would be to risk another attack by my brother's assassins. Perhaps when Tate returns . . ."

Bridín nodded, but didn't accept his answer. Not that it mattered. She had no intention of being here when Tate returned.

Chapter Twelve

TRISTAN PICKED UP the platter and carried it with him to the door. He didn't think his efforts at convincing Bridín had done a bit of good to his cause. She'd shown no signs of listening. Hearing, yes, but not *listening*.

Except . . . for that softening he'd detected in her voice when she'd asked him about his mother. Only natural she'd respond to that, he supposed. And she likely would have felt that response no matter who'd been telling the tale. Be it Tristan of Shara or the Lucifer of Christendom. She had a heart as big as the Sharan sky. Always had. It was one of the things that made it so impossible for him to wish her ill, ever, even though she'd been the most serious threat to his rule. She had the capacity to care for someone who was hurt. Even when that someone was him.

And she'd lost her mother as well. So naturally, his similar loss would move her. Not enough to change her mind, however. He was beginning to wonder if anything ever would be.

"Am I confined to this chamber, Tristan?"

He stopped, his hand braced on the open door. "Of course not." Then he turned to face her again. "Bridín, I've told you, you're not here as my prisoner, but for your own protection."

"As long as you refuse to let me leave here at will, I am a prisoner. Though you paint it with pretty motivations, Tristan, it doesn't change the facts."

He drew a breath and sought patience, though his supply was running severely short right now. "You're free to roam the house, Bridín."

"And what about the island? Am I free to roam it, as well, or will I find bolted doors and sealed windows should I try to leave?"

Tristan studied her, looking for signs she was up to something. Then again, it really didn't matter if she was. There was only one way off this island. By boat. And the only boat hereabouts was well hidden, in a secret cave she couldn't find even if she knew it was here. "Fine," he said. "Explore the island, but be careful, Bridín. Never forget, this was supposedly a wizard's home. The home of a man not only powerful, but dangerous."

She lifted her delicate brows. "So nothing's changed, then, has it?" And then she tilted her head. "What do you know of the man who created this place?"

Tristan held the door for her as she passed, and it seemed to him that she looked around her with a newly curious eye. Good. Something to amuse her would keep her distracted, and perhaps she wouldn't try anything foolish. For a little while, at least.

"If he is the same man I'm thinking of—the only Sharan wizard I know of ever having been banished—he was one of the masters assigned to tutor children in the temple. Hundreds of years before my time, it was, but I've heard the tales. He was incredibly powerful. Some said frighteningly powerful. Some even claimed he'd unlocked the secret to immortality."

He walked beside Bridín along the corridor, and she pushed open one door after another as they passed, peering inside, seeing chambers much like her own. Small, each with a stone hearth and little else besides cobwebs and dust. The ceilings were vaulted, but not as high as it seemed they should be. The hall, not as wide. The place seemed like a small replica of something bigger. Bridín wondered if the legend was true, if it really had been built by someone from the other side. She walked slowly along the dim, chilly corridor, dragging one hand over the cool, rough stone of the wall.

"Why was he banished?" she asked, peering through the last of the five wooden doors.

"Several of the children he tutored took ill, in succession. One after another. Each seemed to have contracted some sort of wasting illness, wherein they would grow thin and pale and weaker with each passing day. At the same time, this wizard seemed to be growing ever stronger and more powerful. And . . . he never seemed to age, or so I'm told."

Stepping away from the door, Bridín faced him, wide-eyed. "He was stealing the children's vitality? Somehow taking it for himself?"

"That was what the superstitious minds of the

time concluded," Tristan said. "Naturally, we've since realized it was more likely a form of malnutrition. Once our people began slipping out of the dark side to gather food, the illness disappeared."

"Then he was punished for something he didn't do?"

Tristan shrugged. "He was banished, not only from our dark realm, but from all of the enchanted world. Word of the deaths spread, along with the tale of the alleged cause. He'd have been stoned to death had he remained."

Again that softening in her eyes. "But if he was innocent—"

"Innocent people are believed guilty of crimes all the time, Bridín."

He referred, of course, to her steadfast belief that he had killed her family. But she refused to rise to the bait, and instead stuck to the subject at hand, much to Tristan's disappointment.

"He came here, then?" she asked.

"So the tale goes. It's said that the sickness of the temple children began to fade shortly after he left. Enough to convince even those who doubted of his guilt. So he came here, and built a castle for himself, a miniature replica of the temple where he'd lived before. And then he conjured the magical mist that enshrouds the place to this very day, guarding it from mortal eyes forevermore."

"This place," she whispered. So like a child, she was, eyes wide with wonder. "Is it, Tristan? Is it this place?"

He tipped his head to one side, better to appreciate the full, parted lips. "It very well could be. This place is quite similar to the temple where I was raised." He looked around him, and shuddered. "A bit too similar."

"You hated it so much then?"

He stared down into her curious eyes. "It was a living nightmare for a child. I'd never have come here if I'd known it was so like that other place."

"How is it similar?"

He took her arm, possessed suddenly of a need to touch her. The warmth of her skin heated his palm where he held her, chasing away the chill of the memories invoked. He led her to the top of the stairs. "The chambers were like these. Small, and each with a fireplace, though there were a great deal more than five in the temple. The front hall is set up in the same fashion, with the hearth on the far wall, and this curving stone staircase to the left. Of course, our kitchens were far larger and more efficient. This one has only a small room with storage space for food, and a cold spring feeding through a space in one wall, for a cooler." They walked down the stairway side by side. "This place has surprisingly modern bathing rooms. Toilets like mortals have, and a hot spring feeding the tub."

"A tub?"

He glanced at her, saw the longing in her eyes. "A hot bath appeals to you, does it?"

"More than you know," she said.

He almost smiled at her. And then he did. Why not? Animosity between them was one of the many things he needed to eliminate, after all. "Come with me. I'll show you." And he led her through the front hall, past the kitchen, and to the large bathing room beyond. "It's close to the kitchen for a reason," he explained. "The same hot spring is piped into the sink there. All gravity-fed, of course. No electricity needed." He opened the door with a flourish, pleased by her slow sigh of surprise.

The tub was closer, in fact, to a small pool, and sunken into the floor. The room was warm, due to the hot springs being directly beneath it. Steam rose from several vents in the floor, creating a mist almost as enchanting as the one that enshrouded the island. A warm, damp mist that was soothing to the lungs. Sunlight poured in through a wall of thick leaded glass that distorted one's view of the outside, and added to the room's warmth.

Tristan bent, moved a valve, and steamy water began streaming into the tub. No high pressure. Just a natural stream. He dropped a stopper into the drain at the bottom, then straightened again.

"You've no need to wait on me, Tristan. I could have drawn my own bath."

He turned slowly, and then went still. Bridín stood in a pool of yellow sunlight, and it glinted in her hair, making it shine like spun gold. She looked like a mystical goddess of old just then, with the sunlight and the swirls of mist surrounding her. And the sight of her took his breath away.

"Were you my wife, Bridín, I would draw your bath for you every night. I'd stir rose petals and vanilla oil into the water for you, and when the tub brimmed full, I'd remove your clothes, and scoop you up in my arms, and lower you into the water. With my own hands I'd bathe you, and I'd wash that glorious hair in henna and myrrh. And when your water began to cool, I'd carry you back to our bed, to keep your feet from touching the cold floor, and rub you dry with towels of fleece. Or kiss the dew from your body with my lips and my mouth. I'd—"

"Enough." She'd lowered her head, and then turned her back to him as he spoke, but he saw her tremble, and thought perhaps the picture he painted for her with his words was one she found appealing. "There is nothing you wouldn't say to convince me, is there, Tristan?"

"No. Nor nothing I wouldn't do." He lowered his hands to her shoulders and gently turned her to face him. "Shall I show you, Bridín, how it will be with us?" He pulled her closer, and she didn't resist. He lowered his head, sliding his arms down along hers until he could lace his fingers in hers. He kissed her, holding her hands, feeling them clench tighter. Her lips softened, opened to him, and he tasted her mouth with his tongue. The fire she could so easily ignite in his soul came to life again, but he battled the blaze. Kept it in check. His kiss was as tender as he could make it, and though he didn't want to, he ended it, and lifted his head to stare into her bewildered eyes.

She blinked up at him. "The tub is filling," she whispered, her voice raw with the hunger he knew she felt. "And I'm capable of bathing myself." She lowered her eyes. "I want you to go now."

"No, Bridín, you don't. Not really. But I will go all the same." He released her and turned toward the door.

"Tristan?"

He closed his eyes and waited, praying she'd ask him to stay.

"No matter what else has gone between us, or what lies ahead . . . I . . ."

He turned to face her, tilting his head to one side. "Go on."

Licking her lips, dipping her head and then lifting it again, she whispered, "I'm truly glad you're alive."

He smiled then, and reached out to stroke her hair, just once. "Well," he said. "That's a start."

"No it's not. It just . . . is."

As she soaked in the tub and plotted her escape from this wretched little isle, she was glad she'd told him. It was little more than the truth. She *was* glad he was alive, despite the trouble he always managed to cause for her. She'd been too angry at his dishonesty to react when she'd first discovered that he hadn't died at his brother's hand. And she was still angry, of course. But now, with a bit of time to mull it over, that anger was tempered by a profound sense of relief, even gratitude, that he'd been spared. She'd mourned him sincerely and painfully. Dreamed of his darkly handsome face, and awakened only to cry herself to sleep once more. She'd missed him. And she was glad he was alive. Truly glad, right down to her soul.

And glad she'd told him. Because who knew when she would see him again? Yes, it was good that he knew how she felt. It eased her mind that she'd bared her soul to him at last.

And now she would escape.

Because she couldn't remain with him. If she never regained the kingdom and the throne, so be it, but she couldn't stay here. She couldn't listen to his tender words, his promises, or see the love shining from his eyes when she knew it was all a lie. It hurt, it hurt too terribly to bear. Perhaps because she wanted so badly for it to be true.

And this was the perfect time to act. Yes, he'd told her she would be allowed to roam the isle, but he was a liar and always had been. He'd likely follow her if she went out alone. Watch her from some secret vantage point. This was the perfect time to escape him. Tristan knew her well, and so knew, too, of her fondness for hour-long soaks in the bathtub. She'd asked him to allow her some privacy. He'd honor that, she thought. So this gave her an hour in which to make her getaway unnoticed.

Tate's absence made this even more perfect. Only one pair of sharp eyes to elude, instead of two.

She didn't undress but instead went to the door and pressed her ear against it to listen. And she heard nothing. Then she went back to the heavy leaded glass window, and found that it did indeed open. The heavy panes were set within wooden frames that hinged on the sides and swung outward from the center like shutters. She flicked the tiny hook and eye free and pushed them wide, then climbed through them. Her hands clutched at the lush green grasses as she pulled herself out of this sunken, earth-hugged bathing room and onto the ground. She rested there for just a moment, kneeling, catching her breath, and glancing around her nervously. Nothing. No one about. Only the lonely stone temple and the sloping grassy lawn. She could hear the waves crashing far below, and could see the spiral path vanishing downward in the distance and disappearing into the dense mists. The lake was loud, so clear and strong thundering in her ears. But invisible beyond those mists.

It was a strange sensation that coursed through her then, as the wind began picking up force, teasing her hair and her dress when she got to her feet. She turned only once, long enough to push the windows closed. And then she hurried away, never once glancing back. She had to return to Rush. She had to expose Vincent as the murderous liar he was, and at least attempt to take back her throne. She had to try her best to see to it her people were well, and ruled fairly and with love, rather than suffering beneath the iron-fisted hand of Vincent.

Her hair whipped out behind her, and the skirts of the black dress billowed like sails. She ran across the lawn and onto the trail: narrow, treacherous, rocky. She hadn't realized how dangerous it was on the way up, since Tristan had been carrying her. Several times her thin slippers scraped over the loose stones, and she nearly fell. Beyond the right side of the trail was nothing. Air. Mists. Rocks and the lake far below. On her left side the sheer rocky wall rose higher and higher the farther she descended. Nothing to grab hold of should she stumble. Nothing to cling to, to keep her precarious balance. Nothing. Yet she ran her hands along that cold stone face all the same. As if simply by touching it, she could retain her connection to the earth. The path grew narrower still. Then broadened out once more only to narrow again. The stones beneath her feet would hold, then crumble and spill over the side, nearly taking her with them. The wind picked up, seemingly having decided to blow her body from the cliffs. And she descended more deeply into the blankets of fog, until she could no longer even *see* the trail before her. And the act of running her hands along the cliff's uneven face became a way of navigation.

And then, suddenly, the whitecapped waves and blue, blue water seemed to take shape amid the fog. She walked farther, as the path leveled off, and broadened, and became a finger of rocks that jutted into the lake. And she knelt there, on that rock, and wished she could see beyond the mists. Wished she knew of a way to get off this wretched island. She was a fairy, yes. But her powers were severely limited without the aid of her pendants. And she was unsure what sorts of spells of this ancient wizard's she might have to get past in order to work her own.

She was a fairy, not a wizard. She could not conjure materials that did not already exist. She could, however, command the elements to do her bidding. In most cases. So . . . assuming there was a boat somewhere on this island—which there must certainly be—she could perhaps bring the boat to her.

Stepping closer to the banks, she peeled off her slippers. Then she stepped into the frigid water, plunging one foot in ankle deep. And she kept the other foot on the wet rock. She tipped her head back and lifted her arms to the sky.

"Wind and water,
Hear your daughter,
Find the wizard's boat.
Wind to blow it close to me,
Water let it float.
With me inside,
Then move your tide,
Return me to the shore.
That I may to my own home flee,
To rule forevermore!"

She finished with a shout, clapped her hands together three times, and knew her spell had been effective. She felt the change in the winds, felt the water move in a different motion around her foot. Squinting in the mist, she watched for the appearance of her vessel . . . Ah yes, something *was* coming. Moving toward her from amid the fog. But it was too big to be . . .

It towered high, rolling toward her at an alarming rate. She turned to run, but too late. The monstrous wave hit her hard, swamped her in cold lake water, and then tugged her in its cruel grip, right out into the depths of Cayuga.

As she fought to find the surface, to find air, Bridín could have sworn she heard the disembodied laughter of the long-dead wizard. Gods, why hadn't she heeded Tristan's warnings?

Tristan had a feeling something wasn't right. It began as soon as she confessed that she was glad he was alive after all. Because the Bridín he knew would never have admitted such a thing. And the longer he thought about it, the more he realized that such declarations were sometimes said when one person wasn't certain of seeing the other one again for quite some time. If ever.

And that train of thought led him to the logical conclusion that his beautiful, mischievous Bridín was up to no good. Probably planning an escape.

He wasn't overly concerned that she might pull it off, of course. This was an island and his boat was hidden. But it was an enchanted island. One filled with mysteries and magic. And Bridín could very easily get herself into serious trouble by rushing headlong where even angels would have sense enough not to tread.

So he returned to the bathroom to check on her. The door was unlocked. He didn't knock. Just turned the knob, half expecting to peer through and see her reclining like a pagan goddess in the tub.

Instead, he found a tub filled only with rapidly cooling water, and a chair pulled close to a newly unlatched window.

Bridín, of course, was gone.

Chapter Thirteen

HE PUSHED THE windows apart, only to be greeted by a gust of wind so sharp and so chilled that it took him by surprise. It tasted of rain, that wind. Black rain. Still he leaned out even farther to tip his gaze skyward, to see that the heavens matched its flavor with their face. Deep, glowering gray, with storm clouds boiling like the liquid in a bubbling cauldron, where before there had been only crystal blue and sunlight.

Something was wrong. Something . . . was happening.

Tristan blinked that notion away, gave his head a shake. It was a storm, nothing more. Apparently his morning exploring Sharan legends with Bridín had affected his own imagination as much as it had hers. She was fine. There was no reason in the world to think otherwise. She was out exploring the island and probably enjoying it. And if she hadn't come in when she'd seen the storm clouds brewing, well, that was understandable. Fairies adored thunderstorms. Everyone knew that. She'd probably plant herself on

213

the highest spot she could find and wait there, arms outstretched, to greet it.

There was nothing wrong. And he was only going out after her . . . just to make sure.

He didn't go back through the echoing stone rooms of the mansion to the front doors. Instead, he stepped up onto that chair and pulled himself out the open windows, just as she had done. And then he rose, and looked in every direction, his eyes narrowing on the mist-enshrouded corkscrew trail, as if he could conjure her image there simply by staring hard enough.

It didn't work, of course, so he started forward. And all the while he battled the grim, deathlike whisper taunting his mind. *If she only went exploring the isle, Tristan, then why did she slip off this way? Why didn't she simply use the doors? You'd already told her she was free to roam the area. So why creep away like this? Unless she's plotting something. An escape attempt, for example.*

He ignored the voice in his head, but with great effort. It made no sense to think Bridín would attempt to escape this island. There was no way off it. No way she could succeed.

But as much as she detests you, Tristan . . .

"Shut up," he muttered aloud.

She'd do anything to get away from you!

"Shut *up!*" He shouted the command this time, shouted it at a voice that wasn't real. One that in all likelihood emanated from within his own mind, giving form to his own doubts and fears. Though it didn't feel that way. The voice felt foreign and malevolent.

He reached the treacherous footpath, and all his attention was needed to focus on keeping his balance. The ever-sharpening, cold wind seemed to blow more mist in upon the isle, and to swirl and toss that which was already there, making it even more difficult to see so much as a few inches ahead. Stones tumbled away. The ground itself, in places, gave beneath the weight of his boot. He hugged the steep edge to his left and continued downward, wondering how the hell Bridín had managed the tricky descent. Why hadn't she turned back when she'd seen how dangerous a trek this was?

Ah, but fairies are fleet of foot and graceful. Her own mother had been one of the very last of the winged ones, who had been, naturally, the most delicate and poised of any fay creature. But the wings were lost unless the lineage was kept pure. Pure royal blood, pure royal *fay* blood. And Bridín's father had been a mere mortal man, smitten and enchanted by the love of her mother.

Winged or not, though, Bridín's agility and grace would have taken her safely down this trail. She could have danced down its rocky surface and never once stumbled, he told himself.

And yet, when he glanced into the shimmering, swirling, seemingly bottomless mists below, he shivered. And for some reason he could not fathom—or did not want to—he walked a little faster, even knowing it was a reckless pace he set.

It was just as he reached the bottom of the towering, volcanolike peak, where the trail spread into a tablet of stone, and the steep angle of the descent leveled off into a smoother shape—that he heard the terrible roar. It was, he imagined, very much like the sound a dragon would make as it swooped down over a defenseless village, flapping its mighty wings and blowing great gusts of fiery breath that would incinerate anything in its path. A deafening, thunderous sound, and he pivoted quickly, his head jerking toward the direction from whence it came. The great wave swallowed the entire shore. With so much force, it struck, that it seemed to push the dense fog aside with its pressure. It crashed down upon itself, frothing and seething and boiling with a living fury. And then it was sucked away again. It receded like a living thing. Like a slippery, stalking creature, stealing away with its booty. It left rivulets streaming after it in an effort to catch up. Puddles and pools amid the rocks where none had been before. The stony hillside dripped with teardrop beads. And the fog began to close in again.

But not before something drew Tristan nearer, closer to the soaked shore. And not before he'd seen it.

A single black slipper, its satin shiny wet, lying bent like a fragile, broken bird, among the rocks. The sight of it sent an impact through him that was not unlike being struck hard in the midsection. The air seemed forced from his lungs with the blow. His jaw gaped and he half ran, half stumbled forward. "Bridín," he whispered. Then louder. "Bridín. *Bridín!*"

He had almost reached the slipper when a smaller, more natural wave swept over it, clutching it in a greedy little grip, and carrying it back into the depths of Cayuga. Tristan could almost believe it had never been there. That he'd imagined it.

But it had been there. He'd seen it.

His gaze scanned the surface as far out as he could see, which wasn't far enough, with the dense fog still hanging over the water. He called her name. Again and again, he shouted to her, but there was no answer. And he started forward, stepping into the water, not even having the presence of mind to remove his boots; such was his panic. Gods, Bridín! He slogged deeper, water lapping over his knees, and then his thighs . . .

. . . and then he paused, tilting his head, frowning. There was something . . . It moved toward him, bobbing in the now serene water. The boat, *his boat,* the one Tate had assured him was tied safely in the hidden cave, floated toward Tristan now as if it were steering itself.

And then it veered outward, away from him, its direction changing, though no one was inside to guide it. Surely some sort of magic was at work here. Some sort of . . .

Magic.

Tristan pushed off with his legs and dove, plunging into the chilled water, sinking deeply and arching upward again. He broke surface and began stroking onward, forcing all the power he possessed into the long, rhythmic sweep of his arms and the steady kick of his legs. The boat kept moving away from him. He could see it just ahead, but still out of reach. And moving. His lungs burned and his arms ached, but he poured still more will into moving faster. And he did. And finally he brought one hand forward swiftly only to have it connect with wood. He gripped that wood, clung to it. But the boat seemed determined to move ever faster, and he couldn't pull himself aboard. He could only hold on and pray that the magic propelling it was Bridín's and not some trick of the ancient wizard, as that monstrous wave must surely have been. He clung to the boat's stern with both hands, and its wake sent water surging up over his face and into his eyes and nostrils. But he didn't let go.

And finally the boat slowed and came to a stop. It sat still, rocking with the gentle motion of the water. Tristan let go and paddled away from it, enough so it no longer blocked his view of the eerily calm waters around him.

And he saw Bridín floating faceup in the water near the bow. Her eyes were closed. Her skin, beaded with droplets and lily white as the lake's water lapped over her face, receded, again, again. Her golden hair spread like tendrils out into the waves while the black of her dress moved like a dark ghost just beneath the surface. Tristan's heart pounded with such force, it seemed it would shatter his ribs, and he lurched toward her, his breathing choked in his throat, and odd, soblike sounds escaping in its place. He reached her, pulled her to him, freeing her beautiful face from the water's deadly kiss. And then he turned to grip the boat's port side, anchoring himself to it with one arm, and lifting her over it with the other.

Her body thudded into the tiny craft, and Tristan pulled himself in as well. Lake water streamed from his clothing, puddling in the bottom. Bridín lay still, in a small pool of it. Not moving. Not breathing. For the first time, Tristan understood fully how she must have felt when she'd believed him to be dead. Looking at her now, he felt the same. He bent over her, clutching her shoulders, shaking her.

"Bridín. Sweet, beautiful Bridín, open your eyes." But she didn't. "Don't do this ... don't leave me, not now." With trembling hands he wiped the wetness from her face, touched her lips. "Live, Bridín. By the wings of the gods, *live!*"

But there was nothing. No sign of life. No movement at all. Sitting up straight, tilting his head up to the skies, Tristan clenched his fists. A cry rose from somewhere within him. Some deep, hidden place. A cry of rage and heartbreak and horror and a hundred other emotions. The sound was swallowed up by the mists, but it echoed in his heart long after he'd uttered it. He was helpless. No wizard's magic could raise the dead. Not even he could perform such a feat.

Only the rarest of the fay folk had discovered the key to unlock the mysteries of death. Only the fay ...

He bent to her again, his spine rubbery, and he gathered her up in his arms and held her close, rocking her, crying freely now, and without shame. His hands tangled in her long, wet hair, and he kissed her face, her closed eyes, her mouth. "I can't let you go, Bridín. I never could. Gods forgive me, this is my doing. If I hadn't brought you here ..."

As he spoke, Tristan felt heat. Burning. A brand searing the skin of his chest, and he straightened quickly, to pull what felt like a glowing ember from his skin.

But it was no ember; it was the twin pendants

he found himself yanking from within his shirt. They'd come alive, those mystical charms. They glowed with a pure white light that hurt his eyes.

"Pendants," he whispered. "If you have the power to bring her back to me . . . do it now. Please, do it now . . ."

He pulled her close again, until the glittering, glowing quartz points were pressed tight between Bridín's flesh and his own. He ignored the pain, just held her there, his arms trembling around her fragile form. And again he tipped his head skyward. "Máire, mother of Bridín and queen of the fay. Hear me if you can. These pendants came from you, fashioned by your own hands and imbued with your own magic. Help me to use them, to save your precious daughter. Please . . . this can't be what fate intended for her. Help her."

As he sat there, tears clouding his vision, it seemed that the mists parted, and then came together again to form the cloudy, hazy shape of a winged woman. No features there. Just a shape. And he heard a voice, soft as a breeze caressing his ears as it whispered, "Why do you cry for her, Dark Prince?"

He blinked, narrowed his gaze, trying hard to see clearly the shape in the mists. "I don't want to lose her," he answered.

"No. Answer me truly this time, or I'll gather my daughter's spirit into my arms and carry her away with me. Why do you mourn her so?"

Tristan's lips parted, then closed again. He looked down at the beautiful, pale woman in his arms, and he closed his eyes. "Because I love her," he whispered.

The wind sharpened then, and when he looked up, the shape in the mists was gone. Panic gripped his heart as he feared he'd answered wrongly once again. Gods, could he do nothing to save her?

But then the pendants heated still more, searing his skin until he grated his teeth against the pain. The glow they emitted grew brighter, until it seemed a sphere of white light spread around the two of them like a bubble. And it, too, was hot.

And then, with one last blinding flash, it was gone. The stones cooled.

And Bridín coughed very weakly.

Bridín shivered with cold, and her lungs ached. She instinctively burrowed closer to the warmth beside her, and sighed as something gently stroked her hair. She felt safe and protected in this cocoon of strength, and she clung to it, savored it as the fogs in her mind slowly dissipated. And then she opened her eyes.

Tristan lay upon the bed, his arms around her, holding her tight. Her head rested on his shoulder, and when she looked up and into his red-rimmed eyes, he smiled very gently. "You're awake."

She felt groggy and lazy, and more than a little confused. She tried to remember getting into this bed with him, and couldn't. She only remembered standing on the shore and summoning a boat to come to her. And then . . .

"The wave!" She stiffened, trying to sit up, but he eased her down onto the pillows, stroking her hair and staring down at her with worry in his eyes.

"It's all right. You're safe now. It's all right." He tucked the blankets around her, easing himself into a sitting position and reaching for something beside the bed. "Here," he said, turning toward her again, this time with a steaming mug and a spoon in his hands. "It's one of Tate's tastier brews. A broth, to strengthen you." He moved the spoon toward her lips, and she let him feed it to her. It was hot and spicy and good. She nodded and he spooned more into her mouth. As he fed her, the concoction's heat seemed to spread through her, warming her limbs and soothing the aches there.

"That's it," Tristan whispered. "Good. You need to rest, Bridín. You need warmth and sleep. You're going to be all right, I promise you that."

She rested her pounding head on the nest of pillows Tristan had placed beneath it, closing her eyes. "What happened?" she muttered.

"One of our wizard host's tricks, I can only presume. You were swept away by a giant wave. Nearly drowned."

She sighed, and shivered again, her memory becoming more clear. The icy cold water sweeping over her, ripping her out into the lake, pulling her beneath the surface.

"You . . . you found me?"

"Thankfully, yes. I found you."

"You saved me?" Her eyes opened again, slowly, meeting his.

"Your pendants saved you, Bridín. I could do nothing to help you."

It wasn't true. She knew that Tristan had

pulled her from the jaws of death, once again. She vaguely remembered seeing her mother, hearing her beautiful fairy voice whispering some great secret to her, but the memory was elusive and hazy. She lifted her hand to her chest, automatically reaching for her cherished pendants. But instead, she felt an odd shape there, a bit of raised flesh that seemed to imitate the pendant's shape.

Frowning, she reached out, her fingers touching the charms where they hung around Tristan's neck. And then she touched his skin just beneath them, and found a similar scar there.

"You . . . you tapped the magic of the necklaces? But . . . how? Only a fairy can—"

"I think, sweet Bridín, that I was helped by a fairy. Somehow."

She closed her eyes again, smiling slightly. "Mother," she whispered.

"Yes."

Sighing deeply, she nodded. "Thank you, Tristan. You're always there when I need you."

"And I always will be. You're my most cherished enemy, you know."

Her smile widened as she thought how appropriately he'd put it. "And you're mine." Slumber crept into her soul in deep blue velvet waves, though Bridín fought it.

"That's it," Tristan whispered. "Sleep now. I'll be near when you wake."

So she slept.

Chapter Fourteen

FOREVER ENCHANTED

SHE HAD LITTLE way of knowing how much time passed as she slipped in and out of a soul-deep sleep. She only knew that every time she woke, Tristan was there beside her. Feeding her that silly broth, or fluffing her pillows or brushing her hair. Scooping her off her feet to carry her to the bathroom when it was necessary. Bathing her with a sponge and a basin of warm water when she needed it. She knew it had been daylight, and dark again more than once. She knew she'd been ill with fever and chills and a wracking cough that seemed as if it would tear her in two. And she knew that no matter what time of day or night she stirred, Tristan would be there by her side.

So it seemed very strange when she woke this time—to a sharp, lucid state for a change—and found him gone.

Blinking her eyes clear, Bridín sat up slowly and tried to take stock. She felt better. Clearer, and not hindered by the recent foggy state of her mind. More like herself than she'd felt since being attacked by that unnatural wave springing to life from the water's formerly calm surface.

Physically she felt better, too. Her head wasn't pounding like before, and the soreness in her throat had eased a great deal. Her limbs no longer ached as if they'd been pounded by a large hammer.

She was well again. That brew Tristan had been spooning into her day and night must have helped. But so had his constant care. He'd coddled her as if she were a small, fragile child. As if he were utterly devoted to her.

Imagine that.

It all made very little sense to Bridín. Of course, he'd wanted her well, since he saw her as his only chance of regaining the throne of Rush. The tenderness in his caring, though, that was beyond explanation. But then, she'd been terribly groggy. Perhaps she'd only imagined the emotion in his eyes.

She was in her room, where she'd been since that first time she'd regained consciousness. Her satin robe hung on the bed's corner post, and she sat straighter, dropped her feet to the cool floor, and reached for it. Now that she was healthy again, she couldn't waste any more time. So much time had slipped away from her already. She needed to find Tristan, and find out whether he'd heard from Tate yet. She was more than slightly concerned for Marinda's well-being, as well as the state of things back in Rush. Her people had waited a very long time for her to return to lead them to freedom from Sharan rule. It wasn't good that they remained subjugated to it while she languished in a soft bed being waited on and coddled.

She got to her feet slowly, waiting a moment to see how it felt. Her legs buckled a bit, but she forced them straight, held to the bed for support. A wave of dizziness receded once she'd stood still for a moment. She pulled her robe on and tied the sash tightly. Then she walked toward the door. Her feet seemed to prefer scuffing to actual stepping, but she managed to make it to her destination. It was as she pulled the door open that she heard voices, speaking softly from below. Pressing one hand to the wall to steady herself, Bridín moved along the corridor and then, very carefully, made her way down the stairs. And as she did, the voices grew clearer.

"The people are suffering incredibly, Tristan. Your brother is merciless."

That was Tate's voice. So he'd returned with his report, then. Bridín eased herself a few steps farther downward, and then, out of strength, she sat down on the stairway and just listened.

"You don't have to tell me of Vincent's lack of honor," Tristan said. "I know it well."

"He's taxing them so heavily, there's nothing left. Taking huge portions of their crops, demanding the craftsmen of the village supply him as well as his troops with all the armor and weaponry they need free of charge. He's doing the same to the clothiers, and the saddle makers and the horse breeders. Takes all he needs and then some, leaving them with no reward, and no means to make up the losses."

Bridín leaned forward, only to see Tristan's stricken face as this news was passed along.

"The people are impoverished," Tate went on. "The ill go untreated. Children go hungry."

"Gods, it's a nightmare," Tristan muttered.

"Oh, but it gets far worse, my lord. The blame for all of this suffering is being placed squarely upon the shoulders of the lady Bridín."

Bridín gasped at his words, and both men turned abruptly. Tristan came to her at a run, taking the stairs by twos until he reached her and gathered her up into his arms.

"What are you doing up?" he asked, carrying her down the remaining steps. "You should be resting."

"I'm better now, Tristan. Please, put me down. I can walk on my own."

He did put her down, but not until he'd reached the only chair in the front hall. He lowered her gently into it, snatching a blanket from its back and tucking it around her.

"Gods, what's happened here?" Tate asked.

"Bridín was nearly drowned three days ago."

"Three days?" She looked up into Tristan's eyes. "Has it been that long?"

He only nodded. "Go on, Tate. I'm sure Bridín wants to hear the explanation for this as badly as I do. How has my treacherous brother managed to lay the blame for his cruelty on her?"

Tate sighed hard, shaking his head and pacing the floor. "He made a public address shortly after the two of you made your escapes. He called on Bridín's followers to find her and turn her over to him. Promised she'd be treated mercifully, but also promised that until she surrendered to him, her people would suffer his wrath in her place. He's convinced most of the villagers that she knows of his actions and has abandoned them—that she's living a life of luxury somewhere while allowing her people to suffer for her wrongs, in her place."

"Wrongs? But, Tate, what wrongs am I to be punished for?"

Tristan sighed hard, and dropped to one knee beside her chair, clasping her hands in his. "Bridín . . . that dawn, before you attacked the castle . . . there were raids, led by a woman who was chosen for her resemblance to you."

"Raids?"

He nodded. "My brother had his men dress in the garb of the forest dwellers and chose a harlot with long, golden hair to ride before them. Several outlying villages were looted and burned. Innocent people were killed. It was, I believe, his effort to turn your own people against you."

Bridín blinked away the stinging heat that rose in her eyes. "And . . . and it has worked."

Tristan lowered his head.

"There is good news, Tristan," Tate put in. "The villagers seem to have made of you some sort of saint. They remember the kindness of your rule fondly and long for those days to return. Your brother is hated, Tristan, but you are loved. At first they believed his lies about you, that you'd sided with Bridín and helped her to escape, attacking your own brother. But if they still believe any of it, they've become convinced it was not your doing, but hers. Little good it does you now, of course. They all believe you dead, thanks to Vincent. But they mourn you, Tristan. Twice now, your brother has had his men sent out to destroy stone images of you, chiseled and erected by the people of the village."

Tristan's head rose and he stared, first at Bridín, then at Tate. "But if they know I'm the one who set Bridín free—"

"They believe she held you under the spell of her fairy's allure, that you were enchanted and couldn't help yourself. And they detest your brother for killing you."

Tristan nodded. "Then there's still a chance . . ."

A deep, wrenching sigh was torn from deep within Bridín's chest. "You've won," she whispered. And Tristan turned to stare into her eyes. "Not only my kingdom, Tristan, but the hearts of my people." She lowered her chin to hide her tears from him. "Serve them well."

"Bridín . . ."

She sniffed and lifted her head again, meeting his gaze squarely. "It's over. The need to hold me here, to try to force me into marriage with you . . . it's over, Tristan, can't you see that now? You can return to Rush"—she bit her lip —"to Shara . . . and you can rally the people to stand with you against your brother. You no longer need me."

"You're very mistaken in that."

She closed her eyes, unable to look at the intensity in his any longer, and imagine she was seeing things that simply were not there. "It's time to leave this island, Tristan. Time for you to return to the other side, and free the people. They've suffered far too long already."

"She's right, Tristan," Tate said. "We have to move quickly. Even if we leave right now, this very night, there will be weeks of preparation needed once we arrive there. We'll move in secret, gathering the forces loyal to you and forming an army. We'll need time to train them, to fashion weapons. It's going to take . . . a month. Perhaps two."

"Two more months of people starving, children dying?" Tristan said, shaking his head slowly.

"It's the best we can hope for," Tate said. "My lord, the sooner we begin, the sooner we can save them all."

Bridín nodded. "You have to go back, Tristan. You have to do it now. Tonight."

"I'm not leaving you behind," he told her. "I won't."

Bridín nodded. "Then I will return with you."

"It isn't safe, lady Bridín!" Tate shouted.

"I'll go into hiding," she whispered, lowering her head to hide her eyes from their view. She didn't want the Wood Nymph reading her thoughts just now. No, not now. Because she knew what she had to do. What her mother would have done. She knew. "Once Tristan regains the throne, perhaps he'll pardon me my . . . my crimes, and I'll be free to live among my people again."

"They'd stone you, surely. Tristan, you can't let her—"

"I'll do more than pardon you, Bridín," Tristan said softly, and he lifted her clasped hands to his lips and pressed a soft kiss to them. "I'll make them understand that you were innocent. I'll make this right for you, again. I swear it."

She nodded, knowing he would try. But it

would be far too late by then. She could not hide
in the forests while her people suffered. She
would not have the blood of innocents on her
hands, no matter how they might revile her. No.
Two months—even one month—was too long to
wait to bring relief to those poor children and
their families. How many more of them might
die of disease or starvation by then? No. She
couldn't let it go on. Not even for one more day.

Once back on the other side, Bridín would do
what she must do—what any good ruler would
do. She would sacrifice her own good, for the
good of her people. She would surrender herself
to Vincent, so that their suffering could end.

He might kill her outright. If he did, so be it.
He might also, she realized, imprison her within
the wretched dungeons below the castle, leaving
her there to die slowly. And if he did that, then
perhaps she could survive until Tristan's victory
over his evil brother.

It did not matter. What she was about to do
could very well be her last act on behalf of her
people.

"We'll leave at dawn," Tristan muttered, but
he didn't sound happy about it.

"What of the wizard's tricks, Tristan?" Bridín
lifted her head, relieved to have something to
think about besides the path that lay ahead of
her. The cup from which she must drink deeply.
"When I tried to leave, I was nearly killed."

Tristan frowned and glanced toward Tate.

Tate rubbed his chin. "That one, it's said, had
a hatred for the fay monarchy that ran very deep.
For his residual magic to work against a fairy
princess who was attempting to escape in order

to retake her kingdom would make perfect sense. But I don't believe he'd act against a Sharan prince returning to take that same kingdom. Still . . . we might take precautions. I'll think on it tonight. And be ready by dawn. Agreed?"

Tristan nodded.

Tate turned as if to leave the room.

"Please, wait," Bridín called, stopping him. "I must know of Marinda. Is she well? Is she safe?"

Tate turned and smiled at her. "I suppose the secret no longer needs keeping," he said. "Marinda is my own wife, and I'd no more leave her at risk than I would cut off my own fingers."

"Your *wife*?" Tristan rose and stared wide-eyed at his friend. "Tate!"

Tate shrugged and grinned at him. "The two of us believed that the two of you . . . Ah, the plan failed, so there's no need going into it now." He shook his head, sighing. "Marinda is fine, lady Bridín, and safe with our own people. I've warned her not to speak out in your defense, lest she endanger herself. And I hope she has sense enough to obey me in that. She sought out your dear friend, the aged mortal—"

"Raze?" Bridín asked, jumping to her feet.

Tate nodded. "Yes, that's the name. He and a handful of those still loyal to you—your cousin Pog, among others—have gone into hiding on the dark side of the forest. And that's where you'll likely have to be staying once we return. Just until it's safe to come back into the kingdom, of course."

"No." Tristan shook his head hard. "Not there. Bridín will not spend even a single night in that sun-forsaken land where I was raised."

"But, Tristan—"

"*Not one night.*"

Tate nodded. "We'll find some other haven for all of them, then." Then he turned to Bridín. "I'm sorry it's turned out this way, my lady."

She nodded, then stepped away as she felt the Wood Nymph probing her mind, and saw his eyes narrow. "I'm feeling tired," she said, as she reached the stairs. "We'd all best get some sleep. Tomorrow will be a trial for all of us."

She did return to her room, but she didn't sleep. She didn't even lie down. It seemed to Bridín that she'd done nothing but lie in that bed forever, and if things went as they very well might tomorrow, this could be her last night among the living.

She didn't want to spend it lying in bed.

Not alone, anyway.

She paced, and she thought of Tristan. Thought of the way it had felt the times when he'd kissed her. The pretty words he'd used to try to convince her to marry him. Thought of how he'd been here, by her bedside, each time she'd opened her eyes for the past three days.

But he wasn't here now. Possibly because he was assured that she was fully recovered, or very nearly so. She didn't want to think it was because he no longer needed her in order to regain the throne. She didn't want to think it, but she thought it all the same. His kisses, his touches, and all of those pretty words had been just ploys. Just methods to make her change her mind. Now that he could return to Rush and take her throne without her—now that her help would be a liability rather than an asset—he was nowhere in sight. No more tenderness in the night. No more sharing his body's warmth to take the chill away from hers. That special way he had of stroking her hair that made her feel utterly cherished. The way he spooned broth into her mouth with as much care as if he were feeding a newborn.

No more.

She bit her lip, stopped her pacing, and looked down at the floor. He'd said he wouldn't return to Rush without her. He'd said he would not allow her to spend a single night on the dark side of the forest, where he'd spent his miserable childhood. He'd promised to clear her name, and to make it right for her.

If he cared so little, then what had all of that been? A cruel joke? A way of saving face? Was he feeling guilty and trying to clear his conscience by throwing her the meager scraps of affection that still remained? Or did he really care for her, after all?

The thought that he might was even more painful to her than the idea that it had all been a lie. Because if he did care, leaving him to face the lonely road ahead of her would be that much harder.

And yet she longed to know for sure.

Dammit, why wasn't he here?

Hot. It was so damnably hot in this room. She jerked angrily at the sash at her waist and shed the robe to resume her agitated pacing wearing only a silky white shift, her feet bare.

He didn't truly care. She might be lying on the floor unconscious in here, for all he knew. If he cared, he'd come through that door, even now that he no longer needed her. If he cared, he'd be here.

Gods, why do I so want for him to be here?

The creak of the ancient hinges alerted her, and she turned to see Tristan stepping into the room, a steaming mug of broth in one hand. He met her eyes, but his were solemn. "I'm sorry I wasn't here when you woke. I hope it didn't frighten you, waking up alone that way."

She blinked rapidly as something deep inside her seemed to thaw. Some icy place turned to mush, and then to liquid. "I . . . was only surprised to find you gone," she said. She paced to the fireplace that was snapping with too much heat. He'd kept the thing roaring ever since her accident. Absently she trailed her fingers back and forth on the mantel, her back to Tristan.

"Are you all right?" he asked. "I know what Tate said must have been a shock."

She blew air through clenched teeth. "To say the least."

And then he was closer, standing right behind her, one hand closing on her shoulder. "Bridín, I—" He broke off, his hand flattening to her shoulder, then quickly moving up to press to her cheek. "You're feverish again. I knew damn well you were up too soon. You're pushing yourself, Bridín."

She turned to face him, the fire's heat searing on her back. "It doesn't matter now. We're returning to Rush tomorrow, Tristan, whether I'm up to the trip or not."

"Maybe." He set the broth on the mantel, clasping her waist and steering her toward the bed. "Maybe not. I'd rather wait until you're stronger."

She planted her feet. "We can't wait. We can't let those people suffer any longer than they already have, Tristan."

He stood there, still holding her waist, and his face went soft and a smile played at his lips. "Even deposed, you're still their princess, aren't you?" He shook his head, looking almost awed.

"No," she whispered. "Not anymore."

He studied her a moment longer. "You're wrong about that. You've always been, Bridín, and you always will be."

She met his gaze, tilting her head to one side. "How, Tristan? How, when they hate me and blame me for every innocent child who's died?"

"Marry me," he whispered.

She blinked up at him, shaking her head in wonder. "You don't need me now. They love you, Tristan. They see you as a martyr. They'll welcome you back with open arms. Why in the name of the gods would you ask me to marry you now?"

He stared down into her eyes, and she saw the emotions swirling in his. "Do you really have to ask me that?"

It overwhelmed her, what she was thinking, what she was seeing in his eyes. And then a bout of dizziness added to the confusion in her mind, and she felt her knees weaken. Tristan's arms closed around her waist, and she heard him swearing softly.

"Dammit, this is all too much on you. Just lie down. Rest. You're not well. Not at all. The water you took into your lungs has been wreaking havoc on your body, and all the rest of this is only adding to your exhaustion. Rest awhile.''

"I don't want to rest."

He eased her closer to the bed, nudged her to sit down on its edge. "I brought some more broth."

"I don't want the damned broth, either, Tristan."

Tristan tilted his head to one side. "Well then . . . what *do* you want?"

Bridín looked into his eyes, and she knew. She knew *exactly* what she wanted. The question was, did he? Did he truly want her as he claimed he did? Even now that he no longer needed her help to regain the throne? Her gaze lingered on his, and he didn't look away. But the black centers of his eyes seemed to grow darker, glossier, and she began to see the firelight's reflection dancing there. The sight made her stomach tighten, so she lowered her gaze, only to find it focused on his mouth. The mouth that had taken her to the heights of ecstasy. Lips full and wet, and so very good at kissing her into a state of frustration.

"Bridín?" he whispered, his voice hoarse.

She licked her lips, swallowed hard, and decided to find out once and for all just how much of his behavior toward her had been part of his act, and how much had been real.

She met his eyes again, held them steady. "Once we return, Tristan, we'll likely have to separate. Me to go into hiding. And you to begin preparations for war."

He nodded. "Tate seems to think it's the wisest course."

"And in war . . . anything can happen. You

could be killed. I could be discovered and murdered by my own people."

"I won't let anything happen to you, Bridín. I swear it. Are you afraid? Is that what troubles you?"

He'd been standing beside the bed, looking down at her, but now he turned to sit beside her.

"Yes, I'm very much afraid. But not of dying, Tristan. What I fear is . . ." She drew a breath, stiffened her spine. "What I fear is that . . . that this might very well be the last night I'll ever spend with my most cherished enemy."

She saw his throat move as he swallowed. "And that would trouble you?"

"Of course it would trouble me. You saw the way I mourned when I believed you to be dead. How can you ask such a question?" She got to her feet and paced away from him, stopping near the fire to contemplate the flames. But they blurred before her eyes. "Never mind," she said. "Go. Leave me and get some sleep. I'm only being foolish and melodramatic."

She heard the creak of the bed springs as he rose. Heard his footsteps, imagined him walking to the door, to leave her as she'd told him to do. But instead the steps came nearer, and a moment later she felt his warmth heating her back. Felt his hand gently pulling her hair away from her shoulder. Felt his warm breath on her neck. And then his lips. She closed her eyes and bit her trembling lip. But still a single tear managed to escape and trickle down her cheek.

"Dammit, Bridín," he whispered. "I didn't come in here because I wanted to feed you more broth. Don't you know that?" He kissed her neck, then his lips worked a path upward, to her ear, tasting it thoroughly before sliding across her cheek and tracing the line of her jaw.

She was shaking; a deep, stirring tremor seemed to emanate from some forbidden place. Some place she'd never explored. "I thought . . ." Her words escaped as a tremulous whisper. "I thought you wouldn't want me now."

"So did I. Foolish idea, wasn't it? I've always wanted you, Bridín. I've hated wanting you. Fought wanting you. And despite all of it, wanted you all the same."

He clasped her shoulders and turned her around to face him. And for a long moment he seemed to be drinking in the sight of her with his eyes. "And I still do," he said softly.

"But if I survive, Tristan, I'll find a way to clear my name."

"I'll help you." And he kissed her lips, softly, slowly, languidly. His mouth moved over hers and she felt herself wanting to melt into his arms.

Finally he lifted his head away.

"I'll win back the hearts of my people," she whispered.

"I have no doubt of that," he said. "You could win the heart of a granite boulder, if you wished it." He slipped his arms around her waist, pulled her closer, until her body was pressed tight to his. She could feel his hardness, pressing into her. And she felt breathless with anticipation. He dipped his head to nuzzle at her throat again, and a heat uncoiled in her middle, spreading its searing tendrils throughout her entire being.

"When I . . . ohhh." She closed her eyes, delighting in the fires he was igniting with his touch. His hands clasped her buttocks and pulled her even harder against him, and his hips moved. She drew a breath, knowing it had to be said. "But if I fail . . . to win back the love of my people . . . ahhh . . . I will be a detriment to you, Tristan. Mmm. If they blame me for all of this . . . don't you see, Tristan? You can't put a woman they despise on the throne as their queen. They wouldn't stand for it."

His teeth closed lightly on her earlobe. One hand slid up her back and over her shoulder to push the strap of her shift aside, and then he was nibbling a path down over her bared shoulder.

"Did you hear me?" she asked him, though she was nearly writhing with need now.

"There's a way," he told her. "There has to be a way, and I'll find it, I promise you that. But not now, Bridín. Now I want . . ."

"I know," she told him, and she slipped out of his arms, taking a single step away from him. And while he stared, stunned by her departure, it seemed, she slipped the other strap down, and let the shift slide from her body to pool around her feet. And she stood there, naked, unashamed, and aching for him, the man she might never be with this way again. Because despite all of her talk, she knew fully well that the odds were against her even surviving the next few days. Let alone convincing her people of her innocence, and ruling her kingdom once more, at Tristan's side.

Tristan stood as still as if he'd turned to stone. Only his eyes moved, dipping to travel a path down the front of her, all the way to her feet, and slowly back up again. And Bridín knew then, by his stricken expression, that he did care for her . . . perhaps more than was wise. In his eyes she saw that he wanted very much to make love to her. And that would be enough. It would have to be enough.

Still he didn't move. "Tristan?" she asked. "Is something wrong?"

He met her eyes, smiled crookedly. "I'm not sure, my lady fair, whether to touch you, or to fall on my knees and worship you."

As she held his gaze steady, letting her hunger for him shine from her eyes, his smile slowly died. "Touch me," she said.

And he swept her into his arms fast and hard, and he kissed her mouth as if he'd been starving for its taste. Burying his tongue inside her, kneading her backside and pressing his hardness between her legs. His passion seemed to erupt, and they tumbled together onto the bed, and she tore frantically at his clothes, eager only to have him naked and warm and touching her everywhere, all at once. Skin to skin.

He helped her, as desperate to shed the clothes as she was to rid him of them. And in moments he, too, was nude, and Bridín's hands were roaming his body freely, making discoveries and eliciting responses everywhere they touched. His shoulders and back, firm and hard with muscle under a layer of tanned, salty skin. His thighs, where hers locked around them, tight and powerful. His chest . . . oh, the smoothness of it, the breadth of it. And his belly, flat and tight, and then her hand closed around the very root of him, and he tipped his head back, grated his teeth and groaned. She moved her hand, learning the feel of him, the shape, and the size and the incredible hardness of him.

He pulled away, staring down at her with fire in his eyes. She reached for him again, but he caught her hands this time, both of them, at the wrists, and held them down to the mattress above her head. "Better that you don't touch me . . . just yet," he murmured, and then he bent to resume kissing her mouth, her face, lower, until he captured one breast, tugging and nibbling at it until she twisted and writhed in pleasure and need. Yet still her hands were immobilized above her head. She could only lie there and move against him while he drove her to the brink of madness with need.

He tormented the other breast in the same manner, then lapped a hot path to her belly, and then lower, and she opened to him when he tasted her there. She whispered his name, then moaned it as his mouth worked her into a frenzy.

And finally he moved up and over her body again, lowering his weight atop her, releasing her hands. She reached around him, clutching his tight buttocks and pulling him to her. And he obeyed her silent command. Very slowly, very carefully, nudging himself inside her. Bit by bit. Inch by incredible inch. She felt herself being stretched, being filled . . . with him. And it was wonderful.

She sighed, and it seemed the elements sighed with her. A gust rattled the window, until the sashes parted and the breeze gained entry. A violet-scented wind swept around them, ruffling the bedsheets and tangling in her hair.

Tristan was trembling now as he continued

moving very slowly deeper inside her. Trembling all over, and she realized that *she* was doing this to him. Making him shudder. Reducing him to this same state of need that he'd brought on her. She pulled harder, and he slid all the way into her, groaning, closing his eyes. He paused there, and she knew he was waiting for her. Giving her time to adjust to the size of him. But she didn't want time. She wanted more of this.

She moved her hips to tell him so, and he responded, pulling back and plunging deeply, again and again and again, his pace excruciatingly slow. And that heat in her belly began to bubble and boil higher. And the wind around them swirled with greater force, faster, keeping pace with their breathing, escalating in time with their heartbeats. The heat inside her boiled higher still as she moved faster, snapping her hips to meet his every thrust. His slid his hands beneath her, clutching her hips the way she clutched his, and lifting her, and filling her to still greater depths. And Bridín strained toward the pinnacle she knew lay just ahead, as the mystical wind buffeted her, and thunder rolled. And she wasn't certain whether the sound came from inside her, or from without.

And when she reached that elusive place her entire body convulsed. The wind became a tempest. The room flashed with lightning that seemed the essence of what she felt, and the thunder cracked like a gunshot. She squeezed him from within, milking him, and she heard his muffled groan, felt his every muscle tighten, and then release all at once as he spilled his seed into her amid the inexplicable storm—the storm created, she was certain, by the two of them. The long-contained emotions of a fay princess and a wizard, finally set free.

Her body relaxed, bit by bit, and the wind died away slowly. Tristan slid his hands up her back, to tangle his fingers in her hair as he kissed her, and kissed her, and kissed her. And then he slid off her body, to nestle beside her. He pulled her close, bundled the covers up over them both, and held her tight in his arms.

And then he fell asleep.

Chapter Fifteen

BRIDÍN WATCHED HIM sleep. He looked so peaceful, so content, a soft smile touching his lips like magic every little while. And she knew what she'd done. She'd let him believe that this was how it would be. She'd given him a hope to cling to that was as unlikely as snow in July, as fragile as a butterfly's wing. He'd made love to her, insisted that he would clear her name, that they would rule Rush together. And the poor, beautiful fool believed it. She'd let him believe it.

And that was cruel.

Because she knew what she had to do when she returned to her kingdom. They might despise her, but the people of Rush were still her people, and her responsibilities as their princess far outweighed the importance of her own happiness.

Or Tristan's.

It would take him weeks to assemble an army and mount an attack on his brother's forces. And in those weeks, children—innocent babies—

would die in the arms of their grieving mothers. Tiny, precious lives would be lost.

She could stop it. Tate had given her that knowledge, though she was certain that had never been his intention. All she needed to do was turn herself over to Vincent, and the suffering of the people would end. She could save those babies, those children. She could prevent the tears those mothers would shed. No one else could do it. Only Bridín. And so she must.

Vincent would likely kill her. It had been his plan all along, she knew that. Oh, there was a slim chance he might keep her alive in order to try to extract information from her, but it was far more likely she'd die at his hands by the time Tristan's armies were ready to attack.

No more children would die, though. If it cost her life to insure that, then so be it.

And yet, it would be hardest on Tristan. Because she knew now that he cared for her, far more than he'd ever admitted. But perhaps there was a way she could spare him some of his grief, make her loss easier on him, when it came.

He stirred as if sensing her eyes on his face, opened his eyes, gazed up at her. "You didn't tell me," he whispered.

"Tell you what, Tristan?"

His smile was slow, a little uncertain. "That you'll marry me, be my queen. Rule Rush at my side."

She closed her eyes, averted her face.

His hand came up to touch her cheek, turning her toward him again. "Bridín?"

"I . . ." A slow breath escaped her, and she

drew it in again with determination. "I can't marry you, Tristan."

All color drained from his face. "You love me. Dammit, Bridín, you can't convince me you don't."

She lowered her chin until it touched her chest. "My husband was chosen for me long ago, Tristan. By my mother. I . . . I must obey—"

He narrowed his eyes on her face, his brows furrowing. "No," he whispered. "I don't believe you, Bridín."

"You have no choice."

"But I do." And he enfolded her in his arms, and he kissed her, deeply and passionately. She didn't even try to pretend. It would do little good. She kissed him back, gave in to the need that seemed to have been a part of her forever.

"We'll be together," he told her. "I'll make you mine, Bridín. I'll never let you marry someone else."

Oh, and he was so right. She'd never belong to another. But as for them being together, he was wrong about that. She'd do what she must. And as he made tender love to her, she cried inside, because she knew that this would be the last time.

Tristan had sensed, almost from the moment he'd come into her room, that tonight was Bridín's way of saying goodbye. He'd known it. He hated knowing it, but he'd long ago learned to see what was clearly before him, even when it wasn't what he wanted to see.

She would leave him when they reached the enchanted forests again. And this time she intended it to be forever. But her reasons were lies, all lies. She didn't intend to marry this other man her mother had commanded her to find. She couldn't. There was something else driving her now, and if it took the rest of his life, he would find out what it was. He'd overcome it. He'd convince her that they belonged together, the two of them. Somehow, he would make her his own. He'd make her love him the way he loved her.

He would.

Tristan lay awake, long before dawn, just looking at her. Relishing this time he had with her, to hold her in his arms. To touch her the way he'd always wanted to touch her.

And eventually, looking at her, knowing that she intended it to be the last time, but not knowing why, became too painful to bear. And he slipped out of her bed, gathered up his clothes, and quietly left her. He returned only once, to leave her crystal ball behind. He wouldn't make her ask him for it, because he sensed doing so might be hard for her. And he didn't want to make this any more difficult for her than it already was. He'd do what he had to do, and she'd do the same. They were both heirs to a legacy larger than either of them. But he knew he'd never forget this night with her. And he'd never love another the way he loved his Bridín. His fairy princess. And he'd never give up on her. Not ever. If she thought he could walk away and let her go now, she was sorely mistaken.

Tristan was gone when Bridín woke. She thumped her fist against the pillow in frustration. Damn him for leaving before she'd had the chance to speak to him, to make him accept that they could not look forward to some happily ever after. He'd ignored her refusal to marry him. He'd refused to believe she intended to marry some stranger instead of him. And he was going to be hurt in the end, when he learned the truth.

She loved him beyond anything she'd ever known.

She was glad that at least she hadn't told him that. It would be easier for him, far easier, if he never knew.

The sun was rising over the lake when she rose to stand before the small window. And she greeted this day with her shoulders back and her chin held up. "Today might well be the day I come to join you, Mother. But I'm not afraid." She bit her lower lip and angrily dashed the cowardly tears from her eyes. "I am not afraid," she said again, her voice firm and hard. And if she said it often enough, in just such a voice, she thought she might even begin to believe it. She turned away from the window then, and was brought up short. The scrying crystal rested on the pillow where Tristan's head had been so recently. He'd brought it to her, left it here for her as she slept.

What did it mean? Was it a gesture of friendship? Of love? Or a token of goodbye? Had he left it for her so that she could find another man to marry, his way of letting her know that his proposal no longer applied? No. More likely, Tristan wanted her to find this other man, so she could see that there was only one in the world meant for her. Tristan, her Dark Prince.

She bit her lower lip and battled tears. It didn't matter. It didn't matter *what* it meant. It was over between them. One way or another, it was over.

Tate had arranged a circle of blue candles around a flat stone table just outside the mansion's walls. Upon the table he'd piled any number of objects. Foodstuffs, and crystals, and even gold coins and flowers picked from the vines that crawled over the stone walls. Honeysuckle and wild rose. The circle of candles glowed in the amber light of dawn, and for once, the wind seemed to have stilled. Amazingly, the candles were not blown out by the breeze that usually rushed in from the lake.

Bridín and Tristan sat upon the ground, just inside the circle. He on Tate's left, and she on his right. Not close enough to touch, she thought miserably, but perhaps that was for the best. She hadn't exchanged more than a stilted, cursory greeting with Tristan this morning. He seemed preoccupied and brooding. Probably worrying about the battle ahead, she assumed, and wished she didn't believe he was this troubled over his feelings for her, and her motives in turning him down, instead. But she did believe it. She knew she'd caused this worry in his eyes, and it cut at her soul. When Tristan looked at her, his heart was in his eyes. It was all she could do not to melt into his arms and confess her love.

"Ancient Wizard of Shara," Tate intoned, standing upright between them, close to the stone altar. "We thank you for permitting us the use of your haven. And we leave you these offerings of peace and goodwill between us."

There was a soft rumble, much like distant thunder, though not a single cloud marred the blue perfection of the sky above.

"We ask your blessing as we take our leave now. Know that we go in peace, and wish you no harm."

Again the rumble, louder this time. Tate closed his eyes, nodded slightly. Almost as if that thunder were speaking to him.

In a quieter voice Tate said, "It will be done."

The rumbling sound died away. The breeze picked up, and the candles were snuffed by a single cold waft of wet wind. Tate lowered his hands to his sides and turned to face Tristan. "The wizard wants it known that he was wrongly accused, Tristan. Seems Bridín's good name isn't the only one you'll have to restore. He harmed no child, loved them as if they were his own, and his spirit is trapped here in this place. He cannot rest until his innocence is proven to his people."

"It's been nearly a hundred years," Tristan said. "Everyone knows by now that it was malnutrition and not the wizard making the children ill." And from the distance, that rumble began again. Tristan searched the skies, and nodded. "But it ought to be a matter of public record," he added. "The wizard's innocence should be written down, and his banishment stricken from the records of Sharan history. I'll see to it."

"I knew he was hurt by being wrongly accused," Bridín said. She got to her feet, brushing the grass and twigs away from the clothing she wore. The pine green tunic, brown leggings, and suede, knee-high boots were back in place. Around her waist was a belt and scabbard, and her own sword hung heavy against her thigh. Her hair was caught up in a tight braid at the back of her head. And the tunic had a hood, which she would pull up when they reached the other side. No need announcing her identity to those who would love to see her dead. She'd march into Vincent's chambers under her own power, not dragged by rebellious mobs.

"It should be perfectly safe to leave now," Tate said. And he led the way to the corkscrew path, and the boat bobbing in the water at its base.

"We have one stop to make first," Tristan said.

Bridín glanced sideways at him, and saw something in his eyes so sad that it made her heart clench. "Where?"

He said nothing. Just took hold of her hand to steady her as she climbed into the boat.

Tristan and Tate waited at the edge of the woods behind her sister's home while Bridín went inside to say farewell. She tried valiantly to keep her eyes dry as she hugged her little nephew and kissed his cherubic face for what might be the very last time. Then lowered him into his cradle and turned to Brigit.

"I just don't understand this," Brigit went on, continuing with the stream of objections she'd begun raising from the moment Bridín had told her she was going back. "You haven't found this man you came looking for. When you came here, you said you wouldn't return until you did."

Bridín shook her head, averting her eyes. "I've run out of patience," she said. "It's been six months and I've seen no sign of this man. I'm tired of waiting. That's all."

"No, it isn't all." Brigit clasped her sister's hands in hers, searching her face. "What's changed, Bridín?"

Lifting her chin, Bridín met her sister's eyes. She sighed heavily, knowing it would do little good to lie. Brigit would only worry all the more. Best to tell her at least a bit of the truth. Not where she was going once she arrived on the other side, or what she planned to do. Brigit would never let her leave if she knew that. But a little of the truth might ease her mind.

"Tell me, Bridín."

Bridín nodded. "I've learned that the people are suffering terribly under Vincent's rule. And you know I can't stand by and let that go on. I'm their princess, Brigit. It's my duty to go back and do what I can to help them."

"And just what do you think you can do?"

She shrugged. "I won't know that until I get there."

"But it's dangerous for you there! Bridín—"

"Brigit, please. I have to do this. Nothing you can say is going to change that, and you're only making this harder than it has to be." Brigit's gaze faltered, and she lowered her eyes. "Hug me, sister, and wish me well. We'll see each other again. I promise you that." And they would. *Be it in this life . . . or the next*, Bridín added silently.

Smiling weakly, Brigit hugged her sister hard. "You're so stubborn," she said, and Bridín heard the tears in her voice. "I love you. Please be careful. Jonathon needs you, you know."

Bridín nodded and returned the embrace before pulling herself free. "I have to go now."

Brigit clung to her hands, but Bridín moved slowly away until only their fingertips touched. Then she turned and hurried out of the house, barely making it through the door before the tears burning in her eyes spilled over.

Tristan held her hand in his as they crossed through the doorway to the other side once more. Otherwise she wouldn't have been able to pass through. Her mother had willed it. She couldn't return without the two pendants that Tristan now wore. So she couldn't have returned here without him.

Mother had known of the protective powers those pendants possessed. And she must also have known of the dangers Bridín would face here in Rush. But Bridín didn't need the protection of the pendants now. She wasn't the one who would ride into battle against a deadly enemy. Tristan needed the pendants more. Bridín would surrender herself and accept whatever Fate had in store.

She squeezed the hand that clung to hers, and Tristan turned to look into her eyes as they stepped together through the doorway. He didn't look away as they emerged on the other side. And neither did she. Though she could feel the differences here. The air smelled differently, softer and lighter somehow, and scented with heady fragrances. The sunlight felt warmer, pure heat and fire on her skin.

Like the fire in Tristan's eyes.

"Bridín, I—"

"Bridey-girl! Lord, but I've missed you!" She

jerked her gaze from Tristan's as Raze limped into the clearing and wrapped her in a bear hug that wasn't as powerful as it had been once. She hugged him back, closing her eyes, wanting to curl into his familiar arms and cry until she fell asleep. Just as she'd done as a child. But she wasn't a child anymore, was she? No, she was a woman now, facing a woman's problems. A leader's choices.

Raze released her and stepped back, scanning her face with his pale cornflower eyes. "Girl, you look tired. Thin." This was punctuated by an accusing glare at Tristan.

"It's only the stress of worrying about my people, Raze. Tristan's done nothing but watch over me. I wouldn't even be here if not for him."

Raze frowned at her, slanted his gaze to the side, to meet Pog's questioning one. Pog simply shrugged and elbowed his way in for a hug. "I've thought about you every day, cousin."

"And I you, Pog," she said. "But how did you know to meet us here?"

Pog nodded toward Tate. "Tristan's man told us you'd likely be coming back soon. We've been camped nearby, waiting."

He hugged her hard, then let her go and searched her face, his own eyes grim. "Bridín, I'm afraid the news isn't good. The people—"

She held up a hand. "I know what's been happening," she said. "They've turned against me. They blame me for their suffering. They believe I'm knowingly allowing it to go on, while living in luxury somewhere safe. I know, Pog."

"I'm sorry," he said. "I've tried to explain, but—"

"There's nothing you could have done." She sighed heavily, blinking her eyes dry, unwilling to shed tears in front of any of them. "It amazes me, how fickle their loyalties can be."

"They were tricked, my lady. They'd never have turned against you without the deceptive skills of . . . *his* kind."

She felt Tristan tense behind her. Felt it even before he spoke. "My brother is as much my enemy as yours, Pog. And I'm just as determined to restore your cousin's good name as you are."

Pog rolled his eyes. "Of course you are. I'm sure you intend to retake the kingdom only to undermine your own rule by vindicating Bridín's name. Makes perfect sense."

"It makes no sense whatsoever," Tristan said softly. "But that's what I intend—that and more."

Again that puzzled glance exchanged between Raze and Pog, while Tristan's eyes burned into her back.

She turned slowly, met his gaze, and heard her heart whisper, *I love you*. Her enemy. Always had, and likely always would, no matter what this day brought.

And she saw the same thing shining in his eyes. But he covered it quickly, breaking contact when Tate cleared his throat.

"My lord, the forces I've gathered are awaiting you deep in the forest, near the crystal caverns. We must go to them now. The sooner the better."

Again his gaze sought Bridín's, caught it, held it.

"My lady," Pog said, "we have safe refuge for

you on the Dark Side. You'll be protected there, but we must go now—"

Tristan shook his head. "Find another place, Bridín. Gather up your loyal ones and find another haven. If I have to think of you . . . *there* . . . I—" He shook his head.

She lifted her hands, clasped his. "I promise you, from my heart, Tristan, I will not linger there."

"Not even one night," he said.

"No. Not even one night. You have my word. I don't want you dwelling on this, Tristan, and becoming distracted. I'll go there long enough to gather those loyal to me. No longer."

"And where will you go?"

Bridín closed her eyes. It didn't matter where. He'd be with her. In her heart, in her soul. His eyes haunting her mind. "I will send word, Tristan, as soon as we've set up camp."

He shook his head. "Not good enough. Suppose something happens to you en route? No, I need to . . . Wait. There is a waterfall. Follow the river north, from the far side of the dark realm. No one will venture that far in search of you. Behind the cascade, there are caves, and you could remain hidden there for weeks, if necessary. The water is pure for drinking, and there is game and fruit in abundance nearby."

She closed her eyes, envisioning the place while her heart twisted. Knowing she would never see it. "It sounds perfect, Tristan."

"You'll go there?" He cupped her cheek, tilting her head up, searching her eyes.

"You know that I can take care of myself, Tristan," she said, and then she smiled, though it felt shaky. "Even against a great wizard, I manage to hold my own. I do . . . what I have to do."

His fingers threaded into her hair. "Then do it, Bridín. Take care. Be cautious. Stay hidden. Dammit, stay alive until this is over. I want you around, fighting over this damned kingdom with me until we're both a hundred and six."

Her lips trembled with the lie as she nodded. And then he pulled her close, very suddenly, and kissed her. His mouth was warm, wet, and possessive. Almost as if he didn't want to let her go. And when he released her, he just stared into her eyes for a long moment. He lifted his hands to his neck and removed the pendants there. And then he lowered them both over her head. She heard Pog's soft gasp of surprise.

"I'll convince you, Bridín," he whispered. "You'll see."

She caught his hand in hers before he took it away from her neck, and then she removed one of the pendants, and pressed it into that hand. "Wear this one," she told him. "And be safe."

He clasped the dainty pewter fairy in his fist, nodding hard. "I'll wear it . . . and when I feel it warm against my skin, I'll be thinking of you."

Her declaration of love for him leapt to her lips, and she bit it back. But she didn't think she could hide her feelings. He must see them in her eyes. He must hear the cries of her heart.

"Be careful," he told her. Then he turned abruptly and strode away into the forest, with Tate following close behind.

"What in tarnation was *that* all about?" Raze asked, staring after Tristan with a frown.

"Come on, my lady," Marinda muttered,

grasping her hand and tugging. "The Dark Side lies in this direction. Come. Hurry, now."

Tristan marveled at what he saw when he made his way to the crystal caverns deep in the heart of the forest of Rush.

Shara, he corrected in silence.

Then he returned to his scrutiny of the clearing that looked to most eyes like a meadow tucked away within a great forest. The entrances to the caverns didn't show. There were tunnels in the ground, covered over by brush and brambles. The caverns honeycombed within the hill that rose at the valley's back, though not a soul would know that by looking.

One of his men had played here as a child, and discovered this place purely by accident. And briefly Tristan wondered how many other wonders this enchanted realm still held hidden within her jeweled cloak. How many other discoveries were waiting for a child's curiosity to find them? And that made him think of Bridín, of exploring these forests with her at his side, and making each new discovery together. It would happen. He'd make it happen.

He drew his mount to a halt and surveyed the area. Several fires snapped and sparked in the valley now, by daylight, but Tristan knew the men would be smart enough not to burn any by night. In one area men sat together, whittling wood with their knives to create long, straight arrows. Over one fire, molten iron bubbled like lava, as it was poured into molds the shape of arrowheads. And the steady rhythm of hammer striking anvil rang like the beat that kept them all functioning, as the smithy forged steel rods into broadswords.

It was easier to work out here than within the caves. And Tristan knew there were lookouts posted, and should anyone venture near, these men and their equipment would vanish into the earth more quickly than a frightened mole. Only the ashes of their fires would remain, leading any enemy to believe they'd camped here briefly and then moved on.

The lookouts had spotted Tate and Tristan as they'd ridden in, but Tate had whistled a particular bird's call, which must, Tristan assumed, be their idea of a password.

Now he sat astride his horse in the very center of all the bustle, and waited as, one by one, men spotted him there. Their eyes would narrow, heads tilting to the side as each elbowed or tapped the man beside him. And within a few seconds, every eye in the place was resting upon him.

And then someone shouted, "Tristan!"

There was a roar, and they all ran forward at once, shouting and reaching up to clasp his hand when they got close enough. Moonshadow reared and danced, snorting and pawing the ground, swishing his tail in agitation. Tristan was glad he was mounted, else he may well have been trampled by his own men.

"Tristan's returned!" someone shouted above the din. "Cease the work! Tonight we celebrate!"

Tristan's mount was led toward yet another hidden entrance to the caverns, this one large enough to accommodate them both once the vines concealing it were pushed aside. Men surged around and beside him, and he found himself in a darkened room as one man rushed around lighting lamps, and another entered from the left, rolling a barrel of ale before him. Several more arrived with carved wooden mugs, and more came bearing instruments. Fiddles and fifes, even a mouth organ or two. Man after man pumped Tristan's hand and welcomed him home. Someone shoved a mug, spilling over with ale, into his free hand.

Lord, but he'd never seen such a hasty change of pace in his life, from working under the sun, to merriment in the confines of darkness. And yet, it happened now, before his eyes. Men danced, and sang, and drank to victory.

And seeing this, he knew how very long they'd been without any cause for celebration whatsoever. And so he let it go on. Eventually every man had greeted him, and he was allowed to recline in a shadowed corner and observe the festivities without taking part. He didn't feel like celebrating. This was just the beginning of the battle, not the victorious outcome. If only Bridín were here. Without her, there seemed no cause at all to celebrate.

The men making music slowed their pace, changing to a soft love song that Tristan recognized as an ancient Celtic one. And he realized that in all the years he'd known Bridín, he'd never danced with her. He'd never crooned the words of this love song to her while holding her in his arms. He'd never . . .

He was being foolish. Within the next few weeks Bridín would be back in his arms again. He'd see to that.

The thought made him smile.

He shook himself as a hand closed on his shoulder. "Tristan, my lord, have you heard me?"

Tristan blinked away his thoughts of Bridín, and focused on the man before him.

"The men . . . they want you to speak, my lord. They want to know of your plan, and where you've been and all."

Tristan nodded, and rose slowly to his feet. The room went quiet as he made his way to the fire near the center.

She rode into darkness. Raze, Marinda, and Pog had her mare waiting, hidden nearby. She'd missed Crystal, and stroked her sleek, lily white neck as she rode slowly, following where Pog led. And gradually the forest grew darker. It was a different sort of darkness she felt closing in around her. A heavy, suffocating kind. The air became stale and cold as they moved on, and finally they emerged into the place where she knew Tristan had been raised. An abandoned village. A ghost town of sorts. With twisted, black-barked trees whose leaves were palest yellow. The vegetation here seemed watery, colorless. White and sickly green. Skinny and drooping, all of it. Even the vines that draped down like specters from the branches under which they passed, trailing their clammy fingers over her face. Spiderwebs. Bridín pushed their touch away from her, shivering in revulsion as she neared the building she knew at once.

Only a handful of people awaited Bridín on the Dark Side of Rush. Mostly relatives and close friends. Very few people she hadn't known personally. It saddened her to realize that this was all that remained of those loyal to her, those who trusted her. Those who didn't actively want to see her head in a basket.

But she'd take care of that . . . soon. Tonight.

The few had gathered in a place that she recognized as soon as she neared it. The temple, much like the house she and Tristan had stayed in at the lake, but on a far larger scale. So this was the place he'd been brought to as a child, the place where he'd been isolated, and trained in the skills of war and of magic. The place where he'd taught himself not to love. Where he'd been convinced that the throne was his sole purpose for even being born, and for living. She liked to think she'd had some small part in ridding him of those errant thoughts, though the pain she was about to cause him might well resurect the very darkest of them.

It was like the other house, and different, too. Darker, more menacing, somehow. The windows here were barred, as if the children brought here were prisoners, never to be freed. She knew the bars might have been as much to keep enemies out as to keep the children in, but doubted a small child would have seen it that way. The stone walls were dark, on the inside as well as without, she noted as they ushered her slowly inside. Not bleached nearly white by the sun like those on the smaller version of the house. Torches, rather than lamps, lined the walls here. Torches she suspected burned all the time, since it was always night here. A cold chill snaked up her spine, and she shivered, imagining Tristan as a small boy, destined to spend his youth trapped in this place, this dark, cheerless place.

No wonder he'd been so determined to win Rush back for himself.

Well, he'd have it. Soon. But not soon enough.

The others were as solemn as if they were attending a funeral. They welcomed her back, yes, but in sad whispers. Her reign was over. They all knew it, just as she did. There was nothing to be done.

A woman had been cooking something in a large kettle over the hearth as they entered. And when the others all sat, Bridín followed suit. Marinda spooned vegetable stew into bowls and handed them to all present. They huddled round the single fireplace in the main room, which was too big and too empty. So much so that every tap of spoon against bowl, every footstep on the cold stone floor, every word spoken in a normal tone of voice, echoed from its barren walls. In natural response, they spoke in hushed voices barely above whispers.

"As a welcome-home feast, it is somewhat lacking," the woman who'd been cooking said. "But it's all we have."

"Thank you. I'm sure it's fine."

"How fare your sister and her family, Sara?" Marinda asked the woman. She seemed more reserved than the rest and spoke in an even quieter voice. She was a fairy, far removed from the royal line, Bridín suspected. She didn't sit tall or show any hint of regal bearing. And she seemed, at a glance, devoid of magic. Or was it hope?

"I received word yesterday," she said, speaking softly. "Her youngest is worse. Anna isn't sure she'll survive the week."

Bridín sat straighter. "But why? What ails the child?"

Sara looked surprised, but then sighed and nodded. "You've been away so long. You've no idea how bad things have become in the villages. No food, no money. The water's been fouled, apurpose if you ask me. Prince Vincent insists the only pure water comes from the castle springs, and he won't give it away. Makes the villagers trade for it, he does. Same for the firewood. And if any are caught hauling even a bit of deadfall from *his* forest to warm their family, or a drop of water from *his* springs, they're tossed into the dungeons. What ails my infant niece is poverty. The cold nights and hungry days." She drew a shuddering breath. "She's been sickly since she was born, poor and gaunt. But she has the most beautiful eyes you've ever . . ."

Sara broke off, choked by tears.

Bridín threw her dish of stew aside and surged to her feet. "Have we a wagon here?"

"Yes, my lady, but—"

"But nothing. See that it's in good repair. What about an ax? Have we one of those?"

"There are tools in the cellars of this place," Marinda said softly. "Old and rusted, but perhaps usable. What are you going to do?"

"I'll tell you what I'm not going to do, Marinda. I'm not going to sit here eating stew while my people—while *innocent babies*—starve to death!"

Sara lifted her head, shaking it slowly.

"They're not your people any longer, my lady Bridín. They've turned their backs on you, believed the lies Prince Vincent has spewed . . ."

"They will *always* be my people," Bridín said. "And I intend to end their suffering."

Marinda grasped Bridín's hand, stopping her when she would have turned to go in search of the ax. "Tristan's army will do that, Bridín. Once he retakes the throne—"

"I heard him myself, saying it would take as long as a month to prepare his army," Bridín snapped. "But if he learns how very dire things have become, he'll launch his attack sooner. Perhaps before he's prepared, and that will only get him killed."

"He might not learn the true state of things right away," Marinda attempted.

"In which case he will wait. And, Marinda, that child will be dead by then, from the sounds of it. And how many others? How many?"

Marinda shook her head slowly, mouth working, no sound escaping.

"Even one baby is more than I can tolerate." She turned to the others in the room. "Find tools, axes, and some rope for snares, bows and arrows if any are to be had, and join me. This forest may be dark and barren, but there is wood. And game beyond the borders of this darkened land. We'll load our wagons with the bounty of the forest."

"We'll be arrested!" one bent and gnarled old man cried.

"No. I'll carry the goods to our people alone, beginning with Sara's sister and her family. I'll trust her to distribute the rest."

"They'll catch you, Bridín," Marinda whispered. "They'll catch you and toss you into the dungeons."

"She knows they will." Raze stood, and clasped Bridín's shoulders with both hands. "Don't you, Bridey-girl? You've had it all planned out since you set foot back here, and probably since you heard about that bastard's ultimatum." She lowered her gaze from his probing stare, and Raze shook his head, addressing the others. "Don't you see? She knows what Vincent's demands are. He wants her in his dungeons, and only when he has her will he put an end to the suffering of the villagers. She knew she had to turn herself over to him the second she heard that decree." He squeezed her shoulders. "Didn't you?"

Lifting her chin, she met his eyes. "How can I sit here in comfort and safety while my people suffer and die?"

"You can't," Raze said. "I've known you too well for too long to think different. But, Bridey, how can you trust that animal to keep his word? How can you know he won't keep right on with the mistreatment of the people once he has you beheaded?"

"I can't be sure. But it's a chance, don't you see? I have to do this. Because if I don't, then those deaths—that baby's death—will be on my conscience."

"I don't want to lose you, Bridey."

"None of us do," Sara said. "My lady, I adore my sister and my baby niece. But I'd never wish you to die trying to save them."

Bridín raised her chin higher, cleared her throat. "He won't execute me right away," she said, and she made her voice loud and steady and strong. "Part of his decree was that he would treat me mercifully. He gave his word."

"His word is no better than horse dung!" Marinda said.

"I know." Bridín fought the waver in her voice and kept her chin high, refusing to let these people see her fear. "But there's also a chance he'll keep me alive, because he believes I can tell him where Tristan is, and what he's planning."

"You can't be sure of that," Marinda went on.

"No. But I'm counting on it. I'll survive the dungeons, and elude the executioner as long as I can. And I'll hope that Tristan's army attacks the castle before I've worn out Vincent's patience. At least this way there's a chance no more babies will die while Tristan prepares his army."

Pog had been pacing, listening to her words. Now he stopped and turned, glaring at her. "There's more to this and you know it."

"What more could there be?"

"Don't play the innocent with me, Bridín of Rush! You know Tristan's soft heart better than anyone. And you know, too, as you've already admitted, that he's liable to rush into battle only half-prepared if he sees the terrible suffering in the village. You think that if Vincent suddenly eases his tyranny over the people, that brat prince Tristan will take the time he needs to truly prepare. So that when he does attack, it will be with a well-trained, well-equipped army, instead of the ragtag band he has now."

"All of which makes perfect sense, my cousin."

"It makes no sense. Let him ride in unprepared if he's foolish enough to do it, Bridín. Let him die in battle if that's his fate. All the better for you when your time comes to fight for your crown."

"No."

"You're as much as handing him the crown. If you die, he'll have only his brother to challenge him for it. And I think that's your intention." The way he said it made it an accusation.

She lowered her eyes, and Pog came forward until he stood toe to toe with her. "You're doing this because you can't bear the thought of him being killed. You're in love with him, Bridín. You always have been!"

She met her cousin's gaze unflinchingly. "What I feel for Tristan has no bearing on this decision, Pog. What I do now, I do for my land, for my people."

"You're sacrificing yourself!" Pog accused. "You're handing your kingdom over to Tristan of Shara without batting an eye!"

"Tristan of Shara is what's best for my people. And right now, Pog, he's their only hope." She turned then, so her gaze swept over all of them. "But know this. My sacrifice will be for nothing if Tristan learns what I've done. Because even if Vincent stopped tormenting the people, Tristan wouldn't wait. If he knew I was in his brother's dungeons, he'd attack the castle, no matter the odds against him. He'd do it even if he had to ride alone against his brother's entire army."

"He wouldn't," Pog said.

"He would," she said, her voice softening. "Twice now Tristan has stepped into the path of a blade meant for me. Twice he's offered up his life to save mine. And he would not hesitate to do so again. You must swear to me that you will not tell him. All of you. Swear it, now. Swear it for the love of Rush, and your families and friends. Your people."

Sara fell to her knees, clasping Bridín's hand, kissing it and wetting it with her tears. "You have my devotion forever, my princess!"

Bridín stroked Sara's hair, and searched the eyes of the others in the room until, one by one, each nodded his acceptance of her command. She drew Sara to her feet. "Come then. We've wood to chop, and game to kill, fruit to gather, and we'll fill jugs with water as well. Sara, there are herbs in the forest that will help your sister's child. I'll help you find them, and Marinda will make for her a broth. Go, find tools," she called, and her loyal ones sprang into action.

Bridín saw the hope in their eyes. Now that they had something to do, something that would help their loved ones, they seemed to come alive. It was good, what she was doing. No matter the outcome, she knew it was good.

Several hours later they loaded the oversize, rickety wagon with several deer and rabbits and game birds, baskets of fruits and berries, corked clay jugs filled to brimming with clear water. Raze worked with pieces of old harnesses he'd managed to put together to form one usable one, hitching Bridín's white mare to the wagon, while Bridín supervised the loading.

"I only hope you get the food to the people before you're caught, my lady," Sara whispered in the darkness.

"I give you my word, I will."

Marinda came between them, with a small leather bag attached to a strap. The bag bulged with its contents, and Marinda reached around Bridín's waist to fasten it there.

"What's this?"

Marinda looked up, not bothering to brush away her tears. "The scrying crystal, my lady. You left it inside. I thought it might comfort you. I've fashioned this pouch for you to help keep it hidden. That evil prince will surely take it from you if he can."

Bridín closed her eyes, and slipped one hand over the curving shape of the crystal ball. Then she pulled her tunic around to hang down over it. "Thank you, Marinda."

"You can thank me by changing your mind," she snapped. "Let Raze or one of the others take these goods to the people, while you stay here, safe with us. You needn't sacrifice yourself this way."

"My people think I let them suffer in order to save myself, Marinda. Unless I go, then what they already believe of me will be true."

"But, Bridín—"

"Hush." Bridín bent low, and kissed the smaller woman's forehead. "You know we'll meet again. One way or the other."

Marinda lowered her head, weeping softly, refusing to say goodbye. Then Raze was there, taking Bridín's hand, leading her around the wagon to where Crystal stood waiting, tossing her mane, eager to be off. "She's all saddled, Bridey. Should you need to run for it, you just jump from the wagon onto her back. Pull this strap"—he touched the bit of harness as he spoke—"and the wagon will break free, leaving you to make a getaway."

"Thank you, Raze." Bridín touched the strap he'd indicated, just so she'd be sure which one it was. Though she had no intention of running from Vincent's men. She knew what she had to do.

"Let me come with you," he said suddenly.

"Raze—"

"I could protect you, Bridey. Watch over you."

She shook her head. "Vincent might keep me alive because of the information I have, Raze. But he'd have no reason to spare your life. Gods, if I had to watch him kill you . . ." She shook her head clear of the ghastly images trying to haunt it. "No. You must stay, and make sure none of them break their word to me by running to Tristan telling tales. All right?"

Raze tilted his head to one side. "You never answered your cousin's question, you know. You're in love with that fellow, aren't you, Bridey?"

Bridín averted her gaze. "How I feel about Tristan doesn't matter," she whispered. "Our fates lead us on separate paths, Raze." She moved forward, stroking her horse's long, sleek neck. "And as for Tristan, he has vows of his own to keep. When he regains the throne, he'll need to take a wife, produce an heir to help solidify his rule." She shook her head, because she knew it was unlikely she'd live long enough to be the woman he chose. "We're sworn enemies, Tristan and I. Always have been, and I'm afraid we always will be."

"And yet he'd ride alone against an army to

save you," Raze muttered. "You know, for a smart woman, Bridey, you're awfully blind about some things."

"If I were blind, as you say, Raze, this would be a great deal easier." She hugged him tight. "I have to go."

"Be careful, Bridey."

"You know I will." She climbed aboard the wagon, patting the ball in its pouch around her waist with one hand. Then she gathered up the reins, waved to all of them, and spoke to her horse. "Giddap, girl. We have a delivery to make."

Chapter Sixteen

SHE SAT ASTRIDE Crystal in a kind of reverent silence as her beloved city came into sight. Rush. Gods, it was beautiful, and it took her breath away every time she set eyes on it. Surrounding the city were high stone walls, all made of marble just as smooth and shiny as glass. And beyond them . . . beyond the walls lay the very heart of her kingdom. And she thought of it as she'd seen it last. The clean, cobbled streets, narrow and twisting among neat stone cottages. Piles of fragrant firewood stacked near the front of each one. The golden glow of oil lamps shining through the windows, made of glass. The thin spirals of smoke writhing from their small chimneys. The merchants' square, lined with larger buildings, businesses, some of stone and others of wood, with their hand-painted signboards swinging in the slightest breeze. The red shoe on the cobbler's sign. The foaming glass of ale painted on the one above the alehouse. The horseshoe drawn painstakingly at the smithy's shop. And the silvery broadsword of the armorer.

She could see none of this, of course, beyond those tall walls. But she could see the shining spires of the castle, piercing the night sky and glimmering nearly white beneath a full moon. Gods, how she'd missed it!

The home of Sara's sister lay on the outskirts of the village, yet still within the city walls. The gate Bridín must pass through in order to reach the woman was guarded by two men in partial armor. One stood leaning back against the wall, while the other reclined in a nest of lush grasses on the ground.

Swallowing her fear, Bridín drew her horse to a halt in the cover of the woods and climbed down from the wagon. She took her sword from its scabbard and placed it across the seat. If she approached them armed, they'd become suspicious. Raze had told her that Vincent had forbidden his subjects to bear arms within the city walls. Only he and his soldiers had the right to carry weapons.

She pulled her hood up to cover her hair, and tucked the long braid within it. And then she stiffened her spine and moved forward. A twig snapped, and the men came alert, their eyes scanning the trees for her. She didn't hesitate but continued walking.

"Hail, guards," she called. "I bring news of the treacherous Bridín of the Fay."

The two lowered their swords and came toward her. Both wearing the blue and white tunics of Shara, over leggings of the same cloth. They wore no helms, though, and she could see them clearly. The larger of the two, with his dark beard and uncombed hair reaching in tangles past his shoulders. The smaller and younger one, smooth-skinned and lean. "And who might you be, that you know of that treasonous wench?" said the ugly one.

"I am but a peasant, sir. A forest dweller, truth to tell. But when I saw the lady today I bethought myself to gain the royal favor by reporting it to the prince. Think you he'll reward me?"

"You've *seen* her?" the smaller of the two men asked, in a voice laced heavily with skepticism.

"Indeed. She's set up a camp three miles to the south, along the river. She has followers there, too. I believe they're plotting against Sharan rule. Might I carry this word to the prince? I don't wish for another to receive my reward. Will he give me gold, do you think? Or land?"

The two exchanged glances filled with greed. "You'll get no gold nor land, wench. Any reward given by the prince will come to us, and rightly so. Aren't we his loyal guards?"

The big man turned to go. The second stopped him, with a hand on his shoulder. "Should we kill her, do you think? So she doesn't run to the prince with tales to discredit us?"

The menacing brute turned to look at her again, frowning.

Bridín bowed low, suppressing a shiver of fear. "I was only passing," she said quickly. "I'll be on my way. You won't see my face again, I vow it."

"Go then, before I think better of it."

Nodding, bowing again, Bridín turned and

scurried into the woods. Then she crouched in the cover of the trees, and watched as the two bickered briefly over which of them should bring the news to the prince. Neither trusted the other to share the glory such a report would bring. And after a moment they both turned and trudged through the gates and into the city, toward the castle with their news.

Smiling to herself, Bridín waited until they'd had time to get out of earshot, before gripping Crystal's halter and tugging horse and wagon forward. She ran, cringing at the creak and groan of the old wagon's wheels, and the clatter of them over the stony road. But when she entered the city, she found all to be quiet. And not at all as she remembered it. Too few lights glowed in too few windows, and the stench of poverty was hideous. The cobbled streets were in need of repair, with gaping holes and broken stones everywhere. She continued running, turning onto a worn path that led along a row of houses in ill condition. Stone cottages with thatched roofs, yes, but the stones were crumbling, and the roofs old and tinder-dry, barely clinging to the houses. Only a few had tendrils of smoke billowing from the chimney.

Sighing in disgust, she quickly located the dark and smokeless home of Sara's sister.

She didn't knock first, simply burst into the house without warning. A tall, bearded man leapt to his feet, raising his hand as if to strike her down.

"Hold! I bring food, and firewood! Hurry and help me get it off the streets before the prince's men see my wagon there!"

The man only blinked at her, shock and disbelief warring with relief in his eyes.

"Who are you," he whispered, "and what is the meaning of this?"

A timid woman crept into the thin stream of moonlight that shone through the open door. She carried a crying baby in her arms, a pale and sickly child Bridín knew at once was Sara's niece. Bridín quickly reached into her tunic and pulled out a corked clay vessel, which she offered to the woman. "This is a potion for your baby," she said. "It will help make her strong again."

"How do you know of my baby's illness?"

"There's no time!" Bridín told them. "This is what you must do. You must unload the goods from the wagon outside, and do so quickly, before we're found out. And you must distribute them in secret to your neighbors." As she spoke she pushed the thatched door open wider, so they could see the wagon heaped with supplies sitting before their home.

"Gods have mercy!" the woman said. "We'll be arrested."

"Not if you hurry and take care," Bridín told her.

The man stepped outside, and Bridín followed. He stared at the heaps of goods in the wagon, and shook his head. "We're saved," he whispered.

"Tell your neighbors that Bridín of Rush has not forsaken her people. Tell them that she only just learned of their suffering and has returned to put an end to it. And tell them that until she can regain her throne, they are to pledge fealty to any ruler who comes in to depose the evil Vincent, who attempted to murder his own brother, and then lied to all the kingdom when Tristan escaped."

The woman sagged in the doorway. The man stared at her, wide-eyed. "Tristan . . . lives?"

"Yes. And he'll soon put an end to"—she looked around her, shaking her head sadly—"to all of this."

Shaking his head in wonder, the man came closer, reached up, and Bridín didn't stop him from pushing the hood away from her hair. Then he gasped and fell to his knees. "My lady!"

"Do not kneel to me, sir. I'm not your princess any longer. But know that I'm innocent of the lies Vincent has spread about me. And that I've returned to do what I must to end the suffering of a people who've been so easily turned against me."

"I'm sorry, my lady! I beg your forgiveness. If we'd known—"

"You know now." She caught his hands and drew him to his feet. "Now, be quick. Unload this wagon and hide these goods. Then take the wagon apart and hide it as well."

He nodded, turning toward the wagon, then stopping to face her again. "These supplies will help a great deal, my lady, but they will not last. What shall I tell the people to do when they run out?"

Bridín lifted her chin. "Has Vincent not promised to end your suffering when I surrender myself to him?"

"Yes, my lady, but . . ." He stopped there, eyes growing still wider. "You can't mean . . ."

"Tell the people," she whispered, "to hold him

to his word." Then she swung into the saddle and pulled the strap that released the wagon from her horse. She kicked the mare's flanks and galloped into the shadows.

And there she waited.

It didn't take long. The guards must have taken word to Vincent in all haste. Within an hour, the streets thundered with the pounding of hooves as Vincent's entire army drove through the city and out its frontmost gates. They would storm into the forest in search of her. The direction she'd given them would take them away from her followers who waited on the Dark Side. And she'd deliberately led them in the opposite direction Tristan had taken. They wouldn't find them. And they wouldn't find her.

Not until they returned.

Raze waited as long as he dared. Until the others had retired to their rooms in this mausoleum, though he doubted they were sleeping. No one would sleep this night. Not while Bridín was off on this mission of hers. And yes, it was exactly what he would have expected her to do. And yes, he'd promised to keep silent about it. But all night he'd been haunted by visions of that sweet-faced little girl facing those dungeons he'd heard so much about. Or worse. Sure, Vincent might well keep her alive in order to extract information of Tristan's whereabouts from her. Information she wouldn't give. And then the bastard would resort to torture. The very thought made his stomach convulse.

The others here would keep their word. They wouldn't tell Tristan what she'd done. They'd do

it because they'd promised their princess they
would, and because they'd been born into a so-
ciety wherein breaking one's word to one's
leader was more than unethical. It was the most
dire form of treason. They'd do it for the good
of their people, as well, because they knew that
Bridín's reasoning was right on that score.

But Raze couldn't keep silent. These people
were not his people. He owed them nothing.
And Bridín was not his princess. To Raze she
was still that frightened little girl who'd run to
him with her nightmares. Run to him for comfort, for protection, for love.

And those things were still swelling in his
heart for her. He couldn't change who he was or
how much he adored her. Nothing could change
that.

So he borrowed a swaybacked donkey from
the makeshift stables, and he set off in the direction of the doorway to the other side. From there
he could head in the general direction Tristan
had headed. And hope that if there really was
magic in this forest, it would help him tonight.

Bridín approached the castle from the rear,
avoiding the few guards who remained posted
around the entrances that were normally used.
The way she planned to enter wasn't exactly
common knowledge. It was a small miracle that
she even remembered.

She smiled and patted the crystal sphere that
hung at her waist. Or perhaps it was a bit of help
from her mother's magic, jogging her memory.
She hadn't thought about this place since she'd

left. But, as children, she and Brigit had played here with their mother.

She parted the branches of the flowering apple tree at the edge of the orchards that backed the castle, to see it again, preparing herself for the bittersweet rush of memories the hidden garden would evoke. But instead of sweet, there came only bitter. The tiny, horseshoe-shaped garden that had been nestled within the curving walls of the castle was now a patch of brambles and weeds. Nothing blossomed there. No sweet, heady fragrances of roses or violets danced on the air. Refuse, waste, littered the ground, and hung from the tops of thistles and burdocks. A vine of poisonous nightshade straggled free of the rest to twist and writhe its way up the gray-stone walls.

Her heart clenched and her eyes began to burn. But she quickly blinked away those unshed tears. This was better than a well-tended, flower-strewn garden would have been. Better to hide the castle's secret entrance, and better to hide her as she made her way to it. She glanced behind her once, just to assure herself the spot where she'd left Crystal out there in the orchard was well concealed. And it was; she couldn't see the mare from here. Good.

She stepped into the jungle of undergrowth, and briars scraped over her suede boots and scratched their way through the leggings. With ungloved hands she pushed aside tangled branches, and felt their thorns pierce her palms. And then she stopped and stood still, turning her hands to look at the twin punctures, and the tiny spiderwebs of blood spreading in her hands.

And she thought of the Christian God, and of sacrifice, and of love.

She blinked at the irony of those wounds in her hands, then shook herself. Time was of the essence. She pressed on, and finally reached the welcome sight of huge gray blocks of hand-hewn stone, one of which was only an inch in depth. A false face to a hidden doorway.

As if it were yesterday, she recalled her mother bringing her and Brigit out here. Slipping away from Grandfather's ever-present guards for once, to enjoy a clandestine picnic in Mother's secret haven. There'd been flagstone paths among the blossom-laden bushes, and a beautiful fountain with dainty stone benches surrounding it. Was it all still there? she wondered. Smothered and buried by the evil brambles that had taken up residence? Were they as beautiful as they'd been before, or cracked and decaying now like the rest of this once magnificent kingdom?

She scanned the briars in the darkness, but stopped herself from searching. Though there may never be another time for her in this sacred place, she couldn't linger here now. She had a mission. For her people. For Tristan.

Facing the castle wall once more, she lifted one bloodied hand and unerringly found the false stone. It pulled free easily. Almost as if it had been ready and waiting for her arrival here.

The opening was a black maw, where once it had been lighted by the glow of Mother's lamp. She'd traversed it standing upright as a toddler. Now she had to bend low as her mother had done then. And her footsteps echoed as she walked. Almost as if someone else were walking through the darkness with her.

The tunnel sloped upward, twisting and turning often, just as she remembered. And with her hand running along one chilled wall, she found her way, until it ended, abruptly.

Bridín swallowed hard and lifted her hands above her head, pushing against the ceiling, feeling it give, knowing she stood now beneath the floor of the chambers that had belonged to her cherished mother, wondering who slept there now, in her place. Tristan had used the royal bedchamber when he'd ruled. And now, in all likelihood, his brother had claimed them for his own. At this moment he was gone, off on a fool's errand. But would one of his servants or guards be waiting, sword drawn, when she emerged?

Lifting her chin, she shoved the trapdoor hard. From above it would seem as if the floor had come to life. As if one of the marble stones were attempting some levitation trick. Praying no one would see it, Bridín pushed harder, sliding the stone to one side and then hefting herself up through the opening.

And when she straightened and looked around, she found herself staring into the warm blue eyes of a woman. A woman in chains.

The woman shook her flaming red mane of hair and looked Bridín squarely in the eye. "You arrived even sooner than I thought you would," she said, and there was something about her voice. The woman's crystalline eyes sparkled as they slowly filled.

Bridín simply stared at her, blinking in the dimly lit room, shaking her head slowly from side to side in dawning wonder. But this couldn't be . . . she couldn't be . . .

"Welcome home, Bridín," the woman whispered. "My beautiful, beautiful daughter."

Chapter Seventeen

RAZE WAS OLD , but his senses were still keen. This place had been good for him. He no longer coughed and wheezed all the time, and had long since thrown away the pills he'd once had to take daily. His body had strengthened. Oh, he was no strapping youth, but he wasn't nearly the fragile old man Bridín remembered. His eyesight was nearly twenty-twenty again.

So he could easily spot the occasional hoofprints Tristan's mount had left in the mossy soft ground. And he followed these for some time, before they seemed to vanish entirely.

Raze found himself at the end of his trail. But there was nothing here. Nothing. He and his donkey stood in an open field, backed by a lumpy hillside. And as the donkey dipped his head to munch on the fragrant grasses here, Raze slid from his back to explore the area.

Burned-out campfires littered the place. Raze hunkered low and held his palm to the ashes. They still emitted warmth. So they'd been here. Many of them. Many more than just Tristan and that little man who seemed to be his chief adviser. The ground showed the imprints of many feet, those of horses and men alike. And yet, there seemed to be no exit route. Raze circled the edges of this meadow slowly, but nowhere did he see where horses had ridden away. It was as if they'd come here and simply . . . vanished.

What did it all mean? Where in the name of God was—

The point of a sword touched the center of Raze's spine, a light pressure making its presence unmistakable.

"Straighten up and turn around, old fellow. Keep your hands at your sides. Do it slowly."

Swallowing hard, wondering from where the fool behind him had appeared, Raze did as he was told. When he turned, he found himself facing a young man with carrot-colored hair that hung to his shoulders in tangles, and a face as smooth as a newborn baby's. "I mean no harm," Raze said softly. "I'm no threat to you, and I'm unarmed."

The young one looked wary, and he didn't sheathe his sword as he clumsily patted Raze's clothing in search of weapons. Satisfied at last, he nodded. "What are you doing here?"

Raze silently wondered at the wisdom of telling the lad the truth. If he was one of Vincent's men . . . Ah, but looking at him suggested he couldn't be. He wore no armor. His clothing was dirty and worn, and he looked as if it had been weeks since he'd seen a bathtub, much less a comb. Raze had seen Vincent's men. Garbed to the teeth in fine fabrics, protected by armor, clean and well groomed, mostly. Barbarians playing dress-up.

"I'm looking for Tristan," Raze said at last. "It's urgent that I speak to him."

The boy's eyes widened in surprise, then narrowed. "Tristan who? You can't mean Tristan of Shara, can you? Everyone knows he's dead."

"He isn't dead," Raze said. "I saw him only this afternoon. He's very much alive, son, but you won't be if you keep me from him. If he doesn't get this news in time because of your overprotectiveness, he'll be furious."

The boy shook his head. "I don't know what you're—"

"Look at me, boy!" Raze commanded. "I'm an old man, and unarmed. I'm no threat to him. Take me to him at the point of that sword of yours if you want, but hurry."

The youth sighed heavily, deep in thought. Finally he straightened. "Turn around," he said.

Biting his lip, Raze obeyed, but he couldn't help wondering if he was about to feel that long blade sink through his back as he stood there.

Instead he felt his hands pulled behind him, and bound tightly. And then a scrap of cloth—torn from the lad's clothing—was fastened around his face for a blindfold.

"All right then," the boy said. "Come along."

"My donkey," Raze protested.

"He'll be cared for. Just come along and keep quiet."

Taking his arm at the elbow, the fellow led Raze in circles for a few moments, to confuse him about his direction, no doubt. Then finally they seemed to be moving in a steady line. There was a rustle as if of branches or leaves. And then

Raze felt solid rock under his feet instead of grass. The air on his face was cooler, and moist. Their steps echoed as they moved onward, turning this way and that. And then finally the lad stopped, and pushed Raze's shoulders so that he sat on what felt like a large, flat-topped boulder.

"Stay here," he said. "I'll be right back." Then his steps moved him away. Raze heard voices, echoing and raised, from a distance, and finally more footsteps, these coming closer.

"Gods. Is that you, Raze?" And a hand tugged the blindfold away.

Tristan of Shara knelt in front of him, frowning in disbelief. He twisted his head to the young man who stood nervously behind him. "Untie him. *Now.*"

Nodding hard, the carrot-top hurried behind Raze and removed the thong from his wrists. As Raze brought his hands around in front of him, rubbing them to restore the circulation, Tristan ordered the young man to leave them alone. And as soon as the lad was gone, he clutched Raze's shoulders in his hands, searching his face with worry in his eyes. "What is it? Something's happened to her, hasn't it? Tell me!"

"Ah, Tristan. You act as if you care about her, and God help me, I hope it's true."

"Where is she?"

Raze swallowed hard, silently asking Bridey's forgiveness. "By now, I imagine she's in your brother's dungeons," he said.

Tristan's eyes fell closed. "No." It was a harsh whisper. But he opened his eyes again and probed Raze's. "How did it happen? Where was she captured?"

"She wasn't captured, son. She went there of her own free will, thinking it was the only way to ease the suffering of those narrow-minded fools she calls her people." Tristan rose quickly, shoving a hand through his hair and swearing. Raze went on. "She knew you needed time to prepare. She also knew you wouldn't take that time once you realized how bad things were in the villages. Children dying every day. Poverty and starvation, filth and disease. She thought that might end if Vincent had what he wanted. She says she surrendered to keep any more innocent children from dying, Tristan, but I think it's more than that. I think she did it for you, to ease the situation enough so you wouldn't go off half-cocked and get yourself killed."

Tristan shook his head slowly. "She knows better. Dammit, she knows I'll come for her."

"She swore us all to secrecy," Raze explained. "She was hoping you wouldn't find out until you'd had the time to prepare your army."

Tristan lifted his head, stared right into Raze's eyes. "But you broke your word to her."

"Seemed like the thing to do at the time."

Tristan nodded. "Thank you, Malone."

"You going to get her out of there?"

"Or die trying," Tristan said. Then he turned toward one of the many tunnels sprouting from this cavelike room, and shouted down it, his voice echoing endlessly.

Bridín fell to her knees where she stood. She couldn't fathom what she was seeing. Couldn't comprehend, or believe, or trust her own eyes. But when she met those of the woman again, she knew. Not why or how. But she knew.

"M . . . Mother?"

Máire smiled softly and lifted her arms. Bridín surged forward, flinging herself into them, hugging her mother hard as tears choked her.

Her mother wasn't hugging her back hard enough, though, and the rattle of those chains told Bridín why. She stepped back, swiping the tears away so she could see the steel cuffs around her mother's wrists, and the lengths of chain that connected each of them to the wall behind her. She couldn't move far at all, couldn't rest, except here on the floor with her arms held above her.

Bridín shook her head rapidly. "What is this? Why are you chained? Where have you been, Mother? What's happened to you? We thought you were dead! All this time we—By the eyes of the gods, Mother, your wings!"

"I know. I know. They're gone, like so much . . . But hush, child. There will be time. Plenty of time, I promise you that. We'll talk of all this later, but—"

"No," Bridín cried. "We'll talk of it now." She stepped closer to her mother, scanning her beautiful face, and then smoothing the wild, uncombed hair. "Gods, I'm so glad you're alive," she whispered. "I've missed you, needed you so." She hugged her again, kissing her face, relishing the feel of her mother's hands threading through her hair before she straightened away once more. "But please, I have to know how."

"Oh, my baby," Máire whispered. "Darling, I wasn't killed during that battle when you were so young. I was terribly wounded, though. Terribly. 'Twas Tristan's own father who struck me down. And he . . ." She closed her eyes, swallowed hard. "He took his sword . . . and . . ."

"He cut off your wings," Bridín whispered.

Her mother nodded, meeting her eyes again. "And left me for dead. I was very nearly so, and many who saw me lying among the dead thought I was gone. But I still had life in me. I'd taken a terrible blow to the head, and was only unconscious. Deeply, deeply unconscious. I knew nothing that happened, and only learned the entire tale later. Enrich of Shara—your Tristan's father—was also wounded in the fight. But his wounds were mortal ones. He lay dying in the castle, but still in command. He sent his sons into the field, with orders to gather up the dead and pile them all together, and then to burn them."

Bridín gasped.

"Tristan was very young then . . . but seventeen, I'm told. And it was he who found me there, and realized I still lived. He didn't know who I was, for he'd never seen my face. But he couldn't bring himself to pitch me into that fire, and didn't dare let on that I lived for fear his father would command him to do just that. A wagon was loaded with corpses, and Tristan himself placed me on top of that heap of death. And then he drove the wagon to the place of the burning. But he didn't go directly there. He veered from the path when he was out of sight of the others, and he wrapped my still body in his own cloak, and concealed me with shrubbery and bushes. He left me there, and went on to finish his grim task."

Bridín listened raptly, shaking her head. "Tristan left you there, alone?"

Máire nodded. "Yes, child. But he returned for me later that night, and took me far away, to a village well beyond the realm of his father. He delivered me to a couple there, and made them promise to care for me, and made them swear never to tell a soul. They gave their word, but only in exchange for the tale of where I'd come from. And he gave it to them, hoping, he said, that it would help later, if I became well again, to reunite me with my family."

A soft hand stroked Bridín's hair. "Tristan's father would have flayed him alive had he ever learned of his son's merciful actions."

"But, Mother, you recovered. Obviously. Why didn't you come to us, let us know?"

"It was months before I was well again, my child. My senses were all stolen from me by that blow to my head. I was blind, unable to speak, or walk. My memory had vanished. When I first regained consciousness I was a mere shell—an empty vessel. But gradually I healed. The first year my hearing returned. The second, my powers of speech. Sometime between the third and fourth years I began moving my arms and legs, and with a great deal of pain and hard work, I was able to walk again. My vision began to return during the fifth year, but the process was a slow one. Even now it isn't fully as strong as it was. And then, very slowly, my memories began to surface. I'd been living as a peasant woman in that faraway village for nearly a decade when I finally realized that I was, in truth, a queen."

She bent her head to kiss Bridín's tearstained

face. "It must have . . . been a shock," Bridín said.

"To say the least. But I remembered you, my daughter. And your sister Brigit. And I knew I had to try to find you, to make sure you were all right. But then I discovered that I still wasn't whole again." She bit her lip, sniffed, met and held Bridín's gaze. "My magic was gone, darling. And it hasn't returned. I'm afraid it never will. I couldn't even pass through the doorway to the other side, though I tried when I learned that was where my family had fled. I was miserable, aching to be with you and completely unable to do so."

"But you knew we'd come back someday."

Máire smiled gently. "Yes, I knew that *you* would. So I returned to my home to live in disguise, as a peasant, and to await the day you'd come back. Alone, and powerless, I had no hope of ousting Tristan's family from the throne. And there was no urgent reason to do so, then. He was a good king, Bridín, and while he ruled there was peace. So I waited, biding my time and telling no one who I truly was. I knew you'd return and I'd find you, and together we would retake our land."

"And I did return," Bridín whispered. "But I failed. I didn't prepare properly, didn't take the time I should have."

"I'd only just heard rumors you were back on the day of your raid, Bridín. And then you were gone again, and I hadn't even seen you."

Bridín swallowed hard, nodding. "But, Mother, how have you come to be here, in the castle, in chains this way?"

Máire lowered her eyes. "Vincent exercises all of his kingly rights, child. He sent his men into the village to bring him a woman. I offered myself to protect the others, because—"

"Because you are still their queen, and they are still your people."

Their eyes met and a shared understanding passed from mother to daughter and back again.

"The same reason you've come here tonight, is it not?"

Bridín nodded.

"I won't ask you to turn back," Máire whispered. "I won't try to change your mind. Because I understand that this is what you have to do."

They embraced once more. "Before I go, Mother, I'll free you. You can go and join the others, help to rally forces and—"

"No, child. I'll stay here. Close to you, in case there's some way I can help." She smiled. "You know better than to argue the point."

Bridín nodded, and straightened away, and as she did, the crystal ball bumped against her hip, reminding her of its presence there. "Mother, if all of your magic has fled, then . . ." She took the ball from its pouch, held it up. "Then how do you explain this?"

"My scrying stone!" Máire's eyes widened and her lips curved in joy. "Oh, Bridín, wherever did you find it?"

"A Wood Nymph gave it to me. Her name is—"

"Marinda," Máire sighed. "Of course. She was . . . like a sister to me. There the day you and Brigit were born, you know."

"No. I didn't know, she never told me."

Nodding, her mother reached out with one

hand, and Bridín held the ball closer so she could touch it. "I filled this crystal with my magic, long ago. Its prisms . . . they seem to amplify it, somehow. And it holds the magic. Once imbued with it, it never fades."

"The ball showed me your face, and told me . . . in your voice, Mother . . . to go to the other side."

She nodded. "Just as I would have told you, had I been there with you."

"It said . . ." Bridín bit her lip. "It said that I would find the man I was to marry there."

Her mother smiled. "And did you?"

"No. Only Tristan." She sighed. "When this is over, I should go back and find him—"

"No, child. There's no need. He's here now."

Bridín looked at her mother, frowning and tilting her head.

"My magic may be gone, but I still have a knack for the psychic arts, darling. He's here. Trust me."

"I don't understand. What—" Her words were cut off, though, by the pounding of hooves from outside. Bridín closed her eyes, bit her lip. "I have to leave you now," she whispered.

"Take the crystal with you," her mother said. "And do not fear, Bridín. Go. Do what you must."

"Are you sure you won't let me free you, Mother? You can slip out by our secret way, and—"

"Go," her mother told her. "And take my love with you."

Bridín nodded once, and slipping the crystal back into its pouch, turned away to step into the hall. She stiffened her spine as she traversed it, and started down the curving stone staircase to face whatever Fate had in store. And yet she wasn't afraid. Her mother was alive, and she could feel only joy in the knowledge.

She made her way to the rush-strewn floor of the great hall, and stood in the center, eyeing the fine tapestries and crystal lamps and hand-tooled wooden furnishings that filled the rich place. Then she drew her sword and waited, facing the main entry doors.

Seconds passed. And then the thundering feet of men sounded, and the doors burst open. A crowd of knights, their prince at the lead, froze in their places to stare at her in shock.

Bridín held the sword balanced upon her palms, and bent to lower it to the floor. "I've come to surrender to you, Vincent of Shara. And my people know I am here. Do with me what you will, but keep your word as their leader, and end their suffering now, as you promised you would."

The bearded man blinked in shock. But it was short-lived. He surged forward, kicking her sword aside with his booted foot, and his shock turned to pure hatred before her eyes. "Wise of you to heed my command, Bridín. But I'll only end the suffering of your precious peons when you tell me all I wish to know."

"Then there is no reason for me to stay." She took a step past him, toward the door, and Vincent reached out to stop her, instinctively, no doubt. But his hand froze in midair before closing on her arm, and he narrowed his evil gaze on the pendant dangling from her throat.

"You cannot harm me while I wear it," she told him. "I'll surrender to you willingly. But I will not submit to torture. And I won't turn this pendant over to you until I've seen proof that the suffering of my people has ended. Do you understand?"

He glared at her. "How like another of my prisoners you are, Princess. The slave who presumes to dictate the terms of her enslavement." He shook his head. "Fine. Keep your pendant, I'll not lift a hand to harm you. And still you will tell me all I wish to know. You'll see."

He turned and waved a hand toward the waiting guards. As she stepped toward them, chin high, Vincent thrust out a booted foot to trip her, so that she landed in the arms of one of his knights.

"Take her to the dungeons, and see that she's guarded well. I'll be along to question her shortly." He met Bridín's gaze. "And you will tell me what you know, *Princess*. I promise you will."

The man held her only briefly, only so long, Bridín knew, as his intentions were good. Once he would have pulled her arms behind her back and caused her pain, but he was unable to hold her any longer. His hands fell to his sides, and she stood straight. She led the way herself, walking ramrod-straight as her two guards followed.

But despite her brave words, Bridín's fear returned now, at Vincent's confidence. He wouldn't keep his promise, he'd said, unless she told him what he wished to know. And what he wished to know was where his brother might be, and what his plans were. So the constraints placed on her people wouldn't end after all. Because she'd die before she'd betray Tristan. No torture, no pain, could make her tell his brother anything about him. But Vincent knew he couldn't hurt her while she wore the pendant, and he'd still seemed certain he could extract the information from her.

The question of how was the stuff of which nightmares were made.

"We can't attack tonight, Tristan. We'd be slaughtered. We're too few. We haven't enough weapons. We—"

"We cannot allow Bridín to be tortured," Tristan said, slamming his fist on the stone table, though the sound of the impact didn't do his rage justice. "I've explained this to all of you. She's innocent of my brother's charges against her."

"Yet guilty of trying to take the kingdom from you, my prince. You cannot deny that. And if we rescue her, she's likely to do it again in the future."

"She's a woman . . . a princess, and she's in trouble. Politics do not enter into this."

"Yes, but by getting half our troops slaughtered in a useless attempt to rescue her, we would hardly be doing her any good."

Tristan eyed his most trusted advisers, knowing they were right. "All right then. How long before we can be ready? I know we'd planned to take a month to prepare, but things are different now. We need to move as soon as possible."

"A week," said one man. "If we work day and night, and send a troop out in search of recruits."

Tristan nodded. "A week. Do it then. You're in charge."

"Me?" The man frowned. "But what about you?"

"I'm going after Bridín. Alone. Tate, I'll need you to draw me a map with all those secret passages in the castle. No one knows them like you do. Go, do it now. The rest of you, stay here. You'll attack exactly one week from tonight at precisely midnight. While Tate is making my map, go and begin to devise your battle plan."

The men looked at him as if he'd lost his mind. He stared right back until, one by one, their gazes lowered and they nodded their agreement. Satisfied they'd do as he asked, Tristan turned to Tate, who quickly ran off in search of parchment and ink. Alone in the cavernous room, Tristan closed his eyes, then squeezed them tighter to keep the tears from flooding out.

Bridín. Beautiful, precious Bridín, in the hands of his bestial brother. Gods, the very thought . . . She might be hurt, even now. Vincent had slashed the pendants from her slender throat once, and could easily do so again. They might be applying the whip to her tender skin and demanding she tell all she knew of him. He could hear her cries of pain and fear echoing in his mind, and he clenched his fists until they trembled.

"No. Gods, no! I swear on my soul, if he's harmed her, I'll kill him!"

A soft hand lowered to his shoulder, and Tristan whirled to face Raze, who stood there behind him, his eyes as misty as Tristan's. "It's true then," Raze muttered. "You love her."

His jaw trembling, Tristan met the man's gaze. "I would die for her."

Chapter Eighteen

BRIDÍN WAS TAKEN to the foulest depths she'd ever known. The castle dungeons. When her mother had ruled the kingdom, she'd wanted the dungeons sealed off, bricked up, and made inaccessible. But her grandfather had argued that a prison of some sort was necessary as a deterrent to crime. Not that he'd ever dared use them as such. Máire would have been furious if he had.

Right now Bridín dearly wished he'd listened to her. She'd never been here before. The door at the end of the long, arched corridor groaned as the guards pushed it open. It was wood at its core, she suspected, but girded on either side with plates of solid steel. Reinforcing strips of iron crossed one another on its face, dotted with bolts every few inches. The four hinges were each as big as her entire head.

Beyond the door, she saw only a curving stone staircase, with a wall on one side and an open pit of blackness on the other. The steps were narrow, their edges crumbling, and the way down steep. It reminded her briefly of the corkscrew trail she'd traveled back at the wizard's hidden house on the lake. But then she shook herself, blinking at the irony of the stark differences between then and now. Then, she'd been with Tristan. Loving him, and perhaps not even aware of it. Wanting him, and all too aware of that. Now . . . now she had very little hope of ever seeing him again. She closed her eyes, saw his face swimming in her mind. His piercing ebony gaze. His raven's-wing hair.

She made her way down the steep stairs, unsurprised when the guards gripped her arms to steady her. So long as they meant her no harm, the pendant would bear their touch, unless Bridín deliberately willed otherwise.

At the bottom of the stairs she was led between two rows of cells, her footsteps echoing in the darkness. And from the depths of some of those holes, she felt eyes upon her. The eyes of her people? And what were they thinking as they saw their former princess marched before them, beaten, captive? Were they wishing her dead? Were they blaming the hell they'd been through on her and her alone?

She couldn't return those invisible gazes. But she held her head high as she was led past the rows of cells and around a corner, into a separate room. The dry, crackling rushes on its floor were old, and the place smelled musty with neglect. But she knew what it was from the moment the guard on her left swung a torch through its arching doorway to illuminate the foul stone walls with dancing shadows. This was a torture chamber, pure and simple. The rack and a table with restraints lay before her. Tools of the hideous trade littered the hook-laden walls. She shuddered with revulsion, yanking one hand away from a guard to close it around the pendant at her throat as she walked all the way to the farthest wall, appalled and amazed that this den of horrors existed.

"Don't worry," the younger of the two guards muttered, and she could have sworn she detected the barest hint of sincerity in his voice. "You won't be harmed."

She turned her back to the wall, facing him as the second guard stepped closer to her side. "You'll forgive me if I put little stock in your assurances," she whispered, her throat taut.

And even as she spoke, the second guard was snapping iron manacles around her wrists. She grated her teeth and tugged at the bonds, as if to test them, only to find herself chained to the wall behind her. Much the same way her mother was imprisoned in the room far above. Except that Bridín's chains were much shorter, only a few paltry links of rusty iron. Her arms were caught up high and outspread, as if she were some bird of prey in midflight, and the wall at her back was cold as ice. The guard knelt in the filthy rushes to apply shackles to her ankles as well, and he didn't need to put his hands upon her in order to get the job done. He simply snapped the leg iron in place and then tugged the chain up until it offered the least possible freedom of movement. And when he finished, her heels touched the stone wall, and there was a great deal of space between the one foot and the other.

She glanced down at her position, then lifted her chin to meet the guard's eyes. "For maximum humiliation?" she asked, her voice soft and dangerous.

"No, Lady Bridín," said the younger one. The gentler one. "For minimum mobility. And only because Prince Vincent fears you—"

"*Frederick!*"

The younger one bit his lip. "He knows of your powers, lady, and doesn't wish us to give you the slightest chance to escape."

"What are his plans for me, Frederick?" she asked, and she held his gaze with her own, willing him to tell her.

"I do not know, my lady."

The older guard sniffed. "Tell him what he wishes to know, and you won't be havin' to find out."

"He won't hurt you," Frederick said. "He couldn't, lady. You're too fair . . . too—"

He stopped as the older one's open hand cuffed him across the back of the head. "She's fay, you fool. And using her wiles to charm you already, you weak-willed runt." Then he shoved Frederick out the door, and she heard them bickering as their steps echoed endlessly.

Bridín hung there in her chains, and wondered how long they would leave her to linger here.

Hours passed. Countless hours. She didn't know if it was day or the middle of the night. Her arms and legs ached and screamed from the lack of movement. And the waiting and not knowing what Vincent intended was driving her mad.

And then he appeared. As if thinking of the nightmare could bring it on, the bastard himself was suddenly there. She looked up and saw him, lounging in the stone archway, head tilted to one side as he studied her.

"Vincent," she whispered. "Let loose these bonds. I surrendered to you of my own free will. I'm not going to try to escape."

He shrugged. "I can't be sure of that, can I? Your kind is known for their cunning, after all."

She clenched her jaw, saying nothing.

"Come now, Bridín, you disappoint me. Aren't you going to beg, even a little?" His eyes skimmed her face. "No, I thought not. Pity."

"Keeping me in chains serves no purpose," she told him.

"Ah, but it does. It amuses me, Bridín. Isn't that purpose enough?" He lifted his brows. "No? Well, then I suppose one must take the torture into account."

She sucked in a breath against her will, then glanced down to see her pendant still resting upon her chest. Vincent, though, was strolling into the room now, walking its boundaries, toying with the tools that dangled from the wall. Irons and hammers and whips and other things whose uses she couldn't even imagine.

"Y-you cannot harm me," she whispered.

"No. Shame that. But I can only guess, Bridín, since you surrendered yourself to me in order to end the suffering of your people, that what I have in mind will be just as effective." He turned slowly, faced the door. "Bring her in."

And Bridín gasped. At once a beefy hand pushed a small child into her line of vision. A little girl, her face grimy with dirt and marred by tearstains. Her once golden hair in filthy tangles. Her arms bound behind her back. The guard pushed her down to her knees in the doorway.

"Tell the princess your name, child," Vincent purred.

Blinking back fresh tears, the girl whispered, "Am-Amelia."

"And how old are you, Amelia?"

"I'm t-ten," she stammered, never lifting her head or looking up. Not once.

Vincent caught the guard's eye and jerked his head to one side. The guard nodded and pulled the child to her feet, leading her away again. Bridín heard the shuffling of those small, bare feet through the rushes, and then the soft sounds of crying.

"I don't understand," she said, even though she was sickeningly afraid she did.

"Simple," Vincent replied, watching her face. "I want to know where my brother is hiding. I want to know what he's planning, and when he's going to move against me. Will you tell me?"

She closed her eyes. "I can't tell you," she said. "I don't know."

"I think you do."

She opened her eyes and met his. "I don't."

"That's a shame. Because I'm going to make you watch while I torture that child. Amelia, wasn't it? By the time I'm finished, I'll be sure of exactly what you know, Bridín. Because I think you'll tell me everything."

She felt the tears brimming in her eyes. "You can't! Vincent, you mustn't hurt that child. I swear to you, I know nothing. I . . . Vincent!"

But he was leaving her, leaving her alone to mull over what he'd said, no doubt. As he vanished around the corner, he called, "Three hours, Bridín. And then I'll be back for your answer." He returned a second later and, smiling, extended his hand. She gasped as she saw the oversize hourglass he held, bit her lip as he slowly turned it over and the sand began streaming through its slender neck. "Three hours," he repeated. "And you can watch it pass, knowing that with each grain of sand that falls, little Amelia comes closer to torment." He lowered the hourglass to the floor, setting it down in a shadowy corner. She could barely see it there, and she knew that was deliberate. It would torture her more to have to squint in the shadows and strain her eyes to see how much time remained, and she'd constantly doubt what she saw.

"You're evil itself, aren't you, Vincent?"

"That might very well be, Princess."

Tristan left Moonshadow tethered in a glade beyond the city walls. He could graze and reach water there, and he was hidden from curious eyes. And if for any reason Tristan couldn't return, he knew Tate or one of the others would come for him. He'd be cared for. Safe.

Safer than Bridín was right now. Gods, when Tristan thought of her inside that towering castle, when he thought of what his brother might do to her in his fury . . . He'd kill him. Surely he would. If Vincent had harmed her in any way . . . Ah, but what hope was there that he had done anything less? He was a brute and an animal, and Tristan couldn't for the life of him understand why he hadn't seen those things sooner. Far sooner than he had.

No, nor indeed why he hadn't realized what Bridín must have been planning all along. He'd been so selfishly focused on his own foolish notions of how to woo her and win her that he'd neglected her safety. Dammit, he knew her well enough to have guessed what she would have done. But he'd been too busy feeling sorry for himself for losing her, even for a short while. Too busy planning out how to win her back again . . . He'd been blind. Stupid and blind. He should have known. He knew her strength and boundless sense of honor and duty. He should have known.

He crept into the city in the pale light of predawn. Crept into the castle by way of one of the hidden entrances Tate had mapped out for him, and made his way through a tunnel—the same tunnel through which he and Tate had escaped this place—to the dungeons. To the cell he'd once been consigned to by his own flesh and blood. The place where his brother had left him to die.

He dropped from the ceiling and landed in a crouch on the floor, pausing there, waiting, listening, scanning the darkness. There was nothing but silence and the occasional flicker of the torch that burned from a wall sconce, emitting soot-laden smoke that burned his eyes and throat. Darkness and the tall shadows of the barred doors. Stone block walls and floors, dirty with the soot and fouled with the stench of all who'd been held here.

Moving slowly, silently, Tristan stepped forward and tried the door. He sighed in relief when it gave way. No one here saw the use in locking vacant cells. All the better for him. He stepped out of the cell and walked silently along the rows of them, searching each cell, perusing the pathetic souls who slept on the floors in many of them, and probing even the darkest corners of the empty ones. When he came to the torch in the wall, he pulled it down, carrying it with him, better to see into the grim shadows. But with each cell he passed, his heart grew heavier, because he didn't see Bridín in any of them.

And when he reached the end of the cells, he thought he'd failed. But then he heard rustling, and a rattle of chains. And he remembered the ancient torture chamber. He'd once used it for storage. But his brother, no doubt, had emptied it of its stores and filled it instead with agony.

Bridín!

He rushed forward, torch held out ahead of him, his stomach turning at the thought of what he might find. And then he paused, just inside the doorway. He stood there, and he stared at her as she slowly lifted her head and met his eyes.

Jamming the torch into a wall bracket, he rushed forward, wrapped his arms around her, buried his fingers in her hair. "Bridín! Dammit, Bridín, has he hurt you? Are you all right? Did he—"

"I'm fine." She lifted her head away from where he cradled it on his shoulder. "He can't hurt me, Tristan, so long as I wear the pendant.

I'm safe. It's you who are in danger. Leave here, now!"

"Not without you," he told her, and he straightened, searching her face. She was so beautiful, and so determined. "I know you wanted to ease the suffering of your people, Bridín, but there has to be another way."

"There isn't."

"I won't leave you here. Understand that. It's foolish to come here like a sheep to the slaughter."

"I'm protected—"

"He's deadly!"

She closed her eyes, and he saw her gathering her wits for the argument with him. Oddly, though, it didn't come. Instead she glanced past him, toward the shadowy corner beyond, then nodded toward the chains at her wrists and sent him a meaningful glance. "Free me, then."

Narrowing his gaze, Tristan gripped the manacle in his hands and pried at it. Then he tugged at the chains. He tried using his sword as a tool, tried countless times to free her. But nothing worked. His callused hands pulled on the chains until they were raw, and still he tried to free her.

"You see," she whispered, and the hand closest to him stroked his hair gently. "It's hopeless, Tristan. You can't free me."

"I can't leave you here."

"It won't be for long," she told him. "Tristan, your duty is to your people now, not to me. You have to get away from here. Stay safe, and don't sacrifice this entire kingdom trying to save one fay female."

"I don't give a damn about the kingdom."

"You have to leave me," she whispered.

But he didn't. Instead he caught her head in his hands and kissed her mouth as if he were starving for her. His tongue thrust inside, tasting her, and knowing he'd die before he left her here to face his brother on her own. And he felt her response, he felt it, recognized it, knew it was for him and him alone. He lifted his head. "You planned this all along," he whispered. "When you said you couldn't marry me, you were only trying to spare me—"

"You're wrong." She turned her head away, averted her eyes. "I'm sworn to obey my mother, Tristan. Now more than ever."

Stunned, he caught her face in his hands. "Why now more than ever?"

"Because she's alive."

"*What?*"

Bridín only nodded. "It's a long story, Tristan. And there's no time for it now. But my mother is alive, and—"

"I don't care," he said quickly, and he knew he'd interrupted her because he was sorely afraid she might convince him she meant what she said. And he didn't want to believe it. He *refused* to believe it. She was his, dammit.

"I love you, Bridín."

He saw the tears pooling in her eyes then.

"You won't be able to get me free," she whispered. "Not in time."

"I will."

She closed her eyes, and he opened his mouth to ask her what she'd meant by "not in time." But then she opened those gemstone eyes again, and focused on his mouth. "Make love to me, Tristan. Just one last time."

He shook his head. It was madness, what she asked of him. Insanity to waste precious time, when he should be digging the chains from the stone with his very fingers if necessary.

She pressed her lips to the skin exposed below the neck of his tunic, and then lifted her fairy eyes to him. And his pulse quickened. His heart accelerated. His skin heated. "I can refuse you nothing, Bridín."

And he put his arms around her. Pressed his hips against her. And she couldn't respond the way he knew she wanted to. But she moved her hips against his, and returned his kisses.

She tugged at the chains, but her arms remained where they were, out to the sides and above her head. She pulled at the leg irons, but her legs remained spread apart and bound tight to the wall. Tristan lifted her tunic and ran his hands up underneath it. He pushed it up high, baring her breasts to his touch, and then he cupped them in his hands, squeezing and holding them. And Bridín twisted herself from side to side in blatant need. He stopped kissing her, drawing his mouth away from hers, to bend his head lower. And he lifted the prize to his lips and suckled and fed from it, and he knew he'd never tasted anything sweeter than the honey of her nipples, the very essence of her skin.

And she whispered at him to hurry, to take her, to do it now. Tristan pushed the hose down to her knees, and rapidly fumbled to free himself from his own. And then he pushed into her. She flung her head back, arms going stiff, legs spread wide and trembling. And he slid his hands around her to cup her buttocks, his knuckles scraping the stone wall behind her. And he held her to him as he thrust himself into her. He took her fast and hard—as fast and as hard as if he truly believed this would be his last chance with her. But he didn't believe it. He never would.

"You're mine," he told her, as he pumped into her, plunging deeper each time. "Mine, Bridín. No man will ever love you like I do." And he kissed her mouth when he felt her come, swallowed her cries, inhaled her breaths. And then he filled her with his seed, and held her tight to him as he spent himself into her.

And still longer.

Until she lifted her head, and trailed a line of kisses over his face. "Right my clothes, Tristan. Hurry, please."

And though he wished to hold her, he knew she was right. Even the few moments of blazing passion had been too much to risk taking. Damn, why had she tempted him that way? He stood away from her, putting her clothing to rights before his own.

"Now. There's not much time—"

"You keep saying that—"

"There's a child, Tristan. A little girl named Amelia. Please, go to her now. Get her out of here."

"I've come here for you," he argued. "Dammit, Bridín, it's *you* I'm taking out of here."

"There's no time to argue. She's a child, so they won't have taken many precautions with her. She should be easily rescued. Please, Tristan. I couldn't think of leaving her behind. Take her outside, through whatever secret way you came in. While you're about, you can find a hammer or an ax to break these chains of mine. But hurry. Please, go now. Hurry."

Tristan swallowed hard, and he thought he detected something in her eyes. Something that should have warned him.

"I'm begging you. She's an innocent child, Tristan, and he plans to hurt her. Terribly. Take her away now, and come back for me."

"I'll take you both—"

"If you don't go fetch an ax, you'll never get me free anyway. Please, just take the girl with you!"

He backed away, shaking his head, knowing she was right. He needed a tool to free her, an ax, as she said. And it would take no more time to gather up a small child on the way out of here.

Why, then, was he feeling this sick ball of dread forming in his stomach?

"Hurry," she whispered. "Hurry, Tristan. Go, find the girl."

He surged forward and kissed her again. "I'll be back," he promised. "No more than a few minutes, Bridín. I swear it to you."

"I know."

And at last he tore himself away, hurrying from the room without looking back, lest he lose his ability to leave her, even for a moment.

Finding the child was an easy task. She was tied by a lead rope to a ring in the wall. As one would tie a dog. She crouched on the wet floor with her hands bound behind her, and she looked terrified.

"It's all right," Tristan said softly, and he bent

to untie her. "I've come to take you out of here."

"No," she whispered. "You came for the princess."

He met the child's eyes, wise beyond their years. "Indeed I did. But she says she won't leave here unless I first take you away."

She frowned. "They all said she was bad. They said she didn't care about her people."

"They lied, child." He stroked the golden hair. "They lied."

Bridín heard the vanishing sounds of Tristan and the girl, Amelia, even as she watched the last few grains of sand fall into the lower half of the hourglass. She'd known he couldn't free her, and she'd known he wouldn't leave her behind. And yet she hadn't been able to be completely unselfish. She'd had to know his embrace, his lovemaking, one last time.

She'd sent him out with the child, knowing that Vincent would come back for her before Tristan could return. But at least the girl would be safe. And Tristan . . . Gods, please, she whispered, protect Tristan. He had to stay alive long enough to oust his brother and free the people. He had to.

Vincent's growl of outrage reached her before she even heard the footsteps of the guards. And then he was there, glowering at her from the stone archway. "What have you done with the child?" he demanded.

"You didn't think I'd let you harm her, did you?"

He panted, breathless with rage. And then he seemed to catch control of himself. He braced his hands on the doorway's edges, narrowing his evil eyes on her. "Guards, fetch me another child. A younger one this time. We'll proceed with the torture right on schedule. You should be able to find a suitable substitute in the village. Go, and hurry."

The large guard, one of the two who'd brought her down here, nodded from behind Vincent and turned to go.

"Wait!"she cried.

He halted, and Vincent looked at her.

"I'll tell you . . . all I know. I'm afraid it isn't much, but—"

"If it isn't enough, Bridín, we'll go on with the torture as planned."

She closed her eyes and prayed she could bluff her way through this. First, though, she had to get out of these dungeons. Tristan would return before long. And if he saw her here, with his brother threatening her like this, he'd leap to her defense and likely get himself killed.

"Well?"

Bridín nodded firmly. "Take me to your war chambers, Vincent. I can show you on the map you keep there, where your brother's men make ready to overthrow your rule."

Vincent stared at her for a long moment. And finally he nodded. "Loose her bonds and bring her up. I'll be waiting." He turned to go, lifting one edge of his cloak to his face and grimacing. "Gods, it stinks down here!"

And then he was gone. Frederick, the gentle, young guard, rushed forward, seemingly as eager to free her as she was to be freed. Unlike Tristan, this youth had a set of keys. And even with those it took several minutes to get her loose from the iron jaws that held her captive.

"There, lady," he said at last, and frowned as he lifted a torch from the wall sconce and examined the red marks on her wrists. "Come along then." Taking her forearm in one gentle hand, careful not to touch the sore spots on her wrists, Frederick led her around the corner and along the margin of stone floor that stretched between the cells. All the way to the far end they walked, with the gruff, older guard hulking silently on her other side. At the very end of the row of cells was the base of that crumbling, curving stone staircase, and Frederick had to let go of her then. Single file was the only sane way to ascend the thing.

Bridín tried hard to plan what she would do when she joined Vincent in the chambers above. Show him some false place in the enchanted forest that surrounded Rush? Lie and pray he wouldn't find out for a while? All that would do would be to buy her some extra time. Days at the most. More likely hours. And what then?

She thought of Tristan as she'd last seen him, wondered if he was even now making his way back to her. To rescue her, or so he thought. Please, let him just run back to the forest unharmed when he couldn't find her. Let him finish his preparations for war as he should, so that he could be successful in his attack against his brother.

She could see her beloved in her mind's eye, so clearly. His smile. His strong, callused hands. The lines at the corners of his eyes. The fullness of his mouth. His—

The stone beneath her crumbled. She felt it fall away as she stepped down upon it. She felt herself pitch sideways, and a quick glimpse below told her she'd ascended nearly to the top of this towering stairway. Stupid, she realized, to let herself become distracted with plotting and daydreaming while walking up such a curving and crumbling ruin. It had been treacherous even with her attention fully on her footing. But this . . . !

The man behind her reached for her, and she glimpsed his face. Frederick, looking mortified. His hand swung toward her as she seemed to hang for a split second in the air, her feet still touching the step, but her body already arching outward, over the endless darkness below. He closed his hand, but she fell away, and all he caught was the pendant.

She felt it snap free of her neck, heard him cry out as her body sailed past him and into the black maw of space beyond the open side of the stairs. She looked at him. For one brief moment she met his eyes, brown eyes filled with horror. And then her momentum pulled her downward, and she was untethered, and plummeting. She heard the men shouting, their feet pounding down the stairs, saw the flicker of their torches, briefly. Then she heard only the dank, stale air whistling past her ears. She didn't cry out. She wouldn't give them that satisfaction. But she did whisper.

"Tristan . . ."

The floor slammed up to greet her, its impact so powerful, the breath was forced from her lungs as she rebounded to fly upward again, and then came down for another blow. She felt the crystal ball split into pieces. The third time she hit bottom, she found blessed darkness.

Chapter Nineteen

OLD MARY RILEY saw the whole thing. She'd been sentenced to thirty days in the dungeons on bread-and-water rations, for the crime of stealing firewood from the prince's forest. What she'd stolen, of course, had been no more than a single limb, no longer than her own leg, and about as big around. It was obviously dead and had been blown to the ground. Not that it had made any difference to that arrogant bastard when he'd passed sentence.

But she'd survived her stay here. Tonight was her final one, and tomorrow she'd be released. She supposed she might have to endure a few of that whip-monger's lashes before she was let go, but she could manage it. She might be old, but she was strong.

Until tonight, she'd thought she'd seen everything. Torture and beatings, and all manner of persons being dragged down here, from the elderly to the crippled to the dying to the very young. Even those women whose bellies bulged with child were tossed into these filthy, vile cells if caught committing what that idiot called a crime.

But never had she seen this kind of cruelty.

She'd come to the bars when she'd heard them approaching, bringing that fair lady from the bowels of the torture chamber to the foot of the stairs. Mary had seen the other man, the one who'd come earlier, and who'd left with that sweet little girl cradled in his arms. She'd heard that one promise to come back for the beauty in the room of horrors. But he hadn't come back in time.

Life offered little enough diversion here, so even seeing the comings and goings of other prisoners became a thing of great interest. But this hadn't been interesting. No, but more like a nightmare. The way Mary saw it, it seemed they'd hurled that poor woman right off those steps. Just tossed her. And she hadn't so much as made a peep, even when she'd hit with enough force to split a melon.

By the gods, she must be dead!

Mary leaned close to the bars in her cell, pressing her face between them, gripping them with her hands. This was the closest glimpse she'd yet had of the nubile young woman. She was beautiful; that was sure even in the harsh, flickering light of the few torches left burning. A face like—why, like Queen Máire's had been, before she'd been killed. Oh, and she'd been the most beautiful . . . But all those fay females were. And this one was fay, or her name wasn't Mary Riley. The beauty lay still, not moving at all, not even to moan, and Mary feared the girl was dead. Then the guards came thundering toward her, holding their torches over her face. And Mary gasped as she saw that torchlight fall upon a golden yellow braid of hair so long, it must reach to her waist.

Gods fury, could it be . . . ?

"The prince will have our heads!" one beefy guard said, punching a smaller one hard in the breastplate.

The second staggered backwards, staring down at the pendant he held in his hand and then flinging it away in horror. "I tried—"

"He wanted her alive! He'll make us pay!"

But the second only remained silent, and knelt beside the fallen woman. He touched her face gently, looked almost . . . guilty. "I think . . ." he whispered. "Yes. Look, she breathes. Fair Bridín isn't dead . . . not yet, at least."

The older one bent over, nodded once. "But how long can she hold on after a fall like that? And when she dies, we'll die with her, you can be sure."

Mary Riley backed away from the bars into the shadows, careful not to make any sound. If they knew she'd seen . . . she'd be as dead as the fairy princess on the floor.

"We'd do well to make haste away from here. Just drag her into a cell and let's go."

The younger guard nodded. But he seemed reluctant. "He'll find her, and tend to her," he muttered as if to convince himself of it. "He'll surely come looking when we fail to bring her up as he commanded. So he'll find her."

The first guard was already opening the steel-barred door of the nearest cell. But it was the second, the one who'd touched her so tenderly, who scooped her up into his arms. There was a jangling sound, and Mary squinted out of her dark cell to see his keys fall from his belt to land on the floor. He didn't seem to notice as he ever so carefully laid the beauty down again, inside the empty cell. As Mary watched in blatant amazement, he removed his cloak and tucked it around and beneath her. "I'm so sorry," he whispered. "I tried to catch you . . ."

"Come on," said the first. "Let's be on our way before *he* arrives."

The two hurried away, no doubt never to set foot in sight of their prince again. Mary Riley watched them go, and then she sat down on the floor and focused her attention on the still form of the woman. And she knew that the body lying wrapped in the blue cloak of the castle guard was none other than Bridín of the Fay, rightful ruler of Rush.

She *hadn't* turned her back on her people at all, then. Mary Riley had never truly believed she had. She'd met the girl's mother once. Queen Máire. Never had she known a woman who exuded such strength and purity of heart. It practically shone from her eyes. No, no daughter of hers would grow up to shun her duty. Young princess Bridín hadn't. She'd come back here, turned herself over to these brutes in good faith, and they'd broken their word not to harm her, and pitched her from the very stairs before her own old eyes. Likely that haughty Vincent of Shara wouldn't keep any of his other promises either, particularly the one about easing the constraints he'd placed on the people once he had the princess in his evil clutches.

Well, Mary Riley had suffered enough under

Vincent's rule. The second she was released, she'd make sure the people knew what was going on inside the walls of the castle. Yes indeed. She'd make sure.

It was only moments later when a third guard came partway down the stairs, glimpsed the princess's broken body lying in a cell, bathed in flickering torchlight, and raced back up the stairs shouting for the prince.

Tristan left the child in the care of a wise woman he knew would protect her, come what may. And from that same woman he borrowed an ax, which he fastened to his belt in all haste, even while making his way back to the castle. But the dread in his stomach did not dissipate, nor did the feeling that he never should have left her behind. That ominous chill had dug deeper into his heart with every second he'd been away from her, and it was that which drove him faster. Like a madman he darted over the twisting, narrow lanes of the village, ducking into the foliage that surrounded the castle proper, leaping roots and ducking vines and dashing around brush and undergrowth. He made his way back to that secret entrance and raced through the tunnel, heedless of the noise he might be making.

But when he dropped from the ceiling into the dank cell, he guessed he'd already known what he was going to find. The cell door creaked as he pushed it open, and the sound echoed. In the distance he heard only a haunting hollow sound of stagnant water dripping from some crack in the stone walls. He stepped into the corridor and hurried through it, his steps loud in the silence, then swung around the corner and through the archway into the torture chamber.

And the chains that had formerly held Bridín's delicate limbs now hung harmless and vacant against the stone wall. Gone. Bridín was gone.

Picking up a torch, he thrust it into the deepest shadows of the room, just to be sure. And then he paused as its dancing light fell upon an hourglass, upright in a corner. Frowning, Tristan recalled the way Bridín had kept glancing at something beyond him, and how she'd kept saying how little time there was left.

Then he closed his eyes and groaned. Dammit, she'd known they were coming for her. She'd known she wouldn't be here by the time he returned. Damn her stubbornness. Damn her courage. Gods, but he loved her beyond all reason.

He turned and made his way back along the rows of cells, peering into each one he passed in search of her, but she wasn't there. He drew nearer the narrow, curving staircase that stretched upward until it vanished in the pitch black distance. The one that led up to the castle's ground floor. And then he went rigid at the plaintive whisper coming from one of the cells.

"My Lord, whom do you seek?" rasped the aged voice.

Tristan turned quickly, spying the elderly woman who clutched the bars, keeping the torchlight as far from his face as he could, lest this prisoner recognize him. "I seek no one," he said, but wondered if perhaps this old woman had seen something, knew something. Anything that could help him find Bridín. "Why do you ask me such a thing?"

She narrowed her eyes, pressing her face tight to the bars and peering at him. "Come closer, boy. You're familiar to me."

Tristan shook his head, averting his face.

"I saw you peering into each cell as you passed. It's her you've come to find, isn't it?"

Tristan's head snapped around quickly. "Her?"

"The beautiful one with the long, golden braid."

Forgetting all about protecting his anonymity, Tristan rushed forward, standing close to the woman's cell. "You've seen her? Tell me!"

"Is it true?" she asked in a whisper. "Is she the princess Bridín?"

Taking a step away from the cagelike cell, Tristan lowered the torch with a sigh, and heard the woman gasp as the light fell on his face. The next thing he knew she was on her knees, head lowered. "Prince Tristan! You're back from the dead!"

"Hush," he commanded. "I'd rather not alert the entire castle to my presence here."

"I should say not," she said, her voice quieter now. "But I can tell you nothing of my lady Bridín, for you and she are enemies, sworn. Both vying for the throne."

"We're more than that," Tristan whispered. Gods, they were *so much* more than that. He shook himself and went on. "We're both enemies of my treacherous brother. Our own fight for this kingdom will be settled only when Vincent has been vanquished, dear lady. I promise you that. But for now, my fondest wish is to see to it she lives long enough to give me that fight, for I relish our battles."

The woman blinked up at him, slowly rising to her feet. Her eyes widened in wonder, and she even smiled, showing her missing teeth. "I do believe you mean that," she said softly. "For your eyes go all misty when you speak of her. Could it be our fay princess has captured the heart of a Sharan prince?"

"Are you going to tell me what you know or not?"

Her smile died, head lowering again. "I'm afraid it isn't good news, my lord. The princess was treated roughly by the guards who held her. Oh, they came for her right after you left with the little girl. But the poor lovely never made it as far as the top of the stairs."

Tristan lunged forward, gripping the bars of her pen as his heart lurched. "What are you saying?"

She met his eyes, her own deeply sad. "They pitched her from the top," she whispered, nodding toward the towering set of stone stairs. "I heard one claim it was an accident, but knowing those kind, I—"

"Was she killed?" he cried, no longer caring who heard him.

"They said she was still alive, sweet prince. Oh, I can see how this news pains you. The guards left in haste, fearing Vincent's wrath. And that prince himself came down here only a scant few moments ago, to find her in the cell where those brutes left her to die."

Clutching the bars, Tristan fought a shudder that weakened him, tried to control the roiling in his stomach. His knees gave out, though, and he sank slowly to the floor, letting the torch fall, still burning, beside him. "Tell me," he whispered. "Tell me all of it."

A leathery hand stroked his bowed head. "Vincent carried your lady upstairs, shouting for the guards to fetch a healer woman from the village. I heard him vow they'd all face the gallows if she died before he got from her the information he wanted." The hand on his head trembled and finally drew away. "My guess, now that I've seen you, is that the information he wants concerns you, my lord. And Vincent seemed to want it badly. He'll save her, if he can, though his motives are as black as his heart."

Gathering his strength, Tristan rose to his feet again and turned toward the stairway. It was only as he started climbing that he saw the keys at the base of the stairs, and shards of convex quartz crystal scattered around. Gods, Bridín's crystal ball! Shattered!

Drawing a breath, he fell to his knees and stroked one large hunk of curving glasslike crystal as he battled emotions threatening to overtake him. But only for a moment. He knelt there and saw a glimmer from the corner of his eye, and when he turned to investigate, he felt the wind knocked out of him. Bridín's fairy pendant, its chain broken. Torn from her throat, no doubt.

Damn his brother for this!

Tristan knotted the chain and draped the necklace around his own throat. Then he stiffened his spine, and converted his grief and fear for her into righteous rage. With a swipe of his hand he scooped up the keys, and returned to the woman in the cell. "What time of day do the dungeon keepers come for the first time?"

"An hour past dawn," she said. "Why?"

"What is your name?" he asked her.

"Mary," she said. "Mary Riley."

Nodding, Tristan lifted the key ring and unlocked her cell. "Mary Riley, as your prince, I charge you with a mission of great importance."

"Anything, my lord," she whispered, bowing her head.

He pressed the key ring into her hand. "First, free the others held captive here. Take them to the tenth cell. There you'll find a secret passage beyond a stone in the ceiling, which will lead you to freedom."

She nodded hard, looking as he pointed the cell out to her.

"Once you're free, you're to spread the word among the people that the princess Bridín is innocent of all my brother's charges against her. Those raids months ago were only a ruse intended to discredit her. The raiders were his men, led by a courtesan who only resembled Bridín. Tell them that she hasn't turned her back on her people, but that she returned here the moment she learned of their suffering, and turned herself over to Vincent in order to end it. And tell them to prepare themselves, for when my troops attack this city, they must join them. It's our only hope of ousting Vincent."

"I will do it," she said, lifting her chin. She stepped out of the cell, and impulsively reached up to kiss his cheek. "Gods be with you, Tristan." Then she hurried away, unlocking cells as she passed them, whispering all he'd told her even before she made her escape.

Tristan returned to the stairs and made his way up, shuddering as he glanced down behind him and thought of Bridín being flung from such a height. *Please, gods of Rush, let her be all right*, he thought. She must be. She *must be*.

At the top, he paused. The door was barred, and if he knew his brother at all, there was a guard posted on the other side. He didn't hesitate but drew his sword, and with his fist, pounded on the door.

He heard movement. A shout. Then the bar slipping free, and the door pushing toward him. Tristan ducked behind it, and when the guard's head poked in, he grabbed the bastard in a headlock and flung him with all his fury. The man flailed wildly, screaming as he plunged through the darkness, and Tristan heard the dull thud and clanging of his breastplate when he hit bottom.

Not another sound.

Tristan slipped into the vaulted corridor, pulling the door closed behind him, dropping the bar into place so as not to alert anyone what was happening. Then he crept through the darkened castle, praying he could find Bridín in time.

Máire sucked in a sharp breath when the chamber door flew open and her detested captor surged through it, Bridín's broken body sagging in his arms. She sprang to her feet, crying out loud, only once before remembering herself. She mustn't give him anything to wonder at. She must let him believe the woman lying like a corpse in his arms was a stranger to her. No matter how her heart twisted at the sight.

Vincent appeared not to have noticed her momentary lapse. He continued forward and lowered Bridín to the bed, slipping his arms from beneath her with more care than Máire had ever seen him exhibit for anything or anyone. Behind him, two of his advisers trundled into the room, comical in their nightgowns and caps. Both looking terrorized—no doubt at the furious bellows that had roused them from their beds. One clutched a candle. It was unnecessary. Máire had long since convinced her captor to leave a light burning when he left her alone here in her prison by night. She was allowed to roam unshackled by day, so long as she was at his side. Likewise, she was free of her bonds by night while he was here with her. Only when she was left to her own devices did Vincent insist on the manacles.

The fool thought himself too hard of heart to be influenced by the charms of a fairy. But Máire knew full well he'd succumbed to hers. Though her magic be gone, she could still manipulate the mind of a man, even one as boorish and cold as he. She shuddered to think of what her time here would have been like had she lost that power with the rest.

"Where is the healer?" Vincent shouted, startling her and causing the two in attendance to jump. "I sent for a healer woman, dammit. Where is she?"

The men looked at one another in helpless appeal.

"My lord," Máire said. "I have some skill at the healing arts. Perhaps I can be of help."

He eyed her in surprise, but no suspicion clouded his gaze. And why should it? She'd been nothing but cooperative with him in all the time she'd been held here. All this time, simply waiting for the day her daughter would return. And now to see her like this. "Release me," she said. "Let me tend the girl before it's too late."

Vincent nodded to the two, who immediately bent to the shackles at Máire's wrists and ankles. She rubbed the spots where the steel cuffs had been, an act so automatic, she no longer thought about it, just did it. Like breathing.

She hurried forward and stood beside Bridín, smoothing the golden hair that had pulled loose from the braid away from her face, feeling the chill of her skin and wincing at its unnatural pallor. A deep purple bruise was already forming high on her cheekbone, and as Máire probed, she found a lump on her daughter's head. She took a moment to blink away tears before lifting her head to Vincent. "I'll need ice from the icehouse. And more blankets. Quickly."

"Go," Vincent ordered the two men who stood hovering uselessly between the bed and the door, clearly wishing to be elsewhere. "Get what she needs, and make it quick."

They hurried from the room almost as one. And Máire felt Vincent's eyes on her as she ran her hands gently over her daughter's limbs and torso.

"Will she live?" he asked.

She took a deep breath, and prayed she could keep the tremor from her voice. "She has a broken arm, and at least two of her ribs seem to be cracked as well, at the very least. There was a severe blow to the head, as well. And I have no idea what sorts of other injuries she might have, inside, where I cannot see them."

"I don't give a damn for her broken bones or hidden injuries, woman. I only want to know whether she'll live long enough to wake and tell me where my traitorous brother is hiding out, and what he plans. So tell me. Will she?"

"I thought your brother was dead, my lord."

"Will the vixen wake or won't she!"

Máire blinked at the anger in his voice. "She might. I'll know more after I've examined her more thoroughly. Perhaps . . . if I knew what happened to her?"

Vincent turned from the bed and pushed one hand backward through his hair. "Damned if I know. I ordered two guards to bring her up from the dungeons. She was found in a cell, like this. The guards seem to have vanished. If they're smart, they'll run to the ends of the earth. If I find them, I'll—" He broke off there, narrowing his eyes at her. She knew how much it always disturbed him when he caught himself complying with her wishes, answering her questions as if he were the slave and she the master instead of the other way around. He gave his head a shake and averted his gaze. "I sent men down to investigate, but I doubt they'll learn anything more."

Máire nodded, deciding not to question him further just now. No need to pique his suspicions. Instead she grasped her daughter's right forearm, one hand gripping it on either side of the break. Then, biting her lower lip, she pulled fast and hard to set the broken bone aright.

Bridín moaned aloud, drawing Vincent back to the bedside. He leaned in close to her face. "Wake," he told her. "Wake, you treasonous wench, and tell me what I need to know!"

"She can't hear you, Vincent."

He glared at Máire, but didn't snap at her for her familiar mode of address. "Damn her, always eluding me in one way or another! It was my intent to do her in long ago, but the brat wasn't in the accident I devised. It took only her adopted mortal parents, instead, while she managed to live on. And while my weak brother had her in his care, there was no way to get to her. Now, at last, I have her in my hands and she still eludes me!" He leaned over the bed, his face hovering inches above Bridín's. "But dammit, wench, you *will* wake, and you will tell me where he's hiding. And then, by the gods, I'll kill you by my own hands!"

"Yelling at her right now is like yelling at the stone walls of this room, Vincent. It will get you no response."

As she spoke, she moved away, her back to him, lest he see the concern in her eyes or note the protective tone of her voice.

"Wouldn't be surprised if she leapt from the stairway herself, just to avoid telling me what she knows of my brother," Vincent growled.

Máire bent to the pile of wood alongside the hearth, tossed several more pieces on the dying fire, and then knelt to paw through the litter and bark beneath the log holder. She chose two stiff, straight pieces of thick cherry bark and returned to the bed, then bent to tear a wide swath from the bottom of her skirts.

"What is this?" Vincent asked, watching her every move.

Máire wrapped each length of bark in the muslin, then placed the cushioned pieces on either side of Bridín's forearm. She used another length of cloth to wind around the two, encasing the broken limb in a soft pink cocoon. "Merely a splint," she explained without slowing her pace. "I'll need to make her a sling as well, and to wrap her broken ribs good and tight. Could you have them bring me linens? Else my dress will be all used up."

"And what is it to me if you go naked, woman, except more convenient?"

Máire lifted her gaze to his, not surprised at his crude remarks. "You wish her to regain consciousness? If you do, we need to ease her pain. Agony this intense will only keep her incapable of telling you anything."

He scowled at her. "Fine, you'll have your bandages. Anything else?"

"Indeed, my lord," she said, injecting a respect she was far from feeling into her tone. Vincent liked her feisty and uncooperative only when he had her in his bed. The rest of the time, she had to curb it or face his wrath. "She'll need quiet, and solitude. Should she take cold or catch a fever now, it would end her so fast, you'd never have the chance to question her. I believe it would be best if we kept everyone away from her, for now, save for you and I, of course."

"I can't dance attendance on a sleeping woman day and night," he huffed.

"Post guards outside the door," she told him, and she kept hold of his eyes with her own, sending as much fay allure as she possessed into his brain, willing him to do as she wished. "Just order them not to enter. The moment she wakes I will send them for you."

He tilted his head, and she saw his indecision. Swallowing her revulsion, Máire stepped closer, lifted a hand to caress his whiskered face. "I've never lied to you, nor tried to run from you, my lord. You can trust me to tend the girl. I vow it."

He stared down into her eyes, and he nodded. Then blinked and pulled himself away from her touch. Máire felt only relief. "So be it, then," he said. "But if anything untoward should—"

He stopped at a pounding on the door. When he yanked it open, one of his guards stood there, and Máire stepped nearer, to hear his report. "My lord, there is chaos in the dungeons!"

"What are you—"

"The prisoners . . . they're gone, simply vanished, every one of them. It's as if they've been spirited away. The door, it was still barred, and the man left to guard it was found dead on the floor. Flung from the stairs, he was. Some of the men say it's ghosts. Spirits of the dead villagers, seeking vengeance on us all."

"Gods' wings, what nonsense!" Vincent turned to send a glance toward Máire. Then looked back at his man again. "You're to stand guard outside this door. No one is to go in or out, except to bring the supplies to my slave. Is that understood?"

"Yes, my lord." The young man bowed once.

"Are you clean, boy? Are you healthy? Been exposed to the fever or—"

"No, sir. I'm healthy and strong."

"Good." Vincent turned again to Máire. "I'm to be sent for the instant she wakes. And then she'll tell me what she knows, or I'll pitch her from the blasted window myself."

Máire nodded, bowing her head in obedience, seething under her breath. The day that bastard laid a hand on her daughter would be the day he lost the appendage. Máire would die first. But she kept her bearing humble until he turned and left the room. And she heard the door barred from without.

Which didn't matter in the least, because she was unfettered now, and she could leave the castle at will, through the passages.

She hurried to the bedside again, drawing another quilt over Bridín's still form, tucking it around her. She should wait until the others brought her the bandages and ice for Bridín's head, and then take her daughter and run.

Ah, but as badly hurt as she was, moving Bridín might very well kill her. Beyond that, once outside the castle, they'd have to move through the very city, in sight of everyone. And while none out there might recognize their onetime queen in the rags of a slave, they would surely recognize Bridín. And since most of those fools believed Vincent's lies about her, they'd likely stone the two of them to death before they'd traveled a mile.

No, the best hope for Bridín right now was to remain here.

And to remain unconscious. Yes. Because if she woke, Vincent would not hesitate to torture her poor, broken body all the more, when she refused to tell him about Tristan. And she would refuse; Máire had no doubt at all of that. No, she must not let her daughter wake again. Not until her body was mended enough to attempt an escape.

Later, when the castle had settled down once more, and Vincent believed her safely asleep at his new prisoner's bedside, Máire would slip through the passage to that once beautiful garden, where she'd known so much joy. Though it was weedy and unkempt, several of her own plants still grew beneath the brambles. And the leaves of one of them would keep her daughter sound asleep for as long as it was necessary.

It would be risking her own life to venture out. Should Vincent come in and find her gone ... he'd kill her. Swiftly and surely, he would.

But if she didn't do it, her daughter would face his cruelty as he attempted to force her to talk. Death seemed to Máire like a far more pleasant risk.

Bridín. Beautiful, stubborn, magical Bridín, tossed from thirty feet or more. Her body slamming, breaking, bruising against a hard, cold floor of solid stone. Bridín, hurting. Dying, perhaps. Gods, no ...

His mind was not on stealth as he slipped through the darkened corridors of the castle. It was only on speed, and on Bridín. His brain whirled with nightmarish images of what he'd find when he got to her. Was she already dead, or maimed beyond hope? Would she even know he was there?

The great hall was dark, deserted, as Tristan moved slowly through it. He was nearly to the first set of stairs when he heard voices. Tristan leapt from the base of the stairs, pressed his back tight to the wall, and prayed for invisibility. There was nowhere to hide. His fingers clutched the wall behind him, clenching and relaxing in a nervous reflexive action as two men in night-clothes came down the stairs muttering to one another. "First she sends us for ice and blankets, and now linens! One would think she was a damned queen instead of a menial slave!"

"Arrogant wench, too, to tell us to leave the linens in the hall with her guard. Telling him not to disturb her, that she'd tap on the door when she was ready for them."

"As if she's nursin' the queen o' the world in that bloody chamber, instead of the most detested criminal in all of Shara."

"Thinks she's important now, carin' for such a valuable prisoner. Gone straight to her head."

"The prince has coddled that one a bit too much. Needs a good taste o' the lash, she does."

The talk continued as the two meandered out of sight, down another corridor and up another flight of steps.

Tristan relaxed, and let all the air rush out of his lungs. The two had walked right past him, but never turned his way. Gods, that was close. He'd best keep his mind on his mission, to get to Bridín. And now he had a clue where she was . . . in a chamber up that first flight of stairs. His fingers clenched in anticipation as he pushed off from the wall, but when they did, a chink in the stone seemed to move. And suddenly the wall turned, sweeping him around behind it like a giant stony hand. When the movement ceased,

Tristan blinked in utter darkness. But his eyes didn't adjust. There was truly no light here. He stretched out both hands, and tried his best to learn the shape of this strange new world.

Walls on either side of him, a ceiling above. He was in a short, narrow corridor. And the wall behind him refused to perform its trick again, though he tried to make it open. Trapped. Dammit. Nothing loomed ahead of him, so he moved forward, aggravated now, to have his mission delayed this way. He needed to reach Bridín. Soon. He had to see that she was all right.

His face smacked hard against rough stone, and he cursed and jerked backwards, rubbing his nose. Then he reached out again, wondering if this hidden passage had come to an abrupt end. But no, it had only turned sharply to the left. Tristan used his hands on the sides to guide him from then on. No use knocking himself senseless.

It was after he'd wandered for the better part of an hour that Tristan spotted a light up ahead, and came up short. Someone else was apparently wandering the secret passages of the castle this night. Someone whose form was small, and feminine, though he could see no detail in the light of the candle she carried.

His heart leapt as he thought it might be Bridín. She was clever enough to fake her injuries, to fool them all until they brought her out of the dungeons and into a room from whence she could make her escape.

It seemed illogical that she would surrender herself only to escape so quickly, but he could only assume she'd realized how much danger she was in here, and changed her mind.

Tristan quickened his pace, but still went silently. He wasn't a fool, and he knew there was a chance this was not Bridín at all, but one of his brother's whores, or worse. He crept closer, closer. And then the lady's hooded cloak fell backward and he saw her hair. Flaming red and wild, not golden blond. She was not Bridín. His heart sank to his feet. But he needed to get the hell out of here, and she seemed to know her way.

He slipped up behind her, clasped a hand over her mouth, and whispered, "Don't scream. I won't harm you, but I need your help and I'm going to have to insist you give it."

The head beneath his hand nodded. He lowered his hand, ready to snap it back in place if she shrieked, relieved when she didn't.

"May I turn around?" she asked him.

"All right."

She did, and held her candle high to examine his face, while tucking a handful of some sort of vegetation into her pocket with her other hand. Then, to Tristan's utter surprise, she smiled. "Tristan," she whispered. "Thank the gods."

He only frowned at her, wondering why this stranger seemed familiar to him.

"You don't remember me, do you?" she asked. "I'm the woman you found on the battlefield one day long ago. The woman whose life you risked your own to save."

"I remember," he said. And he looked her up and down. "You healed. I'm glad."

"Yes, thanks to you. But there's no time to reminisce. Come, this way. Hurry." She left the greenery in the folds of her cloak and clutched his hand in hers, pulling him forward.

"Come where?" he blurted. "Where are you dragging me to in such a—"

"Hush. I'm taking you to Bridín, of course. Gods, but I'm not sure I can help her." She glanced over her shoulder at him, narrowed her eyes. "But you can."

Tristan shook his head. "I'm no healer. But I'd give my soul if it would help her."

"I know that. Otherwise I wouldn't be taking you to her side now, Tristan."

She paused at the end of the passage, held the candle aloft. "I've no idea whether she's still alone in the chamber or not. Could be Vincent awaits my return in there, and if he does, he'll kill me." She set the flickering candle on a ledge. "If you hear him when I go up, then back yourself into the shadows. Let him do with me as he will. Just bide your time and remain hidden, and try to help Bridín when you can."

She lifted her arms above her head to push against the stone. But Tristan settled his hands on her shoulders, stopping her, searching her face with narrowed eyes. "Who are you that you would offer your life for hers?"

He saw the unshed tears in her eyes, glittering in the candlelight. "I'm her mother," she whispered.

"Máire?" He shook his head. "But . . . but how—"

"It's a long tale, Tristan, and we've no time now. But it's true, I vow to you. Now come, let's go and see to our girl."

He nodded, thunderstruck, and lifted his hands to help her move the stone. No sound came from the room above. Though of course, that meant little. Tristan wanted to argue that she should let him go first, and that she should be the one to flee if Vincent was indeed waiting. But before he'd done more than part his lips to speak, Máire was hoisting herself up through the floor. She stood, and there was a long moment of silence. Then she bent over the opening. "It's all right. No one's here. Come up, quickly."

Tristan braced his hands on either side of the opening and hauled himself up and into the chamber that had been his once, and apparently now belonged to his brother. And in his brother's bed . . .

"Bridín!" Tristan ran to her, leaned over her, and stroked her pale face, whispering to her as his heart tied itself into knots. Her tunic and tights were torn and dirty. Her hair mussed and pulling free of the braid. Her beautiful face bruised purple. Her arm in a splint. A poultice of something—ice, he realized when he touched it—pressed to a lump on her head.

"Bridín. Live, my angel. Live. You can't end our battle this way. You have to fight with me, Princess, right to the end." He stroked her hair, then bent and pressed his lips to her eyelids. First one, and then the other. But there was no response.

"You can save her, Tristan."

He lifted his head and turned it slowly. Máire had replaced the stone in the floor, and now stood at the foot of the bed. And as he stared at her, she nodded her head, dropping her gaze to a point high on his chest. Numbly he lifted his hand to the spot, and felt them there. The pendants. And they were warm, unnaturally warm. He lowered his chin to look down at them, and his eyes widened as he noted the faint glow that suffused them.

"The pendants," he whispered.

"Yes, Tristan. They'll heal her. No one can die while wearing them. I still had all of my powers—the most powerful magic in all the world, that of a fairy queen—when I fashioned those pendants for my daughters. And I made sure they would protect them, always."

"No one can die while wearing them," he repeated numbly.

"No. Not even you."

He nodded his head, and then knelt beside the bed. He bent forward and pressed his lips to Bridín's. And when he straightened again, he lifted his hands to the chains around his neck.

The door opened. There was a harsh shout, a curse, and then his brother's sword pressed to Tristan's spine. "Don't move or I'll slice you in half, you sniveling pest! Guards!"

Tristan closed his eyes. *No one can die while wearing the pendants.* He closed his hand around the pendants and ripped them free, tossing them to Máire and whirling on his brother at the same time. He knocked the sword away, reaching for his own and lurching for the door simultaneously.

Vincent lunged after him, but Tristan made it to the door, knowing he need only get Vincent away from the bedroom. Give Máire time enough to drag Bridín into that passageway, put the necklaces around her slender, satin throat.

That was all. Nothing else mattered except that Bridín be all right.

He surged through the doorway only to be met by a wall of resistance. But he clasped the guard's armored shoulders and flung him aside. Then he ducked to one side of the door, drawing his brother through it.

Their swords met with a thunderous crash of steel, again and again and again. But Tristan's eyes were on that open doorway. And he only looked away when he saw Máire peer through it. She met his eyes, nodded once.

He knew at that moment that Bridín was going to live, and so would he, dammit. She was his, and he wasn't going to die and leave her to marry some other fool. Not unless dying was the only way to save her life.

He knew now how little everything else mattered. The kingdom, the throne. The freedom of these ungrateful people. Nothing mattered so much to him as Bridín. Her life, and her heart, and her love.

She'd freed him just as surely as she now fought to free her people. Freed him from the chains his own father had wrapped around his heart. From the belief that he'd been born only to rule this land. What hogwash. He'd been born to love her. Nothing more.

He focused himself fully on the fight, to give Bridín and her mother time enough to escape and make their way to safety. And he held his own, too, might even have won, except that several guards appeared at his back within the next few moments. The tips of their swords drew blood as they poked into him. Tristan stopped fighting, because he'd have died at that moment had he not done so. He lifted his hands in surrender, and let his sword clatter to the floor. Time. All he could do now was bide his time, and wait for another chance to save himself.

He could only pray he'd bought Bridín enough time to escape. Her mother enough time to heal her. If he had, then he'd succeeded. Even if he couldn't manage to get out of this alive, it would be worth it.

Chapter Twenty

BRIDÍN SLOWLY CAME awake. Very slowly. She didn't know where she was, or what was happening to her, for a few moments. And then she became aware of pain. A pain that screamed with the shrillness of a madman, and echoed all through her body. Her head. Her torso. Her back and arms and legs. She was on fire. Being burned alive.

But the burn seemed to flare brightest in a single spot at the place just below her throat. And as her body was pulled and pushed and dragged and jostled, the screams of pain seemed to recede, like waves slowly rolling back out to sea. They all grew smaller and smaller as the heat in the middle of her chest grew larger and larger. As if it were absorbing all the rest, drawing all that horrible pain into its fiery embrace and then holding it there, or burning it away.

And even as she registered the odd sensations, they altered yet again. The pain in her body blinked out like a candle pinched between her fingers. And the spot on her chest burned like a firebrand dropped there to smolder. She lifted a hand to her chest to pull the searing ember away from her flesh, and then paused when her hand closed around the red hot shape of the thing that was burning her so.

And she knew that shape.

A winged fairy, made of pewter twined around a quartz crystal point. And tangled with it was a second, her questing fingers soon discovered. Its mate. Its twin.

"The pendants," she whispered. And that thought brought another. "Tristan!"

Her eyes flew open wide even as the pendants in her clenched fist began to cool. And she searched the pitch blackness around her, eager to see him, to touch him, to tell him . . .

But the person who leaned over her, touching her face and whispering so gently, wasn't Tristan.

"No, darling, it's me. It's Mother. Are you better now, my sweetheart?"

Bridín blinked. "Mother?" And slowly her memory returned. Her mission. To turn herself over to Vincent in order to save her people. Her discovery—that her mother was alive, and then their reunion and Máire's explanation. The hugs. The tears. Then her surrender to Vincent, and her reunion with Tristan. The way she'd made love to him despite the chains that held her—the way she'd thought it might be for the last time.

Because she knew Vincent was coming for her. And he had. His men, guiding her up those stairs . . .

Those stairs . . .

She gasped and pressed a knuckle to her teeth to prevent herself from crying out.

"It's all right," Máire whispered. "You're all right now, darling."

"I . . . I f-fell."

"I know. But you're all right, and we've escaped Vincent. Together. Both of us."

Bridín blinked away her tears and nodded. Yes, they'd escaped. And she was well. She could feel her body healing at a pace too rapid to be believed. But she knew, of course, that it was all due to the pendants. Their powers and . . .

She touched them again, turning to her mother in the darkness. "Tristan?" she asked, her heart in her throat.

And she heard her mother's sigh. "Vincent has him," she whispered.

Bridín closed her eyes. "No. Gods, no, he hasn't risked his life to save mine! Not again!"

She saw her mother's eyes fall closed. She said nothing, but Bridín knew. She knew.

"Come now, on your feet. You ought to be able to walk by now." Her mother helped her to stand, and Bridín blinked in the darkness, finally attempting to take in her surroundings. The familiar dampness and chill made goose bumps raise on her arms, and she rubbed them away.

"We're—"

"In the passages, Bridín. I didn't dare try to carry you through the village the way you were. Now, though—"

"No. Mother, I have to go back! I can't just leave him—"

"There's nothing you can do for him by going

back, child," her mother said, and she gripped Bridín's shoulders as if to drive her words home. "You'd only be imprisoned or killed. If you want to help him, Bridín, you have to do it from beyond these walls."

Slowly Bridín shook her head. "There won't be time. Vincent won't imprison him this time, Mother. He'll kill him."

"If killing him outright is Vincent's plan, daughter, then I'm afraid it could already be too late. We've been cowering in these walls for over an hour now."

"No . . ."

"But if Tristan *is* still alive, then our best chance lies out there, with our people."

Gently she steered Bridín forward, then crouching, pushed away the false stone that blocked the opening. She drew her daughter with her into the pale pink light of dawn. "Come," she whispered. "We'll have to hurry, before the villagers begin to stir. We mustn't be seen."

Bridín lifted her chin, met her mother's stare. "Maybe being seen is the only thing left we *can* do." The fresh morning air bathed her face, filled her lungs. The air of Rush. Her kingdom. Her people. She didn't need to go find any man to help her, no matter what her mother's crystal ball had told her. There was only one man she wanted, and he was inside that castle right now, perhaps breathing his last. Bridín had never backed down from a fight, and she'd never given up on something she wanted. She wasn't about to start now.

Let the mobs stone her for her imagined

crimes, if that's what they felt they had to do. It wouldn't matter. If she lost Tristan, nothing would matter anymore.

She turned to stare back at the castle walls towering above her. Gods, what might they be doing to Tristan right now? Was he even alive? And was the horror she felt at this moment the same as what he'd been feeling not long ago, when he'd looked up at those same towers knowing she was trapped somewhere inside?

It was: she knew that now. He loved her, had told her so again and again. And yet she'd never told him how much she loved him, had she?

She closed her eyes, swallowed hard, and stiffened her spine. "I'll be back, Tristan," she whispered. "I swear it, I'll come back for you." Then, clutching her mother's hand more tightly, she turned toward the thin cover of the apple trees and darted away. When she judged they were a safe distance from the castle, deep in the orchards, she put her fingers to her lips and whistled. Then stood still, waiting.

Seconds ticked past before she heard the fast trot of her horse's hooves pattering over the soft ground. Bridín reached up and caught Crystal's bridle before she even ground to a halt. She stroked the mare's nose and led her up in front of Máire.

"Get on, Mother."

Máire's brows drew together and she cocked her head. "Bridín—"

"Get on and ride like the wind. Find Tristan's men in their forest hideaway and bring them. Hurry!"

Biting her lip, her mother faced her, eyes fear-filled, reluctance in her very stance. "Bridín, I can't just leave you here—"

"I love him!"

Their eyes met and held as the wind picked up, bringing the morning along with it. Bridín's hair whipped her face, and she pulled the braid around in front and untied the knot that held it. With her fingers working automatically to loose her hair, she held her mother's gaze. "I love him," she whispered again. "I don't care if I lose the entire kingdom in the end. It doesn't matter. But if he dies, Mother . . ."

Her mother held up a single hand to silence her, and nodded once. "You're a woman now. You'll do . . . what you have to do." She ran one hand over Bridín's hair as the wind helped her free it from its braid. Then she turned and swung into the saddle. "I'll be back as soon as I can," she promised. And then she dug her heels into the mare's sides, and they shot off through the orchard toward the nearest gate.

Bridín turned and ran, fast as she could go, taking a path that would lead to the shops that lined the innermost streets of the city. The merchants' square. That was where the people would be congregating at this early hour. That was where she would find what she needed. She didn't pull up her hood, but left her hair flying free for all to see.

The wind whistled past her ears as she ran. Her body heated and her pulse soared. She dug deep for the strength to face whatever she would encounter, and then emerged, her momentum carrying her to the crossroads at the very center of the merchants' square, where the old fountain still bubbled and splashed, though its water was no longer crystalline, but brackish and coated in green slime.

One or two passersby turned their heads as she drew herself to an unsteady stop near the fountain. Not enough, though. And yet she was still unarmed, except for the dagger in her boot. She turned her head to the right and spotted the armorer's shop where Gaston was just sweeping off his stoop. And she strode to it, pushing past him without apology.

"Well, now, if that wasn't the—" His words stopped with a choking sound as she whirled to face him. She stood in his shop now, he in the doorway staring. "P-Princess Bridín?"

"I need arms. Quickly! A sword, a shield."

He only gaped at her, shaking his head, working his mouth, though no words emerged.

"I'll find them myself," she snapped, turning on her heel and tearing through the place until she located a plain broadsword and a small mace. She slipped the sword into her scabbard, clutched the mace in one hand, and snatched up a battered shield that was probably here for repairs. Then she marched right past the still-gaping proprietor and into the street, shouting as she walked across it toward the fountain.

"People of Rush, hear this! Bridín of the Fay has returned!"

Several shocked faces turned in her direction. Several other people ran off, only to return seconds later, tugging someone else by the shirt-sleeves. Bridín knew she wouldn't have much time. Given what they believed of her, they'd likely form a lynch mob within a minute or two.

She'd best say what she had to say and get it done before she lost her chance.

She leapt up onto the cement edge of the fountain, keeping her shield raised in case she ended up fighting her way back to the castle. Already some twenty people were gathered around her, creeping nearer, with more appearing from the small buildings and side streets every moment. Yet no one moved to attack her, and she found it odd, fully expecting it at any moment. Bridín faced them all, hearing their whispers growing to a louder murmur, seeing them point her way while leaning and speaking to another. What were they saying? *There she is, the guilty one. The one who betrayed us. The one who . . .*

She shut off her thoughts like snuffing a candle's flame, thinking only of Tristan, and cleared her throat, and spoke again, her voice emerging, to her surprise, strong and clear.

"I don't care what you believe I have done," she told them. "I have no time to explain or try to defend. If you would see me stoned or beheaded for my crimes, then I'll willingly submit. You have my vow on that."

There were several gasps, and more muttering, but it died as soon as she spoke again. "Before my sentence is carried out, know this. Tristan of Shara is not dead, as his brother told you he was."

"Tristan? Alive?" someone shouted.

She had to hurry. Soon someone would report her presence here to the castle guards . . .

"Vincent lied! He plotted to steal the throne from his own brother, plotted to murder Tristan in cold blood in order to take the kingdom. But only part of his vile plan worked. He got the crown, all right, by means more foul than any pigsty's stench. But he didn't murder Tristan, though he tried. His brother—your prince—Tristan of Shara, was tossed to the dungeons to die of the wounds he received at his own brother's sword, but he escaped."

"Escaped." The word echoed around her as the crowd repeated it. "It's just as old Mary said," another voice blurted. "The prince *is* alive!"

"But now Tristan is once again in his brother's evil hands. He put himself there in order to save my life, and I am not going to allow him to die there! So I walked into Gaston's shop, and I found what weapons I could carry." She held up the mace and shield as she spoke. The murmur grew louder. "And now I'm going back to that castle for Tristan of Shara, prince of this kingdom, a man who never once lied to his people, or allowed them to suffer the way you suffer now. A man you all loved. I'm going. And if I go alone, then so be it. But I know that any one of you who is half the man Tristan is will join me."

Heads turned. Men looked at one another, blinking, shocked.

"Join me now!" she shouted. "It may well be your last chance at freedom from Vincent's reign!"

She leapt down from her makeshift dais and turned, striding forward just as one of Vincent's soldiers turned his horse round the corner, glanced up, and caught sight of her. Scowling, he drew his sword, kicking the horse's flanks and surging toward her. The crowd gasped. Bridín slipped the mace into her belt and yanked the dagger from her boot. Then she stood her ground, staring him down with the wind in her face. And just when he swung the sword at her in a deadly arc, she crouched low and flicked her small blade outward. His swing missed, but she heard the blade slicing the air over her head. She sprang upward again as he whirled the horse around.

"Join us, knave!" she shouted. "Join us or die!"

He growled like a bear and surged forward again, sword drawn. But the stirrup she'd sliced on his first pass gave way, and he tumbled to the ground in a clatter of armor. His sword fell and skidded away.

Bridín lunged, stepped on his chest to grip the horse's mane, and pulled herself onto its bare back. "So what is your choice going to be, people of Rush? Will you snivel under Vincent's whip like cowardly dogs, or will you fight for Tristan the way you know he would fight for you?"

There was a long moment of silence. The crowd had grown to fifty by now, with more straggling in all the time. No one said a word.

Bridín sighed heavily. She'd done her best. "I've no more time. Tristan could be dead by now." She pulled the horse around, pointed it toward the castle.

"Fight," someone said. It wasn't a loud voice, nor was it male. It was the voice of an elderly woman. Bridín turned to look at her, as everyone else was doing.

"I told you it was the truth," she said. "Told you she was back."

"Bridín never wronged us," someone else said. "She brought food and supplies when we'd have starved. I say we fight by her side."

"I'm with you, Princess!" someone yelled.

"Go, then! Find weapons, kitchen knives and pitchforks if you've nothing more. Tell your neighbors! Gather everyone you can. Hurry!"

People scurried in every direction, vanishing into shops and houses and sheds. Then they quickly reappeared, all of the men, and many of the women, while the old and sick were left behind to see to the safety of the children. They came to gather around Bridín's dancing mount, carrying hammers and hoes and anything else they could think of that would make for a weapon. One woman carried a frying pan. Another, no more than her broomstick.

Bridín felt her chest swell with pride for these people. Her people. Always. Then she started her horse forward, moving toward the castle. There was no time for strategy or cunning, nor army enough for a frontal assault.

The only option then was the passages.

She rode into the orchard with her army surrounding her, and then bade them all stay put, and stay low, while she moved ahead to remove the false stone from the wall. And then she guided them into the passages, single file and one by one, so as not to form a huge crowd near the castle walls which might draw notice.

Then she went in after them, crowding past the last third of the group, cutting them off from the rest, and pointing them to a tunnel that sloped downward. "This way takes you to the kitchens. Enter there and work toward the great hall. Fight, do you hear? Fight for your lives! For your freedom. For Tristan!"

Nodding, they scurried, their cloth soles sounding like skittering mice on the stone.

Bridín made her way forward again, cutting off another section of fighters and showing them the route to take that would emerge in the chamber where she'd found her mother.

The rest she led forward until she found the opening that led them into the westernmost tower room. A prison, like the dungeon, but one never used. From there they would work their way down, checking each room until they found Tristan.

She prayed it wasn't too late.

Tristan's hands were bound behind his back, and he'd been forced onto his knees in the throne room. His brother, sitting proudly in the seat to which he had no right, swung his booted foot upward one more time, catching Tristan's chin and sending him over backward. He hit hard. Harder than last time. He wished Vincent would grow tired of amusing himself with petty torture and get to the task at hand. If he'd untie Tristan's hands for only a moment, he'd take the chance to kill the bastard.

Heavy hands gripped Tristan's shoulders, lifting him again to his former position.

He prepared himself to take another blow. He could stand the pain. He could stand anything, so long as he knew *she* was safe. And he wouldn't give up, either. He'd fight for his life with his dying breath, dammit, because now . . . now he had so very much to live for.

Bridín.

Damn, Vincent wasn't going to rob him of this.

He'd got her out of here; of that much, he was certain. He prayed her pendants had worked to heal her, and she was all right.

The boot connected again. Tristan felt his chin split open before he hit the floor this time. Men reached for him.

"Leave him," Vincent said. "I've decided."

"Decided what, my brother?" Tristan lifted his head, staring through swollen eyes at Vincent's scowling face. "To stop scuffing up those shiny new boots of yours on my face?"

His words came hard, forced through a throat that was tightened by pain.

"Decided how to kill you," Vincent said softly. "Believe me, nothing would suit me more than a public beheading. But that would mean admitting to the peons out there that I'd lied to them when I told them you were already dead." Vincent pulled his dagger, ran a thumb thoughtfully along its tip, until blood beaded on the blade. "Still, I do long to see your head in a basket, brother. So a private ceremony will have to do. A block, an ax. No fanfare. No crowd. The inner courtyard, I believe. Otherwise we'll bloody up the floors."

He lifted his gaze, locking it on one of the two guards behind Tristan and nodding once. "Take him. See to it the ax and block are made ready. I do believe I'll do the honors myself."

The men tugged him to his feet, holding him by the arms and turning him around. He needed a chance, dammit. Just one break, one moment with his hands free—

He frowned, jerking his head up at a flash of movement from above as they passed through the great hall. Tristan looked up, his eyes unfocused, watery with pain. But sure enough, he saw the flash again, the flash of a sword, and then he heard a grunt.

The others heard it, too, because they glanced upward. But whoever was up there ducked low. The guards who held him shrugged and looked ahead again, but then they hadn't seen the flash of that sword . . .

Or that other flash, which had seemed an awfully lot like that of golden hair catching the rays of the sun.

He glanced up once more, only to see her there. Bridín, peering over the railing at him, then pressing her hand to her mouth in horror.

Yes, he supposed he looked a sight right now. But gods, what was she doing here! He'd risked his life to get her out! What does she do but return, making his sacrifice worthless.

He blinked, and then he smiled. One hell of a woman, she was. No wonder he loved her so. He looked again, to try to tell her, with his eyes, to get out of here while there was still time. But too late. She was gone. Perhaps he'd imagined her. He gave up searching for her as the men pulled him forward, out the far side of the great hall and down another corridor, to a door at the end. But he did glance once more over his shoulder, and this time it was to see a castle guard fall down dead in the great hall, and a blond woman jerking her blade from his chest.

The men opened the door to the inner courtyard. The place was a perfect square, completely surrounded by the castle. There was grass below, and sky above. And walkways on the upper levels, where spectators could line the low walls and lean out to watch whatever special events went on here. A large area, it was. And one apparently put to use a great deal since his brother had taken over. For there had been a pole erected that spanned the width of the square, mounted to the castle walls on either side. Looking up at it, it was as if the sky were sliced in half by a log. From that pole, ropes dangled, unmoving since no breeze entered here. At the end of each rope, a noose, and below each one, a small footstool. And the chopping block and ax stood in another corner. A whipping post fitted with metal shackles for the victim's hands and feet was at the center. Gods, his sick brother had turned the inner courtyard into a place of torture, of private execution. For his own twisted pleasure.

"The block, he said," one guard reminded the other.

"You two aren't much for loyalty, are you?" Tristan asked. "I was your prince. Still am, by rights."

They looked at each other and shook their heads, and Tristan knew these were two of his brother's hand-chosen thugs. Men brought into Tristan's trust by Vincent, but loyal all along only to his brother. His enemy.

One cupped his nape and forced his head down, while the other lifted the leather belts that dangled from either side of the block beneath his torso, and fastened them tight around his waist and shoulders, holding him there.

Tristan looked down at a filthy, stinking basket, coated in vile, blackened blood, and buzzing with flies.

Then he glanced back at the doorway, half expecting to see Bridín appear there. But instead, he saw his brother. The bastard was smiling.

Chapter Twenty-one

BRIDÍN HAD TO duck into an opening off the hallway when Vincent of Shara came striding down it. She bit her lip, closed her eyes, and battled a full-body shudder. She pressed her hand to the pendants at her throat, as if to reassure herself, but found only one broken chain remained. She'd fought hordes of men to get this far. It was little wonder, she supposed, that she'd lost the pendants along the way.

The others were still fighting off the group of soldiers who'd intercepted them in the west wing. She'd battled her way through the fray, intent only on getting to Tristan in time. She had to do so, because without the pendants, there'd be no hope of healing him once this foul deed was done. And there'd be no time to try to retrieve them.

And she had managed to get to Tristan before the bastard killed him. But what help would she be to him now? There were three of them out there. Two guards and a prince, against one woman. What could she do?

She glanced down the hall the way she'd come, but there was no help in sight. Then she looked the other way, the way Vincent had gone. He stood in the doorway to the inner courtyard now, as if pausing for maximum effect, leaning against the door's arch, staring out at Tristan, blocking him from Bridín's view.

She felt helpless. Afraid. Impotent.

"Is that ax good and sharp?" Vincent intoned, pulling a pair of calfskin gloves onto his hands as he spoke.

That bastard!

The feeling of helplessness and fear fled. Anger surged up to replace it. Bridín turned to search the room she'd ducked into . . . only, it wasn't a room at all, but a landing at the bottom of a narrow, curving staircase. And if she remembered correctly . . .

She sheathed her sword. The mace and shield had fallen to the floor in the west wing as she fought her way through the castle guards. But the sword was enough. All she would need. Her rage was her best weapon right now. She mounted the stairs and raced up their spiraling steps, emerging at another landing and lunging through the arched doorway that led to the balcony. And then she stopped, staring down over the stone wall to the scene being played out in the courtyard below her.

Tristan, bound to a block, facedown over a reeking, filthy basket. The two guards standing a few feet away, their backs to her. Vincent, reaching for the ax and testing its broad, curving head with his thumb. Closing his hands around the handle, testing its weight. Lifting it.

She couldn't reach them in time. Vincent lifted the ax overhead, and she turned her eyes away reflexively. They fell on the noosed ropes dangling from the pole that stretched below her.

"Before you die, brother, know that your precious Bridín will be the next to feel the edge of this blade."

And Bridín dove over the stone rail before she'd realized what she was about to do. She heard a screech, like the battle cry of some wild animal of the forest, and belatedly realized the cry was her own. She plummeted downward, stretched her arms out and caught the nearest length of rope, and her momentum swung her forward with the force of a hurricane as she clung to it. She lifted her feet at the last possible moment, and when they connected with Vincent's chest, the man was hurled backward. He slammed into the far wall, the ax flying from his hands, the wind knocked from his lungs. She saw him gaping as she let go the rope and landed on the ground beside Tristan, yanking her sword into her hands at the same time.

A guard came into her peripheral vision, but she whirled and sank her blade into his belly before he could strike her down. His mouth opened wide, eyes bulging as he staggered. She yanked the bloodied blade from his body and turned to face the second. But this one was ready. Crouching low, sword uplifted as the man faced her waving his own, she made a quick grab for the dagger in her boot with her left hand, and sliced through the bonds that held Tristan's hands behind his back. But there was no time to cut the ones that held his body to the block, because her opponent lunged at her, swinging his sword, slicing the flesh that covered her rib cage, and then dancing back before she could return the blow. She felt the white-hot cut, felt the blood seeping down her side. She'd jerked away in reaction to the pain, leaving the dagger resting on Tristan's back. Anger, fury, pain, all melded into action then, and she went on the attack, swinging, advancing, thrusting her sword at the bastard until he'd backed up all the way to the wall. He swung his sword, aiming it at her head, but she ducked and it hissed above her. She rose, driving her head into the man's soft belly, and he doubled over with a grunt. Springing upright, she raised her sword above him.

"That will be quite enough, Bridín of the Fay. You've been lucky, but your luck has just run out." She felt the point of a blade at her back, and froze where she was.

"Turn around," Vincent said. "I want to see your face when you die."

Drawing a breath, Bridín turned. But when she did, she didn't look at Vincent. Instead, her gaze moved beyond him, to where Tristan lay facedown on the block, his hands behind him gripping her dagger, sawing fiercely at the one remaining strap that held him down.

Vincent lifted his sword, pressed its tip to her chest, slowly twisted his hands back and forth on the hilt. She forced herself to look at him, not at Tristan. If Vincent saw where she was looking, he'd catch on. The man behind her was still bent over, trying to catch his breath, gagging and choking.

Hurry, Tristan. Hurry.

"It won't matter if you kill me now, Vincent. Your reign of terror is over. The people know the truth now."

His eyes widened, but he quickly erased any hint of alarm from his features. "What does it matter? Hmm? I have an army. I can beat them into submission again easily enough, or starve them there. I rule by fear, fairy woman. Not by the whim of my subjects."

"And is your army three hundred men strong?" she asked him, stalling for time. "Because the village is, you know. And every one of the villagers is willing to fight to rid themselves of your rule."

He narrowed his eyes at her. "They wouldn't dare . . ."

"Oh, no?" She cocked her head to one side. "Listen."

Vincent did, and he heard what she did. The distant clash of steel, the faint but growing shouts. And finally the thunder of hooves. "What—"

"That will be the army Tristan has amassed. Now your men have his followers as well as mine to contend with. How do you think they'll fare?"

"Damn you!" Vincent shouted. "Die, you treacherous wench!" And he pulled up and back with the sword, clutching it tight, about to drive it right through her.

The man behind her muttered, "Look out!" but it didn't come in time. As her eyes dared one last glimpse at Tristan before she died, she saw his blade finally cut through his bonds, and he rolled over and threw the dagger all in one fast, desperate motion. The blade flipped end over end and embedded itself deeply into Vincent's back.

He howled as his sword clattered to the ground. Bridín dropped to her knees, snatched it up, and whirled to defend herself against the attack from behind her, but there was no need. The lone remaining guard was already fleeing into the castle.

When she turned again, Tristan was on his feet, looking down at the lifeless form of his brother, crumpled in the dirt.

He lifted his gaze to Bridín's, and they stood there, in silence, eyes locked, words unspoken. Tristan parted his lips to say something, but a shout interrupted him. And he looked up toward the balcony where the sound had come from. She did, too, and saw villagers there, fighting, dying. Some still wielding their makeshift weapons, but others, many others, swinging the swords of their enemies. The ones they'd already killed.

Before her eyes, more of Vincent's men fell. Unnecessary deaths, all of them. She met Tristan's eyes again. "Go to your men," she told him. "Tell them it's over. Vincent is dead. The kingdom is yours."

He took a step forward. "Bridín—"

"No, Tristan. It's you the people rallied to protect. You they erected monuments to when they believed you dead. You who brought them out of subjugation to a madman. You're their leader now. They want you . . . not me."

There was a dull groan as another man fell.

"For the love of the gods, Tristan, stop this carnage before more men die!"

He lowered the hand he'd held out to her, cupped the other to his mouth, and shouted, drawing the attention of the men fighting above. "The day is won!" he called. "Vincent of Shara is dead!"

One of the men on the balcony shouted some question down to him, and as Tristan gave orders to spare the rest of Vincent's men unless they insisted on fighting on, Bridín crept back into the castle.

She was tired, aching all over, cut and bleeding. But none of that hurt so much as her heart did. For now that the battle was over, she realized that Tristan had indeed won. He'd won his kingdom, the love of his people, and dammit, he'd won her heart. But now, how could she tell him that? If she pledged her love after all these weeks of resisting him, then he'd always wonder, wouldn't he? He'd always wonder whether it was him she loved, or the crown he could place back upon her head.

Oddly enough, that crown no longer seemed to matter so much. Once, retaking her throne, her birthright, had been the only dream of her heart. Her only wish.

Now . . .

She glanced back through the doorway, glimpsing Tristan once again. Now she knew there was something more, something far more precious to her than any kingdom or any crown. But now that Tristan had *his* heart's desire—

Doubts crept into her mind. Would he even still want her now? Surely he'd have no need to woo or try to win her. No need to make love to her, or fill her heart with wild imaginings of how it could be with them. No need of her at all. She'd be a detriment to him now.

Maybe it would be better for Tristan if she simply left him alone. Lowering her head, turning away, she started back through the castle, ready to leave it for the very last time, stepping over the dead and wounded along the way.

In the great hall, a soft cry brought her head up, and she spied her mother. Máire burst into tears and ran to her, enfolding her in a strong embrace and kissing her cheeks. "You're all right. Oh, my darling, I was so afraid for you!"

Bridín clung to her mother, numb, afraid to cry because if she began, she thought she might never stop. "I'm sorry, Mother. I failed you."

"What a silly thing to say!"

"I didn't do as you told me. I didn't find the man as the crystal said I should do, and now I've lost your kingdom—"

"Our kingdom, daughter. And what makes you think you have lost it?"

Bridín lowered her head, shaking it slowly, too drained to explain. "Let's just go. To the forest, to—"

"You're wounded!" Máire drew away from Bridín, staring down at her bloodied tunic. "Come, I'll tend you in my chamber."

Poor Mother. Didn't she realize it was no longer her chamber? Or her castle or her kingdom?

But she led her by the hand, and Bridín was too tired to fight her. They went up the stairs, and as they did, she tried to let her mother down gently. "It's Tristan the people want, Mother. I'm so sorry, but the kingdom . . . it's his now. Surely you can see that?"

Her mother continued to the top of the stairs, pulling her along the hallway to the bedroom where she'd so recently been held prisoner. "Tristan survived the battle as well, then?" Máire asked.

"Yes."

"I'm so glad. I don't mind abdicating, you know. I'd had my fill of leadership long ago. Though I will admit, it was exhilarating leading Tristan's men here, riding at the front of an army on the attack." She sighed, pushing the door open, pulling Bridín to the bed and easing her onto it. "But my time is over, darling. My magic, long gone. This is your time, Bridín. Your turn to—"

"Mother, haven't you heard a word I've said?"

"Of course I have, darling. And now I have something to show you."

Bridín frowned, leaning back on the pillows, sighing in frustration. Her mother pulled a small, convex bit of glass . . . no, crystal, from within her dress. "I found this, below in the dungeons where you fell. It's a part of the scrying crystal."

Nodding, Bridín closed her eyes.

"Look at it, daughter. And tell me what you see."

"It doesn't matter whose face I see in that broken piece of rock, Mother. I won't go in search of him. I won't marry him. I can't. Not now. I might have lost Tristan, but I will never love any other man. Never!"

She heard her mother's sigh, then felt her

weight leaving the bed. "Perhaps you'll look at it later."

"Never," she whispered. She was so tired. So utterly exhausted.

"All right, darling. You rest. I'll tend your wounds and . . ." Her mother's hand touched her neck and then moved away. "Your pendants?"

Bridín shrugged. "I lost them . . . in the battle."

She felt a warm hand smoothing her hair. "No matter. I think the need for them has passed." The hand continued stroking, and Bridín felt herself sinking into blissful sleep. "That's it, child. Rest. Rest. My poor baby, to have grown up without a mother's love, and all because of the wicked Vincent. It was he who murdered those kind mortals who adopted you, my darling. Oh, but you must have known it, sensed it."

Bridín's eyes opened again and she searched her mother's face. "It was Vincent who killed them?"

"Who else?" she whispered.

And then her mother began singing an ancient Celtic lullaby. One Bridín vaguely remembered from her youth. She felt tears burn her eyes as she realized how very wrong she'd been about Tristan, about so many things, and for such a long time. She counted her regrets as she finally drifted off to sleep.

When she woke, it was night again. She couldn't believe she'd slept for so long. She sat up in the bed, only to find herself undressed, and her mother humming a tune as she poured a steaming pail of water into the large tub someone had dragged into the room.

"Mother? What . . ."

"Ah, you're awake! Good. Come on, now, into the tub. We haven't got much time as it is."

Bridín frowned hard. "Time? Time for what? Mother, what in the world is going on?"

Her mother beamed at her. "A celebration, of course. The wounded have been tended, the dead buried. My, but the men have been busy. And the women, too, restoring this place to order after such a horrible day."

Bridín groaned. Gods, the last thing she felt like was revelry.

"The people have been freed from months of oppression and hardship, daughter. Surely you wouldn't deny them this celebration. Why, Tristan sent out a troop of hunters for game, and the cooks have been working all the day through. There's to be feasting and music. And of course, the coronation."

"The coronation," she muttered.

"Tristan saved your life, countless times, Bridín. You told me so yourself. You owe him this, if nothing more. Your presence at this event. Now, come along, hurry. How is your side?"

"My . . ." Blinking, Bridín looked down at her wound, only now remembering to think of it. But there was nothing there save a rapidly fading pink mark. "How did you—"

"Raze, that dear man, he found the pendants clutched in the hands of a dead man. Brought them to me right away. Don't tell me you didn't notice?" Bridín glanced down to see one pendant dangling at her throat. She opened her mouth to ask what had become of its mate, but her mother didn't give her the chance. "Now will you get busy, dear?"

She didn't want to get busy, but it seemed she had little choice. All those villagers who'd heeded her call to arms and stormed the castle at her side would expect her to show them her gratitude. And she couldn't deny that she longed to see Tristan again, to speak to him, to try to figure out whether there was any hope for the two of them, after all they'd been through.

Her mother tended her as if she were a small child again, washing and brushing her hair, singing as she worked. Then she brought out a gown of glittering emerald, and Bridín caught her breath.

"It was mine," Máire told her. "Tristan was kind enough to show me where our belongings were stored when his father's armies took this kingdom from us so long ago. I was amazed they weren't all destroyed, but I suspect that young man had a hand in their preservation."

"You've seen him?" Bridín asked, unable to stop herself.

Her mother smiled. "Of course. We had much to discuss, that young man and I. Now get dressed, and go stand by the window so your hair will dry in the breeze. My goodness, I'm not even dressed yet myself. I'll send for you when it's time."

"But—"

Her mother sailed out of the room like an errant breeze. Bridín shrugged in puzzlement, and took the brush with her to stand by the window.

Some time later, her mother, and Raze, looking splendid in a suit of fine satin, came for her. She felt as if she were in a dream, wearing the beautiful gown, her hair trailing down her back brushed to a golden sheen, as she walked with them through the twisting corridors, but not down the stairs. No. They took her instead to the frontmost balcony, and from within the shadowy hall she could see out there. Tristan stood near the rail, hands gesturing as he spoke to the crowds lining the outer courtyard below. He wore green as well. Glittering green leggings and a tunic with a red stripe bisecting it diagonally across his torso. His sword hung at his side.

Her mother drew her to a stop there in the shadows. She was about to tell her this wasn't right. That she ought to be on the street below, with the others, not here. But then she caught Tristan's words, strongly, loudly spoken, and she fell silent, listening.

"It is a great battle we've won today," he was saying. "Together we've ousted a ruler who abused his power, tormented his people, and wronged so very many of you that I fear no reward can ever make it right. But there is one wrong my brother did that I can correct, and I would do it now."

"The crown," someone shouted from below. "Put on the crown!"

Bridín dragged her eyes from Tristan's broad back, to see the crown of Rush . . . of Shara . . . resting on a satin pillow, perched on the rail before him.

"Not just yet," Tristan said, and she heard the laughter in his voice. "As I said, there is a grave wrong that needs to be righted. While you all cry for me to wear that crown, there is another person you're forgetting." He paused, turning his head, scanning the crowd below. "You know by now that the charges my brother lodged against your princess, Bridín of Rush, were false. But not all of you know how she returned here, and surrendered herself to him in order to save you, the people she loves. She risked her life for you . . . for all of you. And she was nearly killed because of it. And none of you know that a few hours ago, I lay with my head on the block, my brother hefting the ax above me . . . and again she risked her own life, this time to save mine."

He turned then and looked toward her, his eyes intense, glittering, black. He held out a hand. Bridín stood motionless, still, unable to move. Her mother leaned forward, holding something up in front of her face. That blasted broken piece of crystal again.

"Look, daughter," she whispered. "Just *look*."

Bridín did look. And she saw the reflection of Tristan's face glittering at her from the stone. She blinked, and stared at her mother. "You . . . you mean . . ."

Her mother only nodded, and then nudged her forward until she had no choice but to step out onto the balcony beside Tristan.

He smiled gently, but nervously, at her, then turned again, staring out at the crowd. "So I accept this crown you're so eager to lay upon my head. I accept it . . ."—he reached forward, picking up the glittering crown from its pillow—". . . and I bestow it, gladly, upon its rightful owner. Bridín, princess of this kingdom now and forevermore to be known as Rush." He placed the crown on her head.

The crowd gasped in shock. And Bridín understood that shock too well. To see them like this, two sworn enemies who'd battled all their lives over this kingdom, one simply giving it over to the other.

Tristan drew his sword, dropping to one knee to lay it at her feet. He bowed his head. "I am your man of good faith, lady. My sword is yours to command."

"Tristan, you can't . . ."

The crowd remained silent, stunned, waiting and watching expectantly to see what she would do. Whether she would accept.

Tristan glanced up at her and his heart shone from his eyes. "I love you, Bridín," he whispered, for her ears alone. "And if this is the only way to prove that to you, then I can. And I will. And I have." He lifted his hands to clasp both of hers, staring up into her eyes. "There's no need for you to go out in search of this man your mother says you must marry in order to regain your throne. I refuse to believe you ever truly wanted to do that, Bridín, so now you don't have to. I give it to you. Because the thought of you with another would kill me, and because it is yours, by right, by birth, and from my heart. If I have to live without you, Bridín, so be it. But please . . ." His voice broke. He cleared his throat and forced himself to go on. "Please, don't listen to her. And don't doubt my love for you any longer."

He bent his head again, and that's when she saw the necklace—her pendant's twin—dangling around his neck. Her mother . . . she'd given it to Tristan. She glanced back at Máire. Máire nodded at her to go on.

Bridín turned to face her people, blinking

away tears. "I can only accept this crown on one condition," she said, loud as she could, though her voice choked with emotion. "It no longer suits me to be just your princess. I want to be your queen. And to do that, by our own law, I must marry. I must marry the man who is to be your king. And I know now, thanks to my own mother's magic, who that man is."

There was a murmur, growing louder from the spectators. Tristan lifted his head, staring up at her with a hint of alarm in his eyes, waiting.

"In all my life," she said softly, gazing down into his eyes, "there has been only one man I have ever loved. With all my heart and soul. And I will marry none other than the man my mother chose for me, long ago. If he will have me."

Slowly Tristan rose, facing her.

"Will you, Tristan?"

"It's . . . it's me?" His eyes were so wide, so beautiful.

"It's always been you, Tristan. And always will. How could I marry any other when I love you with every breath in me, my darling? If you refuse me, I swear, I'll die alone, because there can never be any man who can touch me the way you do."

He smiled then, and reached out to run one palm gently over the side of her face. "I can't believe . . . Gods, I thought I'd lost you."

"Never, Tristan." She blinked away tears, but they rolled unchecked down her face all the same. "So tell me, do I dare hope . . . you'll be my husband? My king?"

"I'll be more than that. So much more," he whispered. Then he swept her into his arms, and bent his head, and kissed her mouth with a passion that should have burned the entire kingdom to the ground. The roar of the crowd then was deafening. But it was nothing compared to the thunder in her heart.

Tristan held her close then, cradling her head to the steady beat of his heart as if he couldn't bring himself to let her go. And he turned, with her tucked there against him, to face the people again as they shouted and cheered.

Bridín snuggled close to him, unwilling to be away from him even for a moment. And she wouldn't have to, she vowed. Not ever again.